I WILL NOT BEG

Mountain Masters & Dark Haven Book 9

CHERISE SINCLAIR

VanScoy Publishing Group

I Will Not Beg

Digital ISBN 978-1-947219-14-4
Print ISBN 978-1-947219-15-1
Published by VanScoy Publishing Group
Cover Art: The Killion Group

Warning: This book contains sexually explicit scenes and adult language and may be considered offensive to some readers. This book is for sale to adults only, as defined by the laws of the country in which you made your purchase.

Disclaimer: Please do not try any new sexual practice, without the guidance of an experienced practitioner. Neither the publisher nor the author will be responsible for any loss, harm, injury, or death resulting from use of the information contained in this book.

AUTHOR'S NOTE

To my readers,

The books I write are fiction, not reality, and as in most romantic fiction, the romance is compressed into a very, very short time period.

You, my darlings, live in the real world, and I want you to take a little more time in your relationships. Good Doms don't grow on trees, and there are some strange people out there. So while you're looking for that special Dom, please, be careful.

When you find him, realize he can't read your mind. Yes, frightening as it might be, you're going to have to open up and talk to him. And you listen to him, in return. Share your hopes and fears, what you want from him, what scares you spitless. Okay, he may try to push your boundaries a little—he's a Dom, after all—but you will have your safe word. You will have a safe word, am I clear? Use protection. Have a back-up person. Communicate.

Remember: safe, sane, and consensual.

Know that I'm hoping you find that special, loving person who will understand your needs and hold you close.

And while you're looking or even if you have already found your dearheart, come and hang out with the Dom's of Dark Haven.

Love,

Cherise

ACKNOWLEDGMENTS

As always, huge hugs to my crit partners—Monette Michaels, Bianca Sommerland, and Fiona Archer. I love you guys.

Thanks to Saya and the superb editing staff at Red Quill. Y'all are wonderful to work with.

So many smooches go to my awesome beta readers, Barb Jack, Marian Shulman, and Lisa White who must be masochists, always coming back for more. I'm so thankful to have you.

Fuzzy hugs for the ShadowKittens—my Facebook readers group. Y'all keep me laughing, thinking...and returning to the keyboard.

Finally, y'all can thank Autumn who has been pushing for Sir Ethan to get this book. (I hope it meets your expectations, Autumn.)

PROLOGUE

Well, Toto, we're still in Kansas. In the back seat of her Master's parked Mercedes, Piper Delaney stared out the car window at the country estate. The hot summer sun gleamed off an imposing mansion, which overlooked exquisitely landscaped acres.

Yes, she was still in Kansas, and somewhere along the way, she'd lost her rainbow. Biting her tongue to hold back a sigh, Piper shifted her position, trying to ease her throbbing ankle. Master had refused to allow her the use of a cane. If this summer party was like all the rest, he'd keep her fetching and carrying for hours. He'd say the pain was what she deserved for being clumsy.

Only...she hadn't been clumsy.

Her teeth ground together to stifle a curse. Attracting Master's attention was rarely a good idea—and never after a long trip. His temper was volatile at the best of times.

Running her hand over her head, she felt the prickle of patchy stubble, and tears filled her eyes. She'd begged him not to cut it—but her long black hair was gone.

Her breathing hitched.

Last night, as Piper was bringing Master his wine, the new

slave girl had tripped her...deliberately. Piper stumbled, turned her ankle, and spilled the glass of wine on his lap.

Oh, he'd been so *angry*. Hitting her wasn't enough. He'd gone and butchered her hair with scissors because she wasn't worth dulling a razor.

She felt so ugly and dirty. Ruined. His title shouldn't be Master or Owner; it should be Defiler.

Blinking hard, she looked out the window. The Mercedes was parked in a diagonal line of cars on the grassy guest lot behind the big country house. On the back patio, the house staff was serving up drinks and finger foods. Across the broad expanse of beautifully landscaped grounds, BDSM equipment had been set up. The tall Xs of the St. Andrew's crosses along with stockades, whipping posts, and other equipment created dark blotches against the vibrant green lawn.

Chatting and gesturing, Masters strolled the grounds with their slaves scurrying after them like obedient dogs.

In a moment, she would be limping after Master Serna...a step behind his new girl.

She'd actually been looking forward to this party, to being around people—her favorite thing in the world. She'd even been happy to have another slave in the house, at least until slavegem turned mean. Master Serna got a kick out of encouraging her to be cruel to Piper.

So much for a possible friend.

Piper wanted to cry. Like the miserable worm she was. Because she was pitiful. A waste of space. *Worthless*.

A rumble of conversation came from outside the car. Her owner was introducing himself to a man. Maybe he'd find a new client. Be in a good mood.

Her life revolved around his moods now. She hadn't been like this—not always. Whatever had happened to the joyful, confident girl she'd been? Two years ago, she'd started her second year of college filled with enthusiasm and energy. She was going to change the world. Help people.

Then she'd met Master Serna. When he'd first come into her life, she'd still been...a person. Thrilled by his attention, she'd fallen in love and happily given him whatever he asked for.

Piece by piece, he'd taken away who she was. Reducing her to...nothing. To someone who was—

"Girl."

She jumped, and the irritated snap in his voice sent fear shuddering through her. "Master?"

"Come here, worthless."

Hastily, she scooted out of the backseat, smoothed down her tiny pink skirt, then limped around the car to the back where another Dominant was talking to her Master.

Master Serna was dressed in black leather pants and a sleeveless vinyl shirt, which showed off his barrel chest and muscular arms. Kneeling at his feet, slavegem wore a pink halter and micro-skirt that matched Piper's. The slave gave Piper an ugly stare.

A flicker of movement from the open car trunk caught Piper's eye. Another glance showed only Master's toy bag beside the heavy sheet metal box containing his sports equipment.

"I don't meet too many people from the West Coast," Master was saying to the other Dom. "Long way to come for a party."

"Yolanda and I are old friends, and I had business in the area." The other man's English-accented voice had a mesmerizing resonance. "Unfortunately, I found out one of the Masters I hoped to see today dropped out of the lifestyle."

Standing quietly, Piper tried to look at the Dom from the corner of her eyes. Silvery-blue suit. Dark hair. A flash of deep blue eyes. She hastily lowered her head.

"Oh, do you mean old bleeding-heart Bob?" Her owner chuckled. "Fenton made himself unwelcome in the community. Hasn't been around for over a year."

Piper's hands tightened at her sides. Master Fenton had intervened when another Master almost whipped a slave to death. Later, he'd notified the authorities when a big shot Dom in the lifestyle raped a submissive. This community covered for their leaders just like the Catholic Church had with their pedophile priests. When Master Fenton pushed for accountability, he'd been driven out.

"I'm sorry to hear that." The English Dom's voice had chilled.

"People come and go. It happens." Master Serna's voice had a gloating note. He'd led the group that forced Master Fenton out.

"I'm going to send worthless here for a drink while I set up. Would you like something?" Master leaned into the car and started to drag his heavy toy bag out.

Something moved in the trunk. Piper heard a high *mew* and saw the bag had trapped something small and furry against the sheet metal box. "Master, *wait*."

When he ignored her, she yelled, "You're hurting it!" and pushed him to one side so she could move the bag.

Freed, the kitten blinked up at her. *Alive*. Thank God. But it didn't move.

Piper leaned in. "Are you all right, baby?"

As she reached for the tiny cat, Master clouted her across the face and knocked her off her feet.

Stunned, she landed hard on the driveway. Her skimpy clothing gave no protection, and pain flared as her bare skin scraped over the rough concrete.

Owwww. Rolling up onto her knees, she knelt, head bowed, tears filling her eyes. Muscles tense, she awaited the next blow. Would a pleading apology or silence placate him better?

In her peripheral vision, she saw the kitten flee across the lawn toward the house. Good. That was good.

The other man's velvety voice was calm. "It's lucky your slave moved quickly, Serna. Yolanda is quite fond of her pedigree felines. Damaging one would not have endeared you to her."

Oh, God, this wasn't good. Left alone, Master would have smacked her a few times and forgotten about her. Now, he'd stew over the Englishman's words. His anger would grow.

And he'd whip the skin from her back tonight once they got home.

The conversation above her head went indistinct as she concentrated on sitting perfectly still. On not letting any whimpers escape. After a minute, the rushing of her pulse in her ears died down, and she managed a deeper breath.

The Masters were still talking about people they knew in the community.

"In the kitchen, the cook mentioned that Horn's slave had left him," the Englishman said.

"Ran away, you mean?" Master's voice had gone cold.

"Since slavery is against the law in the US, you can't call it running away. No slave contract is legal, and BDSM slave contracts aren't upheld in any court."

The clipped words struck Piper like hard summer hailstones, and she almost—almost—looked up.

When she'd said she wanted to leave, Master told her that even if she tried to get away, the law would bring her back. Because of the contract she'd signed. He'd brandished it at her, the big formal document with her signature at the bottom. Last year, she questioned other slaves, and they'd said slave contracts were valid. That the police wouldn't help her since she'd signed a contract.

But the contract wasn't legal? Wasn't binding?

Master growled under his breath. "How'd a slave get out of his house? Didn't Horn have locks?"

"Ah, well. They were at a party like this, and she announced in front of everyone that she was done with being a slave and would someone call her a taxi."

"The fucking bitch. Someone did, I bet."

"Of course. If there is no consent, then everything that follows is considered assault." The Englishman's tone lightened. "By the way, I left a bottle of The Botanist from the Isle of Islay in the kitchen. I think you might enjoy a glass. Can you send your girl to bring us drinks? The cook will know where it is."

"Right. Of course." Master cleared his throat. "Worthless, fetch us drinks."

"Yes, Master," she whispered. She pushed to her feet, barely feeling the blood trickling down her scraped shoulder and gashed leg. Hope sped her steps toward the house even as terror clawed at her guts. Could she do this?

Backtracking the stream of waitstaff carrying filled platters, she found the kitchen. It was a madhouse of people swirling around a tall wiry woman.

Gaze snagging on Piper, the cook looked her over with narrowed eyes. "How old are you?"

"T-twenty-one."

"She's an adult," a server muttered.

"All right. What do you need, chickie?" The cook added spice to a bubbling pot.

"Um. The"—she didn't know his name—"the English Master asked for two drinks from his Botanist."

A wave from the cook sent a server off to fulfill the request.

Standing beside the door, Piper struggled as terror started to overcome her courage. Her hands clenched. The contract wasn't legal. She could be free.

Speak up. Now. As she straightened her spine, old scars pulled painfully. "Ma'am."

The cook looked at her again, expression unreadable.

Piper swallowed, searching for what to say. The Englishman's smooth voice came to her recall, offering her the correct words to use. "I don't want to be a slave. I'm *not* a slave. Can y-you call me a taxi?"

"I'll be damned." As Piper stared, the cook actually grinned before glancing behind her. "Yo, boy, fetch my car keys and purse. Go tell Yolanda I'm taking a long break."

Five minutes later, Piper was in the cook's car being driven to a Wichita women's shelter.

A month later, she was in San Francisco, far, far away from her previous Master.

CHAPTER ONE

A*lmost five years later*

Piper ran up the stairs to her one-bedroom apartment on the fourth floor. Sure, she could use the elevator, but she hadn't made it to the gym for a week, and she needed the exercise. Stella's contended that women who'd been abused should make staying strong a priority. Learning self-defense was also high on the organization's priority list. *Get strong; stay strong* was Stella's motto.

Couldn't argue with that. Piper had been a terrified, cringing mess when she'd been dropped off at the San Francisco shelter. After she'd healed, the shelter sent her to Stella's Employment Service, an organization that was so much more than a job-hunting firm. There, she'd gotten advice, found friends, and eventually landed a job. Several jobs, actually. It'd taken her a good year to climb out of the quagmire of abuse. To integrate the person she'd been before with the person she'd become. Was still becoming.

Scars remained, emotional and physical, but she no longer...

mostly...looked in the mirror and saw "worthless". *I'm Piper Delaney, and I cringe for no man.*

Except for last week. Embarrassment curled her shoulders inward. For years, she'd been the badass in her empowerment self-defense class...right up until last week when her sparring opponent had resembled the Defiler—and Piper had frozen. Completely.

Dammit. Scowling, she took the steps faster. Over the past year, she'd started having problems with anxiety along with a few panic attacks. Apparently, PTSD had a delayed version—and wasn't that a sucky thing?

She lifted her chin. So, fine, she'd deal with the stupid panic attacks. And she'd get her ass back to the self-defense class, and there would be no more freezing like a wussie. Or missing days. She half-groaned and laughed because Saul would undoubtedly give her extra sit-ups as a punishment for the time lost.

Still puffing from the stair climb, she entered her apartment and savored the silence. No roommates. *Yay.* Rent in the city was horrendous, but last month she'd finally been able to afford an apartment of her own. One she could decorate to her tastes. She'd painted one wall of the long, rectangular dining-living room a royal blue, which looked amazing with the Brazilian hardwood flooring and set off her white couch and blue-and-white chairs. Pictures and pillows added pops of gold and green colors. Maybe the view of the commercial building across the street wasn't great, but her tall windows provided wonderful light, and the plants lining that south wall flourished.

She smiled at the lingering scent of ginger cookies. They hadn't lasted long at the office. Baking cookies and giving them away was the best of all worlds. She got to eat cookie dough, made people happy, and being generous kept her butt from outgrowing her jeans.

In the living room, she curled up on her squishy couch and pulled out her phone to check messages. The downside of owning a business was that free evenings didn't exist. Not that anything should happen on a Friday after five, but Murphy's Law meant if she didn't check in, the world would fall apart, right?

Her business of providing household managers and services required a huge amount of juggling.

Notepad at hand, she listened to the voicemails from Chatelaines. Two of her business friends wanted to do lunch next week. *Absolutely yes*. They were both crazy fun.

There were a couple of scheduling requests. Easy enough to accommodate.

The last was from a client's daughter. "Piper, I'm calling from the hospital. Dad fell yesterday, and the doctor says he had a small stroke."

Piper stiffened. "Oh, no." *Not Mr. Middleton.* Everyone adored him. He'd been one of her first clients when Chatelaines first opened. He'd thought a household management service was a brilliant idea and had encouraged her to expand her offerings. He was the sweetest man.

Stubborn, too. As the message continued, Piper frowned. It seemed he was refusing to live anywhere but his home.

"So, Piper, can you set up and oversee whatever help he'll need to keep him safe in that big house?"

Oh boy, that wouldn't be easy. But...do-able. She hummed under her breath. His appointed chatelaine would need to talk with the hospital discharge planner. Although the hospital's home health service would arrange therapists and equipment, Chatelaines would need to round up everyone else, including people to stay with him 'round the clock at first. That would take a bit of time.

Wait...Dixon knew Mr. Middleton. As a paramedic, PT assistant, and charmer extraordinaire, Dix could persuade Mr. Middleton to be patient as arrangements were made. But Dix would need to see him first thing in the morning, even if it was a Saturday. Without some assurances, Mr. Middleton was liable to simply walk out of the hospital.

She glanced at the clock. Dix and Stan, who lived across the hallway, were having their rooftop party today. That would be a perfect way to hand over the rest of the cookies. Dix loved old-fashioned gingerbread. Last Christmas, he'd helped her bake—and frost—gingerbread men. And he'd insisted on eating the cutouts he'd decorated with mustaches, bowties...and enormous *erections.* She'd almost busted herself laughing.

Yes. She'd take cookies to the party and bribe her favorite employee. Although an inducement probably wasn't needed. Dixon adored Mr. Middleton.

First, she needed to shower to remove the *odeur de chien*.

Earlier, a somewhat intoxicated friend called to ask Piper to walk her two golden retrievers. Piper grinned. Mickey'd been totally lusting after the guy she'd met at the bar.

Piper could have found someone to walk Mickey's dogs. Chatelaines contracted services like cleaning, landscaping, personal care, and dog-walking, and kept extra help—like Dixon—on staff for flexibility. But she hadn't wanted to hand over the task. Hey, she'd worked as a dog-walker on arriving in SF and still missed playing with the fuzzies.

Although now, she smelled like dog. Golden retrievers loved to snuggle.

And Piper gave people—and animals—what they needed.

Jumping to her feet, she headed into the shower. Clean up. Dress. Get pretty. Because men would be at the party and finding a man-friend was on her list of goals.

Turning on the water, she grimaced. *Stupid goals.*

Why were business goals so much easier to achieve than personal ones? She'd already checked off most of Chatelaines' objectives. Well, until recently when a new service-provider company started infringing on her market. She'd have to up her game to find new clientele. Otherwise, business life was good.

Achieving her physical goals? She was doing fairly well.

Her social goals? She had lots of friends.

But when it came to a romantic interest? Total fail. Each

year, she added *find someone to love* to her list. Each year, she'd try, date once or twice, and give up.

This year, she hadn't even tried. It was turning into summer, and she'd stalled long enough.

Breathing in the soft fragrance of her lemon and lavender soap, she sighed, because there was no guy to enjoy her scent.

In college, she'd loved the boy-girl dance. Flirting, dating, those first heady steps to becoming lovers. Then her stepbrother Jerry had introduced her to Master Serna, his friend from the Kansas City race track.

A shudder ran through Piper as she remembered the headiness of feeling submissive in the presence of a Dominant. She'd been so thrilled. Convinced she was in love.

She'd opened the door to her own nightmare, and there she'd stayed, stuck for far too long because she'd been so very gullible.

Now, after the Defiler, the boy-girl journey was either a boring desert of sand...or a dark maze filled with terrifying creatures.

Even though the shower was still steaming, the water felt cold on her skin. Getting out, she dried off and then pulled out the mascara and shadow to enhance her brown eyes. She might not be gorgeous, but she was pretty and interesting...and her big eyes were totally great.

As she made them even more striking, she bit her lip. Dating was a problem, no doubt about it. Average nice guys simply didn't interest her—at least, not sexually. The dominant types were what turned her on—and, ever since the Defiler, they were also the types that sent her anxiety skyrocketing.

Surely, she could find a pleasant vanilla man where there was some chemistry. She just had to keep looking. And she would.

There, a plan for the evening. Get Dixon nailed down for Mr. Middleton and meet a nice, attractive man to date.

What to wear, what to wear...

Her bedroom closet was easy enough to get into. The day

after moving in, she'd removed the door and stored it under her bed.

She eyed her clothes. It was the first day of June. Red would be good. Heck, red was always good. She chose a scarlet forward-ruffle midi skirt and added a black, red, and white striped sleeveless top. Black stiletto sandals because her five-foot-three body liked the extra inches.

A small black crossbody clutch with appliquéd leather tea roses held her phone, business cards, and keys. Glittering hoop earrings sparkled nicely against her ebony hair and matched the stacked bracelets on her right wrist.

Because sparkle meant party, right?

Carrying a plate of cookies, she went down the hall and took the elevator to the sixth floor.

On the rooftop terrace, mini olive trees alternated with planter beds containing herbs and red geraniums. Bright and sunny, the terrace was perfect for parties—and this gathering was in full swing. People at umbrella-topped tables nibbled on finger foods. Wood benches and lounge chairs held more guests. Some millennials were sunset-watching at the waist-high railing. A bigger cluster of people surrounded the bar area where Jameson Stanfeld, Dixon's roommate and lover, was helping a hired bartender.

In his usual button-down shirt, jeans, and cowboy boots, Stan was serious eye-candy. As she approached, she saw a handsome chestnut-haired man trying to flirt with him—not that the Homeland Security Special Agent was reciprocating.

Breaking off his conversation with the man, Stan pointed at her. "There you are. Dix tried to find you an hour ago."

Piper smothered a smile. In San Francisco, his Texas accent was just plain fun. "I had a couple of dogs to walk."

Stan frowned. "I know you have people who work on-call. The owner isn't supposed to have to fill in like that."

"This was for a friend, not a client."

"Soft-hearted Piper." He shook his head. "In that case, what would you like to drink?"

"Uh, I'm not here to—"

"Piper!" Blond, slender, and far cuter than she was, her friend Dixon let out a whoop of delight and dashed across the terrace. His enthusiastic hug almost knocked her off her feet, and she staggered back.

Right into another man's hard body. "Careful, love." Gripping her upper arm to steady her, he rescued the tilting plate of cookies.

With Dixon wrapped around her, she couldn't even turn to thank the guy. She could only laugh and hug her friend back. "Dixon, you're incorrigible."

"I'm so glad you came." Wearing a bright blue tank and floral shorts, her friend released her. "And you give fantastic hugs, sweetpea. Oooh, I have a great idea. You should grow a dick, then Stan could keep us both as pets, and we'd have awesome three-way sex."

"Wh-*what*?" Sputtering a laugh, she shook her head. "How much have you had to drink, you doofus?"

Blowing his blond hair out of his eyes, he gave her a smug look. "Lots. You're way behind." His gaze stalled on something behind her. "*Hey*. Ethan's got cookies. That's *your* red plate. Did you bring goodies?"

"A bribe, Dix, they're a bribe."

"Oh, I'm really bribable." He blinked his big brown eyes. "Wait. Why am I accepting bribes?"

She snickered. Was he even sober enough to know if he could fit Mr. Middleton into his schedule? Worth a try. "It's like this..." She launched into the explanation.

"Oh, that sucks donkey balls." Dix scowled. "He's a great old guy. I'll go by the hospital first thing in the morning and talk him into staying put till we're ready for him."

"Perfect. You're wonderful."

"Of course, I am." Dixon focused on something behind her, then puppy-whined. "*Piperrrrr*, tell Ethan those are *my* cookies."

Piper turned and saw the man holding her plate.

Whoa, Stan had major competition for the *most-devastatingly-handsome* prize. Tall, broad-shouldered, leanly muscular with stunning royal blue eyes. Somewhere in his thirties. His dark brown swept-back hair, mustache, and well-shaped stubble beard were mind-bogglingly masculine.

Model-perfect chiseled features were marred by a slightly crooked nose—probably from being broken. Looking closer, she could see a few scars on his face. One was almost hidden by his right eyebrow. An elegant cheekbone bore a tiny scar. Her gaze dropped to the hand holding her plate. More white scars disfigured his golden tan. Like with her self-defense instructor, the man's skin held the map of fighting.

When she saw interest light those blue eyes, she realized she was gawking at him like an idiot. *God, Piper.*

His piercing gaze sent her back a step, and then, instead of ogling her body as so many men did, he studied her face.

A disconcerting hum of arousal swept over her—something she hadn't felt in far too long.

Chemistry, it was just chemistry. But...*wow*.

After a second, he turned to Dixon and flashed a smile. "I do believe these are now *my* cookies. For you Yanks, possession is nine-tenths of the law, is it not?" He deliberately took a bite of a cookie.

Dixon pouted. "I thought you were a nice person, Ethan, but that's sadistic behavior."

The man's masculine chuckle didn't ease Piper's realization that Dixon might not be joking. Stan and Dixon were Dominant and submissive. Of course, their lifestyle friends would be here.

A cold chill ran up her spine.

As she turned away, a woman in her forties hurried across the terrace to halt in front of Ethan. A silver choker with a dangling heart proclaimed her a slave for anyone in the know. Reddened and swollen eyelids said she wasn't a happy slave.

Piper's stomach tightened.

"Sir Ethan, for you." The slave offered the man a drink as if the glass were a golden chalice made for a king.

Sir Ethan. At a non-lifestyle party? How pretentious. Even the Defiler hadn't used D/s titles when out in public.

Not my business.

"Thank you, Angel." Sir Ethan handed her a cookie. "You may have one glass of alcohol." His voice was deep and smooth. Almost familiar.

Because of the English accent, he sounded almost like the Dom who'd shown Piper how to free herself. Annoyance prickled her nerves. No one should sound like her champion. No one.

"Thank you, Sir. But could..." Holding the cookie, Angel gave a surreptitious glance toward the exit.

His lips firmed. The Dom's answer to the unspoken question was clear.

Angel's shoulders slumped. "Yes, Sir."

"Let's get you something to drink, sweetheart." After handing Dixon the plate of cookies, Ethan put an arm around his slave and led her away.

Piper relaxed. Maybe the Englishman wasn't completely heartless. At least he was getting the woman a drink.

"Here, Piper." Having abandoned helping the bartender, Stan handed her a glass of red wine. "Start on this, pet. You're going to stay for a while, aren't you?"

Pet, hmm? Obviously, Stan had been drinking, since he usually kept that dominance stuff firmly reined in.

As for his question... Did she want to stay at a party that undoubtedly contained Masters and Doms? "Not long. I...uh... have work to do."

He raised a disbelieving eyebrow.

"He's a human lie detector." Dixon snickered. "You're screwed, Pip."

"Why leave?" Stan asked. "You love people, and as a business owner, you know making contacts is part of the job."

"So there," Dix muttered.

"Of course. You're perfectly correct." Arguing with Stan never seemed to work for Dixon; she doubted she'd have better luck. Of course, sneaking out of a party was a time-honored tradition, right?

"Hey, Abby." Hand in the air, Dixon waved at a woman. "C'mere. I have someone for you to meet."

In a sedate green top and tan dress pants, Abby had short fluffy blonde hair and calm gray eyes. Professional, quiet, and the total opposite of Dix's exuberance.

"Abby's a university professor," Dixon said. "Abby, this is my boss, Piper Delaney."

Piper held out her hand. "It's good to meet you, Abby."

"And you." Abby shook hands, then smiled at Dix. "Last I heard, you had three jobs. Which one of your bosses is this?"

"Piper owns Chatelaines Services." Stan stole a cookie from the plate Dixon held, handed it to Abby, and took one for himself.

Dixon gave him an affronted frown. "Those are *my* cookies, Sir."

Another *Sir.* The love—and power exchange—between Stan and Dixon was what Piper once wanted. It wasn't their fault that their relationship occasionally reminded her of how her search for a Dom had led her straight into hell.

She gave herself a subtle shake. Dixon's Master was a good man.

"Chatelaines is an intriguing name. What does your company do?" Abby nibbled on the cookie, then took a bigger bite with a pleased hum.

"Everything," Dixon said smugly before Piper could answer. "It's named after *la chatelaine,* the female head of a medieval *château*—the keeper of the castle. Now, in the twenty-first century, our chatelaines will help run your home. Grocery shopping needed? Sure. Arranging cleaning services? Sure. Do your dogs need their shots? Your chatelaine will set it up and a dog-person will take the dogs to the clinic for you. Car problems? Your chatelaine will arrange for someone to take the car in. Landscaping a mess? Your chatelaine will oversee the contractor. Need to host a Christmas party for your employees? Chatelaines will get it done—and provide a host or hostess if you need one."

Abby's hand stalled on the way to her mouth. "That sounds like having a butler and wife rolled into one."

Piper took over. "Basically, yes. Just imagine having someone to handle the frustrating minutiae of your life. When you get home from work, there's food ready to microwave and clean clothes in the closet. If a faucet gets a leak, someone else will deal with the plumber. Someone will deal with your washing, mending, ironing—and buy your clothes, too. These days, people in the workforce need that kind of pampering."

"That's...amazing." Abby thought for a second. "Doesn't such versatility require an immense amount of people on staff?"

"We have a few on staff, but we also use third-party companies. A chatelaine not only arranges, but also oversees whatever services are needed for each client."

Abby's eyes lit. "Are you taking on more clients? Do you handle the Tiburon area?"

"We are, and we do." *Yes, yes, yes.* As Piper handed Abby a business card from her clutch, she was relieved the English Master had left. She sure didn't want to work for any Dom. Rich people were tricky enough. "You can find the extent of our services and pricing on the Chatelaines' website. If you think we can meet your needs, call and we'll get an appointment set up."

"I'll do that. We totally need you." Abby gave her a firm nod.

Need. That word filled every hollow in Piper's heart with contentment.

For the next hour, Piper wandered from group to group,

meeting people—and not a one came across as being a Master or sadist. She was having a wonderful time. Socializing was totally her crack.

Returning from the bar, she walked past the concrete planter boxes and veered to avoid the English Master who was talking with another man.

Obviously returning from the restroom, his slave, Angel, joined the men, waiting silently until Ethan noticed her and nodded permission to interrupt.

Angel motioned toward the door, saying something softly.

Sir Ethan cut her off with a quiet few words and pointed firmly to the bench.

Tears running down her cheeks, the poor woman sat, not joining the conversation, head bowed. Her whole body curved inward in misery.

Piper wanted to pitch her glass at the bastard Master, or better yet, to throw him over the railing. To watch his body go splat on the street six stories below. That poor woman.

Did Angel know she didn't have to stay with him? That she had choices?

Piper hadn't known.

Behave, Piper. She bit her lip. Their relationship wasn't any of her business. Angel wasn't a friend. Was a complete stranger.

Still.

As Piper moved closer, Ethan's male friend responded to a hail. He motioned toward the person who'd called, obviously asking Ethan to go with him.

Ethan set his hand on Angel's shoulder.

The slave sniffled. "Would you like another drink, Sir?" She still hadn't looked up at him.

Piper didn't hear his reply, but when he followed the other man, the poor woman seemed crushed. *Damn him.*

Time to woman-up and do something. Piper joined Angel on the bench. "Hi. I couldn't help but see that you don't want to be here. Do you want to leave the man you're with? Is he keeping you against your will?"

"I-I-I..." Angel's eyes widened.

Oh, mistake, Piper. Slaves with strict Masters didn't speak unless given permission. "It's all right. You don't have to talk. But did you know that it's illegal to keep you in slavery? That no slave contract is valid in the US?"

The woman stared, her mouth dropping open.

"It's true." Once free, Piper had looked into the subject. Thoroughly. Everything about the Defiler's contract had been wrong. God, she'd been so naïve. "I know it's scary to think of escaping, but I can help you. Get you to a shelter where you'll be safe. My car is here, and I'll take you wherever you want to go."

"You will?" Angel's voice cracked. "Will you take me to—"

"Excuse me, but what is going on?"

Piper jumped.

Seeming far taller than Mount Shasta, Sir Ethan stared down at her. His face was all hard edges, and his eyes held less warmth than a Kansas blizzard. The sheer power in his gaze turned her bones to water.

His friend stood beside him, just as broad-shouldered and muscular, his black hair in a long braid. An amused expression didn't mask his dominant nature.

Fear was a rushing roar in Piper's ears. *Be strong, be strong.*

"Angel." Sir Ethan turned to his slave. His brows pulled together.

Oh, no. Jumping up, Piper interposed her body between them. "Don't you hurt her; you leave her alone."

Sir Ethan's black-eyed friend lifted an eyebrow. "I think there might be a misunderstanding here."

"I doubt that." Heart pounding like a jackhammer, Piper felt her right hand fist and rise.

"No, oh no." Angel wrapped cold hands around Piper's wrist. "It's all a mistake. My fault. This sweet woman thought you were cruel and wanted to help me, that's all."

Silently, Ethan regarded Angel and Piper, then his lips quirked. "She wanted to save you from the evil Master?"

Piper eyed him, unable to speak. Her heart had lodged somewhere in her throat.

He shook his head. "There is no need for rescue."

Piper didn't let her skepticism show on her face...or the doubt that was growing. Had she jumped to a wrong conclusion?

Angel patted her arm. "Sir, if you'll give me a moment...?"

The sharp blue gaze swept over Piper again. "That might be best. We'll be right there" He motioned to a table a few paces away. Too close for Angel to be able to escape without being intercepted. "Call if you need me."

As the two men moved away, Piper's courage emptied out, leaving only fear behind. She swallowed down nausea and looked at the other woman. "You don't want to leave him."

"No. Oh, I'm so sorry. I've been befuddled all day long. It's nothing to do with Sir Ethan. My Master is..." Angel's eyes turned teary. "I didn't want to be here, and all I heard was that you'd take me where I wanted to go."

"But he's not abusive?"

"No, Sir Ethan is very kind to me. Really." Angel patted her hand. "You are so sweet. And brave—I saw how you stepped in front of me. Truly, I'm where I belong right now." Her tone was resolute. Her gaze level.

"It seems as if I messed up." Piper frowned. Although Angel had been crying, her skin held no marks of bruising, welts, or scars. She hadn't cringed when she'd spoken to her Master. "I'm sorry if I caused problems for you."

"You haven't, truly. I can't believe you offered to help a stranger. You're amazing." Angel squeezed her fingers and let go. "I'll just go explain."

Frowning, Piper watched as Angel joined the two men—and no, the slave didn't look as if she was worried about being struck.

Averting her gaze, Piper felt her face heat. *Way to go, Piper. You just caused a scene. A little one, but still...*

After a minute, she pulled in a breath and rose to her feet. Unable to help herself, she glanced back over.

And met the Master's gaze.

She didn't look away, even though the pit of her stomach slid downward several inches.

But he didn't glare at her. Instead, the laugh-lines at the corners of his eyes crinkled.

Her face went hotter. Knees feeling like jelly, she hurried in the other direction.

"Girlfriend, have you been in the sun too long?" Dixon stepped in front of her and patted her cheek. "You're all flushed."

Great. Lovely. Just shoot me now. "I'm a little warm. There's actually sun out today."

"You obviously need something with lots of ice. Come with me and we'll talk Stan-the-Man out of another drink."

"Right. A drink would be good." *Maybe.* She set her hand on her quivering stomach. That whole confrontation had frightened her spitless. Hopefully, she hadn't shown it, but God, Dominants scared her. Attracted her and scared her. Talk about a double-edged sword.

She pulled in a breath as she followed Dixon past groups of people. How many of them were Masters? Her skin prickled. This was like being in a horror movie and discovering a scattering of the guests were really vampires waiting to slaughter her.

Chills played tag up her spine before she gave herself a shake. *Enough*.

Turning her thoughts in a new direction, she remembered she had a goal in mind for this party. "Dix, how about an introduction to some nice single guys. Non-kinky ones—you know, *vanilla* guys."

"Dudette," he protested. "Not even a few sprinkles for fun?"

She thought of Sir Ethan. What kinky sprinkles would he be into? The thought created a disconcerting pulse in her depths.

Ignore the chemistry, dammit. "No sprinkles. Just vanilla," she said firmly.

Sitting at a table with Xavier, Ethan rubbed his lower lip as he watched the feisty little woman being introduced to a group of people. Piper—that was her name. A little below average height, sweet curves. His first impression when she was hugging Dixon had been *cute*. But she was far more complex than that.

Quite an intriguing woman.

He glanced at Angel who stood in front of him. "I'm ready for your explanation now."

Malik's slave looked thoroughly chagrined. "I'm afraid I gave the young woman the wrong impression, Sir. She thought I was a slave being held against my will. She said she'd take me to a shelter."

About what he'd thought—and very commendable. It was rare someone would step forward to intervene.

He glanced at the man beside him—his best friend since boarding school—and saw the same respect in his eyes. When Xavier's mother had fled her husband, Ethan had learned about the harsh reality of abuse.

However... He frowned at Angel, recalling the sentence she'd started with Piper: *Will you take me to...* "You aren't being held against your will, sweetheart."

"No, Sir. But"—her eyes pooled with tears—"I heard only that she'd take me wherever I wanted to go."

"Ah. I understand." Heart aching for her, Ethan sat the slave next to him and took her hand.

"I'm missing something," Xavier said. "Where did you want to go, Angel?"

"To the hospital. To be with Malik." Her Master had been hospitalized yesterday after a car accident.

Xavier gave Ethan a quizzical look. "That sounds reasonable to me."

"Angel, tell Xavier why you are here at a party rather than still at hospital with your Master," Ethan ordered softly.

"Because he had surgery today, and the nurses wouldn't let me sit with him." Anger thinned her voice. "Sir Ethan thought this party would keep me occupied. Master didn't want me sitting in a waiting room all day and night."

"Of course he didn't." Xavier gave her a level look. "I'd give my Abby the same order."

Angel's shoulders slumped. "I just...just want to be with him."

"But you can't." Ethan edged his tone enough to snap her out of her funk. "Not today."

Knowing he'd be stuck in hospital for days, Malik had asked Ethan to serve as Angel's temporary Master. Some slaves suddenly deprived of a Master had problems. By keeping her under command, Ethan could provide some emotional stability.

Softening his voice, he added, "Tonight you'll need to get your rest, pet. Tomorrow, Malik will be awake and hurting."

"Yes. He'll need me then." She nodded, her chin lifting. "I'll be there for him."

"Yes, you will. He's lucky to have you." Married a dozen years, the two were an inspiration. Still deeply in love, although he doubted the feisty little Piper would believe it.

Ethan saw she'd joined a group of people. Mostly men. Her melodic laugh rang out across the terrace.

Interesting woman. Afraid, but courageous. Confident, yet her gaze was haunted. Those wide, vulnerable eyes had roused his protective instincts.

As if sensing his attention, she looked around. When she met his gaze, she turned her back, although her muscles remained tense as if he'd pounce on her from behind.

Xavier chuckled. "You worry the fuck out of her, don't you?"

"So it seems." If he hadn't had Angel with him, he would have enjoyed worrying her some more.

CHAPTER TWO

"Tomorrow is Sunday. Neither of us has to work. Why don't you invite me upstairs?" Leaning against the red brick wall of her apartment building, Piper's date offered her an expectant smile.

She managed not to sigh. Brian, the accountant she'd met at Dixon's party yesterday, was a very nice man. Exceedingly handsome. Intelligent, stable, pleasant, nice. But there was no chemistry, at least on her part. He apparently felt otherwise.

But her reaction to Sir Ethan had shown her what chemistry could be. Even with past lovers, she'd never gotten such a dizzying zing.

"I'm sorry, but I never take a day off. This isn't a good time for me." She stopped as she realized she'd verged into dishonesty. *Bad Piper.* An open-ended brush-off wasn't fair to him and unworthy of her. "Brian, you're an awesome guy who deserves someone great. But that someone isn't me. Although I had a wonderful time tonight, platonic is how I feel."

In fact, she'd have had just as much fun with one of her friends and not had to deal with any sexual pressure.

His eyes widened in disbelief. He probably didn't get turned down often. "Oh. Right. Then...right."

He leaned in to kiss her anyway, and she set her hand on his chest. Why did they always try? Didn't anyone know what platonic meant?

With a slightly annoyed huff, he straightened. "Well. Okay. It was fun. Anyway. Have a nice rest of the night."

"You, too." See? He really was a nice man.

As he walked away, she sighed. What was wrong with her that there was no chemistry? Another failure. She held her purse with the key fob up to the access reader, heard the lock disengage, and slipped through the door into the marble entryway. *Forget running up the stairs.* Tired of it all, she took the elevator.

Once in her apartment, she washed her face and changed into pink and black floral leggings and an oversized black tank. Back to normal, Piper flopped down among the colorful pillows on her comfy couch. Alone. "So much for dating nice guys."

Silence filled the room, darkened the corners, and scented the air with loneliness.

Even despite the Defiler, she'd still hoped to find a companion to share her life. Someone to watch scary movies with—because he'd be the kind of man a woman could hide behind. Someone who liked to have fun—because laughter was always better when shared.

She shook her head. Long ago, during Piper's group therapy, the counselor asked for everyone's idea of the perfect evening. The other women came up with fancy dinner and dancing, concerts, tropical evenings. Piper had liked all their ideas. Hey, she was totally social. However, her dream evening was staying at home—a fireplace with low flames, sharing drinks and snuggling together on a comfy couch. Reading together. And sex. Surely, there was a man out there she'd actually want to have sex with. Someone who would make her girl-parts tingle.

Someone who would love her as much as she'd love him. Would care for her.

Someone she could serve.

Wait, no. Not that. What was she *thinking*? As jitters scraped over her nerves, she pulled a pillow into her arms. She didn't want to serve a man. Okay, tending to people filled a need, but that was people. Not one man. Not a Master. Never again. *Uh-uh*. Looking after others was her *career* now, not something to give for free. Or for *love*.

Hopes or not, she might not be capable of having a healthy relationship. Not anymore. She wasn't cynical about love. Some people, inside and outside the lifestyle, found wonderful partners. Look at Stan and Dixon. But maybe it wasn't for her.

Because I'm worthless.

No, no, that wasn't true. She scowled, determinedly replacing the thought with healthier ones. *I'm worthy. I'm smart and kind, and I run a fantastic business and make great cookies and have amazing friends.*

Her time as a slave had left her pretty messed up. Then again, her self-confidence hadn't been rock-solid before the Defiler—not since Piper was ten and Mom married super-religious Gideon. Although this was the twenty-first century where unwed mothers were a dime a dozen, her stepfather had been repulsed that Piper was born out of wedlock. Just by existing, Piper had exposed her mother's shameful behavior—and Gideon's son would point out Piper's bastard status at every opportunity.

Gideon had been polite but cold. Eventually, her mother had followed suit.

It'd hurt to know she wasn't wanted.

That was then; this is now. Scowling, she pulled herself out of her pity party. So she just had to work harder to appreciate herself. And, face it, she was pretty damn cool.

Speaking of cool... She went into the kitchen and scanned the tiny cartons in the freezer. There—vanilla ice cream with chocolate chunks. Sweet with something to crunch on.

Dammit, why couldn't Brian have lit up her libido? He was fully as good-looking as Sir Ethan. But, nope. Even when Brian had held her hand, put his arm around her, and nuzzled her neck, she felt no sizzle.

Whereas merely a look from Sir Ethan had sent excitement shooting through her. Oh, he'd scared her, too. But at this safe distance, she could admit the damn Dominant had turned her on.

He'd known that she was scared of him.

She'd amused him.

Scowling, she scooped up a bite of ice cream. As the sweet vanilla melted in her mouth, she bit down on the dark chocolate chunks.

Like an ogre chewing on bones.

Crunch, crunch. Take that, Sir Ethan.

On second thought, she was angrier with herself than him. Her attempt to stand up to him had left her almost puking with fear. It just wasn't fair that the only men who had the right chemistry for her were scary-ass Dominants.

Slumping back on the couch, she took another big bite of ice cream.

Maybe she should see about getting help. There was no question that her unhappy childhood followed by the Defiler had left her with issues. When first in SF, she'd had counseling, but stopped the minute the therapist sounded disapproving of BDSM. Maybe she should try again with a more open-minded therapist.

Meantime, she'd continue avoiding Doms and Masters. Wasn't that funny though? Because, after being a slave, she understood them, what they needed, what they liked, and...

She straightened. *Hmm.*

Chatelaines' new competitor advertised itself as being old-fashioned, like having a '50s style wife at home. Much like what Chatelaines did, but from what she'd heard, the new company's attitude was conservative to the point of looking down on anything other than heterosexual, married lifestyles.

Five of Stan's and Dixon's guests had enquired about hiring

Chatelaines, possibly because she'd been with Dixon and obviously comfortable with his D/s relationship.

Working with people in alternative lifestyles wouldn't bother her staff. She made a point of hiring open-minded people and using open-minded contractors.

Perhaps, rather than avoiding Doms, she should try luring them in. Not as lovers, but as clients. She felt her heart pick up a beat. This might be the answer to her company thriving, despite the new competition.

But...*Dominants*. Oh, God, what good would it do to have a thriving company if the owner died of fear? Could she interact comfortably with Masters like Sir Ethan?

Despite the ice cream, her mouth went dry.

Anger rose inside her—at herself. All this anxiety was intolerable. She couldn't—*wouldn't*—live in fear. She'd managed to get past being a slave, become independent, found friends, and made a living. It was time to work on her neurosis about BDSM and Dominants. At the cold chill that ran through her, she pulled the blanket off the back of the couch and huddled under it.

Stop it, Piper. This was an excellent direction for Chatelaines, no matter how much stress it might cause her personally. She just needed to get comfortable being around Doms. To stop avoiding them. To stop being scared. Because there was nothing to be scared about. Most Doms were nice people.

Aaaand telling herself that wasn't helping at all.

On her last vacation, the woman on the plane next to her had been terrified of flying. Her patronizing husband kept repeating that planes rarely crashed, and she should relax. Like saying it over and over would help?

Piper half-grinned and started her own reassuring chant: *Don't be scared; most Doms are nice people. Don't be scared; most Doms are nice people.*

Yeah, no. Didn't work for her either.

CHAPTER THREE

The Yanks had a saying—*Thank God it's Friday*—one with which Ethan had to agree. After changing out of his suit into jeans and a soft chamois shirt, Ethan Worthington walked down to the ground floor, to what Simon's woman had taken to calling his man cave. Xavier's Abby called it Ethan's English pub.

He smiled slightly. The ladies had a point. To the right, the theater section was filled with chocolate leather furniture, the left held a pool table. Stonework arched over the wet bar in the corner. A table and chairs, along with a cozy sitting area, had a view out the door and windows to the patio and small garden area. With the dark wood, leather furnishings, and vintage boxing posters, the big room held the ambiance of his favorite pub back in Oxford.

He heard a thump and glanced toward the couch. Admittedly, pubs rarely allowed cats. "How are you today, Churchill?"

The tan feline stalked across the room and strategically positioned himself at Ethan's feet. Fluffy brown tail wrapped neatly over white-mittened paws, he looked up hopefully. *Cheese?*

"Not today, I'm afraid." Ethan put ice into a glass, pulled out a bottle of The Botanist, poured, and sipped. The complex flavors swept over his tongue. Mint, coriander, apple...more. *Nice.* The Scots distilled a mean gin.

A meow caught his attention, and he looked down into blue eyes almost the color of his own. Churchill stood up, expectations plain.

Chuckling, Ethan set his glass down on the bar. Lifting the portly, eighteen-pound feline required both hands, especially when the cat went limp. The breed was called "ragdoll" for a reason. With the cat against his chest, Ethan picked up his glass and settled into his favorite chair, the one with a view out the window.

Churchill curled into a comfortable ball on his thighs and gave Ethan's hand a happy cheek-rub.

"Sorry, Church, it's been a busy week." A busy month, actually. The tech arena was in a time of flux with some areas stagnating, and others with, to date, unproven inventions. As owner and CEO of the Worthington Tech Group, he held the reins in a variety of companies—too many companies, he sometimes thought—although diversification helped with overall stability. He loved what he did. Guiding new technology and making a profit even while doing things right—ethically, environmentally, and productively—was an exhilarating challenge.

Under his hand, Churchill purred away. Unlike other cats Ethan had owned, Church didn't hold a grudge. And, thank God, the feline was more even-tempered than the prime minister he'd been named for. Maybe because he was afraid of being tossed out to starve on the streets. Again.

Years ago, after purchasing the Russian Hill house, Ethan had found Churchill in the tiny garden area, half-starved, flea-infested, with matted fur and a raging abscessed tooth. The vet suspected the owner hadn't wanted to deal with illness and simply tossed the cat out.

Being lovers, not fighters, ragdoll cats didn't survive long on the streets.

Ragdolls were also incredibly sociable. "Sorry that I've been away so much. You're missing Angel, aren't you?"

Churchill heaved a small sigh and did a few pushy-paw movements as if in agreement.

Picking up his glass, Ethan swirled the liquid and listened to the silence in the house. Yesterday, Malik had been discharged, and Angel was finally home with her Master.

As Ethan set his glass down, he noticed Angel's duty list on the end table. Malik had written out what he hoped Ethan would do for her each evening: assign her a journal subject, ask questions about it, and administer a spanking. Assign cooking or cleaning—although Ethan hadn't bothered since she'd been so exhausted each night. Instead, he'd picked out light-hearted movies and, remembering times at Malik's home, had her settle on a cushion at his feet. She'd needed the sense of being under control, something she'd lost with Malik in hospital.

They'd managed well enough.

Taking another sip of his drink, Ethan stroked Churchill. Although the house felt uncommonly lonely now, Ethan didn't particularly want a slave, and Angel wasn't what he looked for in a submissive.

Not that he was looking. Not now, probably not ever.

How many times could a man be burned before he stepped away from the flame? After Nicola's treachery and death, he hadn't dated for a couple of years. After that, his attempted relationships had taught him that wealth attracted far too many women who didn't care who he was as long as he had money. There were days he felt like a fox running from a pack of hunting hounds.

Didn't that sound bloody egotistical? He was simply tired of being fawned over.

That brought to mind a woman who hadn't wanted to win him over—the little black-haired beauty who'd tried to protect Angel at the party.

He grinned. "You should have met her, Church. Although I don't usually go for cute or feisty."

Piper had been intriguing. And oddly familiar. Had he met her before?

No, he would have remembered that thick shoulder-length, black hair. The perfect bow curve of her upper lip. The musical sound of her laughter.

He'd never met her before.

Since he'd never seen her at Dark Haven, he doubted he'd ever see her again.

A pity that.

CHAPTER FOUR

With an adorable black cockapoo named Blackie trailing after her, Piper strolled through Abby and Xavier's home, giving it the white-glove treatment. The cleaning crew had finished the second cleaning. The landscapers had now had over a week to work on the grounds.

Initial shakedown complete, it was her turn. The assigned chatelaine would normally have been with her, but Ivy was on bereavement leave.

"The sink in the guest bathroom has a slow drip," Piper said into her phone. Awesome devices, smartphones. Dictating sure beat taking notes on a clipboard, especially since her handwriting was almost illegible.

"Get the maintenance guy to change out the hallway light to something brighter."

"Make sure the cleaning crew works on the blinds next time. They're still dirty."

The sound of a door startled her, and she turned.

As Abby entered from the garage, Piper winced. The owner was home early.

"Hi, Piper. I wondered whose car that was. I didn't know

you'd be here." As Blackie yipped and enthusiastically spun in *my-owner-is-home* circles, Abby bent to pet him.

"I'm sorry. We like to check things out in person after the first week, but I'm done, and I'll get out of your hair."

Abby eyed the phone in her hand. "You're calling the cleaning service to yell at them?"

"No. They did fairly well." Piper showed the display of her phone. "I'm just making notes on anything the landscaping or cleaning crews might do better."

"Notes? Can I see?"

Piper smiled. During the initial interview, she'd learned the professor was brilliant—and curious about everything. "Sure. Here."

Taking the phone, Abby glanced through the list. "Wow. I never noticed half these things, and the rest, I admit, I just didn't bother to tell the services about."

"I've learned we women often feel too awkward or even guilty about asking for what is our due."

Abby's mouth curved in a rueful grin. "It's embarrassing that I know exactly what you're talking about."

"I know, right? But a chatelaine doesn't have that psychological hang-up when defending the client."

"That's a very interesting observation."

"Being picky is part of the job," Piper said. "Ensuring there aren't any annoyances, no matter how small, in a client's life. Heaven knows there are enough things to irritate a person outside of the home."

"There's a truth." Abby smiled. "Is it permissible to offer a chatelaine a glass of wine? I'd love to ask you some questions about how you got into the business."

Piper hesitated. Wine with a client was undoubtedly against proper business protocol. Then again, guys were always having alcoholic good-old-boy lunches, right?

"It's a beautiful day. We can go outside and sit on the patio," Abby coaxed.

The mid-June weather was gorgeous. How could she resist? "I'd love a glass of wine."

One glass of wine led to two along with nibbling on cheese and crackers. Abby was appallingly easy to talk with, and it was fun to hear about how in love she was with her husband, Xavier. Every time Abby talked about him, she practically glowed.

"But you grew up in Kansas? How did you end up here in San Francisco? Did a company move you here?"

Piper thought of the long drive. Arriving destitute, living in the SF shelter. Finding Stella's Employment. "A bad relationship convinced me to get far, far away from Kansas."

"One of those, hmm? I know how a bad relationship can mess up a person's life." Her tone wasn't...exactly...bitter. "Dixon says you're an amazing boss, by the way."

"He's an amazing employee. Everyone from clients to staff loves him." Was there anyone who could think of Dixon and not smile? "When the apartment across from his came up for rent, he got the manager to give me first shot at it." In San Francisco, people fought over rentals like seagulls spotting a tasty tidbit on the beach.

Abby grinned. "Dixon has a way about him."

"I so owe him for the apartment. It's like living in the heart of San Francisco." Although Abby's Tiburon place had amazing views of Angel Island and San Francisco across the way, living in the bustling city center suited Piper right down to the ground.

"That makes sense." Abby picked up a slice of Gouda. "You seem like a people person. Being around your friends would be important."

"It is." Feeling a twang of unhappiness, Piper ran her finger through the dampness on the table. Despite having wonderful friends, she had no one who knew about her past as a slave. It was too humiliating, and unless a person was submissive, she wouldn't understand the compulsion to serve. To give a Master...everything.

At the silence, she looked up to see Abby studying her.

Before the woman could speak, footsteps sounded, and a tall man stepped out onto the patio.

It was Sir Ethan from Stan and Dix's party. The Master-class hardass.

Piper froze, even as excitement fizzed in her blood. She'd dreamed of his hard handsome face, of the dark stubble-beard along his jawline—and dammit, he was even more devastating than in her dreams.

His perfectly tailored, elegant suit showed off his broad shoulders as he walked out onto the patio. He set a bottle of wine and two glasses on their table. "Ladies."

"Ethan. How nice to see you." Abby rose to greet him, and he bent to kiss her cheek.

Remembering how she'd made a total idiot of herself at the party, Piper could feel her face grow hot.

How quickly could she get out of here?

"Blackie cornered Xavier to administer the proper amount of petting, so I've been sent out with the wine." The man's English-accented, sonorous voice smoothed Piper's flaring nerves like a gentle stroke—and she resented that even more.

"No matter what Xavier thinks, Blackie is the boss in our household," Abby said. "Piper, let me introduce Sir Ethan Worthington."

Piper pulled in a breath. Looked up. When the Dom's piercing blue eyes met hers, the bottom dropped out of her stomach.

Then she frowned. Had Abby just introduced the man with his lifestyle title? Did that mean Abby was submissive? Then again, the way authority just poured from Sir Ethan, maybe Abby couldn't help herself.

"Ethan, this is Piper Delaney," Abby finished.

The Dom held out his hand. "We spoke briefly at Stan's party. It's good to see you again, Ms. Delaney."

Apparently, he wasn't going to say anything about her rudeness or about Angel. Relieved beyond measure, Piper took his hand. It was warm, the palm callused, his grip firm, but not overpowering. The way he studied her as he held her hand sent a wicked lick of heat through her body.

"Mr. Worthington," she said, keeping her voice level. Even if he was polite, she wasn't going to call him Sir. Or lie and say it was good to see him.

But *would* it be a lie?

"Just Ethan, please." Releasing her hand, he refilled her and Abby's glasses before pouring wine in the two he'd brought out.

When he sat at Piper's right, she rose, trying to make her escape look casual and not a rout. "Abby, I'm running late. I need to be going."

Her escape was stalled when another man walked out onto the patio. He was, maybe, six-four and a couple of inches taller than Ethan. The black eyes and a hint of reddish complexion spoke of Native American ancestry, although his features were a striking mix of ethnicities. Spotting his long black braid, Piper recognized Ethan's friend from the party.

Could this get any more awkward?

He bent to kiss his wife, fingers under her chin, tilting her head up, taking his time. Anyone with eyes to see could tell the man was as much a Dominant as Sir Ethan.

Piper's stomach tightened. Only two—there were only two Masters here. She shouldn't feel as if she was surrounded.

Straightening, the man turned to Piper. His head tilted. "You were at Stan and Dixon's party. It's good to see you again."

Thank God, he didn't say, *even though you were very rude.* But the amusement in his eyes was clear.

"I told you I met her at the party." Abby looked between her husband and Piper. "Piper, this is my husband, Xavier, as I'm sure you've guessed. Xavier, this is Piper Delaney of Chatelaines."

His smile changed his entire face from dangerous to compellingly attractive. "It's a pleasure, Piper. I wish I'd known about your services years ago." After shaking hands with her, he glanced at the other man who had risen when Piper stood. "Ethan, Piper owns the company I was telling you about. The one that oversees a household and eliminates problems before they even register as a blip."

"Excellent." Ethan's tanned face, dark beard, and white flashing smile made her toes curl. Dammit, she was *not* attracted to him.

"Ms. Delaney, Xavier has told me that I need you."

I need you. The sentiment every slave longed to hear, and when spoken in his strong, resonant voice, the words packed a potent punch.

But she wasn't a slave any longer or even a submissive. No way, no how. Despite the delight shimmering through her.

Get a grip, Piper. He was interested in her company's services, not in hers. Certainly not in her as a slave. The man already had a slave.

Attraction or not, he scared her. Lord, marketing to people in the BDSM lifestyle was a crazy goal. Fate had been eavesdropping, hadn't it? Filling her request before she'd a chance to reconsider.

She was going to put on pointy boots and kick fate into next week.

With an effort, she tore her gaze from the English Dom and smiled at Xavier. "Being recommended is a wonderful compliment. Thank you."

He nodded, sipping his wine.

Ignoring the flutters in her stomach, she forced herself to pull a card from her vest pocket. Only a fool turned down a possible client, whether he was a Master or not. She set her card on the table. "The website has information about our services, pricing, and any other details you might need. If you—"

He picked up the card and gave her an easy smile. "I looked Chatelaines up a couple of days ago. Let's make an appointment."

His entire posture, the look in his gaze...it all shouted

control of himself and everything around him. Her heart skipped a beat and then another. Obviously, fear and attraction were a completely unhealthy mix. He wasn't good for her.

"An appointment. Of course." When she swallowed hard, his eyes narrowed slightly, and he regarded her closer. Hastily, she pulled out her phone and opened the calendar app.

The next day worked out for them both.

"I'll see you tomorrow, then." Why, oh why, did her emotions tumble around as if she was excited at the thought of seeing him again? How insane was that?

With a determined effort, she kept her outward expression calm, her voice perfectly polite and dignified as she bade him and Xavier goodbye.

As Abby walked with her to the front door, Piper figured Sir Ethan would never realize how much he unsettled her. Probably. Although his gaze had been far too observant.

God, please don't let the Dom know how much he unsettled her.

Ethan sipped his wine, his gaze on the door. "That's a very interesting woman." Her beautiful watchful eyes—the darkest of browns, velvety soft—were filled with secrets. And from her wariness and her defense of Angel, Ms. Delaney had been hurt in the past. By a man. Maybe by a Dominant?

Her heart-shaped face had a stubborn chin and dimples that said she knew how to laugh. But she hadn't laughed. In fact, he doubted she could have fled any faster.

He glanced at Xavier. "I'd like to blame her hasty retreat on your *my liege* effect, but I appear to be the one who unsettled her."

Nicknamed *My Liege* by the submissives in his BDSM club, Xavier grinned. "She watched you like you were liable to pull out a whip at any moment. She was far braver at the party."

"She was." Why the difference?

Leaning back, Ethan listened to the soft murmur of women's voices coming from inside the house. At least, Ms. Delaney was comfortable with Abby as she had been with Angel.

Angel. There, that was the reason. Ethan tilted his glass toward the house. "At the party, she felt she needed to defend Angel from me. She had to be brave."

"I think you have it." Xavier grinned at Ethan. "She's a pretty little submissive, isn't she?"

Bollocks. Why was it that married men liked to play matchmaker? It was almost as annoying as being single and pursued only for his bank account. "I doubt Ms. Delaney is looking for a Dom. Even if she were, I need her company's services, Xavier, not hers."

"Of course," Xavier said smoothly. "I realize that."

"Do you also realize that you're a daft wanker?"

A sputter of laughter sounded, and Abby settled into her chair. "I'm not sure I've ever heard you swear before."

"You should have heard Worth when we were in boarding school." Xavier took her hand. "Not that I understood half of what he said the first year. Teenage Brits have a vocabulary all their own."

"I was quite displeased when I realized the Yank had no clue as to the filthy names I was calling him. Those were some of my best insults." Ethan heard the sound of a car leaving and asked Abby, "Did Ms. Delaney tell you what upset her?"

"No." Abby nailed him with a stare. "I like her, Ethan. Don't intimidate her or scare her off, all right?"

He picked up his wine and swirled it. "I'm not intimidating. Where do you come by these notions?"

It was exasperating when both Abby and Xavier burst into laughter.

Fine. He leaned back in his chair and considered how he'd go about being un-intimidating. Because, oddly enough, he didn't want to frighten Ms. Delaney.

Quite the contrary.

CHAPTER FIVE

"This is totally inadequate service." Voice just short of a shout, the middle-aged executive was red with anger. "I want my money returned."

The demand was unreasonable. Piper smoothed the front of her charcoal blazer, but the stalling action didn't alleviate her fear. She started to shake. Who was she to expect fairness? She was nothing. No one.

No. Stop that. Rosalie, the man's chatelaine, had requested Piper's presence for support—not to watch the owner of the company go belly up. Piper firmed her spine. "I'm sorry you feel that way, Mr. Tannehill. Can you tell me what the problem is?"

"I asked her to do some cleaning. I mean, look at this place!" Mr. Tannehill waved his hand and scowled at the short, dark-haired chatelaine standing beside Piper. Rosalie was thirty and one of the most experienced and conscientious chatelaines in the company.

Piper looked around. Truly, the place was a mess. Obviously, the man had given a party the night before. Glasses, spilled alcohol, scattered bags of chips, and plates with old food littered the surfaces and the carpet.

"I can see you need the room cleaned," Piper said gently to

the client before asking Rosalie. "Did you call a cleaning company?"

"Yes. They'll be here within two hours."

"I need it cleaned now," Tannehill snapped. "This is intolerable."

Now? No way. "Since cleaning services usually schedule a week in advance, it's impressive that Rosalie found you someone who could fit you in today."

"Yeah, yeah, yeah. Two hours. In the meantime, she can pick the place up."

Piper folded her trembling hands tightly in front of her. *Be strong, be strong.* "As I explained in our initial interview—and as is noted in the contract—your chatelaine's job is to supervise the various services. She does not do the cleaning."

His lips curled up into a sneer. "Then *you* do it. Or I'll let everyone know that Chatelaines' services are completely inadequate."

She opened her mouth to cave in—to bow her head and clean the room. Rosalie's under-the-breath, *"Not in this lifetime"* snapped Piper out of her head.

Piper owned the company. She didn't do cleaning. What was she *thinking*? That she was still a slave?

She forced her voice to stay level. Calm. "Mr. Tannehill, I'm sorry, but..."

"But what?" He figured out what she was going to say, and his face darkened further. "I should never have taken a chance on a company run by a woman. Fucking bitch."

At her chatelaine's shocked expression, Piper swallowed. She'd instructed her staff they weren't to tolerate verbal abuse from the clients. Now it was up to her to set the right example.

"Mr. Tannehill, I can see the terms of the contract are unacceptable to you, so we'll consider our services terminated as of this minute. You'll be refunded for the remainder of this month."

Before the man could let loose any more profanity, she motioned for Rosalie to leave and followed her out the door.

Once outside, Piper leaned against her car, shaking like a leaf.

"What a horrible man." After casting a glare over her shoulder, Rosalie turned to Piper. "Hey, boss. Are you all right?"

"I... Yes. Sorry." Piper straightened. "I hate confrontations." Assertiveness was difficult when braced for blows or caustic insults that would shred her already damaged ego.

"Oh. Sometimes I forget that most people aren't used to conflict. My family's Italian, and we yell about everything." Rosalie huffed a laugh before her expression sobered. "I'm sorry about calling you. I just didn't know what to do when he demanded that I clean his place."

Seeing Rosalie's worried expression, Piper took her hands. "You did everything right, including calling me. I daresay this would have happened sooner or later with Mr. Tannehill. He's the kind of person to push the limits and see what he can get away with. It's better to boot him from our client list now."

"Oh, good. I'm glad you're not mad."

"Not with you. But do remember to fill out an incident report for the records, please."

"Will do. I'll also cancel the cleaning service and tell them to leave him to his mess." Rosalie grinned, then glanced at her watch. "I need to get moving."

"Me, too." Next up was the initial interview with Ethan Worthington. Dread curled chilly fingers around Piper's spine. Mr. Tannehill had been bad enough, and he wasn't even a Dominant. Why had she thought dealing with Mr. Worthington personally would be a good idea?

No, stop right there. Mr. Worthington had been nothing but polite and controlled.

Besides, her self-defense instructor said fears shouldn't be avoided or ignored. Fears were to be confronted—over and over if needed. As Piper started up her car, she grinned. Self-defense instructors were probably all sadists. *Look at the great occupation I found, Ma. Not only a willing victim, but the client will even* pay *me to pick on her.*

The upscale Russian Hill neighborhood where Ethan Worthington lived was one of steep tree-lined streets, tiny parks, and fantastic views. Pockets of trendy shops vied with gorgeous Victorian and Edwardian homes, a scattering of high-rise apartments, and a serious lack of parking.

As with many houses in space-impacted San Francisco, Mr. Worthington's stucco-and-wood home was tall but narrow. Gray with white trim, the three-story building nestled side-by-side with other Victorians.

Like many of her clients, Ethan Worthington was wealthy. Doing her usual research, she'd found he owned and ran the Worthington Tech Group, a conglomerate of mostly tech companies. He had a reputation for being fair and honest, and employees rated his companies as wonderful places to work. All good.

He still made her want to flee. Being attracted to him scared her even more.

A bleep on her phone signaled a new text.

"Play the message," she said.

Over her speaker came the text-to-speech: "Ms. Delaney, I left the garage door up for you. Do park inside."

God, he was watching? A glance up at the house showed only dark windows, yet he must be standing there, looking down at the street with those too-sharp eyes. Her heart thumped hard.

She pulled in, parked, and slid out of the car.

All right, here goes. Taking a moment, she dusted off her gray, tailored pants, pulled her matching blazer on over the pale blue blouse, and twitched it straight. Her black flats were spotless. Hair still tidily French braided. Perfectly professional. Perfectly boring. She slung on her work satchel cross-body. *Ready*.

The anxiety that had diminished flared up as she stared at the door.

He was a *Master*.

No, he was a client. Just a client. Abby's husband, Xavier, was a Master, too, after all. He'd been polite, and Abby was thoroughly likable.

Piper closed her eyes and worked on her breathing, trying to get herself in the right frame of mind. *Listen, observe, recommend.* She could do this. Had been doing it for years now.

Her mouth was so dry she couldn't summon enough spit to swallow.

Before she could move, her client walked through the garage's interior door. Intimidatingly tall and built. Sharp-edged, darkly handsome face. As she moved forward, she focused on the small unevenness on the bridge of his nose. He wasn't perfect. The man wasn't a god. *Remember that.* "Mr. Worthington."

In a white button-up shirt and tailored pants, he'd obviously come from work. But he'd discarded whatever tie he'd worn and undone the top two shirt buttons for comfort. His rolled-up sleeves showed hard, corded forearms with a slight scattering of brown hair. "Just Ethan, please."

It was a client's prerogative, choosing how to be called. However, she had no intention of extending him the privilege of calling her by her first name. Especially not a Master. "Ethan, then. How are you doing today?"

"Quite well, thank you." He led her to an elevator. With a graceful gesture for her to enter the elevator, he pushed a button on the wall to close the garage door. "Would you prefer to talk first or look around?"

"Let's do both."

He pushed the button labeled ROOF. "All right. We can start with the top and work our way down.

The elevator opened onto the rooftop patio.

Walking out, Piper stared. The whole of San Francisco lay at her feet. Farther away, the bay sparkled in the sunlight, and the graceful beauty of the Golden Gate Bridge brought tears to her eyes. Her voice came out a whisper. "I've never seen such a lovely view."

"It's why I'm still here." He stood right beside her. Only inches away.

Reminded of who he was—*what* he was—she stepped back.

He lifted an eyebrow. His sharp gaze considered her face, her tensed shoulders, her hands rubbing her slacks. "Forgive me, but you seem somewhat unsettled. What can I do to make you more comfortable?"

Feeling her fingers tremble, she folded her hands at her waist. "I'm not—"

His gaze lifted from her hands to her face, and he gave a Dom's slight shake of the head. The one that meant *don't lie to me*.

She swallowed. Could she tell him she didn't like Dominants? Nope and never. "I had a rather upsetting incident before I arrived." That was true enough, and in all reality, she might have been able to disguise her anxiety if not for Mr. Tannehill's unnerving virulence.

"I see." He studied her for another second, and his voice softened. "Would you feel better if we postponed our appointment until later?"

Later? *Never* would be good. She could get one of her chatelaines to do the intake.

However, if she chickened out now, would she ever have the courage to deal with her fears? A coward was not the person she wanted to be.

And he was being incredibly kind. She lifted her chin. "No, but thank you for being so understanding."

Without waiting for an answer, she pulled her notebook from her satchel. "What would you like done in this area?"

His slow smile seemed to show...approval? He motioned toward the wicker furniture and the foliage plants in huge pots. "The standard cleaning. Maintenance of the flooring and trim. The pots are on automatic waterers, but the plants need trimming and fertilization."

She nodded, checked boxes on her forms, added notes as he

continued. As if knowing how she felt, he'd stepped away from the personal and was being all business, and somehow that made him even more likable. Despite seeing her vulnerability, he wasn't taking advantage. Was giving her space both physically and emotionally.

How rare was that?

She followed him downstairs.

With warm taupe walls and off-white carpeting, the master bedroom took up half the third floor. Tall windows along one wall filled the room with light.

The black solid steel canopy bed made her stare. Extra crosspieces connecting the top bars. She knew—*knew*—he used the frame for bondage.

Heat crept into her face even as she took a step away from him.

His gaze followed hers. A slight crease of his cheek told her he'd noticed her flush. Again, he didn't take advantage, didn't make any suggestive comments, or move closer.

She'd never met a true gentleman before. Not until now.

The second floor was an open design with kitchen and dining area opening to a huge great room. On this floor, he'd gone with more traditional décor. Off-white walls and glossy dark wood floors and very uncluttered. Subdued Oriental rugs divided the separate spaces. In the living area, two long matching couches faced each other with a coffee table between. Two armchairs in the same brown and sand upholstery bracketed the fireplace. In fact, the large foliage plants were the only asymmetrical elements in the rooms.

This was a man who valued balance...a lot. She made a note to the landscapers that trimming should be kept symmetrical, and another to the cleaning service that he'd want everything returned to its proper place. Leaving a chair out of alignment? He'd notice.

She caught his scent—clean and fresh with a whiff of leather—and realized he was behind her. Reading over her shoulder.

"Interesting observations," he said mildly.

She held her breath.

"Nicely accurate, Ms. Delaney. Very good." His voice held no anger. Her comments hadn't even dented his self-confidence. If anything, he sounded impressed.

He led the way downstairs to the ground floor. The three-car garage occupied the front. The huge room in the rear was obviously where he spent much of his time.

Dark wood paneling. Chocolate leather furniture. A theater area to the right with a screen that took up most of a wall. The pool table space to the left held a corner bar and small table. Black and white posters of famous boxers covered the walls above a shelf of trophies and a pair of boxing gloves.

A man cave. Dark, comfortable, and in fine taste.

Across from the bar was a small sitting area with overstuffed suede armchairs bracketing a matching love seat. "Oh, you have a cat."

On the ottoman, a huge cat blinked and sat up. It had medium-length white fur with a chocolate brown mask, ears, legs, and tail.

"You are so pretty." Delighted, Piper knelt down. "Hey, there, sweetie." She offered a finger.

Rather than tensing, the feline gave her hand a friendly cheek rub.

She stroked the silky soft fur and grinned at the rumbling purr. "You are totally beautiful."

Ethan took a seat. "This is Churchill, who would appreciate someone to visit him on weekdays."

Churchill took a long leisurely stretch and hopped onto Ethan's lap with no doubt that he was welcome there. When the cat took his time settling into a sprawl across Ethan's thighs, the intimidating man didn't seem to mind. His lean hand stroked down the furry back, setting the cat to purring again.

An anxious knot in Piper's chest relaxed. *Aww.*

As Ethan rubbed the cat's cheek, she could almost feel those scarred knuckles on her own skin. Wanted to feel them there.

She turned her gaze away.

"I'd like someone to come on weekdays around noon to give him some playtime and petting," he said.

"Our cat-sitters will fight for the privilege." Heck, she'd be tempted.

But Ethan had a slave. Did the woman not like cats? Where was Angel anyway? What must it be like to live with such a formidably masculine Dom?

Oh. My. *Not thinking that. Uh-uh.* She cleared her throat. "What schedules will we be working around? You gave me your hours, but..."

Ethan scritched under the cat's chin. "There is only me."

"Oh." He and Angel must not live together or even close. Long-distance M/s relationships were popular these days. "All right. Did you want to complete the paperwork now?"

"There's always paperwork, isn't there? Let's get it over with." With a wry smile, he glanced at the cat in his lap. "Since I'm pinned down, would you get us something to drink while we work, please?"

"Of course." She rose.

"The wet bar has a variety of refreshments. I'd like some apple cider." He tilted his head. "It's quite good. I think you might enjoy a glass."

Inside her head, a bell sounded. A chime of recognition. She'd heard that smooth accented voice saying just those words before. *"I think you might enjoy a glass."*

Frozen in place, she stared at him. Those deep blue eyes. Dark hair. That accent and unmistakable voice.

It was *him*. Her champion. The Master who'd talked about a slave who'd gone free. The Master who'd said a slave contract wasn't valid. His words had been the catalyst that had let her escape.

"Ms. Delaney?" He was watching her, one eyebrow up.

"I'd love some cider. Thank you." She hurried over to the wet bar beneath the sleek wall-mounted widescreen TV. Finding the cider in the small built-in fridge, she busied herself pouring two glasses. Her emotions felt ragged, like ripped-up fabric. Fixing him something to drink steadied her.

Over the years, she'd wondered if the English Master had deliberately spoken to inform her that she had options. Had he known he was giving her an escape route?

Maybe.

Probably not.

She stomped on her need to thank him. It wouldn't be wise to mention she recognized him. He'd want to talk about the past.

Never.

She handed him the glass of cider.

"Thank you." He studied her intently for a long second before saying, "Let's get started on the paperwork."

Taking a seat, she pulled out the standard contract. "Bear in mind, it can take a while to get everything properly streamlined, to learn your preferences, to see other areas where we can make a difference. Please, never hesitate to call me if you have any concerns or questions, no matter how minor, or if you find something one of the services could have done better. I'm reachable by email, text, or phone—however you're more comfortable communicating."

"Your younger clients text; the older ones will call?"

She laughed. "You got it. Personalities skew that way, of course. Introverts will text or email, extroverts like to hear a voice or have a meeting."

The smile that tugged on the corners of his mouth let her relax.

After filling out her part of the forms, she scooped the cat from his lap so he could read through the papers. As she settled down in an armchair, Churchill rubbed his muzzle energetically against her thigh before going limp again.

"He likes you." Ethan read through the list of preferences for cleaning, products, times, etc. His brow lifted. "You have an excellent memory."

The compliment sent sparkles of happiness through her. "Part of the job."

He scrawled his signature at the bottom and set the notebook on the ottoman before leaning back and sipping his drink. "You appear to be feeling more at ease."

Her breath caught for a second. He was uncannily observant. Distressingly so. She'd learned the hard way that a Master who discovered her vulnerabilities could use those fears against her.

She breathed out slowly. Talk about paranoia. Ethan had merely made a comment. A kind one, actually. "You have a relaxing home."

"You said you had an upsetting incident before you arrived. Did you handle the person? Is the problem resolved?"

She stared at him. "What?"

"You're a friend of Abby's, Piper. If I can help, I will."

"It's..." She shook her head, unable to find the right words to put him off.

"Can you tell me what happened?" His smooth voice had softened to low and coaxing.

He was the Master she'd always considered her champion, the one who'd thrown a line to pull her out of the abyss. How could she tell him no?

She couldn't meet his gaze. "Nothing horrible occurred. A client who'd had a messy party wanted his place cleaned immediately. Since the cleaning service wouldn't arrive for a couple of hours, he ordered the chatelaine to do it and was unhappy when I reminded him that his chatelaine was there to manage other services."

"In other words, he was rude."

"Well, yes."

"I hope you told him to bugger off."

She choked on her drink and sputtered a laugh.

The spark of amusement in the Dom's eyes almost set her off again.

"I was far more polite than that. In fact, I almost caved in and started cleaning for him. But his assigned chatelaine was there, and I needed to set a good example, and—" She shut her mouth with an almost audible snap. What the heck had she just confessed? "I—"

Ethan didn't look surprised. Or judgmental. Or...anything. Instead, he put his legs up on the ottoman. "Your company is successful partly because you have a talent for service. You learn what makes your customers happy and give them what they need."

She nodded. That had actually been why she'd started her company.

"However, a gift like that backfires when you run into someone you can't please." He hit the nail right on the head. What with running a conglomerate, he must know a lot about people.

"That sounds about right," she agreed glumly. "Even knowing he was out of line, I still feel uncomfortable over leaving him unhappy."

"I daresay." He gave her a level look. "Have you ever been in a hotel room where the temperature is preset and you can't change it?"

What kind of question was that? "Yes."

"Guilt is like that thermometer. When providing an ethical gauge, guilt is useful. Sometimes, though, the regulator has been preset by our parents or society and no longer fits who we are today. If your childhood conscience conflicts with proper adult behavior, you might need to recalibrate your gauge."

Trust a tech company owner to come up with such an odd analogy. She took a minute to work through what he was saying and...he was right. Her guilt about Mr. Tannehill was excessive. In fact, she shouldn't be feeling any remorse at all. "That's a good way to look at it. Thank you."

"You're very welcome."

"Well, I need to be going." She rose and set the cat in her spot.

Churchill gave her an indignant look worthy of a true prime minister.

Gathering the completed paperwork, Piper smiled at Ethan. Look at this—she was actually comfortable. She'd made it through an entire initial interview with a Dominant.

You go, girl. Facing her fears worked, didn't it?

Then he rose. Absolutely confident, devastatingly masculine, terrifyingly powerful. She wasn't sure if her inability to breathe was from fear or attraction.

She should assign someone else to handle his account. She must. "If we could set up an appointment so I can introduce you to your chate—"

"Ms. Delaney," he interrupted. He put his hand on her arm, which silenced her completely. His fingers were warm and strong, as he turned her toward the kitchen area. "I forgot to tell you there are spare cat supplies down here."

"Um, what?"

"Extra tins of food. In case Churchill feels peckish when a sports game lasts too long."

The wry amusement in his voice made her laugh. And relaxed her. Who could fear someone who doted on his furbaby? "I noticed the boxing gloves on the shelf. Are they yours?"

"My first set, yes." Although he didn't smile, a subtle laugh line appeared to the right of his mustache. "I was a skinny lad. My father hoped it would toughen me up."

His corded forearm looked harder than a baseball bat.

"Was his plan successful?"

"Indeed. I did take to the sport." He chuckled. "It proved useful in boarding school."

"Boarding school. You didn't live with your family?"

"My mother died when I was young. My father"—he shook his head slightly—"wasn't comfortable raising a child."

No one had hugged Ethan as a boy; that was so obvious. Pity made her heart ache. She knew how it felt to be unwanted. "Did you know anyone at the school? Was it an okay place?"

He touched her cheek lightly. "You have a soft heart, poppet. I made friends. In fact, the boarding school was where Xavier and I met."

Abby's husband? "I thought Xavier was American."

"His father sent him abroad for school. We got to be friends when I saw the idiot Yank charge in to rescue a nerd from several upperclassmen."

She knew the answer before she asked. "You helped him?"

"Five-to-one is bad sport." Ethan's jaw hardened, and she knew he'd never side with the bullies. "I simply stepped in to assist. It was the first of many fights we shared."

He motioned to a framed photo next to the trophies. Two lanky teens. Ethan had a fat lip. Xavier had a black eye. "By the time we won the brawl, we were friends."

Of course, they'd won. She'd watched him move—always aware and balanced with rippling muscles like a cat. Xavier would flatten an opponent quickly, but if Ethan got angry, she'd bet he'd take the time to inflict some damage first. For sport. "It's good to have friends."

"Yes. When I came to the States"—his gaze darkened—"Xavier was the first to welcome me."

Seeing the pain beneath his stern expression, she reached out. Before he noticed, she pulled her hand back and put herself into professional mode. "I need to get going."

She would have Rosalie take his account. Or...maybe not. He was a champion, saving nerdy kids and lost slaves. He was *her* champion. How could she let someone else look out for him?

Tending his needs herself would be a small way to pay him back.

She smiled at him. "Most of the services you wanted will start tomorrow. I'll touch base with you on Friday. Once everything is in place, I'll set up an appointment to see what needs to be fine-tuned."

Satisfaction glinted in his eyes. "*You* will."

He'd picked up that she'd planned to hand him off to someone else? "Yes, Sir." *No, no, no, Piper.* She cleared her throat. "Yes, that's right."

He didn't move to touch her. Simply smiled. "I'm very pleased. Thank you."

The glow from his smile lasted all the way home.

CHAPTER SIX

Piper considered cookies to be a far finer dessert than cake. More options and designs. Perfect finger food for a fast lifestyle. Putting in oatmeal let a girl pretend a cookie was healthy. But men seemed to like cake better so that's what she'd baked.

Besides, chocolate cake batter was awesome.

Balancing the plastic carrier, Piper crossed the hallway and tapped on Stan and Dixon's door.

A few seconds later, Dix opened it and grinned. "Hey, girlfriend." His gaze fell on the cake, and his eyes widened.

See? Men—so predictable. "This is gratitude-cake to thank you two for inviting me to your party. Chatelaines won five new clients this week, partly because Stan reminded me that making contacts is part of a business owner's job."

"Trust Stan to point that out." Dix rolled his eyes. "Personally, I go to a party to enjoy myself. But it's all good, especially if we get goodies. C'mon in."

His voice rose. "Everybody here likes cake, right?"

What did he mean—everybody?

A chorus of enthusiastic agreement came from three women in the living room.

Piper took a step back. "I'm sorry, Dix. I didn't realize you were entertaining."

"Pffft." He grabbed her wrist and towed her in, kicking the door shut behind him. "People, this is Piper. She's my boss and likes me anyway."

"Hi, Piper," Abby called from where she sat on one of the dark leather couches. "It's good to see you."

Piper could feel herself flushing. Abby would have heard her gloating about getting new clients. Why didn't the floor open up and drop her down a nice big hole?

"Gratitude-cake, hmm?" Abby smiled. "I should bake one, too, since Stan and Dixon are the reason I now have Chatelaines, and I can get out to see my friends rather than catching up on household tasks."

"Wait." Next to Abby, a slightly older woman with shoulder-length, champagne-colored hair held up her hand. "Is Piper the owner of the household management company you've been gloating about?"

"The very one," Dixon said proudly.

"Perfect." The woman's smile grew. "I'm Rona. Simon and I want to hire Chatelaines, too."

Well, wow. Piper glanced down at herself. Black leggings and barefooted. Her worn-thin, red lounging cardigan. Under that was her ragged T-shirt. The graphic was a wand-holding coffee cup saying: ESPRESSO PATRONUM.

This wasn't the way she usually looked when talking business. *Suck up and deal, Piper.*

"It's nice to meet you, Rona." Piper sat in a leather armchair and summoned a professional mien. "I don't have business cards with me, but Chatelaines has a website and—"

Rona's laugh stopped her. "We've already checked it out. You're on my to-do list to call on Monday."

Five minutes later, they'd set up an appointment.

Sitting back, Piper grinned at Abby. "I'm going to hire you to run public relations."

"It's all you, Piper, and Chatelaines." Abby shook her head. "I always hated having the cleaning crew or anyone showing up when Xavier and I are at home. Now, they don't. Everyone schedules around our hours, and we still have food in the fridge and meals ready and a clean house. It's like having magic elves or something."

Shining satisfaction filled Piper. "That's the goal."

The third woman, a brunette with multi-colored streaks in her hair, pouted. "I'm Lindsey, and I wish I could hire you, too."

"I feel your pain, sweet thing." Dix brought an empty glass from the kitchen and set it on the rustic wooden coffee table before dropping down beside Lindsey. "Stan and I don't have a budget that allows for hiring chatelaines—let alone buying small nations like Rona and Abby."

"Pffft. All that money stuff is Xavier's. Professors sure aren't overpaid." Abby wrinkled her nose.

"Likewise." Rona clinked her glass against Abby's. "Hospital administrators make good money, but nothing like what Simon brings in."

"Maybe I'm a little relieved that Zander isn't rich. It would be weird." Lindsey was about Piper's age with a slow Texas drawl. "Y'all's guys are great, but over-the-top rich people are a tad scary."

Aren't they just? And sometimes pretty obnoxious, Piper thought, remembering Mr. Tannehill. Then again, Ethan was rich and had been a complete gentleman. A completely ripped, drop-dead gorgeous, panty-melting-voiced gentleman.

Lindsey gave Piper an apologetic look. "I'm sorry; that rich comment was kind of rude, wasn't it?"

"You're fine. I'm not rich, and I know what you mean." Piper smiled at Rona and Abby. "Thankfully, the wonderful people outweigh the others."

"Boy, she's tactful, too." Picking up a pitcher, Lindsey filled the empty glass and handed it past Dixon to Piper. "I should have asked if you like Hawaiian margaritas."

Piper glanced at the orange-red, slushy liquid. "I like margaritas, so probably?"

Lindsey had an infectious grin. "My family has a margarita-in-the-evening tradition, and a friend out near Yosemite gave me this recipe. It has the traditional tequila and triple sec stuff, but with strawberries and pineapple for a tropical slant."

Piper sampled and smiled at the fruity burst of flavor. "That is yummy—and yay, I don't have to drive home."

"Me, neither." Dix poured himself more. From the flush on his face, he'd already had one or two. "Knowing these three, someone will pick them up."

"That's good." Piper looked around. "Where's Stan? Is law enforcement prohibited from these gatherings?"

"That'd be fun to try to pull off. But no, he's not here because he's working tonight." Dixon's smile slid off, leaving unhappiness behind.

Uh-oh.

Lindsey bumped her shoulder against his. "Dix, ol' buddy, what's wrong?"

"Nothing." He sat straighter and shrugged.

"*Nothing* shouldn't make you look so unhappy, Dixon." Piper curled her fingers around his and lowered her voice. "Do you want to talk? We can go get some air if you want. Or...drunken parties can be great for drunken confessions."

She might have known the last would hit him right. He snorted and collapsed back against the cushions. "I'm good at drunken confessions."

"What did Stan do to upset you?" Abby asked with the insight Piper had noticed was typical of her.

"He hasn't done anything...yet." Dix took a big gulp of his drink. "See, a friend of his from Texas, another Homeland Security agent, is here for some case, and he's working with Stan. All the time. The Delicious Darrell is sexy as hell and an agent, and he has the hots for Stan."

Piper blinked. "Oh." That could ruin a person's whole week.

"He even found himself an Airbnb rental right here in our building," Dixon said glumly.

"Here? That must bite with a capital B." Lindsey scowled. "Talk about having your house invaded by rodents. Okay, mice are really cute, but that guy sounds more like a big, fat rat."

Rona tucked her hair behind one ear. "I can see why you're unhappy. My question is—is Stan interested back?"

"I don't know how he wouldn't be." Dixon slumped against Lindsey.

The brunette put her arm around him. "There, there, sugar. I don't think anyone has a chance with your Stan. That man loves you."

"He does." Dix nodded morosely. "But I'm so yesterday. Sure, I'm a pretty face, but that guy is like Stan's equal, not some high school dropout with a GED. Sure I got an associate's degree, but still..."

Outrage filled Piper. How could he possibly think he wasn't amazing? "You're a skilled physical therapy assistant, Dix. Every person you care for asks to have you back. That just never happens."

"I think Stan knows what a prize he has in you," Abby chimed in. "The way he looks at you hasn't changed; he adores you."

Dixon sighed. "For now. It feels like we're...I don't know... growing apart."

Feeling anger rising, Piper sipped her drink. If Stan didn't wise up, maybe she'd have a little talk with him.

"You know, Zander's jobs often drag him away for a week or two. When he gets back, or if we feel disconnected or"—Lindsey smiled ruefully—"have been arguin', we visit Dark Haven and, you know, catch up. Flogging makes the ass—and heart—grow warmer, right?"

Flogging? Piper choked. "What's Dark Haven?"

Lindsey's eyes widened. "Oh, hell, I forgot you were here, I mean, I knew you were here, but I forgot you were...weren't..."

"Dark Haven is the finest BDSM club in the city," Dixon said. "Abby's husband owns it."

"Dixon!" Abby's professorial glare should have turned Dixon to ash. "Uh, Piper, it's not like that. Okay, yes, it is like that, and Xavier does own the club, but he wouldn't... No one at our house will beat on the cleaning crew or chef, and we wouldn't leave anything embarrassing out in the open."

After a second of surprise, Piper realized that, first, Abby wasn't sober either, and second, she was worried the BDSM stuff might frighten away Chatelaines.

Piper giggled, and how unprofessional was that? She frowned at her glass. That margarita stuff packed a kick.

"Ho, I just bet My Liege keeps lots of embarrassing stuff at home. Can you imagine the maid's face?" Dixon lifted his voice higher. "Ms. Abby, I thought these ropes were to hold your black satin sheets in place, only they seem to be attached to the headboard. Or...or..."

Snickering, he held up a hand. "The dog walker gives Blackie a 'pull toy', and you figure it out when Xavier realizes his leather gag is missing."

As the women burst out laughing, Abby's light complexion turned bright red.

"We're all fairly normal," Rona said to Piper, still chuckling. "Please, don't kick Abby off your client list."

"No worries there. To be honest, I've been looking for ways to show that Chatelaines welcomes alternative lifestyles." Piper shook her head. "People shouldn't have to worry that people entering their homes are judgy or close-minded. That's just wrong. We're in *your* space, not ours."

"See," Dix crowed. "That, right there, is just one of the reasons I work for this woman."

"Whew." Abby slumped back in her chair. "Thank you, Piper. That's a relief."

Rona eyed Piper. "You know, one way to show you're kink-friendly and to gain new clients would be to put your business card on the Dark Haven bulletin board."

"That sounds great." Piper beamed. "Would you—"

Rona shook her head. "The rule is that the card has to be put there in-person. Not by someone else."

"Awesomesauce." Dix bounced on the couch, almost spilling his drink. "That means you have to visit the club."

"Oh God no." Her horrified response netted her four sets of eyes.

Lindsey lifted an eyebrow. "That didn't sound kink-friendly."

Blunt Texans. Piper rubbed her hands over her face. "No, it didn't, did it? It's like this..." And then the words dried up. How could she explain? Did she want to explain?

Abby studied her for a second. "Could it maybe have something to do with that past relationship you spoke of?"

"Wow, you're really good at that sociology stuff." Piper realized someone had refilled her glass and took a healthy swallow. "The relationship was"—another gulp eased the constriction in her throat—"with a Dominant. It wasn't a healthy one."

When Dix took her hand, totally supportive, tears burned her eyes. "Sorry, sorry." She blinked hard.

"Did you get help afterward?" Rona asked softly. "Counseling?"

"I did. Really." For a little while. "God, I was a mess, and it helped. It's just... Although the counselor understood abuse, she didn't understand why I willingly entered *that* kind of relationship. She thought submission was a sickness all its own, so I ended up stopping."

Lindsey's mouth dropped open. "Whoa, little doggies, no wonder you're sensitive to being judgy about your client's choices. You've been there."

"Yes." Piper eyed the fluid in her glass. "I'm doing fine, really. But sometimes I have trouble being around... Well, you know how some Dominants kind of exude power with every word?"

Every person in the room grinned.

"I have trouble with that. Sometimes." Although she'd done all right with Ethan...eventually. Piper half-smiled at Abby. "Like when I was at your house."

"Ohhhh. Is that why you left before I could even ask you to stay for dinner?"

"That's why."

Abby lifted her eyebrows. "You took Ethan on as a client. How did that go?"

"Better than I thought it would." Piper smiled. Especially after she'd realized he was her champion.

"Was Sir Ethan nice to you?" Dixon shook his head, answering his own question. "Of course he was nice. He's like, the opposite of Lindsey's Enforcer."

"What?" Piper asked. "Enforcer?"

"Oh, Lindsey's Dom helps take care of enforcing the club rules, and he loves it since he's a total sadist." Dixon waved his hand in the air and made a high buzzing sound. "If you were an annoying mosquito, DeVries would smash you and leave your guts splattered everywhere. And he'd laugh."

"*Dixon*." Lindsey giggled. "Zander isn't *that* bad."

The looks the brunette got from Abby and Rona telegraphed...yes, the sadist was that bad. Still, however mean he was, Lindsey had the contented glow of a woman who loved her partner and was cherished in return. So did Rona and Abby.

Piper had no glow. She pushed aside the feeling of envy. She was alone because she wanted to be. Well, not really, but it was still her choice.

"Now, Sir Ethan," Dixon continued. "He'd look at the mosquito and say 'Sorry' like the Brits do, and then he'd set the naughty bug outside. In winter. To die. But there would be ever so much courtesy."

Dixon's imitation of Ethan's posh English accent was deadly accurate and reduced everyone to helpless laughter.

Abby wiped tears from her cheeks. "Well, Piper, I'm glad you took Ethan on."

"Yes, I even decided to stay as his assigned chatelaine. I need to get over being neurotic, and I won't do it by hiding."

"Very good." Rona smiled. "I can recommend some kink-friendly counselors if you ever feel the need. Also, if you want to visit Dark Haven, I'd be delighted to go with you and guard you."

"Me, too," Dixon raised his hand.

"And me," both Abby and Lindsey said together.

"You guys. You're going to make me bust out crying." Piper tried not to sniffle.

"Can she get in?" Dix asked Rona and Abby. "What with all Xavier's rules?"

"I'll talk Simon into running a quick background check that'll satisfy the requirements." Rona leaned forward to ask Piper, "Do you miss...well, not your previous Dom who must have been horrible, but anything about the lifestyle?"

Hmm. Did she miss anything? She already knew that dominance turned her on. It always had. But the actual lifestyle?

"Yeeesss," she said, drawing the word out. "I loved feeling useful. And filling his needs was so satisfying, as if serving added an extra helping of happiness on top of love. Then he changed. It all changed and twisted into something ugly."

Abby made a sad noise. "I know how it feels when desire and the beginning of love turn wrong, but if you add D/s into it... Boy, I can't imagine how messed up I'd be if Xavier wasn't the person I thought he was. I've handed over so much of myself. Given him so much trust."

Lindsey nodded. "What I was thinking."

"Dark Haven is a safe place, and I think a visit to the club might be good for you." Rona sat back. "With escort provided, of course. This was a part of your life that you valued. If you decide to reclaim some of it, that'd be great. If not, that's all right, too."

Abby grinned. "You can see how she ended up a hospital administrator, can't you?"

"I can, yes." Trying to ignore the anxious shivers tap-dancing over her ribcage, Piper smiled at the others. "If you're willing to do some handholding, I'm up for it."

"*Yes*," Dixon crowed. "A Dark Haven foray with a newbie. I love it."

As Abby led the conversation into a different direction, Piper swirled the last of the liquid in her glass. What were the chances that Ethan was a club member?

She might see him there. Just the thought kicked up her heart rate...and somehow eased her shivers.

CHAPTER SEVEN

It had certainly been an interesting week. On Saturday, Ethan walked through Dark Haven, enjoying the female vocals for Bishop Briggs' "White Flag". He smiled, thinking of another assertive female—his very efficient chatelaine who'd been turning his home on end.

A chef coming in and leaving easy-to-reheat meals was proving to be most pleasant. She hadn't changed his cleaning crew, but now when they came through, the house was not only spotless, but everything was in place. Churchill had voiced his approval of his new midday pampering.

Ms. Delaney had called on Friday to touch base and made an appointment to see him in person next week. It was a win for him that she'd kept him on as her personal client.

She hadn't planned to. At the end of the initial appointment, he'd caught on that she intended to assign him to a different chatelaine. So much for his attempt to be un-intimidating.

He truly did like her. He'd enjoyed seeing her turn to mush in Churchill's furry paws. Her delightful organizational skills. Her insightful comments. Her melodic laugh when he managed to coax one out of her. The way she'd flushed at seeing a bed designed for bondage. Her warm heart that had her offering to help Angel.

But...was he interested in someone who really didn't like him? No...he didn't think so. Ms. Delaney had been at ease with men—other men—at Stan's party. Her wariness with Ethan had started when she'd seen him acting as Angel's Master. Because he was a Dominant.

He shook his head, remembering the delight in her expression when he'd complimented her. She was a submissive, one who loved to serve. Yet being around him—and Xavier, for that matter—made her fearful. Everything inside him wanted to help, to comfort and reassure her, and fix what was wrong.

The curse of being a Dom.

Speaking of being a Dom...he needed to concentrate on Dark Haven tonight.

Halfway down the stairs into the dungeon, Ethan stopped to check out the action from above. Interesting scenes and the energy in the room was excellent. He'd said something like that once to a new submissive, and she'd stared at him as if he were crazy, asking if he could seriously judge the energy from the quality of the moaning and slapping floggers.

Actually...yes, he could.

His gaze stopped on the four St. Andrew's crosses near the front. Lots of flogging and canes.

Unfortunately, a newer Dom in one scene was getting sloppy. That'd be his first stop.

Spanking benches occupied the center of the room. A Top there was working over her wife with a paddle. From the wife's shudders and breathing, the Top was doing a fine job.

Michael was using a violet wand near the back. No need to oversee the older Dom; he was always careful. Wax play was going on center back. Ethan didn't recognize the Top. Possibly a visitor—someone taking advantage of the various reciprocal memberships of BDSM clubs. He'd check out that scene second.

"Hey, mate. How are you doing?" Wearing an irritable expression, Mitchell climbed the stairs, leading an older submissive by one wrist.

"Quite well, thank you. Did you run into a problem?" Ethan glanced at the submissive.

"Deirdre here interrupted a scene to ask questions and implore the Dom to do her next." Mitchell's Aussie accent was thicker than normal with his annoyance. "I intervened before he went ballistic on her arse."

The woman's face twisted in anger. "I just wanted—"

"Did I give you permission to speak?" Mitchell growled.

"N-no, but—" She wisely stopped.

The Aussie sighed. "I'm too tired and grouchy to think of a proper discipline tonight. You got any suggestions, Ethan?"

"I can see she has trouble holding her tongue, so start by gagging her. Of course, you'll provide a non-annoying toy in case she needs to safeword."

Mitchell nodded, rubbing his head as if it hurt. "*Defo*."

Definitely, Ethan translated before considering the submissive. "What's her favorite activity?"

"She asked the Dom for a flogging, said she loves it."

"Then you have an easy punishment. Get two Tops. One flogs her—"

When the woman brightened, Mitchell's brows drew together. "Hey, mate, this is supposed to be punishment, not a reward."

Ethan glanced at her. "Stand right there and do not move." He led Mitchell up the stairs out of hearing. "Have the non-flogger interrupt the scene every time she starts enjoying herself. Let the two Tops move away and chat, so she knows no one is paying attention to her. After a few minutes, start the flogging over. Interrupt it again. Repeat the cycle half a dozen times until she understands exactly how devastating an interrupted scene can feel. Then have them send her home—without satisfaction—like the self-involved brat she is."

Mitchell pursed his lips. "Effective and fucking cruel. Thanks."

"Not a problem." One concern down. Now for another. "While you set this up, I'll let Xavier know you're done for the night. He can find another enforcer or police the submissives himself. You're too tired for frustrating messes."

"I can"—Mitchell sighed—"bloody oath, you're right. Thanks."

Ethan glanced at the woman. She met his gaze and looked down immediately. Ah well, maybe she was teachable—and he was glad it wasn't his job. "Deal with her, then go home and get some rest."

Mitchell chuckled. "You know, you intimidate the fuck out most of the Tops. Guess they've never seen your Daddy Dom side."

The Aussie's sense of humor was as crooked as Lombard Street. "Go."

Once on the dungeon floor, Ethan saw the flogger had grown even sloppier. Moving to where the Dom could see him, Ethan waited.

The Dom noticed, knew Ethan could shut his scene down, and walked over. "Is there a problem?"

"Only if your submissive doesn't enjoy pissing blood."

"Say what?"

"Did you forget where the kidneys are located?"

Almost involuntarily, the Dom turned, saw the welts across the woman's right and left lower back, and winced. "Oh, shit."

"You need to flog inanimate objects until you have better control. There's a class on Saturdays where you can practice and get suggestions." The Dom nodded. "For now, perhaps you should wind down with some sensation play and end the scene nicely so your submissive is happy."

Relief swept the Dom's expression as he realized Ethan wasn't killing the session completely—just the flogging portion. "Got it." He huffed a breath. "Thanks. Really."

Pleased, Ethan nodded. Although most Doms wanted what was best for their submissives, some couldn't take correction at all. Good man here.

The second stop was the wax play scene. The Top was doing well.

Now, to find Xavier. There he was, watching a caning.

Walking over, Ethan enjoyed seeing how Abby was snuggled up against his friend. After Xavier's first wife died unexpectedly, the Dom had closed himself off for years. Abby had changed all that.

Wasn't it odd how submissives believed they needed the Doms more than the Doms needed them?

"Good evening, you two." Ethan smiled at Xavier and then at the short professor whose deep blue corset and tiny skirt emphasized her curves.

She smiled up at him.

"Do you have a moment?" Ethan asked Xavier.

"I'm guessing there's a problem somewhere?"

"I'm afraid so." After explaining about Mitchell, Ethan added, "I think some of the tiredness is because he's ill-suited to be the bad guy, at least with submissives. We're much alike in that." Doms with over-protective natures often found it difficult to punish a submissive, even when well-deserved.

Last year, deVries had policed the submissives, and the sadist had enjoyed the hell out of it. But his little Texan, Lindsey, wasn't comfortable seeing him discipline subs—at least the female ones.

"You might hand over enforcement to the Pedersens." Ethan nodded toward a married couple in their late fifties. She'd started as her husband's submissive and, as often happened, had discovered her inner dominant. The two were polyamorous and bi with a side of sadistic. "They like to teach and are ready for a challenge. Perhaps give them Mitchell's assignment tonight."

Brows lifted, Xavier studied them. "I'll do that."

Before he could move, Abby tugged at his sleeve. "My Liege? May I be excused?"

"Is it time for Rona and her visitor?" Xavier glanced at his watch.

"Yes, Sir."

"Of course. Go meet them."

As Abby went up on tiptoes to thank her Dom, Ethan smiled. There was nothing prettier than a submissive asking permission. Yes, he was old-fashioned that way, wasn't he?

"Wait a moment, fluff." Hand on Abby's arm, Xavier turned. "Worth, Simon planned to supervise Rona's visitor, but he and deVries are running late. Can you keep an eye on her?"

"You'll let a non-member play?" That wasn't normal.

"Simon ran a quick background check on her. She's been out of the scene for a while, but isn't new."

"Ah. Of course, then. She can wear one of my *ask-permission* collars." He held out his arm. "Abby, might I escort you upstairs?"

As Abby laughed and took his arm, Xavier gave him a chin lift and headed for the Pedersens.

Upstairs, Ethan paused near the left stage. Tied to a post, Mitchell's mouthy submissive was being lashed into a happy subspace until a second Dom interrupted the flogging. The gag barely muffled the submissive's frustrated whine when both Doms moved away.

Off to one side, Mitchell was leaning wearily against the stage. A smile touched his lips as the submissive's whining grew more audible. Noticing Ethan, he nodded.

The punishment was going well. The Aussie had chosen two Doms who were careful and trustworthy, so Ethan nodded back and motioned toward the exit. *You can go home.*

Relief filled Mitchell's face, and he headed for the door.

More slowly, Ethan and Abby followed and stepped into the entry.

Lindsey was working the reception desk. "Hey, Sir Ethan. Abby."

"Good evening. Xavier told me Rona is bringing in a visitor. Do you have her file?"

"Yes, Sir. Here you go." Lindsey handed over a folder of papers.

Ethan stepped behind the desk and read the name on the file. *Piper Delaney*.

Here was an intriguing challenge for the evening. He'd definitely have to keep an eye on her—something he'd have done in any case. In fact, the thought of putting a collar around her slim neck was disconcertingly appealing.

He flipped through the pages of the background check that Simon's security company had provided at very short notice.

Piper had arrived in San Francisco around five years ago. Worked various jobs—maid, pet-sitter, shopping service for a year, then came up with enough money to start Chatelaines. Was in the black within two years. No arrests or record. Before California, she'd lived in...

His brows drew together. She was from Kansas?

"Hi, Lindsey. Good evening, Ethan." Rona stood on the other side of the counter.

"Ethan? Um, hi." Piper stared at him. Color swept up into her face. She hadn't expected to see him here, apparently.

Well, the same went for him. It would be nice if she was as pleased as he was. He smiled at her. "Welcome to Dark Haven."

She noticed the file in his hands. "Is that the background check that Rona's husband ran?" Eyes the color of melted chocolate met his, and a dimple appeared in her curved cheek. "Did Simon discover I'm a notorious embezzler?"

Ethan laughed. She'd be the cutest crook in the prison. Big brown eyes. Her upper lip was a perfect bow in a mouth designed for smiling. She had dimples, God help him.

He checked the summary at the end of the file. "I fear Simon overlooked your career in crime, Ms. Delaney."

"Whew, that's a relief. And it's Piper."

He'd wondered how long she'd hold him to the formal address. Running a finger down the page, he saw no red flags in the summary. "Then, Piper, it appears you're good to come in and play."

"Oh, good. I guess."

Second thoughts already? "Xavier asked me to stand in for Simon and provide a collar for you."

"A collar?" Piper's color disappeared. She stepped back.

Rona set a hand on Piper's shoulder. "Steady, honey. You've been in a club before, haven't you?"

"Only once. Briefly." Piper bit her lip. "What do you mean about a collar? I'm not a slave."

Her spine was so rigid she might fracture right there.

Abby took her hand.

Ethan suppressed his need to tuck the frightened subbie close. "Piper, I'm not talking about a slave or ownership collar. The one I'll give you is a signal that you're under my protection, and anyone wanting to play with you must ask me for permission first. This way we can ensure you"—*don't get in over your head or get bullied*—"are well-matched with someone."

"It's a good defense," Lindsey said. "Even though the club's private, sometimes newbies get in over their heads or get targeted by creepazoid Tops. No one messes with Sir Ethan. His collar will keep you safe."

He wasn't going to leave everything up to the warning on the collar. Not with this big-eyed submissive. He intended to keep a damn close eye on her.

A collar. Piper touched her neck. The thought was appalling. Since getting rid of her slave collar five years ago, she'd avoided anything tight around her neck. She didn't wear chokers or turtlenecks.

But... Ethan and Lindsey's explanations made sense. She glanced at Rona and Abby. Both nodded approval.

"Ethan is one of the club directors and has been since the club opened. You can trust him," Rona said.

Piper nodded slowly. The older woman wouldn't recommend anyone lightly. Nonetheless, a shiver ran through her, not because of the skimpy red corset and tight leather skirt she was wearing. He wanted her to wear a collar.

Visiting a BDSM club had been a stupid idea.

"Hey, look, girl. There's the board with business cards." Hooking her elbow in Piper's, Abby pulled her over to a bulletin board. Nice and prominent on the wall where people waited by the reception desk. There were categories for the various services.

This was, after all, a big reason why Piper was here. "You're pretty sneaky, Professor."

Abby grinned.

Okay, get the card up, take a walk around, and if she was still uncomfortable, she'd leave. No big deal.

Rona tapped an empty space and offered a thumbtack. "How about there?"

Two sneaky women.

"I bet you're a very effective administrator, aren't you?" Piper pinned her card to the board.

"I'm excellent." Rona put an arm around Piper's waist. "Your turn, Sir Ethan."

Still behind the reception desk, Ethan shook his head at Rona reprovingly before opening his toy bag.

"I couldn't resist," Rona told him.

When Abby snickered, Piper asked, "Did I miss something?"

"I like to tease him about the *Sir* because it is his real title in the vanilla world. He's a baronet," Rona said. "One of the submissives found out, started calling him that here, and it caught on, even though most don't realize it's his actual title outside of the scene."

Piper choked. She'd thought he was all sorts of pompous for

using his D/s title outside of the scene and clubs. He was a baronet?

"I know. It's odd, isn't it?" Abby shook her head. "It feels wrong to call him Sir Ethan outside of the club, yet it's incorrect to formally introduce him without his title, any more than I'd introduce a minister without the Reverend. He keeps having to say 'Just Ethan' afterward."

Aaaand, he'd heard them.

Holding a red leather collar, he stood just on the other side of the reception desk. When Piper's cheeks turned hot with embarrassment, he winked at her. "A baronet isn't particularly impressive in England, but you Yanks do love titles."

"We really do," Lindsey said. "At least you didn't get stuck with *My Liege* like Xavier."

"God is merciful." He motioned to Piper in a *come here* gesture. "Let's get you collared so you can enjoy your evening."

Insane. She had to be insane. Her muscles tensed in protest as she walked around the desk to where he stood. Waiting. Anyone seeing him would know he was a Dominant down to the last cell in his body.

Even if he wasn't wearing all black.

But he was—and...wow. Perfectly tailored black pants and black suit coat over a shade lighter black turtleneck. A black pocket square with silver trim. Black gloves tucked under a black leather belt. His sleek watch was silver and black. He was as elegant as Daniel Craig's James Bond, only with a lethal edginess.

All she could think of was how black clothing didn't show blood.

"Look, Piper." Ethan ran his finger over the silver stripes embedded in the red leather collar. "The striping indicates to club members that you are a guest."

Understanding how that would be a protection, she tried to smile and failed miserably. "Sounds good."

He lifted the dangling tag that was engraved: PROTECTED

BY ETHAN. "This tells them to ask me even before asking you. You're not my property, Piper, but you are protected."

His low, quiet voice didn't diminish the air of command or force of his personality. As she looked up into his watchful gaze, she did feel protected.

She forced the words out, "Thank you. Sir," and bowed her head to accept the collar.

He fastened the buckle without fumbling as if he'd done it often. After snapping on a padlock, he tucked the key in his inner coat pocket.

Mouth dry, she ran her fingers over the soft leather. The shaking inside her increased.

A furrow appeared between his brows. "Come here, poppet." He drew her firmly into his arms until her cheek rested against his chest. "I want to feel you take a real breath."

"Sorry, sorry." Even as she pulled in a breath, her legs felt appallingly weak.

Arm around her waist, he held her up, taking her weight. He felt so...solid. "You're fine, sweetheart. No one will hurt you here. Actually, if you walk around with Rona and Abby, no one will even think of bothering you."

She almost laughed at the thought of anyone giving Rona trouble.

"I'll keep an eye on you as I make the rounds," Ethan added.

Why did he have to be so kind? And so compelling? Each breath brought her the scent of his aftershave, a masculine pine and leather scent, like a trail ride through the English countryside.

"Rounds?" She tilted her head back to look up at him, seeing the strong line of his neck, the dark beard stubble along his jaw.

"Dungeon monitors watch for problems. Some of us also wander about to offer added instruction or discipline. My focus is the Dominants."

Lindsey finished checking in a threesome, then grinned over her shoulder at Piper. "Sometimes he gives a newbie Dom a lesson right there in the dungeon. Or he'll rescue a submissive who got herself into a scene she wasn't ready for, especially if the Top wasn't paying attention. Sir Ethan's our Top Cop.

His lips quirked at Lindsey's irreverent title, then he ran a finger down Piper's cheek, bringing every nerve to attention. Her skin tingled at the slow caress.

"Go with your friends, Piper, and have fun. We'll keep you safe."

Safe. A Dom who promised she'd be safe.

Impulsively, she wrapped her arms around him for a grateful hug.

When he hugged her back, her heart skipped a beat. This was her champion, the man who'd been there for her when she'd been so far down in hell that she hadn't been able to see any hope above.

He hadn't changed at all.

Safe.

An hour later, Piper followed Rona and Abby across the long ground-floor room. For the last hour, they'd been downstairs in the dungeon, viewing the scenes. An hour had been a long time. Despite her interest in everything, she'd had to keep fighting her anxiety.

The place was filled with Dominants, and far too many things sounded like her nightmares.

Still, she'd been proud of how well she was maintaining her composure...right up until she'd seen a Top using a knife. He'd barely drawn blood on the bottom's back. But when he'd picked up a scythe blade, Piper had shuddered, cashed in her *I'm cool* cards, and called it quits.

It'd been a relief when Rona and Abby admitted they weren't into knife play.

"Looks like most of the gang is over there at the table," Abby said. "I'll go see if I can find Xavier."

As the professor peeled off toward the rooms to one side, Rona led the way to a group of a dozen people seated at shoved-together tables. She stopped behind a tall dark-haired man and touched his shoulder. "This looks like a fun party. Might we join you?"

"Lass, here you are." Smiling, he rose and took a kiss possessive enough that Piper could only hope he was Rona's husband.

Black eyes, silvering black hair, deeply tanned, the man was totally handsome in a rugged way. Like Sir Ethan, he wore a suit, but with a white shirt. His tie was patterned in various gray tones, and she choked back a laugh.

He noticed her focus, and his grin was a flash of white. "Don't you like these shades of gray?"

Piper snickered.

"Don't encourage him," Rona said. "He made me read the book *out loud*, pointed out anything that was incorrect, and whenever I turned red, that's what we did that night."

Oh boy. "Isn't the hero of *Fifty Shades* a sadist?"

Not answering, the man held out a hand. "You must be Piper. I'm Simon, Rona's husband."

Just from the sheer weight of his voice, Piper mentally added *Master* to his name. "It's good to meet you."

Still holding her hand, Simon turned and raised his voice. "People, we have a visitor. This is Piper."

As the people around the table welcomed her, he seated Piper on his right and Rona on his left.

Looking around, Piper realized there were a lot of Dominants at the table and several were giving her interested looks. Oh, no. She started to feel like fresh meat in front of piranhas.

Then, the chair on her right was pulled out. "Did you have a good tour, Piper?" Sir Ethan asked.

She realized she was leaning toward him—toward safety—and hadn't answered.

Frowning slightly, he studied her in that way he had, then his arm curved around her shoulders with a comforting heaviness. "It wasn't that bad, was it? You looked as if you were interested in the scenes."

He must have been keeping an eye on her down in the dungeon. Like he'd said. As she relaxed into the curve of his arm, she could feel his warmth. "Sorry. My mind took a detour. Yes, I enjoyed seeing the dungeon."

"Piper is an interesting scene name." A hard-faced blond man in black leathers across the table eyed her. "Do you play the flute?"

Nice normal conversation. She could do this, especially with the security of her champion right next to her. "Piper's my real name. My father loved 'The Piper at the Gates of Dawn'."

"You mean Van Morrison's song?" the blond asked."

"Van Morrison took the title from the book, *Wind in the Willow*," Sir Ethan said and glanced at her. "Do you have a habit of saving baby otters, poppet?"

He'd read one of her favorite books. She smiled up at him.

"Those dimples should be outlawed," he murmured, touched her cheek with a finger, then frowned slightly. "We keep it warm in here, but you're freezing. Did you scare her to death, Rona?"

He shucked off his suit jacket, settled it around Piper's shoulders, and pulled her against his side. Turning slightly, he lifted his hand.

A waiter skidded into the table with his haste in answering the summons. "Sir Ethan, can I serve you?"

Can I serve you? Can I give you my body? My heart? My soul? Piper's flinch must have been palpable because Sir Ethan turned to study her for a long moment.

To her relief, his attention returned to the waiter. "I'd like a hot chocolate with a shot of Bailey's in it, please. Tell the bartender that I'll make sure the submissive doesn't play tonight."

"Right away, Sir." The young man almost sprang across the room.

Piper heard Rona's husband huff a laugh. "The effect you have on submissives is truly appalling."

Sir Ethan chuckled. "It's the accent."

"Um." Piper started to talk, then bit her lip. What was the protocol in speaking? The Tops and bottoms were all mixed together. Was she allowed to ask questions without being given permission?

"You may talk, poppet. This is the free-for-all table." Sir Ethan motioned toward several tables farther back, roped-off with a sign: FORMAL PROTOCOL OBSERVED HERE. "The stricter Masters sit back there."

But Sir Ethan had a slave. Shouldn't he be over in that spot?

"You had a question?" Master Simon asked.

Did she? Oh, right. "Sir Ethan told the waiter to tell the bartender I wouldn't play. What was that about?"

"Ah. We had hoped people would know better than to play after drinking, but a couple of unfortunate incidents showed we were overly optimistic." Master Simon's voice was grim.

"To enforce the rules, when you get a drink, you also get a metal bracelet. One that is removed on the way out." Sir Ethan pointed out a dungeon monitor at the head of the stairs. "Braceletted people can't get into the dungeon. An alarm sounds if a bracelet is detected, and he'll turn the person away."

Pretty high-tech. Pretty wise. Piper remembered more than a few "unfortunate incidents" when the Defiler had been drinking. She dropped that line of thought immediately. "That's a wonderful system."

"Did you enjoy your tour of the dungeon?" the blond Dom across the table asked her.

"I did. There was certainly a lot of variety."

"Right, I remember hearing you weren't a beginner. Where did you play before?"

She stiffened. That wasn't something she would talk about.

Not here, not ever.

"I'm *free*." Lindsey circled the table, a wide smile on her face, multi-colored hair bouncing on her shoulders. She came up behind the nosy blond and leaned against him. "Hey, sexy Dom, wanna play?"

To Piper's surprise, the man's hard lips curved into a smile. He pushed his chair away from the table far enough that he could yank Lindsey into his lap.

Lindsey giggled.

"You're a mouthy one, and you're overdressed." He started stripping her. "Xavier asked me to demonstrate heavy caning."

"Wait, wait. Noooo, I want to sit with Rona and Piper." One hand over her mouth cut off her wail. With his free hand, he unhooked her bustier with impressive dexterity.

Once done, he rose, set her on her feet, and took her by one wrist. "Time to go play."

"DeVriessss." Her whine of protest went nowhere.

Motioning to a male submissive sitting at the end of the table, deVries went up on the raised stage on the right.

Piper watched as he fastened the male to the St. Andrew's cross. He put Lindsey in a kneeling position to the side, cuffing her hands behind her back. Was that a punishment or a reward, not getting caned? To be left out of a scene?

Not wanted. Ignored. Forgotten.

"Please, deVries. Zander, Sir, Master, I want to play, too." Lindsey was whining. Begging. "Please, pretty please, Master?"

Begging.

Cold chilled Piper's skin. *Chained to the doghouse. Naked. No food, no water. Stupid worthless slave. Not good for anything. Maybe I'll leave you out here until only your bones are left.*

Was that grass under her palms? The icy cold of the night wind? Her voice, begging for food, for water, for warmth. Begging...

The weight of the memories compressed her ribs until her chest wouldn't expand. Where was the air? There was no air in the room. Blood roared in her ears, filling her world with only that sound.

Something gripped her waist. Lifted her. A hand cupped her chin. "Easy, Piper. There's nothing here to be afraid of."

There was. There *was*.

"Eyes open. Look at me, Piper. Right now." The voice held the steely edge of command.

Training took over. Her eyes opened.

A burning gaze met hers. Held hers. "You're having a panic attack, poppet. It'll pass soon, and you'll be fine. Now breathe with me—only with me."

"Can't get air."

"There's air enough, sweetheart." Total assurance in his voice. Total authority. "Breathe in. One-two-three-four. Out. One-two-three-four."

Fighting the terror of no air, she forced her lungs to match his pace. In. Out. Slowly, the crushing feeling around her chest eased off. Each breath was a bit deeper. The roar in her ears diminished.

Crinkles appeared at the edges of the keen eyes. "Better. That's better, poppet."

Poppet. It was Sir Ethan. She blinked and realized she was sitting on a table with his discarded jacket beside her. His unyielding hand was curled around her left upper arm. Her chin was firmly held in the Dom's palm, forcing her to look at him.

Oh...God. She closed her eyes as humiliation replaced the panic attack. Yes, she'd had a panic attack, one that had swept her up so fast and hard she hadn't had a chance to fight it off. Her voice came out a whisper. "I'm so sorry."

To her surprise, he chuckled. "You're back to normal if you're apologizing."

Releasing her chin, he ran his hands up and down her arms. "Still cold, though." He put the jacket back around her shoulders, scooped her up, and resumed his seat, this time with her on his lap.

"No, wait." Her feeble effort to rise was curtailed easily as his incredibly muscular arms tightened around her.

"This might help." Master Simon tucked a subbie blanket around her before resuming his seat beside Rona.

Rona. Master Simon. Turning her head, she saw Abby next to Xavier, both watching her.

Her whole body shriveled with embarrassment. Her head bowed. She'd made a spectacle of herself. Interrupted the Masters. Too humiliated even to apologize, she turned her face against Sir Ethan's hard chest and wished she could disappear.

"Ah, pet, it's not that bad," he murmured. Anchoring her with one arm around her waist, he ran his hand up and down her back with long firm strokes. "You're not the first person to have a panic attack here. You won't be the last."

He'd called her a person.

"I'm not a person. I'm worthless." The whispered words came from deep inside, from painful, horrendous training. She was so worthless it'd become her name.

The hand stroking her back stopped. "Bloody hell."

To her dismay, Sir Ethan sat her upright, gripping her upper arms and holding her out so he could see her face. She dropped her gaze under his intense scrutiny.

"No, Piper. Look at me." The steel-edged command was quiet...and impossible to refuse.

Her head lifted.

"There we go."

Ethan stared at the little subbie on his lap. *Worthless*. The name brought back memories from years before. Back when that plonker Serna had abused a slave he'd called worthless.

This was her.

If Piper hadn't whispered and said she was worthless, he wouldn't have recognized her. When he'd met her—it'd been in Kansas, hadn't it?—only stubble had covered her scalp. She'd been so emaciated that her ribs had looked like a washboard. A previous beating had left her eyes and mouth bruised and puffy.

Worthless. What kind of git names a slave that?

Ethan ran his finger over her stubborn chin, remembering how she'd saved Yolanda's cat from being crushed. She must have known how her Master would respond and had acted anyway. Brave soul.

When he'd told Serna about the runaway and that slave contracts weren't valid, he'd felt as if he was planting a seed—the idea she might be free. He couldn't presume to know what she wanted; perhaps she was content with Serna. But he'd given her a direction and a potential ally. Years before, Yolanda's cook had escaped an abusive husband.

Piper wasn't the first woman the cook had taken to safety, but she might be one of the bravest. Far too often, mistreated slaves lacked the courage, drive, and optimism to leave, because those were the traits that an abuser would first destroy. Somehow, Piper had kept enough of herself intact to be able to get out. To make a new life—a good life.

But abuse always left wounds behind.

His mouth tightened. He'd not let those scars hold her back from whatever she wanted to accomplish here.

She was still trembling as he cupped her cheek, forcing her to meet his gaze. "Are you really worthless, Piper?"

Her flinch showed how deep the question hit. Her jaw firmed. "No. No, I'm not."

"Correct. In fact, I'd say you're rather amazing." Gently, he tucked a strand of black hair behind her ear. "No matter what Serna told you."

Just the bastard's name made her tense up. Then her eyes narrowed. "You know who I am."

"Yes. I'm proud of you for having the courage to leave."

She must have been able to hear his sincerity. Her body relaxed.

"I'd also say a part of you still believes the lies he fed you."

"No, I don't."

Ethan waited.

Her gaze fell. "Yes, a part of me does."

"How often do you have panic attacks?"

"I didn't have any...not at first. Now, for the past year or so, I've had...some." She bit her lip. "It was worse here. Being around so many Dominants."

Good. She saw the cause and effect. "I'm not surprised. Everything here, from power exchanges to impact play, would remind you of your time with Serna and how you were brainwashed."

At the simmering rage in his voice, she drew back slightly, realized the anger wasn't at her, and curled back into his embrace.

It pleased him immensely that she felt secure enough with him to take comfort from being in his arms.

But her hands were clenched, her muscles still stiff. "What's wrong, Piper?"

"This might happen again. Maybe anytime I'm around Dominants. I thought Chatelaines would be a good match for people in the lifestyle, but it's a totally bad idea." Despair was a low hum in her tone, like a mountaineer who used his last breath to surmount a peak only to find it had concealed a higher summit.

Pity wrenched his heart.

Pity was not what she needed now. "I don't agree."

A sound captured his attention.

Abby was drumming her fingertips on the table and scowling. "No, nope. Sorry, Piper, but if you think you can escape being our chatelaine because my husband has a bossy personality, you have another think coming."

Piper froze, obviously having forgotten their conversation wasn't private.

As Ethan loosened his hold, she sat up to look at Abby. Xavier set his hand on his wife's shoulder, showing he stood behind what she said.

"You nailed it, Abby. That's exactly what I was going to say." Rona's voice made Piper twist that direction.

Simon's grin appeared.

Even aside from Chatelaines being a fantastic service, Ethan doubted the women would have let Piper back out. She might not know it, but she'd just gotten adopted.

With a visible effort, Piper pulled herself together. Breathing deliberately. Pulling her shoulders back. Straightening her spine. Her head lifted.

When she looked at Rona and Abby, her smile was genuine. "Of course, Chatelaines wouldn't abandon you. We have a contract."

Bloody brave. He hadn't known the young woman long, but she made a Dom proud.

Seeing the same stubborn courage as Ethan was, Abby blinked away tears. "I really like you."

Piper's breathing stuttered for a second. "I like you, too."

She turned to Rona. "I'm sorry I messed up this visit. But at least I know this isn't a good place for me. I should—"

"Should return here over and over until it no longer affects you," Ethan stated. Ignoring her wide eyes, he gave her a stern squeeze. "You've come this far. Finish the journey."

"You don't understand. I'm liable to have a meltdown at any point just from seeing or hearing something that sets me off."

"Yes, you probably will. I'll be beside you to pull you out."

Her mouth dropped open. "You?"

"Me." Ethan frowned, somewhat disconcerted at how resolved he was. He'd normally consider the pros and cons before making a commitment like this. But the thought of anyone else helping Piper wasn't palatable.

He glanced at Xavier. "I will need to cut back on my enforcement duties."

The club owner nodded. "Mitchell isn't the only enforcer who needs a break. You're off until you say otherwise."

"Very good. Thank you."

"Visiting here is a fine beginning. Dark Haven should provide ample opportunity to defuse quite a few triggers," Simon said. "But as a chatelaine, she must associate with Dominants on their own grounds."

"True." At his home, he had tried to set her at ease, yet she'd still been quite anxious. "Being alone with unknown Dominants isn't, perhaps, wise at this point."

Piper's color had improved. "Usually I conduct the intake interview so I can decide which chatelaine will be the best fit."

She gave Abby a wry smile. "I continued as your chatelaine this month, because your assigned one is on bereavement leave."

"And we're enjoying having you." Abby grinned and added, "Maybe you should take an assistant with you for the initial interviews. Having someone else present might help."

Piper nodded. "I've considered training someone else to do intakes. This would be a good time."

Excellent. Ethan smiled. Her mind was working again, figuring ways to work around the handicap. "That's a fine temporary solution. But there will be times you won't have someone with you. What will you do about relieving this fear permanently?"

"Do? There's nothing to do. I can't risk having a panic attack at a client's."

Having followed Ethan's reasoning, Simon exchanged glances with Xavier. The three of them had been friends for so long that spoken communication wasn't always needed. Both nodded at Ethan, agreeing with his solution.

"No, you can't risk panicking at a client's." When she frowned at his ready agreement, he cupped her chin and tilted her head up again. "Unless the client is me."

"You..." Her breathing sped up.

"Uh-uh, poppet, stay with me." He tightened his grip on her chin, keeping her gaze trapped with his. "Breathe in.... Slower. Breathe out. What color are my eyes?"

"Wh-what? Blue."

"What do you smell?" He kept his voice stern. Demanding.

She gave him a startled look. "Um, leather. Perfume. Sweat."

"Very good." Mindfulness and staying anchored physically could help derail increasing anxiety.

"Breathe with me again." He kept her under control for a minute.

"I'm...I'm okay."

"Yes, you are." He released her and brushed her hair back out of her face. "We can work on your reactions at my home. One-on-one. However, an hour or two won't suffice."

"*What?*"

"Piper, are you willing to give up your Saturdays to try to get past this?"

"I don't understand. What are you asking?" she asked.

He almost smiled at her appalled tone. "Saturday morning through late Saturday night. At my home." Ethan tucked her back against his chest, feeling the fine trembling of her small frame. "We'll work through what sets you off and help you learn to either avoid or avert your reaction."

"No. Absolutely not. Never."

Of course that would be her initial response. Quite understandable. Nonetheless, he could see how much she wanted to get past this weakness. He waited, feeling the way her tense muscles started to relax. How her breathing slowed again.

"Don't...don't you have a slave already there? Angel?"

There we go. Her mind was working. "No, she's not staying with me any longer."

"Well..." When Piper stiffened again, he knew what new worry had surfaced.

"No sex, poppet. You'll serve as a submissive, but you don't need the complication of anything sexual." Not yet and probably not with him. No matter how appealing she was.

His interest in a serious relationship had died years ago in betrayal and blood.

CHAPTER EIGHT

H*appy first day of summer.* Carrying a caramel macchiato and a cappuccino from Starbucks, Piper strolled back to her office. She breathed in the salty sea air and smiled at a gaggle of tourists who were staring up at the Transamerica pyramid. Even after five years in the city, she still marveled at the pyramid. The spectacular skyline. The energy in downtown San Francisco.

God, she loved living and working here.

Inside the commercial building that housed Chatelaines' offices, Piper went up the stairs to the second floor and down the hall to the reception area she shared with four complementary service businesses. A good location was the price of doing business with a prosperous clientele, and the Financial District was pricey. Sharing the reception area, conference room, and kitchen space had made it possible.

"Hey, Margot, I brought you a coffee." She set the cappuccino on the silvery-haired receptionist's desk.

"You're a doll. I was perishing for caffeine."

"I know the feeling. A couple of friends and I had a *Pride and Prejudice* movie night and stayed up way too late. But"—Piper heaved a sigh—"Mr. Darcy, right?"

"Mmm, no question." Laughing, Margot sipped her coffee. "Thank you for this."

"You looked as if you were starting to slow down. How's your husband doing?"

Margot rolled her eyes. "He's intelligent, strong, brave—and the man-flu turns him into a whiny two-year-old. He woke me up at 3 a.m. to find the aspirin for him. The bottle was on the bathroom counter right where he'd left it four hours before. If the flu doesn't kill him, I might."

"No woman would convict you." Grinning, Piper headed through the door marked Chatelaines.

The large room to the right was filled with cubicles for her chatelaines and contractors. Her office was to the left with a solid oak desk and a subdued gray-and-white color scheme.

Every Monday morning, her staff would meet in the conference room to get everyone in sync and exchange complaints and hints. She'd have the opportunity to dispense encouragement and direction as needed.

Boy, she herself could use some encouragement and direction right about now. Only the subject matter wasn't one she could broach with anyone. *Hi, I'm going to go be a slave on Saturday, and I'm not sure it's a good idea. What if I have a panic attack? Or the stress makes me even more neurotic than I am already.*

And what in the world should I wear?

As she sat down at her desk, a buzz from the receptionist made her jump. "Ms. Delaney, I have a visitor for—Wait, you can't go back there!"

The Chatelaines' door opened, and a slim, blond man strolled through and into her office. "Hey, sis."

The receptionist was right behind him. "Ms. Delaney, should I call for security?"

It was *Jerry*. "No, it's all right. Thank you." As the receptionist walked out, closing the door behind her, Piper stared at him. Along with the surprise at seeing her stepbrother came the usual unhappy feeling...at seeing her stepbrother.

She rose to her feet. "What do you want, Jerry?"

"Can't a brother want to see his sister?" Lean and handsome and smiling, he started to come over to her as if for a hug, rethought, and leaned against the wall.

Once upon a time, she'd worked so very hard to earn a smile from him.

"You're my stepbrother, not really a brother. Or so you told everyone." When her mother married Gideon, Piper had been ten and thrilled to have a big brother. Three years older, Jerry had hated his new stepsister and used her hero-worship against her every chance he got. When not ripping her ego to shreds, he'd conned her into doing his chores, into giving him money, into taking his punishments. The only times he was ever nice to her was when he wanted something.

"Oh, Pipsqueak, we were just kids, and teenaged boys are jerks." He shook his head. "I'm sorry for those days. Can you accept my apology?"

She breathed out, torn. He had a point—he had been a teen. He was apologizing. It'd be rude to just blow him off. She sank into her chair. "I..."

"May I sit?" He motioned to the chair in front of her desk. When she nodded, he sat. "Our parents are gone, Piper. You and me, we're the only family we have now."

The reminder set up a hollow ache in her chest, the knowledge she was all alone in the world. After escaping the Defiler, she called home and discovered her mother and Gideon had died in a car crash months before. She hadn't been close to them, and yet Mom's death had been a ghastly blow. "I don't think so. I never felt like I belonged. I don't see that changing."

"I'm sorry I made you feel that way." Remorse filled Jerry's expression. "I want us to be family. I came all the way out here just to reconnect with you. Please tell me it's not too late."

All the way from Kansas. Just to see her. Her heart softened...until wariness sent a cold breeze up her spine. "How did you find me?"

"I asked Dad's executor. He gave me your phone and old address out here. It took some research to get your business address, but I'm good with finding things out."

He always had been. Her mouth tightened as she remembered how he'd dealt in gossip. How he'd been paid by his classmates for his silence. Surely he'd outgrown that by now.

Leaning forward, he regained her attention. "I think the West Coast agrees with you, sis. You look really good." His gaze was admiring, and she flushed slightly. As a girl, she'd wanted so badly for him to approve of her. Apparently, she hadn't lost that yearning.

Yet she'd grown up and changed. Had Jerry? "What are you *really* here for?"

"Aw, Piper. That hurts." His expression turned sheepish. "Actually, since you asked, I've got a problem I hoped you'd help me with. You know the money my father left you?"

She snorted. "There wasn't much. Gideon left me one-twentieth of what you inherited. According to the lawyer, it was a token amount to keep the will from being contested."

"It was still a lot of money. I need it now." At her disbelieving stare, he shrugged. "I ran into some bad luck. Took out a loan, and the lenders want their money returned now or else."

Her sympathy faded. Oh, she recognized the pattern. "You got money from a loan shark to gamble with."

"No, I learned my lesson about gambling. Finally. Too late." He rubbed his eyes. "I know I was a disappointment to Dad. I changed."

Had he changed? Hope was a tiny flare inside her. "Then what was the loan for?"

"To start my own business of flipping houses. I have a couple of employees and everything. But, you know, the regular banks wouldn't take a chance on me."

He was actually *working*. Turning his life around. She smiled. "A business of your own? That's awesome." They had that in common, didn't they?

"I love it. Unfortunately, the profit is coming in slower than I'd hoped. You know how that goes."

All too well. Those first months after starting Chatelaines, she'd scrambled like mad, trying to cover the bills. "Yes, I do."

He sighed. "I'm in a bind and need to pay back the loan—before they come after me and break my legs."

Oh God, if he got hurt when she could help, she'd never be able to live with herself. "I can't believe you went to a loan shark."

"Stupid, I know. I was just so excited to start my own business." He tilted his head. "Can you see your way clear to giving me the money my dad left you?"

The stab of resentment made her sit upright in the chair. Her inheritance hadn't come from his dad—it'd come from her mother. Besides, she'd already spent the money, setting up her business.

"Let me think about it." She did have some money in savings and the business account. She could cut back on her own expenses if it'd help him out. "What's the name of your business?"

He hesitated...just a little too long.

She stiffened. Was there even a business? "Let's see one of your business cards." Every businessperson she knew had business cards.

"I haven't gotten around to getting any made."

"Because you don't have a business. You're gambling again."

His *I've-been-bad* expression had worked like a charm on their parents. "Pretty stupid, I know. But I'm really in a bind. You don't want to see me hurt, do you? We're family. The only ones left."

She set her hands on the desk and tried to muster her resolve. How many times had he conned her out of her allowance or her babysitting wages when they were kids? Because she'd been desperate to win his affection.

Love didn't work that way. "I'm sorry, Jerry. Your dad bailed you out over and over for your bad choices. I won't."

"Piper, Piper, you know that money should've been mine. All the money. You and your mother came to us with nothing. You shouldn't have gotten any of Dad's money at all—he wouldn't want you to have it."

The hurt of being rejected lingered even now. Rabidly conservative Gideon had despised her for being illegitimate. If she thought of the money as being all Gideon's, it felt wrong to have accepted it. She pulled in a breath. But that was only one way of looking at it. There were others. "Inheritance isn't based on emotion. The law says married people share, and that means I should inherit something from my mother."

"She would have left the money to me over you."

Maybe. Maybe not. Mom had loved her until Gideon's attitude prevailed. Until she'd been made to see Piper as an uncomfortable reminder of her sin.

The year Mom had married Gideon, Piper'd learned the difference between wishes and real life. She hadn't gotten the affectionate father she'd dreamed about. She'd lost her mother's love. She sure hadn't received a protective big brother.

"The money isn't yours, Piper." Jerry held his hands out in a physical appeal. "You need to give it back; you know you do."

No, she didn't know that. She was no longer an affection-starved little girl. Instead, she'd acquired defenses—like rejecting emotion in favor of logic. "Gideon left you a ton of money in stable investments. You lost all that money gambling?"

The flex of his cheek muscle was as loud as a shout.

He'd gone through well over a million dollars? Her disgust gave way to growing unease. Jerry had always felt entitled to whatever she had.

"I'm sorry, Jerry, but no. Go back to Kansas. There isn't anything for you here." She rose to her feet. "I have work to do. If you'll excuse me..."

He shook his head sadly. "Oh, Piper, I know you'll find it in your heart to help me. You're a good person. If I get crippled when you could have saved me so easily, you're going to feel horrible."

Even as worried guilt swamped her, he opened the door and stepped out, passing Dixon.

Dixon gave him an appreciative smile, then danced into the room with a cute hip shimmy. "Hey, girlfriend. Are you ready to give it another go? I'm off on Saturday, so this time I can be with you."

"Maybe. I—" She realized her stepbrother had stopped right outside her office. Was listening.

Eavesdropping had been one of his habits as a teen. He'd blackmailed several of her high school friends, threatening to reveal some infraction to their parents—drugs, sneaking out, screwing around. They'd paid him off for his silence.

Leaning forward, she buzzed the receptionist's desk. "Margot, please show my visitor to the door." She lowered her voice. "Call security if he doesn't leave promptly."

Hearing the first part of her order, Jerry turned a forlorn look on her. "I'm sorry you feel this way, sis. But we'll talk. Soon."

Having taken the chair in front of her desk, Dixon turned and watched as Jerry walked past Margot and out. "Mmm, he's gorgeous. But he reminds me of some Doms I dated before Stan. Smooth, saying all the right shit, but just out for what they can get."

Dix had a good eye.

Piper rubbed her face, wishing she could erase the last few minutes. "So it seems. I thought at first there was more to his visit." That he'd changed and wanted to really be her brother.

Even now, she wondered if she'd made a mistake and treated him too harshly. What if he got hurt by the loan shark? Her mouth twisted. If there even was a loan shark.

"Old boyfriend?" Dix asked.

"Stepbrother. He wanted money, and I said no."

"Poor Pips." Dix's brown eyes filled with sympathy. "Steplings can be difficult. Our sweet Abby has a stepsister who is a direct descendant of Cinderella's wicked steps."

"She does?" Oddly cheered, Piper relaxed in her chair. "Poor Abby. She and I'll have to compare notes."

"Over alcohol. Her tale of woe requires at least a glass of wine and"—Dixon looked at where Jerry had disappeared—"I'd say yours might call for tequila."

Piper actually laughed. Friends could brighten the ugliest of days.

CHAPTER NINE

On Saturday morning, Ethan leaned against his kitchen counter and watched Piper use his espresso machine and start to relax. Finally. In the short time she'd been here, the nervous little submissive had dropped her purse, stumbled over the ottoman, and tripped on a chair.

However, being set to a task eased her nerves. It appeared that serving was not only her talent but also her comfort zone.

As the cup filled, she glanced at Ethan. "Cream? Sugar?"

"A teaspoon of sugar, please." He glanced at Churchill, sitting at Piper's feet. "And the prime minister would enjoy a splash of cream in his bowl."

"Of course." Piper's dimples appeared. "Prime ministers always get their way."

As Churchill lapped up his morning beverage, Ethan escorted Piper downstairs and out to the patio. "Let's talk for a bit before we do anything else."

He took a seat on the wicker chair, removed the cushion from another chair, and set it on the concrete.

Her gulp was audible, then she gracefully knelt on the cushion, started to put her hands behind her back, and hesitated.

Very good. Each Dominant had his own preferences for a submissive's posture. "Hands on your thighs, palms up. Eyes on me." Although a submissive's kneeling was a potent reminder of the exchange of power, arms behind the back became uncomfortable quickly.

When she complied, he nodded in satisfaction. Although he didn't typically require kneeling when not in scene, he'd stick to a moderately formal protocol while Piper was here. Something close to what Serna might have demanded. "This is the default kneeling posture. I'll tell you clearly if I require anything else."

"Yes...um, how do you want to be addressed? Sir? Or..."

Or *Master*? Considering her past experience, he could understand her distaste, maybe even fear, of the word.

"Sir works fine." He kept his voice calm and slow. "I'm not your Master, Piper. In all reality, I don't enjoy the title or the responsibility. To do it right requires more time than I have."

A line appeared between the lovely arches of her brows.

"Ask, poppet."

"Why would... A Master has everything done for him. Why do you say it requires your time?"

"Was Serna your only experience with BDSM?"

She tensed at the name, then nodded.

Arseholes like Serna were why Dark Haven pro-actively searched for ways to educate and police their own. "Thankfully, the bastard isn't a typical Master. In fact, I'm disinclined to consider him a Master at all. Pond scum would be a more appropriate title."

Her eyes widened. "Really?" She cringed, and her shoulder muscles tensed.

Bloody hell. Undoubtedly, Serna had also punished her for asking questions. For talking. "Yes, really." If she spent time around decent Dominants, she'd discover what a piece of garbage Serna really was.

"The position you're in now is what I require when we're in D/s mode. I think you're observant enough to know when that happens. If we're watching television or reading in a companionable state, then sit where and how you prefer. For meals, I'll let you know."

Her fingers curled inward as her anxiety increased.

He hated to be the cause, yet the more ill-at-ease she was, the sooner they'd discover her triggers and how to circumvent them.

"On Saturdays, while you are under my authority, I consider your body mine. However, I'm not interested in micro-managing anything, including your personal care. Use the bathroom as needed. Shower as needed. I do expect a high degree of cleanliness, and I'd like your pussy to be trimmed short or shaved. If I feel you aren't tending my property carefully enough, I'll step in." He hardened his tone slightly to see how she'd react.

Ah, there it was.

Her face went pale, and her hands clenched. Her breathing started to race.

Leaning forward, he bracketed her face with his palms. "Look at me, Piper. Breathe with me now. In...out. In...out."

Her cold fingers curled around his wrists, hanging on. Anchoring herself. Her eyes were like brown velvet, focused on him—and in spite of the fact that he'd brought her close to a panic attack, she trusted him enough to accept his command, to let him pull her out.

The knowledge sent sweet warmth through his veins.

As her breathing slowed, he caressed her cheek and let her go. Reluctantly. Her skin was like silk. He was close enough to catch the scent of her hair and body—a light feminine musk, a hint of lemon, and fresh lavender.

She was far too appealing. This would test his control. Especially since she needed to be able to tolerate a man's hands touching her—a Dominant's hands.

"Tell me how you feel right now," he said softly, forearms resting on his thighs.

"Okay, I'm okay."

"That's utter rubbish. Try again. Can you feel your lips?"

Her teeth worried the lower lip.

So pink. Was her mouth as soft as it looked? *Out of line, Worth.*

"Yes. Um, I was cold, but it's better, and the roaring in my ears went away."

"Very good. Are you shaking?"

She pressed a hand to her abdomen. "Some. It's better, too." Her brows drew down. "Did you push me on purpose?"

It seemed her brain was also working again. "Yes and no. I wasn't lying about my requirements; however, I was more blunt than normal. We have a job—you and I—to discover what sets off your anxiety. You do have other or additional choices such as talking with a counselor about those triggers. I do recommend that, you know."

Her mouth tightened. "Maybe. Eventually."

He'd let this slide for the moment, but eventually, he'd push harder to get her to see someone. "Once we find your triggers, you avoid the ones you can. I'll work with you on detecting an attack early enough to avert it and on how to pull yourself out."

"That sounds good. I'm game." She frowned up at him. "But, Sir Ethan, I didn't realize how time-consuming this would be for you. Why are you helping me?"

Such a sweetheart, worrying about him rather than herself. However, her surprise that a Dom would exert himself for her needs was simply wrong. He ran a finger along her jaw. "Haven't you heard that a Dom might not give a submissive what she wants but *will* give her what she needs?"

Her gaze dropped. "No. I heard: '*You're property. Nothing. I don't give a damn about you; I don't have to.*'"

That was an obvious Serna quote. The bloody arsehole. "Sorry, but the lifestyle does pull in a few vicious wankers like Serna. Have you realized he was an abusive sadist?"

Although she nodded because her intellect knew the truth, he had a feeling that emotionally she wasn't convinced.

"You've done a magnificent job of turning your life around"—he smiled at the pleased flush that swept her face—"but you have a few steps yet to go. You *need* help climbing them. A good Dom doesn't leave someone hurting when he can help."

She swallowed and nodded.

Piper felt weird. Even as chills ran over her skin, sunshine lit within her soul from Sir Ethan's honesty. And his scorn when he spoke Master Serna's name.

"We've learned one trigger—you fear to disappoint a Master and incur punishment." A corner of his mouth tipped up. "I didn't even say the word *punishment* before your panic attack kicked off."

"You didn't need to," she said wryly.

"What other triggers do you have? Do you know?"

She'd thought about it since last weekend. "An angry or"—she bit her lip—"or a bored Master." Because hurting and humiliating her had been the Defiler's favorite way to get un-bored.

Disgust swept over Sir Ethan's face and disappeared a second later. He stayed in such control of himself that she was in awe.

"What else?"

"Being called names." Her hands closed into fists. *Please don't ask more questions.*

"Ah." Understanding softened his face. "I know it's hard, Piper. However, it will be more difficult if I stumble across a trigger by accident. The more prepared we can be, the better. What names are the worst?"

Her mouth was so dry. She couldn't do this. *Couldn't.* She shook her head—and realized the motion said she was refusing him.

She froze with terror. Now he'd—

Leaning forward, he lifted her up and onto his lap as easily as he would his cat. "Shhhh. It's all right, poppet. We'll get you past this," he murmured, holding her—hugging her—against him.

As he stroked her hair, she pushed her face against his neck. He was so tall she felt surrounded by him. His elegantly clean scent was beginning to smell like comfort.

He wasn't angry with her.

"Tell you what—can you write the names down? You don't have to say them out loud."

As part of counseling, years ago, she'd journaled. Had written the poisonous words. She nodded against his neck.

"Brave girl."

His approval washed over her, a spring rain carrying away the muddy remnants of snow.

How could he be so nice and still be a Dom?

But Stan was like him in the way he cared for Dixon. Were other Doms like Sir Ethan? Was he right—that she'd had a rare and horrible Master? One who wasn't even really a Master?

"Ah, how could I forget?" Sir Ethan shook his head. "In scene, I usually use the stoplight system for safewords where red means everything comes to a halt. However, since we don't know each other, if you say no, I will stop immediately. If you say wait, we'll pause and discuss what's bothering you."

She stared at him. He was openly giving her...control. The ability to break things off. How amazingly wonderful.

"Piper, did you understand what I said?"

"Yes, Sir. Red or no means you will stop." Her voice wobbled as she added, "Thank you."

His expression was unreadable, but his eyes were gentle. "No thanks are needed for something as essential as safewords."

He was so wrong.

"Time for a break. Why don't you settle in? I'd like lunch for us both in an hour. Soup and sandwiches are fine." Sir Ethan rubbed her shoulders. "We'll go out this afternoon to find you something to wear at Dark Haven tonight."

Oh God, oh God.

"Ah, there's another fear," he murmured. "What are you afraid of right now, Piper?"

"I own a company. I can't... If no one respects me, then—"

"Stop." The iron in his voice sent chills through her. He gripped her arms and sat her back so he could see her face. "Is being humiliated what you're concerned about?"

Terrified about? "Yes, Sir."

He considered her, gaze on her face. "I occasionally use humiliation as a disciplinary measure, but never lightly. It serves well as a punishment for someone who *deliberately* breaks the rules, thinking no one will find out. Piper, you haven't done anything to merit such treatment."

Her fingers were still curled tightly.

He huffed a laugh. "You're not thinking of punishment, though. You're afraid I'll treat you like a slave in public or select a sleazy outfit that would humiliate you in Dark Haven."

The pain in her chest showed she'd stopped breathing.

"Take a breath, poppet." He waited until she complied, then ran his knuckles down her cheek ever so gently. "Trust me a little further, sweetheart. My job is to build you up, not to destroy you."

Wait—what? "But I'm a submissive. Your job is to reduce me to—"

"No. Bloody hell." His jaw tightened, and she froze at the anger in his face. Then, to her wonder, the anger disappeared under his steely control.

"Piper, some of the strongest people I know are submissive. They are not diminished in the least by giving up their power."

That didn't make sense.

"Consider this. Drill sergeants are the most capable beings in the universe."

Thinking about the Marines and army people she'd known, she grasped what he meant. She nodded.

"Yet sergeants answer to their officers. Their captains." He paused. "Captains don't reduce their sergeants to less. Sergeants are valued for their skills, knowledge, and strength. Rather than running them down, their officers send them for more training. Build them up. Reward them for their abilities."

He laid his palm against her cheek, his thumb under her chin, his gaze an unearthly blue. "That's how a good Dom treats his submissive."

Oh.

CHAPTER TEN

Early that evening, Piper finished scrubbing the countertops and looked around with satisfaction. Cleaning and tidying up gave her a feeling of control. Calmed and centered her.

Sir Ethan had figured that out quickly. Then again, all day, he'd been determining who and what she was, as if she were a fascinating puzzle. He watched her closely. Asked her questions. Instructed her to take different positions. Used different tones—loud, irritated, bored.

Each time she grew anxious, he intervened. His calm voice and his careful, gentle hands on her arms would break the cycle before she lost it. In fact, he paid such close attention, he usually sensed her panic before she did.

With every episode, he taught her techniques to fend off the panic and made her practice. After, he'd assign something quiet and easy to do. He'd discovered that doing something for him calmed her faster than meditating or doing crafts or puzzles.

That was why she'd been cleaning the kitchen.

She leaned against the counter, taking a moment before returning to him. Aside from a quick shopping trip for her fetish clothing, the day had been...intense.

That wasn't what had her stalled in the kitchen, though. It

was because of who he was. If he'd been white-haired and beer-bellied or...someone else...she wouldn't be quite so rattled. But he was her English Dom, the champion who'd visited her dreams over the years.

And he was so very dominant. When he told her to do something, if she didn't panic, then, oh God, she slid right into the melty elevator-going-down submissive space.

Just his firm voice could do that. His smoky, resonant voice stroked over her like rich velvet.

When he looked at her with those eyes—a penetrating dark cobalt, the same deep color as the glass bottles her mother had collected—everything around her faded, leaving only him.

Her reactions were out of line, dammit. He was just being a caring Dom. Helping her out as he would any other needy submissive. *Remember that, Piper.*

She found him in the master bedroom, selecting his clothing for the evening.

"Piper, good." He set his hand on her shoulder, not making her kneel for which she was grateful. Because, boy, her overworked leg muscles felt like spaghetti. She was going to be sore tomorrow.

"Sir?" She bent her head and folded her hands in front of her.

As he studied her in silence, his gaze was an almost physical touch. "You did very well today, poppet, but you're exhausted. I want you to relax until you leave for Dark Haven."

"But..." Her head came up. She wasn't cured yet. "I'm fine. We can keep going."

"No." He tapped her cheek with a finger. "You're done for now." The way he said it, so quietly firm, silenced her objections.

And did more than that. Decisions, choices, plans weren't in her control today, and the awareness gave her a bone-deep contentment.

"Go sit on the couch and relax."

Once she was settled there, he plucked Churchill off the bed and set the cat in her lap. With a pair of pants over his arm, he disappeared into the bathroom.

Churchill made a pleased meow and curled into a ball. As the sound of the shower drifted out of the bathroom, Piper stroked his soft fur. His body was a warm calming weight, and his low purr more soothing than any music.

She'd been ordered to sit. Had nothing to do. Tension drained away, leaving exhaustion behind.

Sometime later, the door of the bathroom opened, making her jump.

Wearing only pants, Sir Ethan smiled at her. "You look better."

She could only nod...because her mouth had gone dry. All day long, she'd tried—really, she had—not to think of him as the sexiest man she'd ever seen.

But now, oh God. He was barefoot and shirtless, with that just-out-of-the-shower clean scent.

The promise of his aristocratic face was borne out by his finely sculpted frame. A spattering of dark hair covered the tanned expanse of his chest and rock-hard pectorals that bunched and rippled when he moved. A scar crossed his chest, cutting downward almost to the corrugated leanness of his abdomen.

He turned away to open the closet.

Wide, powerful shoulders. More muscles on each side of the furrow of his spine. Excitement swept through her, leaving every nerve sizzling. As he pulled on a shirt and his steely biceps flexed, the temperature in the room skyrocketed.

Buttoning his shirt, he turned to her. "After I leave, take a long bath and dress in the outfit I bought you. Rona and Simon will pick you up at nine."

She stared. "I thought I was going with *you*."

"I must be there early, and you need some time and space." He walked over to the couch.

"But..."

"Enough, pet." He tangled his fingers in her hair, gripped a fistful, and drew her head back. The confident ease of the maneuver reminded her of who was in control.

She swallowed under his unyielding gaze.

"You've done very well, Piper, but this has been more difficult than either of us anticipated. I want you at Dark Haven tonight."

"Yes, Sir," she whispered.

"We'll take it slow and easy. Although I will be touching you more."

A shiver ran through her.

"If I leave you alone, do you promise to find enough courage to show up?"

"Yes, Sir. I will."

"Good girl." His gaze warmed with approval. With understanding.

No wonder some submissives had so much trust in their Doms. Something she'd never had. Something she'd always wanted. Instead, she'd found only pain.

Why couldn't she have found Sir Ethan first?

Something seemed to crack deep inside her ribcage, letting out all the emotions that had been trapped inside. Her breathing turned ragged.

Yanking free of his hand, she buried her face in Churchill's fur.

"No, sweetheart." Sir Ethan set the cat on the floor, sat beside her, and with firm hands, pulled her against his hard chest. "When you're unhappy, this is where you belong."

Tears filled her eyes. She tried to push back, to escape.

"Shh." He kissed the top of her head. His arm around her waist tightened, caging her in safety rather than pain.

Face against his shoulder, she couldn't hold back the first sob or the next, and the storm swept over her. She cried.

He...let her. His warm hand moved up and down her back in long slow strokes.

Slowly, as the tempest eased, her mind cleared—leaving her appalled. What was she doing? Hiccupping, she tried to stop, tried to sit up.

His big hand cupped the back of her head, holding her in place. "You've stored this up for a while, pet. Let it out. I have you."

He did—oh, he did. And she dissolved into tears again.

Stockings. Boots. Victorian drawers with lacy edges that came to below her knees. A white puffy-sleeved chemise. Piper did up the hooks on the brown leather corset and fastened the outside decorative row of tiny buckles. She donned petticoats and finished with the full black skirt.

Done.

After checking herself in the guest room mirror, she looked at Churchill who was supervising from the dresser top. "What do you think, buddy?"

He lifted his nose, eyes squinching in approval.

"Okay, good." She bent to exchange a cheek rub. "I think steampunk looks pretty good on me, too. Who would have thought?"

That afternoon, the quick shopping trip for fetwear had been fun, especially since Dark Haven's theme tonight was steampunk. Even better, Sir Ethan chose clothing she was comfortable wearing. He'd been wonderfully kind.

Tonight, she'd be with him at Dark Haven. Yes, she was still scared, but not as much as before.

A glance at her cell told her she was out of time. "Got to get moving, PM. Oh, no, the collar."

Sir Ethan had said he'd leave a play collar on his bed for her. She walked into the master bedroom. Yes, there it was. Sleek brown leather with fleece padding on the inside. It didn't have silver stripes or say PROTECTED BY ETHAN. No, this one simply said ETHAN'S. As she buckled it around her throat, she felt queasy...yet almost pleased. Happy.

No, you idiot. Do not tell me that you're getting interested in that man. That Dom. What kind of weird psychology thing was this? A man terrifies a woman, and she falls for him?

She walked over to the dresser to look at herself, her breathing still a bit fast.

Then, she smiled. On the dresser was one of Chatelaines' engraved silver bowls that the cleaners used to deposit stray items. She'd seen bowls with buttons, change, underwear, ties, socks, jump drives, eyeglasses, pill bottles, and earbuds.

No matter how neat a client was, there was always something.

Sir Ethan's bowl had coins, pens, a tie tack, and a paper. The printing on the paper caught her attention. *SLAVE ROUTINE: Assign cooking chores. Cleaning chores. Have her journal and ask questions about the material.*

The last item on the list was *Spank to tears every night before bed.* A chill ran up Piper's spine.

No. No, he wouldn't.

Heart pounding, thinking only of escape, she turned toward the door.

But she'd promised Sir Ethan she wouldn't run. That she would show up at Dark Haven tonight. People didn't talk much about honor, but it meant a lot to her. She'd given her word.

The doorbell rang. Oh, God, Rona and Simon were here.

Okay, she'd go. Once there, she'd simply thank Sir Ethan and call this off. She'd thought he wasn't like the Defiler, but he was. Spanking just to make someone cry? They hadn't even talked about any kind of pain. He must be far more sadistic than she'd thought.

How could she have liked him so much?

As she answered the door, sadness filled her chest until her heart ached with every beat.

After escorting the general contractor and his crew out, Ethan accompanied Xavier on a leisurely viewing of the interior remodel of the dungeon. BDSM and steampunk went well together. "It looks magnificent, Xavier."

"Yes, it looks good." Xavier led the way up the stairs.

On the ground floor, the changes were mostly decorative. One wall was exposed brick. Behind the right stage was a floor-to-ceiling sepia old-world map mural. Behind the left stage, odd gears and wheels covered dark wood paneling. Industrial light fixtures with Edison bulbs ran the length of the room over the social area of wooden tables and chairs.

Ethan walked toward the rear of the room where the wooden bar was surrounded by vintage leather-and-metal barstools. Black pipe shelving held bottles of spirits as well as more steampunk oddities—leather-bound books, terrestrial globes, and antique knickknacks. "Where did you get all this?"

"Abby and I spent the last year browsing antique stores."

Ethan grinned. She'd probably enjoyed herself thoroughly. Before moving in with Xavier, she'd decorated each room in her home around a different country. Living room—French. Kitchen—Italian. "Nice job of scheduling. You finished just in time for tourist season."

"Tourists." Xavier growled under his breath. "Just what we need, more out-of-town guests with reciprocal memberships."

Reciprocal memberships were arranged with clubs in other locations so someone from another club could visit here, and Dark Haven members could play in a different city. Unfortunately, other clubs didn't always adequately instruct their members as to proper behavior.

Xavier wasn't an easygoing club owner.

The sound of conversation caught Ethan's attention, and he turned to see Simon crossing the room with Rona.

And Piper.

Pleasure filled Ethan at the sight of her.

She looked spectacular in the steampunk attire he'd bought. The deep brown corset matched her eyes and accentuated the curve of her waist. Her shoulders were bare, her full breasts pressed high, reminding him that he needed to discover if being intimately touched was one of her triggers.

Damn, but the day had been difficult. His instinct was to protect her, not terrify her. Certainly not reduce her to tears. Rather than hating him—she'd been grateful. After an episode, she took a few minutes to recover, then would say, "I'm ready."

He'd told her if she wasn't ready to face a memory, a counselor could approach it more gently. But she'd insisted on continuing. She was too brave for her own good.

He'd have to monitor her carefully here in Dark Haven.

It wouldn't be a hardship. She was a delight to be with. The combination of a giving nature and indomitable courage was incredibly compelling.

"Xavier, the new décor is amazing." Rona turned in a circle to look at everything.

"I'm glad you like it." Xavier studied the two women and nodded. "You two fit in perfectly."

"Thank you, My Liege," Rona said.

"Thank you, Sir." Piper curtsied. As she rose, her gaze met Ethan's...and her smile faded. Looking away, she clenched her hands. Her shoulders and neck muscles tensed.

When he'd left her at the house, she'd been open and warm.

After studying her for a moment, he glanced at the others. Simon and Xavier had also noticed. "Excuse us, please."

"Piper." He held out his hand, palm up. "I want to show you the"—no, not the dungeon. She didn't need the edgy dark atmosphere down there—"the wall of gears."

Left without a polite choice, she set her hand in his. Her fingers weren't cold. Weren't trembling. She wasn't afraid of him. At least they'd made that much progress.

As they walked toward the wall, he studied her. "I would like to know what you're feeling right now."

"I'm in awe of what Xavier has accomplished here." Stilted, cool voice. Very unPiperlike.

"No, pet. We're not discussing the décor. I'd rather hear why you've withdrawn behind a wall."

Piper stiffened. Why did he have to be so perceptive? On the other hand, he'd given her the perfect opening to tell him she was done.

How would he react? Would he be angry? She should have called or sent a message with Rona...however, he'd been so nice to her all day. Thoughtful. Stern when needed, and oddly gentle at the same time. He deserved to be told in person. To be thanked properly.

"Piper?"

He stopped by the wall and looked down at her. A Master waiting for an explanation. The Defiler had done that in the beginning—before he stopped letting her talk at all.

No, don't think about that time.

"It's just...it's been a long day." She stared at the floor, disappointed in herself. That was honest, but she was avoiding the real truth. The memory of the list surfaced, and she felt herself close down further.

"Yes, it's been a long day for you. Eyes on me, Piper."

She clenched her teeth and obeyed, feeling as if she had been stripped naked.

His gaze trapped hers, his eyes piercing. "What's going on, poppet?"

Say it. Just say it. "I'm done. We're done." She started to look away, but he was suddenly close, his fingers curling around her chin, holding her so she couldn't retreat. Couldn't hide.

"I hear what you're saying. Tell me how you reached this

decision, please." His English accent was stronger, his voice softer. "And why we didn't discuss this before I left."

Her mouth was too dry. She swallowed, heard the gulp. "I didn't know you were going to"—*hurt me.* She tried to draw away and got nowhere. Anger sparked amidst the jittering anxiety. "I found your list. Sir."

"What list?"

"The one where you spell out my duties and the punishment for each if it's not done correctly."

His puzzled expression infuriated her, and she wrenched her head free. Took a step back. "The one that says you'll spank me to tears each night."

Comprehension filled his face. "Ah, that list." He winced. "Bloody hell, did I leave that out where the maids would find it?"

His only worry was about hired staff seeing it? "So it seems. It was in the bowl where the cleaning crew puts anything they find under or in the furniture."

"That was careless of me." He shook his head. "The list isn't for you, Piper."

"Sure it isn't," she said sarcastically. "I'm sure you write out slave lists just for the fun of it."

The darkening of his eyes was a warning, and she cringed. What was she thinking to speak to him that way?

But she had liked him, and this betrayal was just...just... Tears filled her eyes, and she furiously blinked them back.

His warm hand curled around her nape, pulling her closer.

She flattened her hands against his chest. She didn't want comfort. Didn't want anything from him. He was a bastard who—

"Piper, the list was for Angel."

For Angel? *What?* Piper stared at him. She'd forgotten entirely about Angel. The surge of relief was heady. "Did she run away? Break things off with you? Was the spanking the reason?"

Her resistance was weakening, and somehow her cheek was pressed against the smooth lapel of his suit coat.

His hand moved up to cradle the back of her head as he chuckled, low and resonant. "She didn't run away. She returned to her Master. I was just babysitting...or I suppose one could call it slave-sitting?"

"You were what?"

"When her Master was hospitalized, he asked me to keep her until he was discharged. If you'd looked closer at the list, you'd have seen the handwriting isn't mine. Malik wrote out what she needed to stay busy and also what she required for...mmm...some Masters call it maintenance."

Cold spilled through her. "Hurting her is *maintenance*?"

Sir Ethan stroked a hand slowly up and down Piper's back. "She's a masochist, poppet. Regular spankings keep her leveled out."

"I bet you enjoyed doing *maintenance.*" Piper went motionless, horrified she'd spoken aloud.

When he laughed, relief bubbled up inside her.

"Although it wasn't sexual since Angel is completely in love with her husband, I can't say it's a hardship to spank a soft squirmy female." Sir Ethan's voice was cheerful. "I'd find it much more fun to spank you."

His statement took her breath away. The thought of his big hard hand hitting her bottom. The intimacy of...

As heat streaked through her, he gripped her hair, pulling her head back, forcing her to look up. Chills of anticipation and anxiety streamed over her skin. When he ran his finger over her lower lip, her center clenched in need.

No, please. She didn't want anything sexual between them. She tried to shake her head.

The amusement had faded from his face. His eyes were level, his tone firm. "Spanking isn't something I'd do without discussing it first or without your consent."

He meant it.

Being abused had turned distinguishing a lie from truth into a survival skill. She was very skilled.

Sir Ethan wasn't lying.

As her fear eased away, her strength went with it. She sagged against him.

"There we go," he murmured and kissed her hair. "You need something to drink and time to rebalance. Let's sit down, and we can talk about tonight."

Tonight. As he led her back into the room, she realized the quivers in her stomach had turned into those of anticipation.

Rona and Simon were already at a table. As Sir Ethan helped Piper sit, Rona pushed over two glasses. "I hope root beer is all right?"

Piper hesitated, giving Sir Ethan a glance as he took a chair beside her.

He read her easily. "Yes, you may talk freely until I take that privilege away, and yes, you may enjoy the drink."

The way he said that so easily, naturally, left her feeling as if she was walking on an uneven cobblestone road. She ran her tongue over dry lips. "Thank you, Sir." Her words came out almost inaudible.

He didn't smile, but a crease appeared in his cheek. He pulled her chair closer so they were hip-to-hip. His arm rested on the back of her chair, warming her shoulder blades and marking her as his.

The sense of comfort, of being where she belonged...was terrifying.

And way too arousing.

With astute black eyes, Simon studied her, and then smiled. "I'm glad you got whatever was bothering you straightened out."

To her shock, Ethan told him. "Malik had written out what to do for Angel when she was with me. Piper thought the list was for her, including spanking her to tears every night."

Rona gurgled a laugh. "No wonder you were upset. I'm impressed you even showed up tonight."

It had been a very close thing.

A glance showed Sir Ethan was watching her. His wink held

understanding. Sympathy. He truly wasn't angry. Another knot in her gut untied.

It was going to be all right.

Dark Haven had filled up—and Ethan was enjoying the reaction of the members to the new décor. Xavier had only told people that the theme of the evening was steampunk, not about completely transforming the interior.

Ethan picked up his toy bag, buried his grin at Piper's wary look, and escorted her down to the dungeon. He wanted to evaluate what activities interested her or frightened her. Serna had truly done a number on her, the wanker.

After the abuse she'd endured, it was surprising she was still drawn to BDSM at all. If he could, he'd teach her what the lifestyle could be.

He'd like to show her even more than that. He wanted to touch her, to kiss her, to take her. To see how his ropes would look on her bare skin.

There was more between them than the Dominant and submissive dynamic. When he spoke to her, her cheeks would flush; her lips would part. She had a growing awareness of him as a man as well as a Dom.

He wanted to explore that as well, but with Piper's history of abuse, he'd have to move very, very slowly.

"Everything looks different. This is new." Midway down the stairs, Piper walked out onto the landing.

Since everyone paused on the stairs to check out the dungeon, Xavier'd taken Ethan's suggestion and had the construction crew angle the stairs and build a railing-enclosed landing. It was a perfect height to view all the scenes.

Ethan leaned on the railing beside Piper. "The Tops are acting like they have a bunch of new toys."

Closest to the stairs, some of the St. Andrew's crosses were now black steel X-shapes. Others were covered in decadent black leather. The stone walls hadn't changed, but the rafters appeared to be massive black pipes, giving the room an industrial warehouse ambiance. The far corner held a "floating" black blimp. Chains dangled beneath it for use in suspension or as restraints.

"Let's go on down." Pulling her close, he ran his thumb over the back of her hand—a small hand, but sturdy as well—and led her down the stairs where they'd be close to what was going on. He wasn't about to let her keep everything at a distance.

Especially not him.

When they reached the dungeon floor, he stopped her. He'd chosen her costume with regard to her need for defenses. But she'd been here long enough to relax. It was time to remove some barriers. "Before we walk around, I'd like to see you wearing less."

"What?" Although her eyes widened, she didn't retreat.

Very good. She didn't trust him, not entirely, but hadn't panicked.

He went down on one knee beside her. "Left leg."

When she moved her leg forward, he unlaced and pulled off her ankle boot. She gave him her other foot, and he took off that boot as well.

Rising, he smiled at her worried expression. She knew he wasn't done.

"Remove your skirt and petticoats, please. Leave everything else." He smiled slightly. "You have lovely legs. I'd like to see them."

"B-but..." Even as she automatically undid the waist clasp, he could almost see her internal discussion. He wasn't here as her friend but as her Dominant, and he'd told her what he wanted.

Removing the skirt and petticoats wouldn't humiliate her—he hadn't asked her to remove her undergarments, after all.

Her tiny sigh made him grin.

Her skirt and petticoats dropped into a pile at her feet. She was left in her leather corset and white cotton undergarments—white stockings, thigh-length chemise, below-the-knee lace-edged drawers. The corset pushed up her breasts and drew attention to her waist and rounded hips, contrasting with the innocent appearing white chemise and lacy drawers.

Her velvety brown eyes were wide and vulnerable.

"Beautiful." Ignoring his craving to touch all that soft skin, he motioned to the built-in lockers beneath the stairs. "Put everything away and bring me the key."

Clothing dealt with and key in his pocket, he took her hand and started on a tour of the dungeon. Much like the Shadowlands in Florida, the walls were decorated with functional items. The right wall held Victorian walking sticks, one of which was being vigorously used on a submissive. The Domme's man had an artistic row of welts up his ass.

Feeling Piper's wince, Ethan made a mental note. Hard impact play wasn't in the books, for now.

A black metal safe with hand-sized holes caged a whiny submissive. Her displeased Dom didn't look disposed to let her out anytime soon.

When Piper shivered, Ethan frowned. Had she been caged? He'd have to ask her, but later. This wasn't the time for ugly memories. The scenes were putting her on edge. He kept walking.

Odd-shaped stands of metal and old gears shelved cleaning supplies. Open antique jewelry boxes on top held condoms, gloves, dental dams, and lube.

In the spanking bench area, a Top grabbed a lube packet and drizzled the contents between the buttocks of his restrained submissive.

A glance at Piper showed a mixture of worry and excitement.

Ethan stopped, keeping her from moving away from the scene. "Do you find anal sex painful or fun?"

She bit her lip. "It was exciting. At first."

"Ah." If her lover had been gentle, she'd probably enjoyed the thrill of that kind of sexual submission. But Serna had undoubtedly brutalized her. "When we discuss what interests you, I want your impressions from the beginning of your experience."

"Yes, Sir." Her tight grip on his fingers loosened.

After a second, he realized she was relieved that he planned to discuss her interests. Negotiate.

Putting an arm around her, he resumed their walk. All the new steampunk BDSM equipment was in use. He eyed the steel spider web, thinking Piper would look good there, and...

He halted.

She looked up. "Sir?"

"Sorry, poppet." He gave himself a mental punch. He wasn't here to play; he was here to help. Although being honest—as a Dom must be—he admitted to himself that the longer he knew her, the more he wanted to play with her for his own enjoyment.

Scene after scene went by. She was fascinated by Shibari. Also by wax play when done in a sensuous way. The sadist splashing hot wax on a screaming masochist made Piper freeze.

Pain wasn't her kink. He'd guess most impact toys would be a hard limit for a long while to come.

They reached the area with bondage tables. Rona was tied to one, and Simon was using suction cups on her tender bits.

Piper's eyes widened. Her cheeks flushed, and she unconsciously leaned against Ethan.

Excellent. Now he knew where to begin.

He took her to the back where there was rough stone flooring. Where fire play was allowed. Safety equipment was kept between each bondage table—fire extinguishers, towels inside buckets of water, fire blankets.

"Come here. I think you're ready to try something." He tossed a fireproof blanket over a bondage table and turned.

She stood staring at him.

"Sit on the table here for a minute, pet." Gripping her around the waist, he set her on it.

Her eyes were wide, fear trying to break out. But today, they had—the two of them—started to take control over her anxiety.

He bracketed her face between his hands, leaning down to capture her gaze. "Slow breaths, poppet. This is talking time. Nothing to be afraid of. Nothing happens here unless you agree. Nothing."

A shudder ran through her.

"What color is my coat?"

She blinked. Focused on his brass-buttoned, dovetail coat. "Mahogany."

"Very good. What about my vest?"

"Black. Everything else is black."

Since a man was screaming across the room, he skipped asking what she heard. "Touch my cheek."

Her soft hand stroked across his upper cheek and down to his jaw-outlining stubble. "I'm okay now. And I like your beard. Not too rough, not too soft."

"Thank you, poppet."

Her gaze fell. "Sorry about the panic."

"I'm not." He smiled at her blink of surprise. "This is what we're here for, are we not? To see what triggers panic attacks and help you work past them."

"Oh." She gave him a rueful smile. "I forgot."

"The dungeon is quite distracting." She looked calm again. Time to move on. "Have you ever had a Dom or therapist do cupping for you?"

She shook her head, casting a glance toward Simon and Rona.

Ethan smothered a smile. "Simon is using erotic cupping. My idea—for tonight—is the relaxing type. I'd like you to feel more comfortable in a dungeon."

Her gaze drifted toward Rona again.

"I'll be working on your back, pet. You're not ready for anything else."

A flush rose from her chest to her cheeks. He looked forward to a time in the future when erotic cupping would be fun for her.

Her teeth worried her lower lip. "It sounds intriguing, but you won't get much..."

"There will be no sexual satisfaction for me. Is that what you mean?"

Her flush deepened, and he stroked a finger over her cheek, feeling the warmth. "Piper, a man doesn't have to get off every time he turns around. Even if your ankles are sexy as hell, I won't jump on you."

"I won't—I didn't mean..." Her eyes narrowed. "You're teasing me."

"Who could resist?" Amused, he walked around the table and started unlacing her corset. "This and the chemise have to go."

After setting the corset to one side, he pulled the chemise out from under her, then lifted it up and over her head.

A shiver made her breasts jiggle before she covered them with her hands. Beautiful breasts, almost too large for her petite size. He looked forward to feeling the weight of each on his palm. The areolas were a wide pinkish-brown and already bunched tightly.

He laid the garments on a nearby chair. "If you're not comfortable, you can lie down right now, Piper. On your stomach. Although there will come a time when I won't cater to your modesty."

"I, uh, guess I'm not used to being naked any longer."

"I'm not surprised." As she lay down on the table with her head turned toward him, Ethan removed his coat and rolled his shirt sleeves up, securing each with an elastic band. Taking his time, he prepared the materials for fire-cupping. Alcohol. Small torches of copper-wrapped cotton on a stick that were easier to use than forceps and cotton balls. A firestarter.

Her head rose at the sight of the firestarter. "You're going to burn me?"

"No, pet." He lit the cotton torch on fire, held it in a glass cup for a second, and set the glass on his palm to show nothing horrible happened. "Now hold out your hand."

When she complied, his heart warmed at the trust she was giving him.

He went through the steps again and set the cup on her palm. "The fire removes the air from the glass. When on your skin, the lack of oxygen in the cup creates suction and lifts the skin upward. The Chinese believe it's effective for pain and relaxation."

"You've done this before, right?"

"Many times. I teach a class here every few months."

"Oh. Sorry."

"Piper, a submissive should always check the qualifications and reputation of a Dom. You're quite right to ask." Filling his hand with silicon lotion, Ethan flattened his palms on her shoulders.

She jumped, then relaxed. "I didn't ask about you, though, did I?" Her mouth twisted in self-condemnation.

"You're too hard on yourself." He started a slow massage, noting where her muscles were tightest. He trailed a finger down the small lumps of her vertebrae to the pretty dimples above her ass. Her skin was soft and velvety and far too tempting, so he turned his attention to the scars. Serna had marked her with a variety of implements—whip, blade, flogger, cane—the fucking bastard. "If I wasn't essentially recommended by Xavier and Abby, Rona and Simon, you'd have been far more cautious with me."

She blew out a breath. "You're right."

"Of course I am. I'm a Dom—just a step under God."

When she laughed, her muscles loosened even more.

Sir Ethan was incredibly nice, Piper thought, resting her cheek on the table. Of course, yes, he was a Dom and totally took charge, like how he'd told her to remove her clothes. He hadn't raised his voice, but his authority came through loud and clear. Yet he didn't mind her questions and had even reassured her she wasn't an idiot.

Her lips curled into a smile as she remembered her first visit with Rona and Abby. The baronet Dom really *had* come with the Dark Haven seal of approval.

As she watched him set up his equipment, she could tell he was very experienced. There were no worried pauses or fumbling for supplies. He wasn't using her for a practice subject. She tensed, remembering when the Defiler learned to use a bullwhip and had practiced on her rather than an inanimate object. So much pain, so many scars.

"Subbie," Sir Ethan gripped her nape firmly. "Whatever you're thinking about, let it go."

"Right." She exhaled and tried to relax. "Sorry, Sir."

His warm hands slid over her back, slow and even, massaging the tension away, continuing until she started to melt into the table.

"Much better." He straightened.

Tensing again, she watched him set the mini-torch on fire, hold it in the cup, and blow the flame out. He placed the cup on the big muscle to the right of her spine. The rim was warm and...

Everything under the cup pulled upward with the oddest sensation.

"Breathe, long and slow," he reminded her.

Right, right. "It doesn't hurt."

"No, there shouldn't be any pain today." Another cup, then another. More. A deep tugging sensation came with the suction under each cup.

He slid some of the cups to new places. Did more. Took some off. Moved others.

The dance of warmth zigzagged across her back. As each spot of tension smoothed out, her eyes closed. Somehow the cushion beneath her grew softer and softer...

Eventually, she realized he'd stopped, that nothing was touching her back.

She managed to lift her eyelids.

With the lights behind him, his face was in shadows, but she could see the curve of his lips. "How are you doing, poppet?"

"I don't think I've been this relaxed in years."

"Excellent. Consider this your reward for being brave enough to enter the dungeon and strip down."

A reward? Whoever heard of that?

When his mouth tightened, she realized she'd spoken the questions aloud.

His hard face turned gentle, and he ran his knuckles over her cheek. "I enjoy rewarding good behavior, Piper. Now, are you ready to try the next scary step?"

Scary? No, no she wasn't ready. She'd far rather take a nap right now, with him standing guard. How had he made her trust him?

He was waiting for her answer. *Focus, Piper.* As a submissive, she knew the proper answer to any question posed by a Dom. "Yes, Sir."

"Brave girl. Roll over."

Uhhhh...that would put her breasts on display. Next scary step.

His gaze met hers. He didn't move. Didn't speak.

Right. She could do this. After a second, she squirmed and rolled until she was face up on the bondage table. In the cool dungeon air—and under his gaze—her nipples contracted into tight, aching peaks.

He leaned over her and brushed her tangled hair out of her eyes. "At this point, I'd like to tie your wrists over your head and continue the massage—not the fire-cupping—on your front. Whether I touch your breasts or not, is your call."

Her throat went tight. Fear, arousal, excitement—the unsettling brew of emotions sent her pulse skyrocketing.

"Piper, there's nothing to fear." His smooth English accented voice remained easy and quiet, as effective as a tranquilizer. "The dungeon safeword is red. As I told you before, you can also say *no* or *wait* if needed."

"I understand. But you want to tie my arms and...and—"

"You're asking why I think I should restrain you and touch you in a more intimate way?"

Well, at least one of them could articulate things. "Yes. That."

"Because I get the impression you respond sexually to Dominants, which for many submissives, can mean vanilla men won't attract you." He smiled slightly. "It's a common problem for those in the lifestyle."

"Oh." How reassuring it was to hear she wasn't alone in that dilemma.

"To date someone who can fill your needs—a Dom—you need to move past being terrified of the basics. Shall we see how you do with your arms bound and being touched?"

Move past being terrified. That *was* what she was here for. She looked up at him, seeing the aristocratic chiseled features, the firm lips, the stern jaw. So very controlled. So very patient. If she said no, he wouldn't get upset.

Why did that make all the difference in the world?

This really was the next step. If she had the courage. She could think of no one she trusted more. She could give him this much control. She could.

Be honest with yourself, Piper. She *wanted* him to touch her. Just the thought of Sir Ethan's muscular hands on her skin made her heart thud harder. And touching her breasts? She could feel how tight her nipples were, as if they were calling for his attention.

She could do this—because it was Sir Ethan. "Yes, Sir."

A corner of his mouth lifted. "Yes to bondage?"

She swallowed and took the next step. "Yes to everything." Lifting her arms, she offered him her wrists.

Surprise then approval lit his eyes. Taking her hands, he kissed her fingertips. "I'm proud of you, Piper."

His compliment sent a thrill of happiness through her.

His silence drew her attention, and she realized his eyes had narrowed. Darkened. Turning her hands over, he examined the scars on her wrists. To her relief, he didn't say anything, just wrapped the soft rope into a singularly effective tie around her wrists with a loop at the end. Lifting her arms above her head, he hooked the loop over something at the end of the table.

After setting bandage scissors on the metal rolling tray table, he smiled down at her. "All right, here's the test. Pull on the rope."

What kind of a test was that? Didn't he think his knots would hold? She gave a little tug, then a stronger one.

There was no give. The rope was gripping her wrists, gripping like brutal hands, cruelly holding her down. There was no way to escape, no way to—

"Piper."

The resonant warmth in the masculine voice slid between her and the ugly memories, a shield blocking away horror. With an effort, she opened her eyes.

Sir Ethan cupped her cheek in a big hand and leaned his elbow on the table, comfortably close. Waiting for her to recover. "Do you want free, poppet?"

She'd had a flashback, nothing more. Sir Ethan was here, near enough she could inhale his clean, brisk scent. A breath cleared the constriction in her throat.

She met his gaze and gave him a firm nod. "Thank you. I think I'm good now."

"You're remarkable is what you are." The smile on his face was all for her.

Then he squirted lotion in his palms, rubbed them together, and stroked up each side of her waist, just above her drawers. His hands were hard, not a businessman's hands at all. Like her, he had quite a few scars—a couple on his face, the one on his chest, lots over his knuckles. Didn't boxers wear gloves?

"What put those scars and calluses on your hands?" Her

question popped out followed by her gasp of dismay. *A submissive interrupting a scene with her stupid chatter. Her worthless mouth should be put to better—*

"Piper."

His voice was a tide pulling her back to the safety of the shore.

"Sorry, I'm so sorry."

"Sweetheart, I'll remind you as often as needed that this is exactly why we're here—to find out what triggers you and defuse it. Perhaps to replace some of the ugly memories with better ones." His hands moved over her slowly, exerting even pressure over her upper arms, her shoulders. He firmly squeezed away the knots, leaving warmth behind.

She gave him the proper, "Yes, Sir."

Beneath the dark mustache, his wicked grin was white in his tanned face. "Did I tell you that I want your silence during this scene?"

She frowned, trying to remember. "Um, no, Sir?"

"If I don't want you to speak, I'll tell you. Sometimes I care; usually, I don't. I'll never punish you for not being able to read my mind." He held her gaze, letting her see his sincerity. Letting her absorb the truth.

Another knot unraveled.

"There, that's better." His hands slid up and over her breasts.

She gasped.

Sir Ethan's firm hands were on her. Touching her intimately.

Deep in her core, buds of excitement began to unfurl, blooming with a slow seductive heat.

He ran his palms under her breasts, over, molded them, pushed them together. He kneaded her upper pectorals for a moment before stroking downward again.

Her breasts tightened, the nipples pebbling into hard peaks. Wanting more.

"For the scars on my knuckles"—he lifted his hands

—"they're from boxing. I wasn't always careful about wrapping or using gloves."

She should have guessed that. "And the calluses?"

"Weight-lifting." Smiling at her, he ran his palms over her nipples, and the sensually abrasive scrape sent excitement coursing through her body.

She sucked in a stunned breath.

His gaze lifted from her breasts. Met hers. Forthright hunger was there in his eyes, and as he studied her face—her undoubtedly flushed face—the sun lines at the corners of his eyes deepened with his smile.

He continued massaging downward, her sides, her ribs. When he returned to her breasts, his touch was firmer. His thumbs circled her nipples.

Streamers of need ran in a direct line from her nipples to clit, wakening a restless need. She was *aroused*. The sensation was terrifying. And wonderful.

Leaving her breasts, he massaged the tenseness from her shoulders before returning to tease her some more.

After the fire cupping and under his hard massage, her muscles were limp—even as her breasts swelled until every touch of his hands reverberated through her. Her nipples ached.

She stared up at him, the intense blue of his eyes, and the dark shadow of heavy stubble-beard along his jaw. His lips. What would his lips feel like?

Her pussy slickened—because it was Sir Ethan who was touching her.

His gaze swept over her face, and a crease appeared in his cheek. "I believe that will be enough for this session."

He pinched her nipples slightly and tugged, making her back arch. And then he undid the ropes on her wrists.

The oddest disappointment welled inside her. Because she wanted him to do more.

"You did well, Piper. Good girl." His voice stroked over her in the wake of his hands, approving, leaving warmth behind.

After helping her lower her arms and sit, he tipped up her chin—and she got her wish.

His lips were firm and yet velvety as he kissed her. Slowly. Lingering for a wonderful moment.

As he straightened, she stared at him...and felt barriers dropping. Leaving her open. Defenseless.

Oh, she was in so much trouble.

On the new landing, Dixon did a quick dance step to the *Queen of the Damned* soundtrack that played in the dungeon. It totally added to the dark steampunk atmosphere. Perfectamente. He loved it when Stan would swing a flogger or cane in time with a song's beat.

Dixon's ass was already wiggling in anticipation. It was going to be a great night.

Lindsey had been right—he and Stan had needed a trip to Dark Haven to reconnect. Stan hadn't even needed any persuasion.

"Great decorating job," Stan leaned on the railing.

"Scary as shit." Dixon took in the harsh, almost frightening ambiance in the room and grinned. He and his Dom had dressed perfectly for the evening.

Stan wore black jeans tucked into knee-high, brown leather boots. His buckle-laden, brown leather vest covered hard pectorals and a six-pack to die for. In fact, Dixon's tongue had traced every dip and hollow as they dressed.

Rather than a vest, Dixon wore a chest harness made up of brown leather straps and buckles and a matching leather jock strap.

When Stan tucked his fingers in Dixon's heavy brown leather collar, Dixon shivered happily. His Master always left the collar loose enough he could use it as a handle. Being firmly pushed into place made Dixon harder than a rock.

Moving closer, he breathed in Stan's scent, sighing in happiness when his Master's iron-hard arm curled around his waist. He wasn't the only one with a woodie happening...and he couldn't help himself. Like a heat-seeking missile, his palm was right on target to stroke over his Master's rigid cock.

"For touching without permission, I'm breaking out the dragon tail," Stan growled.

Dixon jerked his hand back. *Oh, fuck a donkey.* Like a contagious disease, the cruel dungeon mood was affecting his Master. Stan was a sadist.

Not an over-the-top one like deVries...except sometimes.

This might be one of those sometimes.

There would be pain tonight, wonderful, heady, cock-spasming pain. Dix's balls started to throb in time with the music.

Stan motioned toward something across the room. "Isn't that Piper?"

"Ha, she made it! Rona said she was coming tonight if she didn't chicken out."

Dixon leaned forward to see better. Hot damn. Not only was she here, but she was half-naked and looking all flushed, confused, and aroused.

Sir Ethan did have a way about him. A shame he only played with females.

"Come, boy." Stan tugged on the collar. "I hear a spider web calling your name. The steel one."

Fuck, yes.

As they crossed the dungeon toward the steel-wire web, Dixon noted—once again—that people with hard-ons shouldn't have to ambulate. It felt like he had a baseball bat between his legs.

"Now, why did I have a feeling you'd know this place?" Darrell Legrand stepped in front of Stan. "We gotta stop meeting this way, JS."

Hackles rising like a dog, Dixon stared at the chestnut-haired special-fucking-agent. Stan's new partner from Texas. Why the piss-in-the-iced-tea was he here?

Karma, you bitch, you're supposed to be on my side.

"Hell, man." Stan stopped with a grin. "I didn't know you were still in the lifestyle."

"Eh, now and then." Darrell's smile widened. "I've had a craving to bottom for someone recently." The desire in his eyes as he looked at Stan said exactly who he had in mind.

"You've come to the right place," Stan said—and Dixon's heart sank. Until Stan added, "There are a lot of good Tops here tonight."

Ignoring the hint, Legrand moved closer, as if Dixon wasn't standing right there beside his Master. "Been a long time since we played together, JS."

Dixon held his breath.

Stan shook his head. "Thanks, but no. I have a subbie who has an appointment with a spider web." Stan did a chin-lift and headed away, still gripping Dixon's collar. "Have fun tonight, Legrand."

"Yeah, I will. I always do...as you well know."

As they headed for the spider web, Dixon tried to recapture the glow of before. His Master had turned the guy down. He *had*. Hadn't even looked particularly interested, but Legrand sure was. He looked at Stan like a starving Doberman, spotting a juicy steak.

Once Monday arrived, Special Agent Darrell Legrand and Special Agent Jameson Stanfield would be working on some Homeland Security case. Hours and hours...together.

Dixon's heart ached like a sorry piece of meat.

At the spider web, he knelt, waiting as Stan set things up. The dragon tail came out of his toy bag along with other impact toys.

Dixon felt no shivers. His hard on had disappeared.

He looked up at Stan through his eyelashes, feeling the pull of the man. So fucking gorgeous, all stern attitude, chiseled features, ripped muscles. With an ability to be tender, loving, beneath all that.

Yeah, he was head-over-heels and wasn't that just a fucking uncomfortable sort of love, anyway?

Miserable, in fact. For the first time since they met, Dix wished he hadn't fallen in love.

Closing his eyes, he tried to get his head into the right space for playing, for being touched and hurt and undoubtedly fucked. Even if his heart ached, he needed to be the perfect submissive for Stan.

Because there was another contender for the position.

CHAPTER ELEVEN

Feeling proud of herself, Piper strode down the sidewalk with long steps. Sweat dampened her T-shirt, and her pectorals and glutes ached in a good way. Because, hoorah, she'd just finished a kickass workout. Embarrassing as it was to admit, Ethan and his muscles had been the incentive. As busy as he was, he worked out religiously. She had no excuse not to do the same.

He was good for her, in more ways than one.

He was also the reason she was losing sleep. For the past three nights since Dark Haven, she'd dreamed of him touching her, of his hands ruthlessly holding her down, of him taking her in a thousand different ways.

She'd be with him again this Saturday, and the thought filled her stomach with happy butterflies.

Slowing, she shook her head as uneasiness crept over her like a black fog. She'd felt this fizzy anticipation and desire. Seven years ago.

No, that wasn't a fair comparison. What she felt now wasn't the same as then.

When she'd been new to BDSM, the Defiler's dominating control had seemed like the answer to all her needs. She'd been too inexperienced to see the red flags—like how he insulted his exes, how he demeaned waitresses. Recklessly, she'd flung herself into his arms and handed over everything. To a total bastard.

She wasn't jumping into anything now.

Sir Ethan was the Defiler's complete opposite. Everything Ethan did—his authority mixed with compassion, his honesty, his communication skills—none of it was a pretense. He was one of the most respected Dominants in Dark Haven. More than that, he was simply a good person. She'd never seen him be less than polite to everyone, rich or poor. He didn't raise his voice or throw his weight around, not even to the submissives.

She liked him.

Okay, she was definitely lusting after him, too. He'd said she didn't need the extra complication of sex when serving him at his house, but she'd be amenable to some complications right now. Each time she heard his resonant voice and English accent, her heart spun into a breakdance, full of leaps and somersaults and kicks.

His hands on her breasts had been...too knowledgeable. Too sexy. She wanted those hands everywhere on her body.

Great. She snorted. Now she was damp from more than sweat.

Laughing, she rounded the corner.

"Piper, here you are." Her stepbrother stood in front of her brick apartment building. "Here, I brought this for you. Happy summer." He handed her a single pink rose.

"Um..." She loved flowers. She always had. "Thank you."

"It's good to see you, sis." He tilted his head. "But, you kinda look as if you had a rough day. Is there anything I can help you with?"

Old comfy gym clothes, sweaty, hair a mess. "I was just—" *No, Piper.* She had no need to justify her appearance, although his offer to help softened her heart. "That's sweet of you, but no. I'm fine."

"Good, that's good. How about I take you out for an early supper? We can catch up with things."

"I thought you went back to Kansas." Jerry was being uncomfortably friendly. She bit her lip as unease grew in her belly. She needed to remember that, as children, the only times he'd been pleasant was before he asked for something. "I'm sorry, but I have to go back to work."

"Then later?" His smile widened. "I found a restaurant last night I think you'd enjoy. You like Thai, I know."

Her dismay swelled under an onslaught of memories. The time he'd bought her a book, then asked to borrow her bike. The time he'd taken her to a party, then put her on the spot, making her pay for the pizzas he'd ordered for everyone.

Now, he brought her a rose and wanted to go out to eat... because he wanted her inheritance. Suddenly, his showing up at her door felt far less friendly and more like browbeating.

She straightened her shoulders. "I'm sorry, but no." Why was it so hard to say no to people? To be honest? It made her feel so ugly inside.

Pulling in a breath, she hardened her heart. "We've never been friends or family, Jerry. I see no reason to start now."

"That's pretty brutal. I guess I don't have any family left at all then." He looked so hurt, guilt swept her.

"I'm sor—" No. This was like refusing a second date. She shouldn't let it get drawn out. "Have a good life, Jerry."

"It might be a really short life if I can't pay off the loan shark, Piper."

"We had this discussion already. I don't have anything for you. Go on home."

"I can't, I'm afraid. That inheritance is mine."

"No, it isn't."

"Piper, Piper, Piper." He shook his head sadly. "If you return my money, I'll stop bothering you."

Until he gambled it away and came back. "No."

"If I don't get any help, we'll be having this conversation a lot. Maybe every day. I'll enjoy spending time with my little sister"—his voice dropped to a whisper—"who was a sexual slave for years."

The threat was there, laid out. Her mouth went dry. If her clients found out about her past, they'd never respect her. She'd lose her reputation, maybe her business. SF was tolerant, but...a woman in business already had an uphill fight. To be known as having been a slave? She lifted her chin. "I doubt anyone would care, but you do what you need to do."

"I will. I do love San Francisco. It's such a small city—I'll probably run into you everywhere."

He'd follow her. Show up when she was with a client. She'd never be able to relax. As ice swept her body, her hand unzipped her purse, reached for her wallet.

No. Think, Piper.

Struggling to keep from folding in on herself, she closed her hand around her purse. "Harassment and stalking are illegal. If I see you again, I'll call the police."

"It's a public street. There's nothing illegal about my being here. Or anywhere else." He never lost his smile as he continued, "You probably have lots of friends coming and going from here who'd love to talk with me."

Her friends. Her work. He threatened everything she'd built here.

"I don't want to cause problems for you. Just give me what should have come to me—and I'll be history." He moved forward. Bigger than she was. "I want my—"

"No!" Her fist shot forward, impacting his belly with a hard thump.

Satisfying.

Terrifying.

As he folded over with a loud groan, she held her bag to the door sensor, heard the lock click, and entered. Quickly, she yanked the door closed behind her.

The door rattled behind her. A glance back showed him scowling at her through the metal-reinforced glass.

She jogged up the four flights of stairs, needing the exertion to keep from breaking down in tears as she had when she was a little girl. Like after he'd thrown her favorite doll down the storm drain. Like when she was sixteen and refused to turn over her allowance, so he'd told everyone she'd fucked her history teacher to get an "A". Her stepfather hadn't spoken to her for a month.

Piper, just stop. There was nothing she could do. She'd made her refusal clear. Verbally and—an edgy satisfaction filled her—physically. Surely he'd give up and go away.

There was no time right now to worry about Jerry—she was due at Ethan's and was now running late. His cleaning crew had been through earlier, and she wanted to do a quick evaluation before he got home.

As she held her purse to her automatic door lock, Stan and Dix's door opened. A tall man with chestnut-colored hair came out, reading a paper as he walked.

"See what I mean about the motivating factor?" Stan followed and pulled the door shut. "Sorry about the detour. I should have remembered to bring my notes to the office."

"Not a problem. I never mind an invite to your place, JS." Standing very close, the stranger set a hand on Stan's shoulder, his body language past friendly, more like intimate.

Piper stared.

Not seeing her, Stan shook his head. His voice dropped to a reproving, "Darrell."

"C'mon, we were good together. Could be even better." Darrell ran his hand down Stan's arm, spotted Piper watching, and stiffened.

Alerted, Stan turned. He started to smile at her, then frowned. "Are you all right, darlin'? You're pale."

She was? Then she remembered Jerry. "Fine. I'm fine."

She slipped into her apartment and shut the door. The sound of their voices and footsteps diminished as the two men left.

That must have been the co-worker of Stan's who Dixon was

worried about. The guy was definitely making a play—and had been in their apartment. Did Dix know? Should she tell him?

Probably not. It seemed like Stan needed a good shaking, but she didn't really know what was going on. At least Stan hadn't jumped the guy's bones, despite Darrell's flirting.

With a sigh, she headed for her bedroom and the shower she badly needed. Workout sweat. Emotion sweat because of Stan and the jerk. Anger and fear sweat because of Jerry.

She turned the water in the shower to hot, waited for the steam to rise, and stepped in.

Tipping her head down, she let the hot water flow over her. The tension in her muscles wasn't rinsing away at all.

Because she really doubted Jerry would simply give up.

Ethan walked into his home, smiling because Piper's car was in the garage. She'd mentioned that Chatelaines liked to do a post-cleaning evaluation the first few weeks.

He had hoped to see her today.

Spotting her all-black trainers under the coatrack inside the garage, he removed his shoes and climbed the stairs.

Her lilting voice came from the living room. "Good job on the kitchen. The cleaners need to work on getting the cat hair off the furniture. Maybe the pet-sitter could do some brushing if Churchill will let her."

Her voice turned to a sweet coo. "Hey, buddy. Will you let our girl brush your fur? Most kitties love it, you know."

At the kissing sound, Ethan grinned. Someone liked cats, and Churchill was particularly lovable.

"You are just what I needed after the day I've had. Thank you, PM."

After the day I've had? Her voice did sound thin. Stressed.

Concerned, Ethan walked into the room.

Her back to him, Piper wore belted black slacks and a dark

red, collared shirt. A matching red scrunchie held her ebony hair in a low tail just past her shoulders. Bad day or not, she still looked admirably professional.

Had that arsehole executive caused more problems? Or was the culprit another of her clients? She was such a sweetheart, it was difficult to believe anyone would give her a rough time, but some people were more shark than human, attacking at any sign of vulnerability.

"Piper."

With an audible gasp, she spun, Churchill in her arms. She took a hurried step back as if fearing to be struck. "Sir."

Ethan waited, keeping his shoulders relaxed, hands at his sides, expression calm. Last weekend, when she'd left Dark Haven with Rona and Simon, she'd been relaxed enough to hug him. Today, tension simmered around her. It appeared the gains they'd made had disappeared. Yet her trust in him wasn't completely gone. If he'd surprised her like this the first day they'd met, he'd have had to peel her off the ceiling.

As he waited, she pulled in a long breath. "Sorry, Sir."

"It's all right." Slowly, he moved closer, lifted a hand, and touched her cheek with his fingertips. She didn't flinch.

Progress.

Her gaze went to the brass wall clock. "Did I mix up your schedule or are you early getting home?"

"I'm early." He took Churchill, gave the cat a stroke, and set him on the recliner.

Piper wrapped her arms around herself in a self-soothing movement.

He'd rather she learn to take reassurance from him, instead. He ran his hands up and down her arms. Her skin was cold. The little muscles beside her mouth and eyes were tense. "Rough day, hmm?"

"Yes." Before he could ask, she added, "I don't want to think about it. This is your time."

"Is it then?" That wasn't an opening a Dom could resist.

Giving her ample time to refuse, he drew her to him. "Come here, poppet."

With a sigh like a lost child, she flattened against him, soft and female. Seeking comfort.

Comfort he could give. He wrapped his arms around her and kissed her temple. Without any hesitation, she hugged him back.

It must have been a truly bad day.

As he simply held her, he was pleased to feel her muscles relax.

She rubbed her forehead against his chest and murmured, "This is very unprofessional." But she didn't pull away.

"Not really, pet. Chatelaines business or not, while you are in my house, you're under my command. When our D/s arrangement stops, we'll move to a purely business relationship."

He rubbed his chin on the top of her head. Her hair was slightly damp and smelled like lavender with a hint of citrus. She must have showered before coming here.

The knowledge made him harden.

"That sounds straightforward. Okay." Although she must be able to feel his erection, she melted against him even more.

With someone else, he'd assume she was extending an invitation.

Slowly, he pulled back far enough to lift her chin and see her eyes. Molten chocolate. Flushed cheeks. Under his gaze, she turned pinker. Aroused?

He ran his thumb over her soft lower lip and felt the quiver. "Piper. Did you want to alter our arrangement to include sex?"

At Sir Ethan's English-accented question, Piper's body sparkled to life, like a Christmas tree strung with an overabundance of tiny lights.

No, foolish body. This can't happen. Only...she wanted to have sex with him. To have something more than merely sex.

She was being foolish. He was a Dom—he simply wanted to

fuck. This once. Nothing more. She licked over her dry lips and saw his eyes ignite. "Yes," she whispered. "I want to include sex."

"Mmm. All right." His hand on her ass pressed her against his hard erection, and with the other hand, he cupped her breast firmly. He showed no hesitation, taking command with an ease that took her breath away.

Anxiety and heat twirled from her head to her toes.

A corner of his mouth lifted. "To me, sex means bondage, oral and vaginal penetration, possibly spanking your ass or light swats in other places, and toys, including anal toys. Several orgasms for you; at least one for me."

Her mind went utterly blank.

"Piper."

She managed to focus on his face. So absolutely masculine and sexy. The dark mustache and beard framed his firm lips, ones she wanted to kiss over and over. When he rubbed his shaft against her, hitting her mound above her clit, a hot shudder shook her. Her whole lower half was turning into a molten pool.

"Did you have a problem with any of that, poppet?"

"What?"

He huffed a laugh. "This is called negotiating with your Dom, pet. Are you all right with that list?"

Negotiating. She knew what it meant. But her brain had snagged on two words. "*Several* orgasms?"

Laughter lightened his eyes. "Is that an objection and/or do you have other concerns?"

"Um. No objection." Several orgasms? Her body hummed like someone had flipped a switch. *Think, Piper.* "Ah...no marks that'll show and a safeword, right? I'm not a slave."

His mouth firmed. "I insist on safewords for anyone I top, slaves as well as submissives. Use the stoplight system—yellow for pause and talk, red to halt everything."

Her last faint worry dissipated like mist on a sunny morning. "Yes, Sir. I understand."

He considered her. "Let's add pink for panic."

"Doesn't yellow or red cover that condition?"

"I want you to catch an anxiety attack before it gets a grip. If I know you're worried, I can help you figure out ways to move past it."

Even when she offered him sex, he was thinking of ways to help her. The center of her chest had gone as soft and squishy as a melting tootsie roll. "Pink. Got it, Sir."

Gripping her low ponytail, he tugged her head back and kissed her. Gently at first. Using his teeth to nibble on her mouth. Tracing her lips with his tongue. As she leaned into him, he deepened the kiss. His tongue invaded, possessed, and lured her into dueling.

As her arms wrapped around his neck, he flattened her against him.

He was erect. And huge.

When he lifted his head, she made a needy sound. *Bad Piper.* Her mouth closed tightly to prevent any more unwelcome stupid-slave noises.

"Piper, I like hearing you. Hearing everything—moans, whines, screams." Even as he touched her cheek lightly, his lips quirked. "Begging is fine also unless I tell you to stop."

Cold shot through her, turning her muscles to ice. She jerked away from him. *Beg. Never, ever, ever.* "Never mind. I'm sorry. I don't want to do this."

He didn't reach for her. Head tilted slightly, he stood still. His eyes pierced her, going deep, dissecting her. His gaze lingered on her breasts—no, on her arms that she'd wrapped around her torso. "Piper. Are you at pink?"

Pink? What the heck did he mean? *No, wait.* Pink was for panic. She rubbed her fingers on her pants. Her fingertips were numb. She was teetering on the edge. *Breathe slow. Look at four things.* Slight bump in his nose. Crease between the dark brows. Corded neck. Button-up shirt. *Hear three things.* Her breathing—still too fast. The hum of the refrigerator. The thump as Churchill jumped onto the couch.

Sir Ethan hadn't moved. His stillness pooled around her like a calm lake.

Her next breath was slower. "Yes. That was pink." She hadn't been prepared for how suddenly she'd dropped into the abyss of terror. "I'm sorry."

Not a trace of anger showed in his face. Instead, he gave her an encouraging smile. "Have you got it under control now?"

"Ah..." She did a quick self-eval and blinked. "Yes. Yes, I do." And without his help. She'd done it all by herself.

"Very good." He moved forward and tapped her chin lightly with his knuckles. "I'm proud of you, poppet."

Proud. Of her. He'd ignored how she'd jumped away from him and snapped out that they were done. Instead, he focused only on how she'd overcome the attack. Her lips curved. She was rather proud of herself, too.

"There we go," he murmured. "Tell me what set you off."

"Um." She wet her dry lips. *Say it. Just say the word.* "B-b-beg." A breath. "I hate that word."

"That's good to know." Questions rose in his eyes, but he didn't ask. Not yet. However, he was a Dom, and all too soon, he'd want to discuss why the word got to her.

Too bad. She wasn't going to talk about it. That time was in the past; those days were over and wouldn't be brought to the surface. Ever.

God, she'd totally messed up this sex stuff, hadn't she? Should she leave? Swallowing, she let herself look at him.

Despite his lazy stance, he simmered with an aura of lethal power. That was his personality—purely dominant. The air of command was amplified by his appearance. A perfectly tailored white shirt showcased broad shoulders. Designer-scruff shadowed a strong jaw. Scarred, deadly hands.

A flutter of desire rose up. She wanted him. Had always wanted him.

He waited, watching her with patient eyes. Giving her the choice. Talk or leave or...continue.

She could continue.

Her gaze lifted, and she saw how his lips were tipping up. When she met his eyes, the floor started to sink. She took a step forward—her choice—and his arms closed around her.

He drew her up onto her tiptoes and thoroughly, mercilessly, kissed away the last lingering hint of anxiety, leaving only excitement behind.

God, how did he do that?

In no hurry, he unbuttoned her shirt partway and slowly traced burning lines over each inch of newly bared skin. He pushed the garment down from her shoulders to her elbows, trapping her arms at her sides. Her bra straps followed, adding to the clothing restraint.

Intent eyes held hers as he cupped her breasts, lifted, weighed, kneaded. "You have beautiful breasts. Did I mention that before?"

She could only swallow. Her breasts swelled under his caresses, the skin tightening. His confident fingers stroked beneath, over, circling. Never touching her aching nipples. She pressed against him, wanting more.

He chuckled and ignored her silent plea.

When he finally touched one nipple and rolled it between his fingers, electricity shot through her in torrid streaks, searing outward and downward. Her eyes closed against the overwhelming urgency.

"Eyes on me, poppet," he said softly.

She forced her eyes open, and he brushed a kiss over her mouth. "I like looking into your eyes, seeing your need, seeing all the things you don't say."

He curled his palm under her right breast, holding it firmly, like a tether, as with his other hand, he rolled the nipple and pinched the tip.

Heat sheeted through her like hot rain. She stared up at him, transfixed by his heavy-lidded stare, secured from even moving by his ruthless hold on her breast. Her legs began to shake.

"Very nice. Let's find a more appropriate location to continue." He unbuttoned the rest of her shirt and undid the front clasp of her bra. "Remove these, please."

She blinked, then slid her shirt and bra off, laying them on the couch.

His gaze was warm as he drew a fingertip over her collarbone, between her breasts, down her stomach, making her acutely aware that she was naked from the waist up. Hot tingles trailed in the wake of his touch.

With a warm hand on the bare skin of her lower back, he guided her to the stairway, up a few steps, and halted. "Pants off."

She swallowed past a suddenly dry throat and unbuckled her belt. After unbuttoning, she lowered the zipper and pushed her pants down. Stepping out, she leaned down to pick them up.

A hand on her nape kept her bent as he stroked along the edge of her thong. Could a fingertip sizzle? His merciless grip on her neck contrasted with the teasingly insistent touch over the exposed part of her buttocks and her hips, continuing until she was so very aware—and resentful—of the barrier of her underwear.

A light tug on her hair straightened her.

Up several more stairs. Her heart rate increased with each step.

He stopped. His murmured, "Thong off, now" sent a shudder of need through her.

She slid the black lace garment down, stepped out, and leaned down to pick it up. His hand between her shoulder blades kept her bent in half.

"Hang onto the railing, please." He curled her fingers around the lower railing, then patted her right knee. "Move this foot up two steps."

Oh my God. Her head spun. Bent in half, clinging to the railing with both hands, she moved her foot up.

"That's perfect, pet." With firm fingers, he kneaded her

buttocks and ran his fingertips over the crease between her bottom and thighs.

She shivered and moved slightly. His palm flattened on her low back to hold her still.

Heart thumping hard, she waited for the sound of his zipper. She wasn't scared; the heat inside her had burned the fear to ash.

"You're such a brave girl." His hand moved lower. Down her buttocks. Brushed over her inner thighs.

Expecting him to *take* her—not *touch* her, she jerked.

"Don't move, subbie." The steel in the mesmerizingly smooth voice froze her in place.

His hand slid between her legs in an unhurried exploration of her slick pussy. His fingers traced her recesses, from puckered rim to her mound. One finger skated past her clit and brushed over the top. Just that lightest of touches sent shockwaves of excitement shooting through her.

Slowly he moved his finger down to her entrance and slid inside. Invading, probing. She jerked at the intimacy.

His low voice was a caress—and a command. "Don't move, Piper."

Curling his finger, he massaged a sensitive area with unerring precision, pressing harder, sending desire roaring through her. Her insides began to gather in a coil of excitement.

He pulled back, then worked two fingers in, stretching her, taking control from her with every touch.

When he stepped back, she barely smothered the whimper of need.

"Up you come, poppet." His grip on her upper arm helped her stand upright.

Her legs were wobbly, her pussy so wet she could feel the moisture on her inner thighs.

He held her steady as he guided her up the stairs to the bedroom.

She'd seen his bedroom before. But this time, the black metal canopy bed was different. Huge. The geometric design above the padded headboard seemed ominous...and erotic.

He stopped her in the center of the room. "Stand right here."

Her heart galloped against the inside of her rib cage. With her head bowed, all she could see were her toes curling in the off-white carpet, his pant legs, and his sock-clad feet.

She was naked; he was dressed.

He walked in a leisurely circle around her, trailing his fingers against her bare skin. "You have a lovely body, Piper. Beautiful legs. I like the curve of your hips, the roundness of your arse." His hand curved over her bottom and squeezed.

He liked the way she looked. The inside of her chest felt as if the sun was warming it.

Moving in front of her, he lifted her chin and took her lips—not gently, but devastatingly possessive and deep. He gripped her hair to pull her head back farther. An iron-hard arm held her against him.

The room swirled, blurring everything except the feel of his mouth, the ownership of his tongue.

"Mmm." He rubbed his cheek against hers, his jawline beard softly abrasive. "Piper, look at me." The command was a masculine rumble in her ear before he straightened.

"Sir?" She met his gaze.

"You told me your limits. Now I'd like to find out what you enjoy." He smiled slightly.

She almost sighed, wanting him to kiss her again. His lips were so firm and yet soft and—

"I need a *yes* from you if you want to continue." He pulled the scrunchie from her ponytail and finger combed her hair to fall in wavy tickles past her shoulders. "Or you can say no, and we'll simply stop at this point. That's allowed, poppet."

As he stepped back from her and waited, her thoughts stuttered. She could tell him no...at this late stage? She could see his thick erection straining against his pants. He wanted her.

But he'd stop. If that was what she wanted. The difference

between him and the one before had never seemed so vast. Her agreement mattered to him. "Yes. Please."

His eyes warmed. "Your courage astounds me, sweetheart." And he gathered her into his arms as if he could see how much she needed to be held. As if he knew how hollow she felt, making that decision for herself. She rubbed her cheek against the crisp smoothness of his shirt. Breathed in the pine and leather scent of his lingering aftershave.

After a long, wonderful time, he pulled back.

He set his hand on her shoulder, undoubtedly feeling her quiver under his powerful grip. He ran his other hand down her front and squeezed one breast, molding it in his palm. His thumb circled the nipple.

Just like that, both nipples spiked with need, and her pussy started to throb. Gaze on her face, he held her completely still as he played. Teased. Tormented.

"Lie down on the bed, please. On your back. Legs open."

The tingling spread over her skin. *Now.* It was going to be now. Breathing fast, she climbed onto the high bed and across the black-and-gray comforter.

Turning onto her back, she watched him strip. She would never grow tired of seeing him without a shirt. A sigh of pleasure escaped her. His biceps and deltoids bunched as he moved, and her fingers longed to touch, to see if his muscles were as hard as they looked. His chest was broad and...

This time she could truly see the long scar that bisected the coarse chest hair. A white scar, so whatever had hurt him had happened a long time in the past.

Her gaze took in the six-pack abdomen and followed the dark happy-trail to a long, thick erection. Of course, even his cock was gorgeous. And really big.

She swallowed hard.

After setting his clothing on a chair, he looked her over in turn. The glint of masculine satisfaction sent an edgy hum along her nerve endings.

Taking a condom from the nightstand, he covered his long, engorged shaft.

He joined her on the bed. Settled between her legs. After pinning her wrists above her head, he set his cock against her entrance and pressed in, slowly. Relentlessly. She was aroused and slick, but it had been years, and she struggled to accommodate him.

And yet, and yet... The ruthless impaling satisfied something so deep inside, she couldn't name it.

He set his arm beside her shoulder, bracing his weight. His gaze on her face, he watched her carefully as his shaft sank deeper until he was sheathed to the hilt.

Barely breathing, she throbbed around his thickness. Slowly, her insides softened. Preparing for more.

He kissed her lightly, then pulled back and pushed in. Not fast, just a deliberate, unhurried savoring. His sensual lips were slightly curved. "You do feel magnificent, pet."

With every thrust, he moved his hips, tilting and changing the angles where his cockhead struck.

One place was...sensitive. Her nerves there startled awake, and a shudder ran through her. Her nipples contracted tightly, and her hips rose.

A corner of his mouth kicked up. "There, hmm?"

His next few thrusts were there, right there, and urgency grew inside her. His strokes increased to a hard hammering. *So good.*

"And you like that, too," he murmured before slowing. Stopping.

When she opened her eyes, he was still, watching her with his perceptive gaze.

"What..." She swallowed. "Is something wrong?"

"No, sweetheart." He took her mouth, obviously not angry or unhappy. "I just wanted you warmed up from the inside first."

Warmed up? Before...what?

He nibbled on her jaw and then released her wrists. "It would please me if you keep your arms over your head."

"Yes, Sir." She wouldn't move them an inch, she vowed, no matter what he did.

His face was gentle when he cupped her cheek and kissed her lightly. "So sweet."

He pulled out slowly, leaving her empty inside, throbbing with need. Unhurriedly, he moved down her body, kissing, nibbling.

As he stroked and kneaded her breasts, bit by bit, his hands grew rougher, building up the anticipation until finally, his fingers plucked her nipples.

She arched up with a moan. And froze in fear, stiffening in preparation for the blow.

"Piper."

He didn't hit her. Motionless, his hands cupped her breasts. When she lifted her gaze to his face, his expression held only... patience. "Poppet, what did I say about you talking or making noise?"

I like hearing you—moans, whines, screams.

"You like hearing me."

"Very good. Do keep that in mind." No anger or irritation darkened his voice. He sounded like someone ordering a cup of coffee. "Eyes on me, Piper."

Oh, God. There was a funny twisting inside at the realization that nothing shook this Dom. Not anything she did. Not even his body's needs. His control over himself—and her—was absolute.

His gaze stayed on her as he resumed playing with her breasts, building up the ache again before he tugged on her nipples. When he rolled the peaks between his tightly pinched thumb and finger, the painful pressure was so intensely pleasurable she moaned again.

"Perfect." Bending down, he sucked lightly on her nipples. A light bite sent heat searing through her before he moved down.

He nuzzled her belly and lower until his breath puffed warm against her mound.

His fingers parted her labia, and he studied her a minute.

The relief that she'd shaved herself that morning made her head spin. The need for him to think she looked all right was huge, insane, because women weren't attractive down there. Not like men and—

"Now that's a lovely, plump cunt," he murmured and stroked a slow finger through her folds, up and down. Circling her clit, rubbing slightly, swirling in her wetness, doing it all again. The memory of how his cock had felt, the thrilling bliss of having him inside her was still with her, and now, his touch on her clit sent her higher and higher.

Christ, but she was beautiful, Ethan thought. Her arms stayed over her head. Her eyes kept closing, then she'd remember his command and force them open again. Wanting to please him. To obey him.

She warmed his heart in a way he hadn't felt in a long, long time.

Leaning down, he teased her briefly with his tongue—although this time, he wouldn't do much oral. No, he wanted to watch her face and hands, her shoulders and stomach as he touched her. Make sure he didn't trip over more triggers. He wanted to discover where she was sensitive, responsive, indifferent. Discover what amount of pressure worked for her, although that would change somewhat with the excitement levels.

He flickered his tongue over the top of her clit and hood and felt the way her hips tensed to rise. The nub was fully exposed, a hard little ball of excitement.

Time to up the game. On his knees between her legs, he slid two fingers into her cunt and curled them upward to massage the pebbly area of her G-spot. With his other hand, he traced a finger in circles around her clit.

Her breathing revved up to fast and shallow.

So beautifully responsive to touch. To domination. She liked some pain on her breasts and nipples. She liked being hammered with a dick. He'd have to try nipple clamps. Maybe light spanking.

He wasn't a sadist, as such. Pain—light to moderate—was simply another tool in the orgasm toolbox. Still rubbing her G-spot, he used his other hand and drew his fingernails from her low stomach, over her plump mound, to barely above her clit.

She gasped, and her cunt clamped around his fingers. Very nice. He did it again, harder, more painfully, leaving red marks on her bare mound.

Her body quivered. Her eyes had glazed with arousal.

Yes, this was a pain she liked. How much pain? Watching her carefully, he lightly slapped her pussy, right where he'd scratched.

Her body went rigid, her cunt a vise around his fingers. So very, very close.

Bending, he closed his lips over her clit, tonguing and sucking it as he drove his fingers in and out. Her hips bucked, and with a delightful keening cry, she came. Her cunt spasmed around his fingers in rhythmic waves as her chest, neck, and face flushed a vivid pink.

"You are truly gorgeous." Pulling his fingers out, he leaned forward and set his shaft at her entrance.

As he thrust into the head-spinning heat, the walls of her cunt beat at his dick. "You feel incredible, sweetheart."

"Oh God, I'm coming again."

He laughed because she was. The spasms increased, fisting his cock, hot and hard. "Let's see how long we can make it last."

He lifted himself slightly to enjoy the sight of his slick cock sinking deep into her.

Since she liked being pounded, he set up a hard rhythm that should satisfy them both. She was tight around him and beautifully soft beneath him. "Put your arms around my shoulders, legs around my waist."

The change in position pressed her lush breasts against his chest and threatened his control.

Her knees gripped his hips. She was still making orgasmic whimpers with each contraction of her cunt.

"Move your knees higher, poppet."

When she complied, her pelvis tilted up, letting him drive deeper. Very, very nice.

A nova of anticipation grew at the base of his spine as his balls drew up, firming to a throbbing hardness. The feeling was...amazing.

A hand under her ass held her still as he drove into her with short, sharp strokes. Fire roared through him, crushing his balls and searing his dick as he came in forceful, jerking jets. The cascading pleasure ripped through every part of him as he pressed deep, and she gripped him with arms, legs, and cunt.

After an infinitely pleasurable time, he tucked a hand under her head so he could kiss her. Her mouth was soft, willing. Giving. A kiss with heart.

He was still buried in her, and the tiny post-orgasmic spasms of her cunt set off matching happy twitches of his dick.

Settling in, he kept kissing her—because he hadn't had so much fun kissing someone in ages.

Piper's heart was like a drug-crazed prisoner, banging frantically against her ribcage. Her thoughts swirled around her brain with almost the same wildness.

She'd gotten off—and more than once.

Sir Ethan had made sure she reached climax. She'd known he was good with his hands, but *oh my God*, she'd never come so hard in her life. Not even with her fingers. Even more, he'd gone down on her, using his mouth, his tongue. Doms—Masters—didn't do that. Slaves did oral for Masters, not vice versa.

As he started to soften and pulled out, she sighed at the empty feeling. At the return to reality. She should—

He slid over next to her and tucked her up against his side. She froze. He was cuddling her? Not shoving her away and telling her to clean him. Not sending her to bed down on the floor.

"Your muscles are tense again, poppet." He rose up on an elbow to look down at her, his gaze like a tender hand stroking her face. "What was that thought?"

"Noth—" She caught herself before committing the punishable act of avoiding an answer. What would be inoffensive? "I was thinking I should get up so I can clean you. If you would like that."

"I probably would at some time in the future." His gaze penetrated deeper than skin level, making her want to hold up her hands as a shield. "But I intend to refuse most of the duties Serna insisted upon."

She winced at the sound of the other's name, then blinked. "You...what?"

"Stay here, pet." Rolling off the bed, he unselfconsciously walked into the bathroom, completely comfortable in his nakedness. She heard him clean up. He returned with a washcloth. "Spread your legs."

B-b-but... Despite the war going on in her head, she obeyed. She knew better than to deny a Master.

The warmth of the wet cloth penetrated and soothed her pussy. Yes, she was sore. It had been a long time. Still, he was a Master. "Sir, this is something I should be doing."

His lips twitched. "I think the way it works—at least in your mind—is: if Sir Ethan wants something, he gets his way." Ignoring her squirms of protest, he gently, but firmly, washed her clean.

"No, that isn't how I think."

His brow arched.

It was. It was exactly what she thought.

Straightening, he drew a fingertip down her body, around a breast, tapping the nipple, watching it rise into a peak. "We'll continue working on your beliefs, Piper. Your fears as well as your assumptions."

His eyes hardened. "The rules and beliefs that were beaten into you need to be examined."

Her supine position put her at a disadvantage. She sat up. "I've been through therapy."

"When?"

"After I escaped."

He nodded, as if unsurprised. "Excellent. Did your counseling help you work through the actual Master/slave dynamics and expectations?"

"Well, no." Not even close since the counselor had acted like Piper'd deserved being abused for having willingly wanted to be a slave. Or...or...had that been Piper's own guilt warping her perception of the counselor's words?

"I see. Did you discuss Serna with your family?"

"No." He hadn't let her call them. Then again, they hadn't come to look for her. Once free, she'd wanted to go home, even knowing she wouldn't be welcomed, but her mother and stepfather were already dead.

One person was left. The thought of Jerry ran through her mind, and she stiffened. "I don't have any family. None."

His gaze took in her stiff shoulders, her jutting jaw, but he simply said, "That's rough. I'm sorry, poppet."

She breathed out, realizing she'd been holding her breath.

He stroked her hair. "I get the impression you've avoided talking about BDSM. That's logical; you never expected to be back in a power exchange. But here you are."

Here she was. Dear God, she was in a Dom's bed.

He chuckled. "Such an expression."

His long pause let her absorb the change several years had made.

"Piper, I want you to think about the service you gave and the rules Serna insisted on. Decide what kind of power exchange you want for yourself. What rules you will follow, not because you feel you have to, but because you *choose* to. That's what submission is all about."

When he tapped her cheek with a fingertip and walked back to the bathroom, she stared after him, feeling the terrifying tug in the center of her chest.

Because he was everything she'd wanted back in the days when she'd first dreamed of having a Dom.

CHAPTER TWELVE

Two days later, Ethan drove through the Financial District. Casting a glance to his right, he smiled.

In the passenger seat, Piper held a box carefully on her lap. After breakfast on the waterfront, they'd strolled past a candy store, and she'd sniffed the air like a pup scenting a steak on the grill.

Ethan had taken her inside to pick out a treat and received quite the education. Apparently, there was candy, and then there was *chocolate*. In the past, he'd wasted far too much money on flowers when he should have been buying carefully selected chocolates for his women.

Of course, the preference might only be Piper's. She truly was unique.

He found her remarkable in so many ways. Her courage in leaving Serna and turning her life around. Her integrity in how she ran her business. Her honesty. Her generosity. Her way with Churchill. Her willingness and joy in submission even after what she'd been through.

Their first time together, Tuesday afternoon, had shown him she was someone very special.

Last night confirmed it. The sex had been superb. She gave as sweetly as she received, and admittedly, he'd never had a finer blowjob. Nevertheless, he needed more than excellent sex to be interested in a woman. Piper was quite simply fun to be with—whether they were cooking, cleaning, watching a movie, or just talking. She had the ability to be both bubbly and peaceful at the same time. And when she submitted to him, she captured his heart.

In just this short time, he'd grown to care for her a great deal—and the realization was somewhat unsettling.

Now he needed to decide whether to continue on this path. To get more involved or to pull back.

Damned if he wanted to let her go.

The light turned red. Stopping the car, he glanced over.

She was looking out the window and smiling at a dog-walker. Two shepherds and a Maltese paced obediently beside the young man.

Piper turned to Ethan. "That was one of my first jobs when I came to San Francisco. I never did learn how to keep the leashes from tangling. All too often, I got wrapped up like a May Day pole."

"I'm sorry I missed seeing it." Knowing Piper, she'd merely laughed at the mess.

As the light changed, Ethan picked up her hand and kissed the center of her palm. "Are you sure you don't want me to drop you at your office?" He'd picked her up there after work last night.

"These are the clothes I wore yesterday." Her eyes widened in horror. "You don't want me to do the walk of shame, do you?"

Women were strange and fascinating creatures.

"Heaven forbid." His lips quirked. "It's not a problem males have—our clothing is bland, and, I'll admit, no man would notice anyway."

"Too true. You guys are pretty oblivious." She realized she'd insulted him and froze...then relaxed. Because she was finally catching on that he wasn't an abusive arsehole like Serna.

Progress.

He halted the car at the curb in front of her building.

She turned to him, obviously expecting a quick kiss.

He shook his head. She'd learn, beginning now, that her Dom liked to do things for her, especially things that kept her safe. "I'll walk you to your door, poppet."

"But, there's no—"

His look silenced her, because she *had* learned when an argument would be futile.

Getting out, he helped her out of the car and walked her across the sidewalk.

"Well, Mr. Worthington, I had a lovely time last night." Her eyes glinted with amusement as she dutifully observed the ending-of-a-date etiquette. "Thank you for the chocolates, for dinner and breakfast. I—"

"You are most welcome." Putting an arm around her waist, he yanked her against him and fisted her hair. A ruthless pull tilted her head back so he could silence her with a long, wet kiss.

She tasted of the chocolate she'd nibbled in the shop. He might begin to understand the appeal.

When he lifted his head, she had one arm around his neck and was mashed up against him, a far better way to end a date than talking. Satisfied, he rubbed his lips over hers. "By the way, this weekend on Saturday, and if you wish, Sunday, we're going to kink camp."

Her brows drew together. "I'm not sure whether to be thrilled or scared. What exactly is kink camp?"

"The Bay area's BDSM groups and clubs host a three day weekend in a campground farther inland. Trees, tents and cabins, and every variety of kink you can think of. We'll drive over Saturday morning, enjoy the camp, and spend the night in a tent."

"Kink and camping." She laughed as she stepped back. "It sounds like fun. Should I bring anything?"

She was energetic and sociable—she'd be delighted with the friendliness of the people there. "Bring casual clothing for two sunny days and a night that might be somewhat chilly."

"I can do that."

"I'll be helping with the setup on Friday afternoon and evening." He didn't like the thought of not seeing her for two nights. "But I should be free after eleven. Would you like to join me for a late-night Dark Haven visit?"

"Yes." She bounced on her toes. "I'm meeting Abby and Dix for a late supper, so that should work out well."

"Excellent. If something comes up, we can readjust. No matter what, I do expect to see you at my house bright and early on Saturday."

Rather than flinching at the reminder, she smiled, her eyes kindling with desire. "Yes, Sir Ethan. Absolutely, Sir Ethan."

"Bratty little subbie." He turned her toward the door, giving her a swat on the ass.

After she was safely inside, he headed for his car, grateful this pair of pants weren't as tight as jeans. Because kissing her left him half-erect every time.

"Hey, Worthington. Good fight last week." The hail came from a passing car. From a member of Ethan's boxing gym who must have watched the matches last week.

Ethan lifted his hand in acknowledgment.

As he drove to his office building on the other side of the Financial District, he considered the happiness buzzing in his veins. Years ago, he'd felt like this—the heady slide as lust for a woman turned into something more.

It hadn't ended well.

Two more attempts at relationships had failed as well. He'd learned his wealth was more important to a woman than he was. Now when he dated, he made it clear that any "relationship" would never progress past informal dating.

Recently, Xavier had been urging him to forget the past and find someone permanent. Was Piper the one? He certainly hadn't intended to get involved with her.

Yet how could he not?

He should think long and hard about where this relationship was going, but...what was the point? Somehow, he'd gone straight past attraction into serious without pausing at casual.

And he was all right with that.

Now he just had to convince one wary, adorable submissive that he would be part of her future.

Hidden in the doorway next to his stepsister's building, Jerry rubbed his jaw. That had been a very...interesting...interaction. One he'd been lucky to see.

The day had certainly started badly. At Piper's office, the fucking receptionist had called security on him. But after hearing her tell the rent-a-cop that Piper hadn't come to work yet, Jerry'd staked out Piper's apartment building.

Now he had some information to work with. His bitch of a stepsister was late to work because she was fucking around. Oh yeah, that'd been a hell of a morning-after kiss he'd watched. The man seemed pretty gone over her. Even bought her expensive chocolates.

From the looks of his suit and car, the dude had some bucks.

Damn her for landing on her feet and using money that should have come to him to start her business.

If he couldn't get it from her, he might have better luck with her rich boyfriend. There had been quite a few revealing tidbits in that conversation. The man's name: Ethan Worthington. She'd called him Sir, and he'd called her a bratty subbie.

Jerry headed down the sidewalk. Some time doing research would fill in the gaps.

Piper should have handed over his inheritance instead of threatening him with the police. And *punching* him.

Bitch.

Before he left this city, he'd do his best to rip apart her fucking perfect life.

CHAPTER THIRTEEN

On Friday night, energized from helping set up kink camp, Ethan walked into Dark Haven shortly before eleven.

"Hey, Sir Ethan. You have a visitor." At reception, Lindsey looked up from scanning cards for three members and motioned toward a man by the far wall.

Tall and thin, the stranger was good-looking in a clean-cut, blond, blue-eyed way. He wore khaki pants, polo shirt, and a pleasant smile. "Ethan Worthington, how are you?"

"Quite well, thank you." Ethan frowned. "Have we met?"

"No, I'm afraid not. Although, I know *you*." The man gestured toward the door. "Would you mind if we went outside where it's quieter?"

Used to new Doms asking for help, Ethan followed him out onto the sidewalk. The night air was thick with fog, holding the briny scent of the bay along with the stench of old urine common in many parts of the city. "What can I help you with?"

"This...is a little awkward, I'm afraid."

Having seen and heard about far too many scene disasters—from ripping out nipple piercings to accidental self-whippings, Ethan set himself to listen without laughing or judgment. "Let's hear it."

"All right. You see, *Sir* Ethan, my sister told me all about you and your hobbies."

What did this have to do with anything? Ethan raised an eyebrow. "Your sister?"

"Your *bratty little subbie*, Piper."

The wording was familiar...and this did not sound like a Dom wanting help. "You and Piper are siblings?"

She'd said she had no family.

"That's correct. She's my little sissy. Of course, there was a reason she didn't tell you about me. My name is Jerry, by the way."

Ethan's gut tightened. This man had an agenda.

"Now, Mr. Worthington, I hate to do this and ruin your evening, but I have to ask you for some money." The light tenor voice remained pleasant despite the subject matter.

Ethan kept his own voice polite, even as he scanned Jerry for hidden weapons. None. "Is this a robbery?"

"No, no, nothing like that." The blond pulled on his earlobe. "It's like this—you have a fine reputation in this city. Your business depends on that reputation. It would be unfortunate if your company's customers discovered how the CEO spends his time. Slaves and BDSM clubs and all that are rather unsavory, after all."

Ethan knew where this was going. Too bloody well. "You want to be paid off to stay quiet. Is that what you're saying?"

"Yes, I'm sorry, but that's correct." The arsehole shook his head. "I hate to ask for money, but it's a tough world."

Ethan smiled slightly, not averse to dragging this out. Because he intended to flatten the bastard before they parted. "If you're short on cash, ask your sister for funds." If Piper really was his sister. There was no resemblance.

"Oh, she needs the money, too. Who do you think targeted you?"

No, Piper wouldn't do that. Ethan straightened. Time to put an end to this lying wanker.

"You don't believe me, do you?" Jerry snorted. "You think I picked you out of a hat or something? Hardly. Piper and I have got this down to a science."

An ugly feeling slid into Ethan's gut. "I doubt that."

"Oh yeah. She does the planning, and I'll admit, I pretty much take orders." Jerry had a rueful smile on his face. "Like yesterday, she shared her chocolates with me—damn good chocolate, thank you—while we figured out how I'd approach you."

She'd given this person the chocolates he'd bought her? Ethan kept his face impassive. "She has a good business."

"She does—and she spends more than it brings in."

If she was having financial difficulties, she should have asked Ethan. He would have helped. But sending her brother to blackmail him? This was utter betrayal.

And still...she *couldn't* be a blackmailer. Not Piper.

"She really gets off on gutting you BDSM bastards. After all, she has a score to settle after the way one of you made her a fucking slave." Jerry smiled. "The money doesn't hurt, though. How else do you think she got the money to start her business?"

Ethan's thoughts fragmented. She'd escaped Serna. Come to San Francisco with nothing. How *had* she gotten the money to start Chatelaines?

No, Piper wouldn't do this.

"And yeah, I need the money, too." Jerry sighed. "I'm the only family she has left. She'd do anything for me."

"Would she now?" When asked her about her family, she'd gone stiff. He'd noticed, but let it go, thinking it was from grief at not having anyone. Instead, she'd been hiding the existence of this bastard.

The taste of betrayal was so bitter Ethan choked on it.

Jerry took a step forward. "We need to wind this up. Mr. Worthington, as rich as you are, you'll barely feel the sting of ten grand."

"It'd be less expensive to simply kill you." With an effort,

Ethan kept his voice level. The last woman to betray him had died. Badly. *Screams and shouting. Nicola choking. Drowning in her own blood.* Shaking off the memories, he gritted out, "I'd enjoy it more, too."

Jerry's friendly expression slipped. "Don't be stupid. I always leave papers with friends, just to keep people like you from over-reacting."

The threat of exposure didn't bother Ethan. That fact Piper had deceived him and planned this... Pain deep in his chest suggested he cared more than he'd realized.

Apparently, she didn't care at all.

Or did she? He frowned, thinking of her open, hearty laughter, her eyes that revealed every emotion. How she responded, holding nothing back. Doubt edged in again.

Did this stupid sod even know Piper? Maybe he'd just picked up some—

"Jerry!" Piper, accompanied by Dixon, came down the sidewalk. She stared at the blond in obvious surprise before her expression turned hard. "I told you—"

"I know you wanted to hit Ethan up tomorrow. Too bad, Pipsqueak. I couldn't wait."

She scowled. "What are you—"

"Enough," Ethan snapped. She *did* know the bastard, was his sister. They'd planned everything all along. She'd played him. Ice closed around his heart, smothering the anger.

He pulled his gaze from Piper. Stepped closer to Jerry. "You'll get nothing from me."

The blond's expression turned ugly. "Listen, asshole. Pay up, or your name will be on the front pages tom—"

Ethan threw a one-two combo, a jab followed by a cross. Jerry's head whipped back and forth. Roaring in pain, the man lunged forward, swinging wildly.

Ethan blocked, and his sharp double jab flattened the wanker's nose. As blood spurted, Ethan delivered a cross, followed by a solid left hook.

Ribs cracking under the impact, Jerry shouted in pain. Ethan finished with a hard right uppercut to the arsehole's jaw that knocked him sprawling on the sidewalk.

"What the fucking-duck is going on?" Dixon shouted. He stood beside Piper who hadn't moved.

Hands over her mouth, she stared at her brother. She didn't even look at Ethan. It was quite obvious where her loyalty lay.

He waited...waited for her to defend herself.

Face dead white, she was wholly focused on Jerry.

Ethan's last forlorn hope died. Pushing his warring emotions aside, he considered the blackmail attempt. Would the two try to pursue this shit further?

They'd have a surprise coming if they did. Last time, he'd left his home. Left his country. *Not again, dammit. Never again.*

"Piper." No response. He let the raging anger inside him edge his voice. "*Ms. Delaney*."

Her eyes were dazed, but her gaze lifted to his hands, his face. She flinched—so fucking guilty—then retreated a step in fear. Of him.

She should be afraid.

The ice storm of emotions inside him chilled his voice. "Stay away from me, or we'll see how you look in police handcuffs."

He started to move, then stopped. "You can consider Chatelaines' contract terminated."

A Master stood on the sidewalk, shrouded in the fog. His eyes were cold, so filled with fury and—*hate*—that everything inside Piper shriveled in fear. Her shoulders hunched. She stumbled back.

After a long second, he turned and walked away. Blood dripped from his fists, leaving horrible spots on the dirty gray sidewalk.

She couldn't breathe.

"Fucking-A, that was intense." The voice came through the

pounding of her pulse. Someone took her hand. "What in the dragon's dick was that about?"

There was no air in the world.

Someone lay on the pavement. Blood over his face. So, so red. Awful. The darkness that had filled the street at the sounds of a beating now enclosed her completely, crushing her ribs with a brutal grip. No air. No light.

"Piper, hey, it's all right. You're okay." An arm came around her shoulder, shook her slightly. "I got you. Slow that breathing down, girlfriend. Slooooow."

Dixon. It was Dix. Fighting the crushing terror, she pursed her lips and exhaled against the barrier. *Touch.* She opened and closed her hands. *Sound.* Heard groaning—and flinched. *Sight.* Opened her eyes to fog, to Dixon's worried face.

The shadows receded slowly, even as fear still shook her so hard her bones rattled. Cold sweat covered her face.

"Yeah, yeah, yeah, there you are, Pipster." Dixon's hands were on her shoulders. "Stay with me."

Her legs wobbled, but she was upright. "Thanks, Dix."

He touched his forehead to hers and moved to stand beside her. So she could see.

See her stepbrother moaning on the sidewalk, hands pressed to his face.

Ethan had hit him and hit him. So hard.

Jerry saw her staring. "Get over here and help me. Jesus fucking Christ."

Her thoughts felt thicker than the fog wrapping the street in gray. Ethan wouldn't assault someone out of the blue. Why was Jerry even here? "What did you say to him, Jerry?"

"Nothin'. Jesus, bitch, he attacked *me*," Jerry snarled.

Why wouldn't her head work? *Think, Piper.* She and Dixon had arrived, seen Jerry, and she'd been furious. Only Jerry'd said something...something about Ethan and tomorrow. Ethan had told Jerry, "*You'll get nothing from me.*"

That was it. Horror speared through her ribs and straight

into her heart. "You are"—her lips were numb, her throat so dry her voice cracked—"always conning people out of money. Did you try that on Ethan?"

"No shit, seriously?" Dix stared at Jerry. "Did you eat an extra bowl of stupid this morning?"

Jerry ignored him and sneered at her. "Get a grip. I didn't do anything."

"You did. Oh, you did." Memories sucked her into the muck of the past. *"Yeah, I gave your brother money. Jerry said he'd tell your father I fucked you even though we didn't." "I paid off your brother. He said he'd get me kicked off the football team." "I gave your stepbrother twenty..."*

Jerry had tried to blackmail Ethan.

Her Ethan.

Incandescent rage moved her forward. Her foot slammed into his face, right where Ethan had punched him. The ghastly sound and feel made her stagger back.

She'd kicked a person. Bile rose into her throat so fast, she gagged.

Grabbing her arm, Dixon let out a hoot of approval. "Go, girl."

"Cunt!" Jerry grabbed her ankle.

"Don't. Touch. Her." With a low growl, Dix stomped on his hand.

Jerry yelped. His attempt to rise was defeated when Dix put more weight on the trapped hand. "Sis. Pipsqueak, you know me. I wouldn't—"

Fury filled her. "You *would*." When he punched at Dix's leg, Piper snap-kicked Jerry in the chest.

At his yell of pain, sickness ran through her, and she shoved it down. Jerry had hurt *Ethan*. "You tried to con him out of money, didn't you?"

Gaze averted, he gave a single nod.

"You, you stupid..." She remembered the ice in Ethan's eyes... as he looked at *her*. As he'd spoken. "*Ms. Delaney.*"

Oh, no, no, no.

"He..." Her voice cracked. "Ethan thinks I helped you." A sound of pain, like a wounded dog, broke from her, and she reeled back.

"Pips, wait." Dixon came after her.

Holding his ribs, Jerry pushed to his feet and retreated a few steps. "Yeah, he thinks you planned it. Gag on that, bitch." Holding his ribs, he lurched down the sidewalk, and the fog swallowed him up.

She didn't move. Ethan had believed Jerry. He thought she was after his...his money?

"Piper?" Dixon's concerned face came between her and the world. He took her hand. "Girlfriend."

"Ethan didn't even ask me if I was part of Jerry's plan," she whispered.

Dix's brows drew together. "He...didn't."

"He believed Jerry. Believed everything Jerry said." She pulled in a shuddering breath. "I thought we had...something. I trusted him, Dix."

The fog was closing in, blurring the buildings, the lights.

"He didn't trust me at all, did he?"

As pain hollowed out her heart, she crumpled to her knees and wept.

In his car, Jerry didn't take his foot off the gas pedal for a good half-mile. His nose was *busted*. His head throbbed like crazy. His chest hurt, his ribs, his jaw. Everything.

Fuck, but that goddamned Brit had hard fists.

But he'd gotten Worthington good. Online, Jerry'd found the newspaper stories about the bastard and his ex. How perfect was it to make Worthington think Piper was just like her? The pain in the Brit's face had been glorious.

Feeling the trickle of blood, Jerry used his shirt to wipe his face. That fucking bastard.

And that fucking bitch, too. Wimpy, whiny Piper. Always following him around when they were kids, trying to get him to like her. As *if*. So pathetic.

When she'd gone to college, Dad kept saying: *Piper is in college. Why aren't you?*

Damn her. But she'd paid—and the comparisons had stopped when she dropped out of school. When she disappeared.

Back then, she read romances—ones full of seriously kinky shit—so he'd introduced her to the most sadistic asshole he knew.

Heh, Serna'd been so pumped at the new tasty treat that he'd tossed Jerry a grand.

Jerry's grin disappeared as pain stabbed into his face, and he moaned. *Fucking Worthington. Fucking bitch.*

A shame Serna hadn't killed her.

When Jerry ran into Serna in Wichita last month, the sadist said his "property" had run away years before. He wanted her back. Bad. Was still searching for her. Jerry hadn't even thought of looking for her until then.

Pulling over, he blotted the blood from his face. Saw the red on his shirt. Rage flooded him. The bitch would regret kicking him.

He had a feeling Master Serna would be pissed-the-fuck-off to find out his ex-property was hanging out in a BDSM club.

Yes, the sadist would pay good money for that tidbit of information.

Once at home, Ethan ran cold water over his bloodied knuckles. It'd been a while since he'd fought without gloves or strapping. Even so, he should have hit the arsehole harder and busted more than his nose.

Hell. Ethan glanced in the mirror, seeing the harsh lines in his face, seeing the idiot who'd trusted a woman. Again. When would he learn?

Piper Delaney had played him like a violin. Had set him up for blackmail. The pain in his heart was far worse than the ache in his knuckles. He'd trusted her. He'd been well on the way to more than just liking her. He'd cared for her.

And she'd shared everything with her brother, from chocolates to information.

Just as Nicola had done with Bradley.

Under the cold water, Ethan's hands fisted as he remembered Nicola's face when he'd confronted her. Her dismay that he'd discovered what she and her cousin had planned. Her whisper as she confessed that although she cared for Ethan, her loyalty to her cousin was stronger.

Just as Piper's was for her arsehole brother.

In the living room, Ethan dropped down in a chair.

Jumping onto his lap, Churchill stared up as if wondering what was wrong. Such big blue eyes.

Piper's eyes were dark brown and the most expressive eyes Ethan had ever seen. Even when trying to hide something, she couldn't. In fact, he doubted Piper could lie to even a five-year-old and get away with it.

Like a multi-legged insect, misgivings crept into his brain. Because, if Piper couldn't lie, how could she have deceived him enough to set up a con game? Being a Dom and businessman for so many years, he wasn't easy to mislead.

Now, Jerry—he'd lie as easily as he'd walk. Could that git have made up a tale about being her brother?

No, she'd recognized the bastard and spoken to him about hitting Ethan up tomorrow.

He frowned. Actually, those had been Jerry's words. Piper had hardly said anything, in fact. "*I told you—*" After Jerry had spoken, she'd looked confused. "*What are you—*"

Ethan stroked Churchill's soft fur. "I don't know, PM. I

might have missed something." Because just the thought of being lied to again, of being wanted for his money had sent fury into his bloodstream. He'd admit he was thin-skinned when it came to the subject.

Could he have over-reacted?

He ran his hand down the cat's soft fur as he admitted, "I was quite angry and said some rather foul things to Piper."

In feline censure, Churchill kneaded Ethan's thighs hard enough his claws pricked skin.

"Jerry knew that I'm a Dom called Sir Ethan," Ethan explained. "He knew I called her a bratty little subbie. He said she gave him the chocolate I bought her."

Hmm.

Aside from those tidbits, Jerry hadn't related any particularly intimate or kinky details.

"Bollocks, did I jump too quickly to believing the knob-head?" Now that he was thinking rather than reacting, he was questioning everything. Again.

Piper Delaney just didn't feel like a liar or con artist. She had too much integrity and courage.

Ethan rubbed the ache that had centered behind his ribcage.

All those years ago, even when terrified of Serna, she'd acted to rescue a kitten. More recently, she'd tried to intercede for Angel. Shared her fears with Ethan. Opened her soul.

Blackmail? No, not Piper. The numbers weren't adding up. The engine was misfiring.

Time to find out why.

"Thanks for the escort service." At the door to her apartment, Piper patted Dixon's hand and tried to smile at Lindsey. "Thank you, and I'm sorry. Will Xavier be angry?"

"Pffft. He'd be angrier if I hadn't helped." Hearing about the fight on the sidewalk, Lindsey had abandoned her reception duties and insisted on making sure Piper got home. "Put a sock in it, girlfriend."

She gently pushed Piper inside.

Stopping just inside the doorway, Piper stared as her two friends walked past her and into the apartment. Her eyes burned with unshed tears, and her throat felt as if a rock was stuck in there. They needed to leave. She couldn't hold it together much longer

Ethan believed she tried to blackmail him.

"Guys. I don't need any more help, and I'm going to—"

"Bawl your head off. I would, too," Dixon tossed his coat over a chair. "That's why we're staying."

"Alcohol." Lindsey was in the kitchen. "Where is it?"

"Pip's a rum girl. It's over the microwave." Dixon dragged Piper across the room, dropped onto the couch, and pulled her down next to him.

"Dix." Piper searched for the right way to reassure and send her friends home, but the words weren't there. She didn't *want* to be alone. Some people were hide-in-a-cave types, but not her. She had other friends she could call, but none who could understand about Sir Ethan, about a D/s relationship the way Dixon and Lindsey would.

"He was a total asshole," Dix stated.

"Yeah." Lindsey had the Bayou spiced rum bottle under one arm and carried a tray with a six-pack of cola and three tall ice-filled glasses. She unloaded everything onto the vintage steamer trunk that served as a coffee table. "I think I'm glad I never had a brother."

Dix took the bottle of rum and started pouring. "Not the stepling. I meant that bastard, Sir Ethan."

"Wait—what?" Lindsey dragged a chair closer and sat, tugging her denim maxi-dress straight. "You told me her *brother* upset her. It was Ethan? Then where is he?"

The brunette looked around as if the Dom would suddenly appear.

"Gone." There was no Ethan, not any more. Just an aching hollow place in Piper's heart. "He's..."

All the stifled sobs broke loose at once. She clapped her hands over her mouth as tears scalded her cheeks.

Slinging an arm around her, Dixon pulled her against his slender frame. "Cry it out, Pips. I would. Ratfarts, but between your dickweed brother and dickmunch Dom, you had an incredulously-crummy night."

The sympathy in his voice made her cry even harder.

It hurt. It hurt so much.

All her life, her parents had taken Jerry's side. He'd talk and talk, and by the time he finished, they'd agree with him. He was the perfect one. If he got into trouble for anything, he'd cast the blame on her, and they'd believe him.

He'd mattered to them; she never had.

She'd thought maybe...maybe she mattered to Ethan. That he liked her some. More than some, even.

But he'd believed Jerry, too.

"...then Ethan got all pissed-off." Dix was explaining what'd happened to Lindsey.

"The brother said Piper was his partner. To blackmail Ethan?" Lindsey asked in disbelief.

"Exactamento. Ethan busting Jerry's nose was a beee-u-tee-ful sight. Only then our dumbass Dom cuts Pips to shreds and walks away. He didn't even ask her any questions or anything."

"Criminy." Lindsey made a disparaging sound. "I hardly know her, and I know she wouldn't do something like that."

"See? That's what I'm talking about." Dix shook Piper. "Here, sweets, drink some of this. You know, I'm starting to like this rum stuff."

A glass was tucked in Piper's hand.

As Piper sat up, Lindsey handed over several tissues before grinning.

"What?" Piper sniffled and wiped her eyes. "What's funny?"

"It's a real girl thing to notice, but you're one of those

gorgeous criers. If Abby cries, she gets all beet-red and splotchy. I'm not much better."

Despite the pain in her chest, Piper found a laugh surfacing. Because it was something only a friend would say. "Well, thank God for small favors, right?"

"That's the spirit." Dix poured more rum in his glass, ignoring the soda. "Speaking of small, it's time for sex curses."

"Sex *what*?" Piper eyed him over the rim of her drink.

Dix lifted his glass and said with relish, "May Sir Ethan's dick shrivel up and fall off."

"Starting with an oldie, hmm? My turn." Lindsey clinked her glass against his. "May Sir Ethan's dick shrink until he has to wear glasses to find it."

Piper could see where this was going. Two sets of expectant eyes settled on her. "Seriously?"

"You bet, pet." Dix put a finger under her glass and lifted. "Take a gulp and subbie up."

It was a diversion, but it worked. Reality hurt too much to face right now. She frowned, trying to remember the old Middle Eastern curse. "May the fleas of a thousand camels infest his pubic hair and his arms be too short to scratch."

Lindsey nodded solemn approval. "It's a classic for a reason."

Dix grinned. "May his cock clog with cum and require a plumber's drain-snake to rooter out."

"Oh, my effing God, that's just nasty." Lindsey shuddered. "So, Piper, how much do you hate him? Do we need to get really mean?"

At the reminder of *why* her friends were cursing Ethan's package, Piper blinked hard. "You guys are great, but he's your friend. I don't hate him. It just hurts." She tried to paste on a smile. "It'll pass soon enough. Really."

"Maybe. But I remember what it feels like to be Dom road-kill." Lindsey's jaw tightened. "May an evil sadist bronze Ethan's balls and nail them up on Dark Haven walls."

Dix's eyes were hard. "With him attached."

Oh, God, what had she done?

Dixon lifted his eyebrows. Her turn.

Don't let the team down. Piper drank half the very tall, very strong drink and subbie-upped. "Before fun-time, may his erections shrink so much that even extra-small condoms fall off."

A huff of a laugh came from Lindsey. "Wouldn't *that* be disconcerting? Hmm. May his dick shrink until no one can find it in the forest of pubic hair."

"A flea-infested forest, no less." Dixon pretended to be pushing through tall foliage. "Where is the little worm? I know it's in here somewhere."

"You guys are crazy." Piper felt the rum hit her bloodstream, and she slumped back on the cushions. Her eyes were irritated and swollen from crying, her makeup undoubtedly streaked down her face, and she didn't care.

"My turn." Dix bounced on the couch. "Wait for it...wait for it..."

"Spit it out, subbie-boy." Lindsey grinned at Piper because... really, was there anyone more darling than Dixon?

Dix held up his glass and intoned solemnly, "May Sir Ethan's balls shrivel to the size of walnuts right before an attack of zombie squirrels."

As he pretended to savagely crack walnuts between his teeth, Piper busted into helpless giggles. Lindsey was laughing so hard, she was snorting.

They were so wonderful. And Ethan had been so *cruel.*

Piper started to cry again.

In the hallway, standing outside Piper's half-open door, Ethan listened to the vicious curses in disbelief. Christ, he should don an athletic cup before going in there.

Beside him, Stan snorted. "Jesus, remind me not to piss off my boy."

"Good luck with that." Ethan glanced at the Dom. "Thanks

for letting me into the building. Could you do me a second favor? Take your submissive and Lindsey home with you."

At the sound of sobbing—Piper's sobbing—Ethan froze. Guilt hit him like a gut shot.

Stan's expression hardened. "I didn't ask you what happened, but I get the impression you hurt Piper pretty bad. I consider her a friend—a damn vulnerable one."

"She is, and I did." The sound of her crying broke his heart. "I'm not sure what's going on, but I'm going to do my best to make it right."

"Fair enough. God knows, we all fuck up at times. But..." The Homeland Security agent's mouth went flat. "The walls in this building aren't soundproof. If she calls for me, I *will* answer."

"Fair enough." He'd do the same for a female friend.

Pushing the door wide open, Ethan walked in.

Lindsey saw him first and stiffened.

Checking over his shoulder, Dixon scowled and jumped to his feet. "No, no, you will *not* be in here." He made a grand sweeping gesture. "Get your aristocratic ass right out of here."

When Piper turned, her eyes were wet, her face tear-streaked.

He'd done that. *Dammit.* How was he going to sort this mess out? Ethan moved to one side of the doorway. "Stan."

The Dom stepped in. "Time to head home, my pretties."

"No. Absolutely not." Ignoring his Master, Dixon crossed his arms over his chest and glared at Ethan. "You'll get to her over my dead body."

Stan muttered to Ethan, "He's the most loyal person I know —and so fucking cute." Walking forward, he grabbed Dixon by the back of his shirt. With his other hand, he nabbed Lindsey's wrist and yanked her to her feet. "Party's over. We're going to let these two battle it out."

"You can't leave him with her," Lindsey protested. "He was—"

"Lindsey." Ethan met her gaze. "Let me make it right."

She hesitated before shooting him a threatening glare. "You'd better."

Dixon wasn't the only faithful friend. It said something about Piper to bring out such loyalty. After Stan dragged them out, Ethan closed the door.

"You need to go, too." Piper had scooted into a corner of the couch. Her knees were pulled up against her chest, arms wrapped around her legs. "There's nothing to make right. Nothing to talk about."

The desolation and finality in her tone were concerning. How much damage had he done? Her arms tightened around her knees. She was shutting him out, physically and mentally. If he pushed too hard, she'd demand he leave. Which was her right.

He sat down close enough his thigh brushed her bare toes. Picking up her drink, he sipped. Rum and coke. Mostly rum. "Dixon and Lindsey are rather intoxicated. How sober are you?"

Startled, she lifted her gaze. "Mostly sober—not completely. They were drinking faster." Her gaze was steady. Her diction was clear.

"Then, may I ask a couple of questions before I leave?"

He saw her submissive side—the need to please—warring with the need to shield herself from more pain. "Then you'll leave?"

"If that's what you want." He picked up an open can of cola and took a drink, stalling as he decided where to begin. "Jerry said he was your brother. I didn't think you had any family left."

Her brows pulled together and then her mouth dropped open. "I did tell you that, didn't I?"

He waited.

"Jerry is my stepbrother." Her dark eyes were haunted. "And, as he told me almost daily when we were children, he's not my family."

The arse-licking wanker. "Does he live in San Francisco?"

"I—I don't think so. I don't know, actually. I haven't seen him for years." At Ethan's raised eyebrows, she sighed. "Our parents died in a car crash. They left him the business and all the accounts except one mutual fund that'd been Mom's, which came to me."

Ethan pulled in a breath. "That was how you started your business?"

She nodded. "He gambled his inheritance away and came here to get me to hand over my money, too."

"I take it you didn't?"

"I told him to go away and never come back." She frowned. "I don't know what he was talking about with the tomorrow stuff. I never said anything about tomorrow."

Ethan covered her foot, warming her cold skin with his hand. "He meant your plan was to blackmail me tomorrow, not today."

Indignation, then anger, flared in her eyes. "I never. I wouldn't."

"No, I don't think you would either, poppet."

"You did, though. You walked away." Her lower lip trembled. "You decided I was guilty without even asking."

He'd hurt her right to the core. He was a gormless idiot, wasn't he? "I'm sorry for that, Piper."

She looked away. "You should go now. There's nothing for you here."

There was *everything* for him here. How could he get her to see that he'd been wrong—but not unforgivably wrong?

"Piper," he said slowly, feeling his way. "After I punched your —" The tightening of her eyes warned him that *brother* would be the wrong word—"Jerry, I waited for you to explain. You never even looked at me. Only at him."

A shudder ran through her. "You waited? I didn't know...that you waited. I...there was blood." She swallowed hard. "You hit him, and he made a noise, and the sound...."

Understanding punched him in the sternum. She'd been abused, often enough that the sight of blood and the sound of a blow would throw her into the past. Yes, he'd cocked this up royally. "You were fighting off a flashback."

Not looking at him, she nodded.

He should be horsewhipped.

"Why did you just leave?" Her eyes were liquid with tears. Her voice was filled with anguish.

"Because..." Piper wasn't the only one to have a brain derailed by flashbacks. He squeezed her foot. "I have a story to tell you."

A story? No. Why didn't he go? Piper could feel the tiny hitches in her breathing that warned of another crying bout.

How foolish was she that her heart yearned for him to stay? Why did she love the way his warm hand felt on her bare feet and how he absent-mindedly stroked the top of one with his thumb.

"I was raised in Oxford, outside London." He didn't wait for her permission to begin his tale. Not this Dom. "My father was wealthy with extensive business interests in manufacturing. After finishing my MBA, I started working with him." Beneath his dark mustache, his lips tilted up. "And then I met a woman. I fear I was rather gullible."

Gullible. Her head came up. Oh, she knew how that worked.

Even though she didn't speak, he nodded. "Yes, I thought you'd understand."

He took a drink of the cola. "While in university, I experimented with BDSM, but Nicola was far more experienced. She introduced me to the Master/slave lifestyle and eventually became my slave."

His eyes were haunted, and his jaw set as the memories drew him away. Hurting him. Had the woman broken Ethan's heart? Piper curled her fingers around his hand on her foot to tug him back to the present the way he did so often for her. "What happened to her?"

He blinked and focused on her. "She was murdered before the police could arrest her."

"Wh-what?"

"Nicola and I had been married two months when police detectives showed up in my office."

Married? Piper felt a jolt of jealousy, but it faded under the pain radiating from Ethan. "What did the police want?"

"They'd started investigating Nicola after her third husband died. Her previous three—wealthy—husbands had died within a couple of months after the nuptials. It was a pattern. She and her partner—her cousin, Bradley—would run through her inheritance, then target a new victim."

His lips curved in a mirthless smile. "I was the latest dupe. The police didn't have enough to arrest her and couldn't track down her cousin so they asked for my help."

Oh, God. Piper stared. What would she do if the police said Ethan planned to kill her? What a horrible dilemma. "Oh, Ethan."

"I couldn't accept it, even though they showed me pictures of her with her previous husbands. But then they gave me her actual history, and none of what she'd told me was true. The police said she and Bradley would research their target, and she would become whatever kind of woman would be most appealing to him. It worked, I must say." His voice roughened "I loved her."

Piper tried to imagine Ethan as a young man, just out of college. He'd have married that woman, thinking of a forever love. "That's despicable."

Unable to be so far from him when he was hurting, Piper lowered her legs, slid closer, and pressed against his side. She stroked his chest slowly, trying to soothe him. "What did you do?"

He sighed. "I let them tap our phone. During a call to her cousin, they spoke in a convoluted code, one that gave very little away. The detectives made some guesses and thought my murder was planned for a Halloween costume party we were to attend. I agreed to go and bait the trap."

Of course, he had. Even knowing it'd all happened in the

past, she still wanted to shake him.

He lifted Piper's hand and rubbed it over his cheek. "When we arrived there, she was so loving I couldn't stand it."

His laugh was bitter. "Using the Dom skills she'd helped me hone, I pushed until she confessed everything. Their plan was that Bradley would knife me during the party. She'd be sure to be in a group of people across the room."

"Murder you during a party? Seriously?"

"It was a crowd. Loud music. People jostling each other. I had on a black pirate costume. Her cousin was to dress as a rival pirate captain and pick a mock-fight with me. Not realizing his intentions, I'd have played along, of course."

Ethan ran his thumb over his lips and shook his head. "By the time anyone realized I'd really been stabbed and was dead, he'd have changed to a new costume and left. It was a good scheme."

A chill ran up Piper's spine. "An awfully cold-blooded scheme. I can't believe she didn't care at all." How could anyone be with Ethan and not care for him?

"Actually, she did care, or that's what she said. She loved her cousin more."

That bitch. "You said she died?"

When his face tightened, Piper couldn't tell what he was feeling. Grief? Regret? Maybe even guilt?

"Nicola and I were leaving when the police spotted Bradley. He saw them closing in, put his knife to a young woman's throat, and told the detectives to stay back. He backed up toward me and Nicola, probably thinking his cousin would aid him."

It had been years in the past...and yet Piper had to hold her breath.

"Someone screamed. While Bradley was distracted, I yanked his arm away from the girl's neck. As the girl scrambled away, Bradley attacked me." Ethan's mouth drew unto an unhappy line. "I blocked his swings—he wasn't that good—then Nicola grabbed my arm. To help him."

If his wife had still been alive, Piper would have killed her. "What happened?"

"I got loose, pushed her toward him, and dived away. I didn't realize..." He shook his head, his jaw tight. "He grabbed Nicola, maybe to hold her for a hostage instead, but she panicked. The knife sliced her carotid."

Ethan took a slow breath. "She died. He went to jail."

Her Dom felt his wife's death deeply. Felt guilty. She could see it in the way his shoulders slumped. Nicola had died, and he'd survived without a scratch.

No, wait. Had he? She'd seen the long white scar on his chest. "He cut you, didn't he? When Nicola grabbed your arm, her cousin got you with his knife."

Ethan didn't answer, but she saw the truth in his eyes. His "beloved" wife had almost gotten him killed. *God.*

Heart aching for him, Piper crawled onto his lap so she could bracket his face and make him look at her. "It wasn't your fault. You didn't start the fight. You didn't take someone hostage. You saved that young woman's life."

"Maybe." He rested his forehead against Piper's. "I'm not sure lives and deaths balance out on a scale. Nicola died."

Had she ever known anyone she could respect like this man?

She didn't want to care for him. No, she didn't, but she did. That stupid wife—how could anyone live with Ethan and choose someone else?

After a second, she realized his arms were around her. What in the world was she thinking? She started to slide off, and he gripped her hips. "Not so fast, poppet. We're not quite done yet."

"Um. What's left?"

"You know how you were thrown back to the past when I pounded on Jerry? You weren't thinking at all, just fighting old memories."

The blood. The pain. She nodded.

"That's what happened to me. When Jerry said you two

wanted money from me, I fell into the past." A muscle tensed in his cheek. "Nicola said she liked me, might even have loved me, but Bradley was her cousin, and she'd do *anything* for him."

The bitter, wry tone in his voice registered after a moment, and Piper's eyes widened. "Is that what Jerry told you I'd do?"

"I'm afraid so, yes. I'd already left everything behind once because I'd been foolish about a woman."

Damn Jerry to hell and beyond for deliberately doing his best to destroy what she had with Ethan.

"You believed him, of course you did." Exhaustion pulled the strength from her muscles, and she slumped against Ethan's chest. "So why are you here?"

"Like you, I was caught in the past," he pointed out gently. "Then my brain kicked back in. You're not a blackmailer. Or a liar."

"You were taken in before. What makes you think that I'm not..." Good grief, was she really arguing for the wrong side? "I mean, never mind."

"I'm not twenty-two this time around, pet." Chuckling, he rubbed his cheek against hers. "With age comes clearer sight."

He'd definitely acquired clear sight. She'd never met anyone who seemed to see right down to the bottom of her soul.

"Reasons or not, I hurt you, Piper. My temporary idiocy made you cry." His arm tightened around her. "I am very sorry."

God, he was a good man. "Forgiven. I didn't do very well either, after all." She hauled in a breath. "Now what?"

"We continue on." He ran his thumb over her bottom lip, and the following kiss was tender enough to make her heart ache. "I can spend the night here if you wish. I'd rather you come home with me. We'll clean up, have another drink, and have vanilla sex all night."

She gave him a disbelieving look. "You? And vanilla sex? Wait, does that mean I get to give orders?"

"Don't push your luck, poppet."

CHAPTER FOURTEEN

Out of foggy, cold San Francisco, Ethan had driven inland to where there was blue sky and warm air, rich with the scent of pine. As he led Piper toward the clusters of tents and cabins, he tipped his face up to the sun. It looked like a good weekend for kink camp.

An electric golf cart, the only vehicle permitted on the grounds, whirred past them, the attached trailer piled high with luggage and toys. Ethan and Piper's bags were on it and would be delivered to the Dark Haven area.

Only half-awake, Piper yawned adorably, then smoothed down her black capris and tugged her dark red tank top straight. "You said we'd be camping out with people, but not much more than that."

"I tried, but someone fell asleep five minutes after she got in the car." Ethan grinned at her indignant scowl.

"*Someone* kept me awake most of the night."

He had. The realization he'd almost lost her had left him needing her badly. They'd made love, talked, and made love some more. "I thoroughly enjoyed it, too."

Her flush was charming.

He pulled her closer. "What would you like to know?"

"Is everyone here in the lifestyle? Like that party in Kansas?"

It was good she'd grown comfortable enough to mention her past, although she never spoke Serna's name or shared details of her time with him. That was worrying.

Patience. He must be patient. She'd tell him all eventually. "The party in Kansas was solely for Masters and slaves. Here, you'll find any kink and any relationship you can think of."

"You helped set up yesterday?"

"Yes, I assist with scheduling and layouts each year and teach a workshop or two. I have a Shibari demo later today." He smiled. "I think you'll enjoy the fun here."

And he would enjoy his time with her.

As they walked past the areas sectioned off for various activities, a herd of ponies—human ponies—stampeded through a littles playgroup. The pigtailed and stuffie-carrying littles—persons letting loose their inner child—abandoned their coloring books to scream and bounce in excitement.

Piper's giggles were a balm on his heart.

Last night had been rough for both of them. Helping her with her past experiences was one of his goals, but it appeared he needed to work on his own as well. Getting blindsided by his emotions was bad enough. Having that moment arrive at the same time as Piper's flashback? DeVries would've called it a clusterfuck.

Speaking of deVries, Ethan spotted the ex-mercenary, now one of Simon's security agents, watching a football game. No it was called soccer here. His submissive, Lindsey, stood beside him, laughing at what was happening on the field. Since the only clothing permitted in the game was footwear, female and male bits were bouncing harder than the soccer ball. One woman ran with her hands clasped over very abundant breasts.

"Ouch." Piper crossed her arms over her own full breasts. "I'm not playing that game, Sir."

Ethan laughed. "We can watch instead." He veered toward deVries.

Lindsey spotted them and squealed, "Piper!"

Before Lindsey could move, deVries gripped a hank of her long hair and held her back. The Dom glanced over, eyebrows lifted, asking silently whether Ethan would permit the submissives to meet.

When Ethan nodded, deVries released his hold. "Go, baby."

The two women met in a collision of hugging, and Ethan smiled. It was good to see Piper acquiring submissive friends who could talk about things that vanillas wouldn't understand.

"Want to get coffee? Simon's already over there." DeVries pointed toward a huge shade tree in the center of the activity areas.

Piper wasn't the only one who was tired. Caffeine would be most welcome. Trailed by the women, Ethan and deVries joined Simon at a table under the tree.

A second later, Rona brought over two cups of coffee along with a cheese Danish on a plate. Gaze down, she waited for Simon's direction.

As Piper joined Ethan, her face lit. "Hi, Ro—"

Ethan's hand over her mouth smothered the greeting, and he bent down to whisper, "Here is something else I didn't get a chance to explain. This weekend, the Dark Haven members in D/s relationships will observe club protocol unless told otherwise." He removed his hand.

Her face turned pink. "Sorry, Sir."

He gave her a quick hug and kiss before pointing at a serving booth. "I would like a plate of donut holes, a scone, a cup of hot tea, and an iced tea, please."

"Yes, Sir." Her face brightened as if the task was a reward. Because, to her, it was.

He loved her joyful need to please him and how her trust in him had grown. He would gently take up the control she was now willing to relinquish. Being submissive was as natural to her as his need to protect and take charge was to him.

They fit.

Ethan took a seat at the table and saw deVries had sent Lindsey off, too.

Seating Rona beside him, Simon fed her bites of the cheese Danish. He looked across the table at Ethan. "I heard you flattened someone outside Dark Haven last night."

Bloody hell. Gossip moved through the club faster than the Chunnel's Eurostar train.

"Give us the story," deVries demanded. "That shit didn't sound like you at all."

Ethan hesitated. This was Piper's past. Yet... His mouth firmed. Jerry's behavior could pose a risk to more than Ethan. "It happened this way..." He explained who Jerry was, his past history with Piper, what had happened on the sidewalk.

Simon's eyes turned dangerous. "Do you think Jerry returned to Kansas?"

Returning, Piper heard the question. Her hand jerked, almost spilling the drinks she held.

Biting her lip, she set the cups, plate, and napkins on the table and waited for her next instruction. Right now, the only thing she needed to worry about was Sir Ethan's satisfaction. Nothing else.

Only...all three Doms were looking at her. Studying her.

Sir Ethan nodded toward the ground, and she went down on her knees in the soft grass beside him.

After a glance at Sir Ethan, Simon asked her directly, "Do you think your stepbrother returned to Kansas, Piper?"

Sir Ethan would be upset if he knew Jerry was still here. She looked down at her hands and equivocated, "It would be crazy for Jerry to stay."

DeVries growled. "Subbies who bullshit annoy the fuck out of me."

Her body tensed at the threat. *Run. Run now.*

Sir Ethan set a hand on her shoulder and turned toward

deVries. "Zander, no intimidation, please. She's suffered enough abuse in the past."

The terrifying hardness disappeared from the Enforcer's face.

"What Sir Ethan said." Lindsey glared at her Dom.

No, no, don't. Mouth dry, Piper gave Lindsey a worried shake of her head. *Be quiet, please.*

Sir Ethan noticed and squeezed her shoulder. "Don't worry, poppet. DeVries won't punish her for loyalty."

"I might." DeVries pointed to the ground. "I haven't caned her ass in far too long."

Lindsey dropped to her knees beside his chair, but a tiny smile graced her lips. She didn't appear concerned.

The band constricting Piper's chest loosened.

Until Sir Ethan rephrased the question. "Piper, give us your thoughts about where your stepbrother might be."

She didn't think she'd reacted, but his jaw went stern. "Has he contacted you?"

Cheering came from the right, and stalling, she turned. At the next tree over, a man was being hoisted in the air from hooks inserted into his upper chest and back. Although his skin pulled up in horrifying tent-like shapes, his face held a look of unbelievable peace.

She made an unhappy sound, and an arm came around her shoulders. "Easy, pet."

Sir Ethan was here. She was all right. She breathed out and started to relax.

Then he cleared his throat, and she looked up at him. His expression warned that, although he would render comfort as needed, his patience wasn't unlimited.

What would he do when he heard about Jerry? She clasped her hands tightly in her lap. "He texted me sometime last night, and I ignored it." The message would only be nasty words and threats. "I don't think he'll try anything. Really. "

At Sir Ethan's *gimme* gesture, she pulled her phone from her shorts pocket. As the owner of Chatelaines, she couldn't be completely unreachable, but she'd set her phone on vibrate only. She pulled up the message and handed the cell over.

He checked the display, and his mouth tightened before he pushed the phone across the table. Simon and deVries leaned forward. The same hard expressions appeared on their faces. Lindsey and Rona exchanged glances.

"What are you thinking, Ethan?" Simon's tone was mild, the look in his black eyes almost terrifying.

"Why, I thought your company might dig up the location of my good friend Jerry so I can pay him a visit." The ice in Sir Ethan's quiet voice chilled Piper to the bone.

"No." She grabbed his hand. "No, Sir Ethan."

DeVries grinned. "Be a pleasure to locate his ass for you, Worth."

"We can find him," Simon agreed. He undoubtedly could. According to Lindsey, Simon owned an international security firm where deVries was one of his badass operators. "However, from what I hear, you thoroughly damaged the man once already."

"I might have"—Sir Ethan paused—"knocked him down."

Knocked him down? More like broke his nose, ribs, and reduced him to a bloody heap. Piper snorted.

And her damned Dom *winked* at her.

Simon grinned. "Your actions might put you in a problematic position in regard to him and the law. I suggest you leave the next visit to someone else." Simon tilted his head toward deVries. "I daresay Zander would be pleased to inform the man that any further harassment of Ms. Delaney will not have a happy ending."

"I suppose I could help out this once." Despite deVries's grudging words, his icy eyes lit with anticipation. "Can't let some bastard pick on our subbies."

Our subbies. Like she was one of them.

Shaking at the relief that Sir Ethan wouldn't go after Jerry and get himself arrested, Piper pressed her face against his hard thigh. The feeling of his hand on the back of her head gave her such a sense of comfort that tears filled her eyes.

"I'll accompany Zander"—Simon lifted an eyebrow—"just to ensure our friend Jerry is capable of walking onto his plane."

"Fuck, you're fussy," deVries muttered.

Plans made, the men started talking about the camp and the upcoming activities.

Slowly relaxing, Piper straightened.

"That's better," Sir Ethan murmured. After giving her hair a tug, he handed her the glass of iced tea. After she drank some, he held out a donut hole. She lifted her hand to take it, but he shook his head with a slight smile and waited.

Oh. She opened her mouth and carefully took the small glazed pastry from his hand.

The burst of sugar grounded her, dispelling the shakiness inside. She took a sip of iced tea, savoring the hint of peppermint, and let out a tiny sigh.

Watching her, Sir Ethan smiled, the sunlines beside his eyes crinkling.

As she leaned against his leg, he fed her another bite.

As Piper accompanied Lindsey and Dixon on an exploration of the camp, she couldn't stop smiling. It was only afternoon, and the day had already been full of fun.

First, she'd helped Sir Ethan set up their tent over in the Dark Haven area. Then he'd said they should make sure the air mattress didn't leak. When she'd given him a puzzled look, he closed the flap, pushed her onto the mattress, and vigorously "tested" it. By the time he finished, she could say with confidence it had no leaks.

Done in after three orgasms, she'd lain in Sir Ethan's arms, listening to the hum of conversation, people walking past the tent, the faint music accompanied by the shushing sound of wind in the evergreens. She'd drifted into a wonderful nap.

They'd had lunch with Mistress Angela, her submissive, Meggie, and Mitchell, a blunt, tough-looking Aussie Dom. Angela had teased Mitchell about the submissives who were giving him flirtatious glances. Meggie had whispered to Piper that, last summer when Sir Ethan had come alone, he almost smothered under all the hungry looks he'd received.

Piper totally understood how anyone might yearn after him. She felt the same way. Even more disconcerting, she found that kneeling at his feet gave her a melty sensation of contentment.

After lunch, other club members joined them, and Dixon and Lindsey got permission to explore the camp. Piper hadn't realized she was giving Sir Ethan pleading looks, but he'd said her puppy-dog-eyes were so irresistible that he would have to dress her up someday in floppy ears, paw mittens, and a tail.

She hadn't quite decided how to feel about that.

Since Sir Ethan had a workshop to prepare for, he'd collared her and let her join Dixon and Lindsey. He'd also murmured something to Stan and deVries about letting trouble loose in the camp.

Piper grinned as she linked arms with Lindsey and Dix. Sir Ethan might have a point.

The camp was full of interesting sights. Forest alternated with open areas. Tents mixed with cabins. Every area swarmed with crazy, kinky people. Sex happened, right out in the full light of day and anywhere. Piper averted her gaze from the Domme who had bent her sub over a stump and was pegging him.

Two people walked by in leather pants and chain halters, then a woman stalked past in a gorgeous cat suit, followed by three lesbians, arm-in-arm. One gave Piper an interested glance before noticing her collar.

There were naked people and half-dressed people. Cosplayers were attired as anything from mountain men to harem girls. One of the organizers wore a top hat, nineteenth-century suit, and kept twirling his long waxed mustache. Another organizer in a schoolmarm's starched white blouse and long black skirt was enforcing her dictates with a switch.

There was simply too much to look at. Piper's eyes got wider and wider.

Alongside the path was a boot-blacking chair where a guy in biker clothing was getting his tall boots shined. The submissive at his feet had black smears and mud on her white shirt—and the most contented smile ever.

Service. Understanding completely, Piper stomped on the moment of envy.

A whine of pain came from the stage of a workshop area. A man was strapped down on a GYN table, feet bound in the stirrups. The top standing over him held up a thin rod somewhat longer than straw-length.

"Oh, no way, little dogies." Lindsey shuddered. "There will be no metal rods shoved up my urethra, thank you very much."

It was a *sounding* lesson.

Piper took a step back. At least that kink was something she'd never had to endure. "Me, neither."

"You're such wussies," Dix said. "Just imagine if your short girl urethras were the length of a dick."

"God, no." Piper stared at him. "You and Stan do that?"

"I tried it." Dixon took in their awe-filled expressions and snickered. "It gave new meaning to *hard* limit. Never again."

As they walked past another clearing, Piper slowed and stared. "What is that?"

A hollow dug into the ground was filled with pillows and a writhing mass of people. No one was groaning or crying, instead, there were giggles and sighs. No one was kissing or groping... "That's not an orgy, is it?"

"That's a cuddle pile." Dix flung out his arms dramatically. "I totally need a hug. Come with me, little girls."

Unmoving, Piper watched as he left his flip-flops on the rim and carefully crawled down the slope. A big man pulled him close, gave him a long hug, which Dixon returned, then passed him on to the next person.

Huh. Piper exchanged a glance with Lindsey.

"I'm game," Lindsey said. "How about you?"

Piper answered by leaving her flip-flops beside Dix's. Her heart began to hammer as she went on hands and knees down the slope toward a woman sitting on the edge of the crowd. The lady was older than Piper, all soft curves as she pulled Piper close. Her hug was long and sweet—the kind Piper had gotten from her mom before things changed. The lady released Piper into the crowd. Then a man was hugging her, a younger man, then another woman, and eventually she ended up beside Dixon on the other side. After giving him a hug, she realized she was close to the edge.

Flushed with laughter, she crawled up and out, feeling more open and whole than when she'd gone in.

Lindsey and Dixon joined her, all smiles.

"Sometimes it's not about the kink or the sex," Dixon said.

"Sometimes it doesn't need to be." Although a lot of Doms wouldn't see it that way. The Defiler would never have let anyone touch his property, worthless or not.

Oh, no. Dismay flashed through her. "I didn't ask Sir Ethan for permission."

Laughing, Dix nudged her shoulder. "Girlfriend, who do you think told me the cuddle pile was over here?"

"He did?"

"Mmmhmm. He said you're a hugger, and you'd love it."

Sir Ethan had thought of her. She couldn't keep from smiling. It was her job—and her joy—to give people what they'd like. She'd never anticipated that a Dom would feel the same and arrange something she'd enjoy.

"You escaped the bullet this time, Pips," Lindsey said, "but you should probably find out where Sir Ethan draws the line. With Zander, if I'm on my own, he doesn't consider a hug as infringing on his territory. But if there was anything sexual going on, I'd get in trouble."

Piper frowned. For this event, she was Sir Ethan's submissive because he'd brought her. Other times, though... Did they have that kind of a relationship? She was so confused.

Farther down the path, another area had people getting foot rubs and back massages. Piper flushed remembering how Sir Ethan had massaged her at Dark Haven. So wonderful. And then he'd had her turn over. His hands on her breasts.... *Mmm.*

Maybe she could give him a massage this weekend and perhaps finish with a dick massage? She grinned.

They passed some diapered age players in a fenced-off area made to resemble a playpen. Diapers—uh-uh. But there were some really cute babies.

Next up was a pavilion tent with an orgy going on. All screams and pounding music.

A girl could get whiplash trying to see everything. This place was insane.

Piper realized she was running her fingers over her collar. It was funny. From hating anything around her neck, she'd gone to being grateful for it. A few people had started to approach, seen her collar, and been deterred. Being marked as Sir Ethan's gave her the ability to relax and enjoy herself.

Even better, the event had a "yes means yes" consent protocol, as in consent was never implied, but had to be spoken. She loved that.

As the sun hovered above the tops of the trees, Lindsey pointed to a raised stage on the right. "Look. Sir Ethan's giving his demo."

On the stage, dressed in black, Sir Ethan stood beside a beautiful brunette who wore only a token thong. In his resonant, English-accented voice, he demonstrated knots as he covered the woman's torso in an intricate pattern of rope.

Piper took a few steps toward the stage, and her jaw clenched.

He was touching the woman's body. Touching her breasts. Speaking to her in a low voice in-between talking to the crowd. When he tied a knot between her breasts, the woman leaned into him.

Knife-edged jealousy ripped right through Piper's chest with a searing pain.

Still on the path, Lindsey looked from the stage and back to Piper before saying something to Dixon. They moved forward and formed up on each side of Piper.

"You know, my mouth is as parched as if I'd been blowing Bigfoot's giant hairy dick." Dixon linked his arm in hers and pulled her back toward the path. "C'mon, I totally need something to drink."

Piper looked over her shoulder. Rigging complete, Sir Ethan had the woman suspended in the air. He gave her a slight push to make her spin slowly. Her eyes were closed, her features slack. She was in subspace.

When the scene was over, Sir Ethan would give the bottom aftercare. He was a most conscientious Dom. But would he give the beautiful woman...more? Piper swallowed.

Dammit, she shouldn't be jealous. She had no claims on Sir Ethan—he was just trying to help her out with her problems.

No, she was wrong. They'd gone past that. Sex. Sleeping at his place. Sharing things, from the ugly stuff like his wife's betrayal to silly personal facts like how she hated figurines and collections that just gathered dust and how he needed balance in his home and life.

Last night, Jerry's lies had hurt Sir Ethan—because she mattered to him.

She needed to stop being insecure and not be jealous. He was merely doing a scene with a rope bunny, a model, who was undoubtedly a nice person.

Who rubbed against him. Again.

Piper glared at the stage. She should slap that woman's face off.

"Now, now, Pips." Dix pried her fist open. "Let's not go off and get all *no-touchy-my-man* on Tanya's ass. You know she doesn't mean anything to your..." His voice faded as he stared at something over her shoulder. Hurt shadowed his brown eyes.

Piper and Lindsey turned.

In the audience, Stan stood beside the guy named Darrell who'd been outside Dix and Stan's apartment. The one who'd flirted with Stan.

Lindsey's eyes narrowed. "Who's Stan with?"

"Special Agent Darrell Legrand," Dix said. All the animation had died from his face. "I told you about him."

"His name is Legrand? Seriously? I wonder if his package is grand as well." Lindsey's gaze was still on the two men.

"Probably." Dix sounded so unhappy that Piper put her arm around him. He leaned against her.

Lindsey took his hand. "Dix, no. Stan wouldn't mess around on you."

"He might. That guy—he's everything I'm not, and he wants Stan. I don't think anything's going to stop him."

Piper set her jaw. "Stan doesn't want him; he wants you." If that wasn't true, she was going to kick Stan's butt.

Piper added, "However, if you want, we can join them and mess up the guy's plans." Being in the crowd and trying not to watch Sir Ethan with that woman would be tough, but she'd do it. She'd do anything Dixon needed right now.

Dixon turned away. "Uh-uh. I still need something to drink. And we both need to get out of here."

Piper gave a sigh of relief.

After his demonstration, Ethan found his pretty submissive with several Dark Haven people, all watching the Disney Beat-a-thon —impact play set to Disney tunes. The song, "I'll Make a Man Out of You," had filled the area with male bottoms getting whacked by female and male Tops. Canes, flogger, paddles. The slapping of flesh in time with the beat of the music was almost mesmerizing.

"Piper." He sat down beside her and pulled her into his arms.

To his surprise, she was stiff, almost resistant, before melting against him. Had she seen something that upset her?

He tipped his head down and kissed her, again feeling her hesitation before her mouth opened, and she sank into the kiss. By the time he finished, she was giving as enthusiastically as she received.

When he lifted his head, he studied her face. The sun had given her skin a pink radiance that a flush of arousal had heightened. He ran his thumb over her wet lower lip.

But there had been that slight hesitation... "Tell me what you've been up to this afternoon."

"There was this place—a cuddle pile." Her face lit as she described it to him.

Excellent. She was learning that touch didn't have to be sexual. Before he could get to the root of the bit of distance he'd felt—

"People. There's a game starting over in the meadow we should join." Xavier rose and pulled Abby up with him.

"I know the one you mean." DeVries stood. "They'll give us weapons. I'm in and so is this little prey."

Lindsey let out a startled squawk as he hefted her to her feet.

Ethan started to smile. This would be a fine game for Piper to experience. "Let's go, poppet."

As Piper walked beside him, she fanned herself with one hand. "I'd forgotten what it's like away from the water." In San Francisco, the ever-present breeze of the cold Bay kept the city in the seventies. Inland, even the evening sun beat down with a vengeance.

"You'll be cooler very soon," Ethan promised. Her wary look made him chuckle.

At the edge of the grassy open space, volunteers were unloading the game's weaponry from a golf-cart trailer.

"Water guns?" She narrowed her eyes at Ethan.

Ethan grinned. "You'll find them quite refreshing."

"But..." She looked down at her clothes.

Before he could tell her that her clothing wouldn't be an issue, one of the organizers—Master Khan—stepped onto the trailer and smoothed the sides of his waxed handlebar mustache.

"Hear ye, hear ye." The booming voice that had served Khan on a battlefield was just as effective in the campground. "This will be an erotic power-exchange game. The ones with the power—they get the guns. The ones without—they get naked. Except for shoes. Tender little subbie soles need to be protected."

Grinning at the ribald comments, Ethan chose a pistol from the stack. A streamlined Super Soaker.

"I like games with weaponry." DeVries picked out a heavier firearm. "Why are there never any games with whips?"

Stan gave the Enforcer an *are-you-serious* stare. "Considering some of the whip wielders you've seen, would you want to let them loose in a field?"

Xavier shook his head. "There's a terrifying thought."

Chuckling, Ethan led the way to the brimming kiddie pool to submerge and fill his water gun. Once the weapons were loaded, the Doms rejoined the submissives.

Piper gave his water gun a frown. "This game seems rigged."

"What are the rules?" someone called.

Master Khan rocked on his heels. "No running. Bottoms must keep their fingers laced behind their back. Once in the meadow, each naked person must visit a number booth in order of one through five and must show all five marks to exit the game. A naked person who moves their hands or has an orgasm will be punished with five switches on the ass from a monitor, remain in place to the count of a hundred with hands over the genitals, and then it's *game on* again. When finished, a naked person can get rewarded nicely by the weapon wielder of their choice."

He wagged his finger. "Of course, the weapon wielder must be agreeable."

"Awww, that's a shame," Lindsey called.

"I'm agreeable, sweet cheeks." A man standing near Lindsey grinned at her.

Ethan heard deVries growl under his breath. "My little brat is going to get her ass warmed."

"That's not exactly a deterrent for her." Xavier was digging something out of his pack. He held up several packets of warming lube. "Anyone?"

Ethan studied Piper. The lubricant might keep a little submissive focused on her senses rather than her worries. "That would be welcome, thank you."

Xavier tossed packets to everyone.

This was going to be fun.

Dixon and Lindsey were naked already. Abby was slowly stripping, and Piper was still dressed.

Ethan gave her a brief kiss. "Remove your clothing, poppet."

"This isn't my sort of thing. Really." Yet the excitement had flushed her cheeks.

"That's all right. It's *my* sort of thing." When her eyes rounded at his lack of sympathy, he barely smothered a laugh. "Piper, you may say *no,* of course. Then we'll have a long discussion about why you didn't want to play a fun game."

Her lower lip inched out into a tiny—adorable—pout. "I didn't come here to have long discussions."

"Exactly. Strip, pet."

Her gaze dropped, and she pulled off her clothes and set them in a pile on the ground. Covering her breasts, she frowned at him—at his clothes—and opened her mouth to say something that would probably get her in trouble.

Meeting his level gaze, she turned red. "I'm sorry, Sir. I don't mean to be disobedient."

A strong, caring woman...who surrendered so beautifully. To him. How could he resist her? He pulled her against him. "I know you don't. I'm pleased you're willing to give this a try."

The kiss he gave her heated rapidly. Because that was what this game was all about—erotic stimulation and entertainment. She needed to learn that BDSM could be, quite simply, fun.

He stroked his hands over her silken skin, squeezed her curvy ass, cupped her breasts—and got a gasp of embarrassed delight. "Now spread your legs for me."

Her eyes widened.

A few feet away, Stan stroked an entire palmful of cold lube over his submissive's dick. Dixon squealed a protest. He'd probably squeal louder as the lube turned *very* warm.

Ethan covered his fingertips in lube and stepped behind Piper. Reaching around, with one hand, he opened her labia. With the other hand...

Piper shivered as Sir Ethan's fingers touched her clit. She jerked, but his body was rock-solid behind her, his chest against her back. She wasn't getting away from whatever he was putting on her.

The liquid on his fingers was cool against her over-heated flesh. As he rubbed the stuff in thoroughly, making her squirm, arousal lit inside.

When he stepped back, she turned. "What did you put on me?"

"Your paperwork said you're not allergic to anything. This is just a mild lubricant that'll keep you warm while you're out there. Did you understand the rules?"

Her face turned hot with her embarrassment. "Hands behind my back. Go to each station in order, one through five."

"No running and no orgasms." He smiled, ran his finger up her pussy again, and excitement streaked through her. As he helped her put her flip-flops back on, she saw an answering desire in his gaze.

The announcer clapped his hands for attention. "Shooters, take a position anywhere you want. Your only rules are no running, no touching, and shoot only for the genitals. All naked genitals are fair game." The announcer's big laugh boomed out. "It's like the opposite of fighting."

A ripple of laughter went through the crowd, and people headed into the meadow.

Piper hadn't moved. Shoot for the genitals? Oh, this was going to be really strange.

"Come along, poppet." Holding his gun, Sir Ethan set a hand low on her bare back, firmly steering her toward the center of the grassy area.

Her friends were being herded out, too. Already erect, Dixon was hopping with excitement. Suddenly, he stopped, touched his shaft, and glared at Stan. "What the jumping genitals, Master? That lube you put on me is burning my dick."

Stan's grin was wicked. "I know."

Piper put her hands over her mouth to stifle the giggles threatening to escape. Because, OMG, this was insane.

As the setting sun warmed her shoulders and back, Piper walked beside Sir Ethan. Her embarrassment was fading since all the submissives were naked.

In fact, the jiggling of her bare breasts was erotic as all get out, and her skin itself seemed more sensitive. Every part of her was...

She stumbled and halted. *Oh, wow.* Whatever Stan put on Dixon was what Sir Ethan had rubbed on her. Because her clit felt hot and cold and tingly, all at the same time. Her weight shifted as she rubbed her legs together.

Sir Ethan swept her with a molten blue gaze, and his masculine grin of comprehension put quivers into her belly. The sight of the thick bulge in his jeans sent hunger sweeping through her.

She'd been worried about that rope-bunny at the demo, but

he hadn't gone with her. He'd come here. To play with Piper. All his attention was on her. The sweeping sense of being wanted and watched-over was amazing.

He was amazing. She stared at him, feeling as if she wanted to go to her knees. Feeling as if she wanted to be held, be kissed.

Expression tender, he touched her cheek lightly.

"Five, four, three," Master Khan shouted. "No touching, people. Weapon-wielders, if you see someone orgasm, hold up a hand so the monitor can punish them. Naked people—get your hands behind your back."

Hauling in a breath, Piper laced her fingers together behind her.

Sir Ethan backed away, pumping the water gun.

Oh, no. Oh, God.

Master Khan's voice grew to a roar. "Two, one, and GO!"

A shockingly hard stream of cold water hit Piper's mound—and below. On her *clit*. She shrieked.

Yells and screams sounded throughout the meadow, and then everyone was moving as fast as possible without breaking into a run.

Piper bounced off Lindsey, turned in a circle—and two more jets of water zapped her pussy. It wasn't just Sir Ethan shooting at her.

In outrage, she saw that every person with a gun was shooting at any target.

Not *fair*. In her flip-flops, she speed-walked away from Sir Ethan toward Booth One. Someone had already messed up; the high whistle of a switch was accompanied by a yelp.

She turned to look—and more water hit her.

Her clit tingled and burned from the lube, making the cold water even more of a shock. A water blast hit her, followed by several caressing splashes. Her pussy swelled, already throbbing. Her nipples were tightly peaked.

Another devastating stream struck her clit, and she heard Sir Ethan's resonant chuckle.

The damn Dom was far too accurate with a gun.

With a gasp of relief, she reached the safety of the roped-off Booth One enclosure.

Helping out there, the Dark Haven Aussie, Mitchell, marked a "1" on her upper arm. "I haven't seen Ethan join in the games before. You're good for him, subbie."

"Really?"

"Really." He grinned and turned to the next person, leaving Piper blinking. She was good for Sir Ethan? She'd never thought of him as needing anything she could give. Mitchell's compliment made her feel as if she was glowing inside.

As the jostling in the pen increased, she remembered there was a game going on. Pulling in a breath, she hurried toward Booth Two.

A long burst of water, directly on her clit, made her stagger to a stop, almost paralyzed with need.

"Keep moving, poppet."

He was evil. *Evil.*

Sucking in a breath, she dodged two other Tops and zigzagged across the grass. A sneaky Domme nailed her good as she approached the station.

She got "2" marked on her arm.

She safely reached Booth Three and collected her number.

By the time she headed for Booth Four, her engorged clit ached and tingled. The intermittent thrumming blasts of water had built her arousal to an excruciating edge. She whimpered with desperation. *Don't come, don't come.*

"Piper." A few feet away, Sir Ethan smiled slowly. "Show me a *Standing Present*, please." His accent hit on the second syllable. *PreSENT*.

It was an order—a Dominant's command prior to inspection of his submissive. *Oh, God.* Flushing, she put her hands behind her head with fingers laced together, then widened her stance.

Sir Ethan's water gun was pointed toward the ground. He glanced to one side and nodded.

At Xavier. He aimed and the powerful stream hit her clit. Before the water stopped, another ruthless torrent came from the right. DeVries.

The devastating sensations brought her right to the explosion point. With her legs so far apart, her labia were pulled open, exposing her very, very vulnerable clit. Her body shook as the pressure in her center grew, as her muscles went taut, as she hovered right on the razor's edge. *Noooo.*

"Sorry pet." With a wicked grin, Sir Ethan aimed and fired. As did someone else—Stan. Mercilessly they shot her. The forceful streams of water, angled from different directions, struck on either side of her clit. Everything inside her seized, pulled together into one all-consuming knot, then her world exploded in a brilliant fireball of pleasure.

She shook as she came, sobbing, "Oh, oh, oh." Her knees wobbled as she gasped for air.

"Now, that's a damned shame. What a disobedient subbie," deVries said in a rough, pseudo-concerned voice. Through blurred eyes, she saw him grin and lift his hand.

Lift his hand. The bastard was summoning a monitor.

A man in an orange shirt stalked over, switch in one hand.

Stan, another complete bastard, pointed to her. "Bad subbie."

"Oh and did a naughty little someone come without permission?" Clicking his tongue against his teeth in a tsking sound, the monitor motioned to her with his switch. "Bend over and grip your ankles, pretty girl. Breathe through your punishment."

She stared at him in disbelief and saw Sir Ethan watching.

When he gave her a tiny wink, her mouth dropped open. He'd known she was close to coming. He'd deliberately *made* her come.

When she glared, the monitor's brows drew together. "Should I make it ten for insolence to your Dom?"

Eeeks. "No, sir. Sorry, sir."

Sir Ethan looked at the monitor and put his thumb and forefinger close together in a *just a little* gesture, then turned his attention to her. He moved his hand up and down. *Bend.*

She folded in half and gripped her ankles. Offering her bottom.

"Count for me so I don't lose track." The man deliberately, sadistically swished the damn switch in the air, terrifying her with the sound, before letting loose.

The sting across her bare buttocks made her jump. But it wasn't too painful. "One, sir."

More slices hit, burning more intensely. "Two, sir. Three, sir."

He moved to her other side and adding the last two in a new spot. Harder. She squeaked. "Four, sir. Five, sir." *Ouch!*

"All right then. You can stand up, girl." The monitor stepped back.

"You were a good submissive, Piper. I'm proud of you." The approval in Sir Ethan's voice made tears come to her eyes. He stood close to her, not touching, but protective, making her want to bury herself against him. His gaze caught hers and held, giving her the slow internal slide of surrender.

His fingertips lifted toward her face, stopped. He shook his head and sighed. "It's time to cup your pussy and count to a hundred, poppet. You get a chance to recover."

That was good because her bottom burned and so did her pussy. *Wait a minute.* "You mean, recover so I can come again?"

His swift grin was answer enough.

She shot him a look that made his grin widen.

"I'll catch up with you in a bit." He gave her a long appreciative look that made heat rise in her face, then followed after the other three Doms.

She scowled when she saw that guy—tall, built, and naked Darrell—trailing after Stan. The jerk. Hoping Dixon wouldn't notice the creep, she started counting.

A couple of minutes later, she finished and hurried toward Booth Four.

The first hit of water on her now overly sensitive clit almost sent her into orbit. Each one after moved her far too quickly into needing to come.

Again.

But she held the climax off.

Others were orgasming. Like when deVries, Sir Ethan, Xavier, and Stan all surrounded Abby, trapping her the same way they had Piper. The professor came with a scream that was half orgasm and half outrage.

Grinning, Piper darted into Booth Five's pen, collected her number, and was done.

Although *done* wasn't really the right word—because she was so aroused, she might just die.

CHAPTER FIFTEEN

Ethan collected his dazed submissive as she wobbled off the field near Booth Five. She was drenched—even her hair had managed to get wet. With the sun behind the trees, the air was chilling, and despite the flush of arousal, she'd get cold quickly.

"Come, pet. We'll sit by a fire pit until you warm up." As he wrapped an oversized towel around her and held her against him, her contented sigh filled an empty space inside him. She was his, his submissive to enjoy, to care for, to cherish. The sense of satisfaction ran deep.

As he tucked her clothing into his toy bag, he noticed a male submissive kneel in front of Stan. Since the subbie's arm was marked with 1 through 5, he was probably hoping to collect a reward from the Dom.

"That jerk," Piper muttered. "He's trying to steal Dix's Master. Can we go hit him?"

My loyal subbie. Ethan kissed her lightly. "No, poppet. Stan will have to fend off aspiring lovers all by himself."

As they watched, Stan frowned, looked down at the man, and shook his head *no* before walking away.

"Well, okay then," Piper said under her breath.

Grinning at her endearing indignation, Ethan slung his bag over his shoulder and walked her down the path. They went past the food pavilion, a workshop, more tents, and came to the various evening gathering areas—the ones with fire pits.

The primal aggressive music of the Hu band's "Wolf Totem" caught his attention, and he guided Piper toward the shadows around the fire pit. Blankets had been spread out on the grass as an invitation for people wanting a place to fuck.

On the far side, away from some enthusiastic activity, he set his toy bag on a blanket that was close enough to the fire pit to feel the warmth.

Standing beside the blanket, Piper turned her head, listening to the slapping, wet sounds of someone having a good time.

When Ethan set his hand on her nape and pulled her against him, her back against his chest, a quiver ran through her. Sliding his hand under her towel, he cupped a full breast. Her nipple hardened against his palm. "I intend to take you hard, sweetheart. I hope you're ready."

"Oh, I don't know," she said. "I'm awfully tired." And the little brat ground her round ass against his dick.

He bit the curve between her shoulder and neck and felt her shudder. "You have my permission to nap while I fuck you."

Her startled giggle made him grin.

As he helped her sit on the blanket, four people appeared out of the shadows—two younger Tops and two bottoms. One was Tanya, the brunette who'd served as his rope model earlier.

"Ethan, um, excuse us? Do you have a minute?" asked one of the Tops. "We had a question about the demo earlier."

Bloody hell, now? Cock aching like a sore tooth, Ethan suppressed his sigh and smiled instead. "Of course. How can I help?"

"You said the chest harness only needed a few more wraps of the rope to turn it into a bondage position for sex. Can you... We wanted to try that." The young man flushed and patted the rope hanging out of his leather bag.

"It would be easier to show you than to explain," he said slowly.

Tanya knelt and bowed her head, waiting for his permission to speak.

"Yes, Tanya?"

"I'd love to serve as your rope bunny again, Sir Ethan, if it pleases you."

Sitting on the blanket, Piper ignored the talk as she thought about the game that had just finished. Had she really scurried around naked, orgasmed in public, and giggled so hard she'd almost fallen over? Who would have thought sex and dominance could be...fun?

When one of the bottoms spoke, Piper realized the woman who'd been in Sir Ethan's rope demo was offering to be his model again.

Piper stiffened. Sir Ethan had chosen this blanketed area so they could make love. Or fuck like rabbits. Both. But that rope-bunny seemed to think Sir Ethan's hands would be on *her*.

"All right," he said to the bunny, then went down on a knee to pull rope from his toy bag.

The woman was beautiful. Tall and slender. *No, no, no.* Jealousy was a murky swamp in Piper's belly.

Tensing against his probable rejection, Piper touched Sir Ethan's thigh before he could stand.

"Poppet?" He rubbed his knuckles against her cheek.

She hesitated. Could she bear being really tied up? Here? Was she crazy? "I can... Could I be...?"

He studied her, then leaned forward and said for her ears only, "I wasn't going to restrain you for an audience, but if you're comfortable, I'd love to tie you." His gaze warmed her more than the towel around her.

"I can do this. I'd like to. Please, Sir."

"Excellent." He stood and lifted her to her feet, tossing the towel to one side, leaving her naked. "Thank you, Tanya. My submissive will help me this time."

My submissive. Everything inside her turned to mush at the possessive words, and it was frightening. The last time she'd felt this way, she'd handed over everything. Herself, her body, her soul.

"Piper." One word. A quiet reminder to stay in the present, to pay attention to him.

Her gaze locked onto his.

"Better." He gave her a smile, then took bandage scissors from his bag and laid them on the blanket. Pulling rope from his bag, he folded the length in half. "I want your weight balanced, hands loose, eyes on me."

He made several turns with the rope, around her ribs, up and under her breasts and over, before folding her arms behind her back, forearm against forearm. Her breasts were lifted upward in the harness. More rope circled and compressed them further, tightening the skin, making her nipples pucker and ache.

His hands moved over her, so sure and competent, smoothing the ropes over her skin. His touch was soothing and somehow heightened every sense in her body. His dark velvet voice stroked over her in the same way as his fingers.

Sir Ethan ran his hands ran down her torso, cupped a breast, touched her hip. "See how this knot is made?"

Half mesmerized by the feelings running through her, Piper leaned her head against his shoulder.

Standing with the other three, Tanya was frowning, lips forming a pout.

As Sir Ethan continued binding Piper's breasts, she realized why the rope-bunny was displeased. Because Sir Ethan's behavior was different with Piper. Despite the inherent intimacy of rope, the interaction between him and Tanya had been about the knots. The design. Warm, but not erotic.

With Piper, he was deliberately arousing her with every touch. When he adjusted the rope on her breasts, he caressed and teased her nipples. As he moved her hair to run a rope down her back, he kissed the exposed curve of her neck. This was sensual bondage, each movement, each knot, each slide of the rope made to heighten her arousal.

And oh God, it worked. She could feel the wetness of her pussy, the tight swelling of her clit.

Standing behind her, Sir Ethan cupped her breasts, his thick cock pressed against her ass as he spoke to the young Tops. "This is the chest harness I demonstrated on stage. At this point, rather than tying off the rope around her waist, I'll restrain her in a convenient position for my use."

She tensed the slightest amount.

He bent, his cheek against hers. "Give me a color, sweetheart. I can stop if you need."

The knowledge that he was so aware of her body, so cognizant of her worries, made her lean back against him. She rubbed her cheek against his, her heart full to overflowing. "Green, Sir. I'm all right, Sir."

"I'm proud of you, poppet," he murmured, then spoke in a normal voice. "Kneel, please."

He gripped her upper arms as she knelt on wobbly legs. His leg was against her shoulder as he stroked her hair, keeping her tied to him with more than rope. "A standard frog tie will restrain each calf against each thigh. An additional rope above and below her knees will add stability to the upper tie."

Down on one knee beside her, he started to wind rope down her legs. Meticulously, knot by knot. Each breath brought her his clean masculine scent. His smoky sonorous voice was a low murmur in her ears.

Flames licked over her skin with each press of the rope, each glide of the strands. Even as the heat increased, the ropes—*his* ropes—enclosed her in a seductive cocoon. Her mind slowed, each thought drifting past like a leaf on a slow river.

He positioned her on her side, bent her right leg, and tied her calf against her thigh. His hand stroked up her inner leg, teased her pussy, then he rolled her over and tied the left leg to match the right.

"That's pretty incapacitating," one man commented.

"Having the extra rope around her knees lets me do this." Moving her as if she were a doll, his hands warm and careful, Sir Ethan tied a rope, securing her knees partway to her chest.

She really would be unable to move, and she didn't care. Everything inside her wanted more—more touches, more stroking. His cock.

He turned her, so her head was down with her shoulders and cheek pressed against the rough fabric of the blanket. Her arms were behind her back. Rather than her knees secured against her chest, ropes held her knees perpendicular to her torso, putting her butt high in the air and also letting him push her thighs widely apart to expose her ass and pussy.

A shiver of need ran through her.

"Any questions?" he asked the four people.

"No, I think we can follow that. Thank you very much," one said. The rest murmured their appreciation, and she could hear them moving away.

"You look very pretty like that, poppet." Sir Ethan skimmed a fingertip along the rope around her waist. Just that single touch focused her attention right there, making everything inside her melt.

Her eyes closed, each breath slower, as she savored his nearness and waited for him to release her.

Instead, she heard a zipper. The crinkling of a condom packet. He knelt behind her. "It would be a shame to waste all this hard work, don't you think?"

Her words were gone, but her body shouted yes.

Moving her knees even farther apart, he settled between them. She could feel the fabric of his jeans against her bare inner thighs.

He was dressed. She was naked. He was free. She was restrained...and in a way that gave him unobstructed access. He could touch her wherever he wanted, and she couldn't even move her hands.

He had all the power—and it made her want him all the more.

Leisurely, using one finger, he explored her pussy, stroking the crevices, fingering her clit, moving the hood up and down. Invading her entrance. Rubbing the small space between it and her asshole.

All her focus narrowed to the slow slide of his fingers as her pussy swelled and ached with need.

"Hmm. The arse-up position always reminds me that there are two holes conveniently available," he mused.

What did that mean? She braced for him to take her, wiggling slightly in anticipation.

Instead, his strong hands parted her buttocks.

She jerked in shock. "Wait, wait." Ugly memories threatened to overwhelm her, but even as she pushed them away, she realized nothing was happening.

He'd stopped. This was Sir Ethan. He wouldn't hurt her. Stroking her back gently, he waited.

She sighed. "Okay."

"Breathe, poppet."

Even as she took the ordered breath, cool lube drenched her asshole.

He paused again, cleared his throat.

Right, right. She inhaled.

"Good girl." Something cool and smooth pressed against her back hole, and he firmly penetrated her with a slender anal plug.

She squeaked at the hot stretching of unfamiliar muscles, the ruthless possession of that very private part of her body. Panting, she struggled against the ropes that bound her arms behind her back, the ropes that kept her bottom so high in the air. So vulnerable.

The feeling of him simply taking her over ran through her, like a high-speed elevator going down.

"Still all right?" he asked gently. His big hands massaged her buttocks. Owning her. "Give me a color."

Red. No, yellow. Despite the shivers that ran through her, she wasn't panicking. Wasn't hurting. "Green. I think, green."

His chuckle stroked over every nerve in her body. "There's no hurry. Take some time to decide." And he resumed playing with her pussy.

Her asshole throbbed, zinging with awakened nerves as he teased her clit, driving her closer and closer to coming, until she was shaking with need. A whine escaped.

"Still green?" His voice held laughter.

Damn Dom. "Green."

"Good enough." He slickened the head of his cock in her wetness and started to push inside.

She whimpered as the anal plug and his thickness stretched her to an almost unbearable tightness. Too full. Her pulse pounded around the intrusions, and she squirmed helplessly.

As he continued his inexorable possession, the ropes seemed to tighten around her. She could do nothing. She was completely under his control, his power. *His.*

Then he was in, a solid, intimate, heady presence inside her. Leaning forward, he kissed her nape, cupping her breasts, sending dark hunger through her.

Even as the walls of her vagina throbbed around him, he began, increasing in speed and power until she could feel the jolt of each driving thrust deep in her core. Taking her hard as he'd promised.

"I like this position for you, poppet." His fingers teased her nipples, tugging, pinching to a mind-spinning pain. "Everything is in reach—and you can't interfere."

When he reached around to play with her clit, his thrusts never slowing, glorious pleasure rushed through her...sending her closer and closer. Anxiety flared, and she fought against coming. It was too much. She'd lose everything if she came. Restrained and coming, he'd have her completely in his power, in his control.

"Piper." His hand flattened on her pussy. His thrusts halted. The pause was long. Alarming. "Can't you trust me, poppet?"

She was panting, excited, scared, and...yes. Yes, she trusted him. For restraints. For orgasms. For both together. Her eyes closed, her muscles relaxed, and she...surrendered.

"There we go." He smoothed one hand over her back, even as his other slid through her wetness, rubbed over her clit, demanding a response. His cock filled her, jarring the sensitive asshole nerves with every thrust, tightening her clit, and the excitement grew inside her, the need filling her until her whole lower half quivered on the brink.

He slowed, his touch lightening, drawing it out, and she could hear her whimpers.

"Nice, very nice. Let's come together, shall we?" He hammered into her, short and fast, even as his finger rubbed directly over her clit, slick and demanding and impossible to deny. The pressure grew, grew inside her until her whole body balanced on the precipice.

And fell. Wave after wave of sensation roared through her, even as his grip on her hip tightened, as his cock thickened and jerked. He came, sending more spasms through her. More and more. The blanket, the ground, the world disappeared.

Even as she lost herself, she knew she was safe, cradled within his ropes and his care.

Two hours later, having cleaned up and rejoined the Dark Haven people around a different fire pit, Ethan stroked Piper's silky hair. Her head was pillowed on his thigh, and she looked as contented as he felt. His mind was quiet—Shibari was an active form of meditation for him—and his body was replete with what had followed.

As a Dom, he was gratified with the trust Piper had given him. It had been a joy to see her in his ropes, see her fall into subspace. To have her trust him with all of her body.

Smiling, he looked around. Stan and Dixon were on a blanket to their left. To their right were Lindsey and deVries.

"Hey, subbie-gang, it's time to make Dom-treats." Never quiet for long, Dixon jumped to his feet. Yelping, he clutched his crotch. His Master got a glare. "I swear, Sir, I think that stuff burned all the skin off my dick."

"Stan." DeVries rubbed his chin. "I've got a rubber barbed wire flogger that'd remove whatever skin is left."

"Hey!" Dixon pointed to Lindsey. "Girl, you just sit your patootie right back down. That sadist of yours isn't getting any Dom treats."

Laughing, Lindsey tilted her face up for a kiss from deVries, which he gave immediately.

Ethan smiled. Finding Lindsey had changed the bitter ex-mercenary. He'd always be a sadist, but he was more open, more comfortable with people. Submissives had far more power than they realized.

Piper yawned and sat up. "Sir. May I have permission to fetch some Dom-treats—whatever they are?"

"Permission granted." Ethan pulled her against him, savored her soft mouth, and released her.

Dixon pulled her to her feet.

When Lindsey joined them, Dixon frowned at the brunette. "Girl, what did I say?"

"Dix, do you really want to spend the evening with a cranky sadist?" Piper asked. "Give him treats and keep him calm."

"Ooooh, good point." Dixon dodged the swat Lindsey aimed at his head, and the three headed for the closest fire pit.

"What the hell are Dom treats?" Stan took a sip of his beer.

"That's right, you haven't been here before." Leaning back on his elbows, Ethan tilted his head up. The moon was full, beautiful in the black night sky. "The serving table has graham crackers, chocolate squares, and marshmallows, the ingredients for s'mores."

"Well, damn." Stan grinned. "I haven't had those since fishing with my pa in Texas."

Ethan had first tried s'mores on a camping trip with Xavier and his previous wife soon after coming to the States. He smiled. Xavier's first and second wives were very different, but Abby was a perfect fit for the man he was now.

Ethan's gaze settled on Piper who was roasting a marshmallow over the fire pit. The sound of her laughter was one of the most beautiful things he'd ever heard.

"There they are." Rona's voice came from the right. She and Simon, then Xavier and Abby claimed blankets near the group.

By the time everyone had exchanged greetings and a few stories, Piper and her crew returned. Carefree and in high spirits. Damn, he liked seeing her like this.

She went to her knees in front of him. "Might this slave give her Master a treat?"

Touching her cheek, he murmured, "Only if you rephrase the question to use first person and Dom."

She blinked and paled, not having realized what she'd said.

In all reality, he didn't find the phrasing offensive, but for her mental health, leaving the slave mentality behind would be best.

Closing her eyes, she pulled in a breath and whispered. "I'm not a slave." When she opened her eyes, she smiled at him. "Thank you. May I give my most favorite Dom in the whole world a treat?"

"That works nicely." Worked more than nicely, actually.

"Prepared with her own two hands, it was," Dixon called.

Ethan bent to kiss her soft lips and tasted marshmallow and chocolate. "I see you enjoyed some treats while you were cooking?"

"Well..." Her lips tipped up at the corners. "I had to taste-test to ensure everything was worthy of my Sir, of course. I've heard baronets are really fussy."

"They totally are," he said agreeably and took a bite of his worthy treat. The golden marshmallow and softened chocolate square were sandwiched between two graham crackers. He'd forgotten how delicious the meld of flavors was. He finished the crunchy, gooey sandwich in a few bites. "Thank you, poppet, that was excellent."

Her eyes lit with the pleasure of a service submissive being complimented by her Dom. It melted his heart.

Without thinking, he tucked her in the curve of his arm, up against his side. Where she belonged.

"Your girl picked up club protocols damn fast." DeVries studied Piper, obviously having heard her refer to herself in the third person. "She even knew the *present* position. Has she had training?"

Ethan started to respond, then stopped. Conversations in the evening were informal, so she could answer for herself. In his opinion, it was time for her to share more of her past, but he'd leave it up to her.

At the question, Piper felt her palms go clammy. Despite Sir Ethan's reassuring arm around her, the world seemed to shake.

DeVries, whom everyone called the Enforcer, waited for Sir Ethan to reply.

Instead, Sir Ethan lifted an eyebrow at her, dumping the response square in her lap. Damn him. Even so, if he'd answered for her, she'd have hated that, too.

"I, uh, had some training. Years ago." She rubbed her hands on her jeans.

Simon looked at her. "Back in Kansas?"

Of course he knew she was from Kansas. He'd done the Dark Haven background check. *I don't want to think about Kansas. About then.* "Um. Yes."

Xavier was stretched out on his side, nibbling on Abby's fingers as she leaned into the curve of his body. He propped himself up on an elbow to study her. "How long were you in an M/s relationship?"

"How did you know?" She turned an accusatory glare at Sir Ethan who must've spilled everything about her past to everyone.

"I didn't," Xavier said, amused. "I do now."

Her reaction had confirmed his guess.

"Sorry," she whispered to Sir Ethan.

He tugged her hair in a tiny reprimand, then moved her into the space between his opened legs so her back rested against his chest. His arms crossed under her breasts, holding her to him. Safety and comfort. Then she realized he'd also trapped her into facing the rest of the group.

Xavier cleared his throat in a warning. Submissives weren't supposed to be slow in replying.

"Two years," she muttered.

"Was that kind of power exchange—slave and Master—not to your taste?" Simon asked. Snuggled against his side, Rona gave Piper a concerned look.

"No. I didn't like the Master/slave dynamic." Keeping her answer as short as possible, Piper set her jaw. That time in Kansas was past. Done with. Not to be thought about. Ever.

Except Xavier, Simon, and deVries were now eyeing her thoughtfully.

"Were you the only slave in the household? Was that part of the problem?" Simon asked. "Having a Master who wanted another slave?"

Even as she stiffened at the question, she saw Dix also react. But he turned to look at his Dom in dismay. Then he slid back, leaving a good twelve inches between him and Stan. Stan turned to frown at him.

Oh, no. Had Dix seen creepy Darrell's behavior during the game? Did he think Stan wanted two slaves?

Her mouth went tight. Bad enough the questions bothered

her, but if talking about polyamory was upsetting Dix... Well, she wouldn't have it.

She forced a light tone into her voice. "No that wasn't the problem. Can we talk about something more fun?" Not waiting for agreement, she added, "Campfire stories are an old tradition, and I'd love to hear how Dixon and Stan met."

Maybe it would remind the two of how much they loved each other.

Pressed against Sir Ethan's chest, she could feel him laugh. "Nice way to change the subject, subbie," he murmured for her ears only. "But you won't escape answering forever."

Yes, yes, she would.

DeVries snorted. "How they met is Tex's story, although she turns green when she thinks about it."

"What?" Piper blinked. Her curiosity was huge, but green didn't sound good. She shook her head at Lindsey. "You don't have to share if you—"

"It's okay." Lindsey gave deVries a good frown, then half-smiled at Piper. Her Texas accent was thicker than normal as she said, "My ex-husband was involved with human trafficking and gun smuggling over the border. I found out, and he died, but it was horrible, and I'd need a lot more alcohol and time to talk about that day."

Piper stared. A criminal ex? She wanted to grab Lindsey up in a hug. At the same time, she was dying to hear the whole story. *Bad, snoopy Piper.* "Really, I don't need to know—"

"We'll talk about it one of these days. Anyway, his partners framed me for his murder, and I ran to San Francisco to hide, but they came after me. Dark Haven was partying at a wilderness lodge near Yosemite, and Simon called in Stan—Mr. Homeland Security criminal investigator." She grinned. "Dixon's first impression of him wasn't good."

"Apparently, I looked menacing. He jumped in front of Lindsey to protect her." Stan smiled, grabbed Dix's hair, and yanked his submissive into his lap.

Dixon squeaked and went silent as the hand in his hair tightened.

"That right there told me I wanted to know him better." Stan ran his knuckles over Dix's cheek while keeping him from moving. Apparently, the Master was finished with having Dix give him the cold shoulder.

Eyes closed, Dix stayed silent.

Piper's heart ached for him. For them both. How could she help?

But she'd learned that interfering in a relationship rarely worked out well for anyone. *Dammit.* Her fingernails must have dug into Sir Ethan's forearms because he gave her a firm squeeze, bringing her back to the present.

Leaning back against him, she could feel the slow rise and fall of his chest. Occasionally, he'd lower his head to brush his cheek against hers or rub his chin on the top of her head. Being in his arms like this, the recipient of his open affection was wonderful. Overwhelming.

Tears welled up because she loved being here. Belonging to him.

And because *this* was what she'd thought BDSM would be like. What Dominants would be like. Blinking back the tears, she looked around. Dixon—being cuddled in spite of his withdrawal. Lindsey—pressed up against deVries who had his arm around her and was playing with her fingers. Abby—lying down, her head on Xavier's thigh. Rona—sitting beside Simon, a blanket over their knees, sipping from the same wine glass.

There were good Doms in the world.

BDSM could actually be fun. Like today with that crazy, embarrassing water gun game. Orgasming in public. No one had tried to humiliate her. Even the switching she'd gotten had been more for fun and sexiness than real punishment. The whole game had been a way to share a submissive with other Tops without any actual touching.

Sex didn't have to hurt.

And restraints could be more than a way to hurt someone. Earlier, Sir Ethan had bound her body and, with every knot, had also tied her feelings to him. He'd positioned and used her for his own pleasure. Demanding it in the way of a Dom. Somehow, it had been everything she wanted.

Afterward, he'd shown her the real meaning of aftercare.

As he cuddled her in his lap, when people stopped to talk, he'd told them *later*, as if holding her had been the only thing he wanted to do. He'd shown no urgency, no sense of impatience. Arms around her, he'd stroked her bare skin and told her how much she'd pleased him.

Looking down, she noticed how she'd curled her fingers around his forearms. Needing to touch him.

Wasn't it funny how the tie between her and the Defiler had started with potential and ended up as a single strand—that of fear. Even her service had been performed out of dread.

With Sir Ethan, the ties between them kept multiplying, weaving into a thick rope. Giving and receiving pleasure in mutual joy. Submitting and serving. Being appreciated, protected, cared for. Laughing together. Sharing meals and conversations.

Now she had this, too—the way he openly kissed her and cuddled her when he was with his friends, showing he was pleased to be with her.

The bond between them kept growing, and how could she keep from worrying? Did she want to risk being tied to another man again? A Dominant?

Even worse, she could feel another strand weaving itself into the rope...a strand of love.

Last time, she'd signed away everything—her freedom, her body, her life. She'd learned her lesson.

Sir Ethan surely wasn't anything like the Defiler, but she was going to take her time.

CHAPTER SIXTEEN

In the kitchen at Ethan's house, Piper took a moment to get her thoughts together. Over the last two weeks, she'd steadily lost ground in the attempt to keep her emotions under control.

And she'd tried really hard.

Well, okay, indulging in too much wine while watching the Fourth of July fireworks from Ethan's rooftop hadn't been a good idea. She'd almost blurted out the lethal *I-love-you* phrase that night. But, honestly, she was only human. Sex and alcohol and Sir Ethan in Dom mode. No one could resist that combination.

She huffed a laugh. Face it, keeping things on an even, cool level was just plain difficult. It was almost trickier with other people around—like when they went out to eat with Simon, Rona, Lindsey, and deVries. It'd been a great night—and she was finally...mostly...comfortable around Sir Ethan's Dom friends.

Simon and deVries had reported that, when they'd visited Jerry in his hotel, he'd been packed to leave. Realizing who they were, Jerry'd actually burst into tears, still traumatized over what she and Ethan had done to him. It was appalling how satisfied she'd felt at hearing that. Everyone had grinned, and Ethan had fist-bumped her. When deVries complained about not having an excuse to beat Jerry up, the laughter had cleansed the room.

So that was done.

Opening the fridge, she glanced at the labeled dishes left by the chef. Curried turkey casserole sounded good. She popped two servings into the oven.

Picking a meal wasn't hard. If only it were as easy to decide how she felt about Ethan. Instead, her feelings were as erratic as...as the San Francisco weather had been. People here expected their mid-July weather to stay in the 60s, not climb to an appallingly sunny 85 degrees, then plummet. She glanced out the window at the fog closing in, blurring the world.

That was her relationship. Confusing. Foggy. Occasional spikes of heat. It could be she was going crazy.

A furry body twined around her ankles, making her jump. "You smelled the turkey, didn't you?"

Churchill gave a plaintive meow, trying to convince her he was wasting away to skin and bones.

"Uh-huh. It's obvious you haven't eaten for weeks." The pudgy cat was probably closing in on twenty pounds.

But his big blue eyes were so pleading. So effective. "Don't tell Ethan, okay?" She dropped a few kitty treats onto the floor.

Purr, purr, purr.

"We're a lot alike, cat." All her life she'd felt starved for love, and now, with Ethan's open affection, she couldn't seem to find her balance. She sure didn't want to act as needy as Churchill did with his kitty treats.

In the living room, she heard footsteps, indicating Ethan had finished his post-workout shower.

"Do you need help, Piper?" he called.

"Nothing to do. We can eat in half-an-hour or so." Oh God, didn't that sound so domestic? How in the world had she ended up practically living here?

She'd noticed the chef, who came in weekly, was now preparing food for two rather than one—and she hadn't been the one to make that change. She had to admit she really enjoyed having food prepared and ready to pop into the microwave or oven. Making meals was boring, which was why she had a long list of take-out/delivery places in her phone.

Baking—and giving the goodies away—was her thing. She glanced at the berry tartlets on a covered platter and smiled.

Although, she had to admit, mixing drinks for a gorgeous Dom came in a close second. She carried out Ethan's gin and tonic along with her rum and coke, then stopped to look at him.

He was stretched out on the couch, his back against the armrest, feet on cushions. Comfortable and drop-dead sexy, like Hollywood's idea of a pirate—sharp blue eyes in a tanned face, brown hair still wet from his shower. Dark mustache and thick stubble-beard. Bare-footed, he was in his usual evening-at-home attire of black drawstring pants and a loose sleeveless shirt that revealed his stilled pumped-up muscles.

What was there about his biceps that made her want to bite into the hard curve?

Laughter glinted in his gaze; he could read her like a book. Damn Dom.

She huffed in embarrassed exasperation. "I'm not going to jump you."

"Now, that's a pity. I wouldn't protest, you know." He wouldn't. Unless they were observing stricter protocols and she wasn't supposed to touch without permission, he liked when she made advances. Of course, that moment of control lasted only a second before he took over. Even when they were "playing" he never lost that air of command.

Shaking her head, she handed him his gin and tonic.

"Thank you, poppet." He sipped, and his appreciative "very nice" sent a glow through her. Doing anything for him, especially when he showed his approval, dropped her right into service-subbie space. Not the fluffy chemical stew of subspace obtained from impact or rope play, but a happy quietude. A blanket of contentment in a beautifully silent world.

Sipping her own drink, she sank down into a chair.

"You look like you had a good day," he observed.

"I did. Chatelaines has two more new clients, both from Dark Haven." She frowned. "Actually, I'm not sure more clients is a good thing."

"You lost me. Why?"

"Having ample money coming in is rewarding, of course, but if the business continues to grow, I'll have to hire managers."

"Considering the hours you work, I'd say you've reached that point already."

"I know, but"—she gave him a rueful smile—"I like being hands-on and knowing my clients are getting the best service. Managers might not be as fussy as I am."

"No one is as careful as the owner," he agreed. "But if you don't expand, you'll cap your profit."

"I know." She shrugged. "As long as I have enough for the basics and some fun, I don't need more."

His eyebrows lifted.

"I know, I know. Being content with less is sacrilege to you rich people."

"You have no respect at all, do you?" His chuckle showed he wasn't offended.

A meow drew her attention. Beside the couch, Churchill stared up at Ethan, butt wiggling slightly. Picking a landing spot.

"Your Prime Minister wants a lap." Piper picked him up, took herself a cuddle, and set the hefty feline on Ethan's stomach.

The Dom made an oomphing sound, although there was no way the cat could dent those rock-hard abs. He stroked the cat. "I think you've gained a couple of pounds, Church. We're both going to be in trouble with the vet."

Frowning, he squeezed the cat's rounded belly. "I get the feeling someone has been giving in to your begging."

Uh-oh. He'd warned her last week that if he caught her slipping food to the cat again, he'd spank her. Her stomach sank as his gaze turned stern. "How many treats did you give him since you got home today?"

She lifted her chin. "None. I haven't been *home*."

"Piper." The very quietness of the single word held more menace than loud ranting.

"Six. I gave him six treats just now in the kitchen."

Sitting up, he set Churchill on the floor and beckoned to Piper with two fingers. *Come here.*

No, no, no. Yet, somehow, her body stood her up and took her the two steps to the couch. He gripped her hand and guided her to a stomach-down, ass-high position over his knees.

Her hands were on the carpet, her feet on the other side of his legs.

"Don't move from there." His English accent was brusque, showing his displeasure. "Was I less than clear about the consequences of feeding the cat?"

He'd been very clear. She had no excuse other than being a sucker for furbabies. "No, Sir."

"Very good. I will not require you to count for me, since even I can count to six."

Punishment got no warm-up, no sexy fondling before his hard hand slapped her bottom. Her lightweight cotton pants provided no cushion, and the blow stung like fire. She sucked in a breath, bowed her head, and gritted her teeth.

The spanking continued without pauses. *Two. Three. Four. Five. Six.*

He had a merciless hand, but at least it was over quickly. Tears burned in her eyes, but she hadn't cried, and—more importantly—hadn't tried to fight or cover her butt. She hadn't moved.

Now, she tried to sit up.

He set a hand in the middle of her back, pinning her against his legs. His other hand massaged her burning bottom. "Why did I spank you, poppet?"

"I-I fed Churchill treats that he's not supposed to get."

"Is spanking an effective deterrent? Do you think you can keep from indulging him in the future?"

"I won't do it again."

"Good enough." He helped her sit up and, despite her efforts to pull away, settled her on his lap.

His thighs were all hard muscle, and her butt *hurt*. She sat stiffly, in no mood to cuddle. Or do anything else with him. The jerk.

Ignoring her resistance, he pulled her against his chest and sighed. "I know some Doms, especially sadists, enjoy punishing their submissives. I don't. Mixing sex and pain in an erotic context is fun. I don't like simply hurting someone."

I don't care. Her jaw was clenched so hard it ached.

Her hand was clenched just as tightly. He pried it open and put a kiss on her palm.

"Don't try to be nice to me. It won't work," she gritted out.

"No?" He ran his hand up and down her rigid back muscles. "You're angry because you were punished. Do you feel I overstepped my bounds?"

"Yes." Or no. Maybe? "I don't know."

"Actually, I did want to talk to you tonight. It's past time," he murmured.

Talk to her. A shard of ice penetrated her heart. *No. Oh no.* He was going to break things off. She'd known this would happen, knew she wasn't good enough for him. But, already?

More tears stung her eyes from a different pain, this time in her heart. She set her hands against his chest and pushed herself back. Tried to stand. "I-I'll get my stuff."

"You'll do what?" Hands on her upper arms, he held her far enough away that he could see her face. His eyes sharpened. "Sweetheart, whatever you're thinking, it's wrong."

"You want me to leave. I get it; we're done."

"We're nowhere near being done." He cupped her face, brushing the tears away with his thumb. "I merely want to discuss the boundaries in our relationship."

She stared into his face, seeing affection. More—actual caring and concern.

"Relationship?" When his gaze trapped hers, she felt her equilibrium go askew.

"Yes, poppet. This is a relationship." His tone was amused, but lifting her chin, he kissed her firmly. Seriously.

She breathed out. He wasn't pushing her away. "Relationship," she said again.

"Yes. In case you haven't noticed, we have a romantic relationship." He stroked her hair back from her face. "But we're also in a D/s one—and that dynamic needs clarification."

Enlightenment broke over her. The spanking. He'd been talking about boundaries.

On the weekends when they were working on her fears, they had certain limits. But this wasn't the weekend. She straightened her shoulders. "I'm not a slave." *Please, don't let him want a slave.* He'd said once he didn't...

"There we go. A good start." A crease appeared in his cheek. "I'm not interested in a total power exchange where I think I own you. I am a Dom, however." He paused. Lifted an eyebrow.

When she didn't speak, he tapped her chin with a finger. "This, poppet, is a negotiation. You have to contribute."

Yes, he was right. *Okay.* He was a Dom. Did she consider herself submissive? Want to do the D/s stuff as his submissive? And how stupid was she to even think that she didn't? Of *course*, she was submissive. She dug deep, pulling up the honesty that he'd demand. "I like when you take control."

"Now we're making progress. Not ownership, but authority is good." His perceptive eyes stayed on her face. "All the time?"

"No." She swallowed. Was he going to be angry? Or disappointed? The thought of disappointing him twisted her emotions into a tangled mess. "I'm submissive. We both know that. But I'm also the owner of a business, have friends, things I do—stuff where I don't want to be answerable to you."

"Very good." His eyes warmed with approval. "Agreed.

Neither of us wants Master/slave or 24/7 Dominant/submissive. So the next question is *when*. I think we both enjoy D/s in the bedroom."

Her cheeks heated because he knew all too well how much she enjoyed being dominated during sex. "Yes."

"I don't care what you wear or eat or do during the day." He brushed his knuckles over her cheek. "I *will* want to select your clothing for the club or for any activity associated with kink."

The constriction around her chest was loosening. She'd panicked because she'd screwed this stuff up so badly the first time, simply handing over everything. "Okay. Yes."

Days were hers; sex was his. That left quite a few hours unaccounted for. "What about the evenings like now or weekends—or when we're just together? Restaurants and events?"

"Now, that's the question," he said softly. His gaze held hers. "How much control do you want during non-sex time, poppet? If I tell you not to feed the cat and you do, is that a D/s infraction or a romantic relationship one?

He wasn't a heavy-handed Dom.

When her lips quirked, his chin rose slightly, telling her he wanted her to share that thought. She flushed. "I was thinking you weren't a heavy-handed Dom, but my butt sure hurts."

His grin appeared and disappeared so quickly that only her heightened heart rate was evidence of its existence.

She spoke more slowly, trying to untangle her thoughts. "You don't have a lot of rules and rituals, and I like that, but if I mess up, I like that you don't blow it off, either." Because that would feel as if he didn't really care.

She sighed, knowing she was consigning herself to more spankings. "And I like that you don't let me go unpunished."

When he'd disciplined her, it felt like he was involved enough in what was between them, in his own rules and regulations, to take the time and effort to enforce them. Not because he liked hurting her, but because the dynamic of their relationship was as important to him as it was to her.

She loved serving him, loved that he required it, loved that he noticed what she did, good or bad, and gave her praise or disapproval accordingly. "It seems like we fall into a kind of power exchange most of the time."

His lips twitched. "You noticed that, did you?"

She hadn't at first, but then she'd realized how she felt more comfortable leaving decisions up to him—although she'd speak up if she didn't agree. He picked up if something bothered her, often before she realized it. What they did on Saturdays was the way they interacted with each other most of the time. Even when they simply watched television, she felt as if she was under his authority.

And he did become more...forceful...in the bedroom. To her great pleasure.

"All right, let's try this," he said. "At home or where it's appropriate—as when we're at Dark Haven or BDSM parties—we observe the power dynamic. Anywhere vanilla, we don't."

"Yes, Sir." She curled against him, her cheek against his chest. He had that wonderful fresh-from-the-shower scent.

"Since you have now handed over control during the evening hours," he paused, deliberately torturing her with anticipation, "each night, you will take fifteen minutes and write out your thoughts on how this is working. How you feel. Where I'm not meeting your needs. Resentments. What you like or don't like."

That...wasn't what she'd thought was coming. Journaling?

From the amused glint in his eyes, she knew she was pouting. She heaved a massive unhappy sigh to accompany the pout. In case he had any doubts about her enthusiasm for his project. "Yes, Sir."

He snorted. "The attitude nets you an extra fifteen minutes tonight, pet."

She barely kept from growling at him, yet pleasure was a lovely ball pulsing inside her. Because he hadn't let her get away with it. Because there was a comfort in knowing the limits and being forced to live up to them. He'd told her once that a fence could be seen as a prison—or as the protection that kept wild animals out of the backyard.

To her, his rules felt like a wall of protection.

He ran his finger down her cheek. "I will be reading your notes, poppet. I'd especially like you to use them to bring up topics you're uncomfortable discussing. I might well write in it, too."

They sat like that for a while—and there was nothing more wonderful than being held.

When the oven timer dinged, they got the food onto the table, and he poured them both some wine. Sometimes he let her do the work and serve him; more often, they worked together as partners.

It was always his choice.

As they ate—with Churchill under the table in hopes of dropped food—Sir Ethan smiled at her. "We'd been talking about your new clients before your spanking interrupted us. I wanted to tell you there are ways to grow a business without sacrificing quality. We can go over some methods if you like."

He was always willing to coach her in business management, finances, or anything else she wanted to learn. Even better, he was never patronizing. He respected her, even if her company was a million times smaller than his conglomerate. "I'd like that, Sir."

"Good. I have a book you might like. I'll get it for you tonight." He rubbed his neck.

She eyed him. "You look tired. Did someone beat you up at the gym? Were you boxing?"

"No to being beaten up. Yes to boxing." His brows drew together. "The tiredness comes from a day spent inspecting one of the manufacturing plants. Their accident rate went up this year without any apparent reason, according to management. I spent the day talking with the workers to see if that was true."

"Did you figure out the cause of the accidents?"

"I did." His eyes turned hard as steel. "Which is why I fired the occupational safety professional and one of the VPs."

"They were cutting corners?"

"Yes. Profiting at the expense of their people." His mouth thinned. "Arseholes."

Of course he was displeased. He was as protective of his employees as he was of submissives. Aristocrat or not, he was incredibly easy to talk to. His laborers had probably shared every single problem.

He must have been talking and on his feet all day. Maybe she should give him a back massage. No, she knew where that would lead, and it sure wasn't rest.

But there were other options.

After they finished eating and returned to the living room, she got lotion from the bathroom. Settling at the other end of the couch, she started massaging his bare left foot.

His sigh of pleasure made her smile. "Piper, you need to stop that"—she froze—"sometime next year."

"Very funny, Sir." She ran her thumbs across the bottom arch of his right foot, pressing firmly. It was wonderful how massaging the knot out of foot muscles could relax everything else.

By the time she finished, he still looked tired, but the signs of stress had disappeared.

At least until his cell phone rang. Darn it.

He picked the phone off the ottoman and checked the display. "Xavier, what's up?"

From the phone came the deep voice of Dark Haven's owner.

No rest for the wicked, hmm? Piper went into the kitchen to fix more drinks and get the berry tartlets she'd baked.

When she set the plate on the ottoman, Churchill lifted his head, ears swiveling in interest.

"Behave, PM," she warned. She and Churchill had differing opinions on where the boundaries lay. The PM respected that tables and counters were human owned and off limits. Piper agreed that any food landing on the floor had hit feline country.

Ottomans and coffee tables however... Diplomatic discussions were ongoing over those territorial boundaries.

Ethan was still on the phone. "I'll talk to human resources and see if they can find something suitable." After a second, he added, "Not a problem. I'll give you a call tomorrow." He ended the call and laid the cell down.

"Problems?" Piper picked up tartlet and took a bite.

"Xavier asked me to hire a woman. She has an arrest record and is getting turned down for jobs. Rona and Xavier both vouch for her. Apparently, she's highly motivated, even beyond the fact she needs a job to get her child back."

That sounded unusual. "Is she a friend of Xavier's?"

"No, the request is through Rona. As a hospital admin, she occasionally runs across abuse survivors and will send them to Stella's for help with job-hunting."

Piper choked. "Stella's?"

"It's a nonprofit company of Xavier's to help women who were abused to find jobs." Ethan shook his head, his eyes sad. "He named it after his mum who died at the hands of his father."

"Xavier owns Stella's," Piper said slowly.

"You know it?"

All too well. "I...um, some of our Chatelaines' contractors hire through them."

His gaze was far too focused, and Piper concentrated on selecting another small tartlet.

Swinging his feet down, dislodging the cat, he stole her pastry right out of her hand. Popping it into his mouth, he pulled Piper onto the couch beside him.

"*Hey*." She frowned at him.

"Very tasty, pet." He didn't let her go. One arm around her shoulders kept her from moving away. His other hand turned her face toward him. "Now tell me why Stella's makes you uncomfortable. And evasive."

Her jaw clenched. "Why do you have to go digging at everything?"

"It's a Dom trait, poppet." He gave her a half-chiding, half-affectionate squeeze. "Answer me, please."

"It...it's nothing important. I'm not uncomfortable." She totally was. "As it happens, Stella's helped me when I first got to San Francisco."

"Ah, I hadn't thought about that." He frowned. "How long did you stay at the shelter in Wichita?"

He knew that? She stared at him. Had he checked on her after hinting she could escape her slavery?

Oh, he totally had.

"I stayed only long enough to get patched up. I was eager"—*hysterical, panicking*—"to get out of the area." *Out of the Defiler's* reach. "A shelter employee was leaving for San Francisco to see her grandchildren and agreed I could go with her. She liked me because I looked like her daughter. She tucked me into the backseat, and by the time we got here, the Wichita shelter had everything set up with a shelter here. Then later, I got sent to Stella's to find a job."

Her eyes burned with tears. "Everyone was amazing."

Ethan cuddled her closer, remembering back to when he'd first set eyes on her in Kansas. He'd seen her spirit hadn't been crushed as Serna had undoubtedly hoped. But the wounds from that time were not yet healed. "I'm sorry you had an abusive bastard masquerading as a Master."

Her shoulders hunched. "I put my signature on that contract of my own free will."

"I doubt you realized what was going to happen. If you were new to the lifestyle, how did you meet Serna anyway?"

She stiffened at the arsehole's name. Withdrawing, mentally and physically.

Bloody hell. "How can I help you if you can't even talk about your time with him?" Or even hear his name?

"I'm past all that." She rose so hastily she tripped over the ottoman. Turning, she scowled at him. "Rubbing at a scab leads to scars, not healing."

"Piper."

"I don't want to talk about it." She wrapped her arms around her waist. "If you'll excuse me, I need a shower." Her face was white, mouth in a tight line. She held herself as if she still felt the pain of an abused body.

As she disappeared into the stairway up to the bedroom and master bath, he didn't follow. Pushing right now would be counterproductive. She needed to know a Dom would respect her limits; however, he wasn't going to give up either. How could he help if she wouldn't talk?

After draining his drink, he picked Churchill up. "She's a stubborn one, eh, PM?"

Unblinking blue eyes met Ethan's. The cat set a paw on his hand.

"You're right, of course. Patience is required."

Sooner or later, perhaps with a counselor, Piper needed to talk about her time with Serna. She still got caught in the loop of thinking she was worthless—and that would probably continue unless she exhumed, then excised the cause. Until then, remembering being a slave would be a form of torture for her.

Anger flared inside Ethan. That arsehole had really done a number on her.

Would facing Serna in person help Piper? Her memories had turned the bastard into a huge, undefeatable monster. Sometimes, viewed with older, wiser eyes, a bogeyman could be revealed as pathetic. Twisted and unstable...but human.

"Suggestions, Church?"

The cat rubbed his head against Ethan's chest while determinedly kneading his stomach.

"Provide ample affection along with teasing out some answers?" Ethan considered. "Good advice. Let's see where that goes."

Meantime, he'd go offer a nonjudgmental hug and let her

know her refusal was allowed. That she hadn't damaged what was between them.

Her shower had been a fast one. When he reached the master bedroom, she was standing in front of the big walk-in closet, staring at the door, something he'd seen her do more than once. Not any door—just the ones on closets.

His brows drew together. He'd noticed the closet in her apartment lacked a door, although the hinges remained. "Do you have a problem with closets?"

Squeaking in surprise, she spun to face him.

He kept his voice calm. Soothing. "Or is it the door itself that bothers you?"

"I'm fine."

She was ignoring his question. He studied the wooden door. It was a typical door. He opened it and flipped on the light. Shelves. Clothes on hangers.

No, look harder, Worth. He turned off the light. It was a big closet; not everyone had big closets. A smaller one would be... claustrophobic. Especially if a person couldn't get out. "Did Serna lock you in the closet?"

The way she flinched told him everything he needed to know.

"The filthy wanker." The fury simmering in his gut came out in his voice and didn't help at all. Abandoning words, he pulled her close, pleased beyond all measure when she came willingly.

No, more than that—she burrowed against him as if she'd found a safe haven.

Rubbing his cheek against her hair, he held her, and her trust in him filled him to overflowing.

Then, being his indomitable Piper, she chuckled. "Do baronets use words like wanker?"

"Probably only the ones who spent summer holidays working in their father's factories. I picked up a whole new vocabulary that way. I quite impressed the lads at the boarding school."

He gave a faint husky chuckle as she leaned into him.

As he held her, he studied the closet. His home—their home—should be a haven.

No matter how brave a subbie might be, she might need help eradicating monsters that lingered under the bed. Or in the closet.

That's why Doms were put on this earth.

CHAPTER SEVENTEEN

A week later, after her self-defense class, Piper had stopped by Alberta's apartment to feed and cuddle Archimedes. When Piper had first gotten to San Francisco, Alberta had been in the same shelter, along with her orange tabby—all that she'd brought from her old life. The two women became friends, cheered each other on as they struggled to create new lives. Poor Archimedes had been the recipient of more than one bout of tears.

Now Alberta was in London at a software developer convention, and Piper had her own business.

Since her friend's Richmond District apartment was near the Presidio, Piper was finishing the day by walking the Promenade Trail loop. Who could resist the spectacular views of the Bay and the Golden Gate Bridge? Smiling, she stopped to watch the dogs bounding into the water to retrieve balls. So much enthusiasm.

Summer afternoons in San Francisco had to be the most beautiful of times. The breeze off the Bay bit through the side of her sweat-soaked T-shirt, while the bright sun heated her back. If only the rest of her life was as sunny.

Oh, and doesn't that just sound pitiful? Her chuckle netted her interested looks from two male joggers. *No, guys, I'm not flirting.* She needed to stop laughing at her own mental commentary.

Nonetheless, she wasn't pitiful, and her life was sunny.

Work was great. Her clients kept referring her service to their friends—the very nicest kind of advertising. Taking Ethan's advice, she'd asked Rosalie if she'd like to move into management. Rosalie was completely onboard with the idea. And it meant Chatelaines was going to grow, which was both scary and exciting.

Socially? Along with her vanilla friends, she now had Dixon and Lindsey who'd pushed right into BFF status. Abby, too. Rona...Piper quite simply wanted to be Rona when she grew up.

Physically? She was better than ever, partly because Ethan's chef prepared meals with tons of vegetables. Partly because Ethan insisted she visit the gym regularly. Her bossy Dom had actually driven her there a couple of times. His concern worked; she felt great.

In fact... Smiling, she broke into a jog—so not her favorite thing—and maintained it for long, long minutes before dropping back to a fast walk. She wasn't even really out of breath. *Go, me!*

But, when it came to her relationship with Ethan, she was so damn confused. He'd called what they had a romantic relationship and a D/s one. The night after their talk about that, he'd said he expected them to be exclusive—no sex with anyone else. Her heart had done handstands when he said that applied to him as well as her.

Then he asked if she was ready to leave off using condoms?

Wow. Just wow. The feel of him without a condom was so, so different. Warmer and slicker and sexier. More intimate, somehow.

Was it normal for the slide into a "relationship" to have been so easy? So natural?

Admittedly, in some ways, they were very alike. Both of them were gregarious and liked to be out and about. He had SHN – Broadway season tickets—for two—so they'd been to plays and musicals. She'd been his date for a charity benefit where he served on the nonprofit's board, and they'd shared a table with Xavier and Abby. Ethan had repaid her by escorting her to a reception given by a cleaning company Chatelaines used and to a friend's engagement party. A few days ago, he'd had the chef make a special meal, and they'd had Simon and Rona over for dinner before they'd all gone to an art gallery showing given by another friend of hers. Between the four of them, they knew almost every person visiting the gallery.

As if to balance out the cultural overload, Ethan had dragged her to a soccer game and a boxing tournament where a friend of his was entered. God, she couldn't believe Ethan fought like that for fun. No wonder he was all hard muscle.

He really was. She licked her lips and broke into another jog.

Face it, he was simply fun to be with. It seemed he thought the same about her. He'd mentioned last night that he was getting out more because he enjoyed taking her places.

When he said things like that, it floored her. Sure, she was used to compliments from men, but they weren't Doms. Weren't *her* Dom.

She realized she was gasping and stumbled to a halt. *Idiot.* A person walking a poodle grinned at the way Piper was bent over, sucking in air. Yeah, this would look good on her gravestone: ***Piper Delaney. Thinking of a man, she had a heart attack.***

But her Ethan was a very special, amazing guy.

If he hadn't unraveled Jerry's bullshit, they wouldn't be together now. He had a lot more courage than she did. And more patience. He'd understood about her unwillingness to talk about her time as a slave, although she knew his patience wouldn't last forever.

Because he was a Dom.

God, she was so crazy. Stupid Piper had gone and fallen in love...with a Dom. With a moan of dismay, she dropped down in the grass next to the sidewalk.

Two mothers chatted as they pushed their babies in strollers.

Out on the Bay, gulls dipped and soared over the glittering water. Barking in delight, a big yellow lab charged into the water after a thrown stick.

Everything around her was alive.

She was alive. And in love. *No, no, no*. "I do not want to be in love, dammit." Not with a Dom.

On the sidewalk, a white-haired man leaned on his cane and frowned down at her. His voice crackled with age and probably a lifetime of cigarettes as he told her, "Love is a gift. The finest gift you'll find in a lifetime. Don't throw it away so casually." Looking older than God, he gave her a stern nod and kept on walking.

Love is a gift.

Would Ethan see her love as being a gift? Dread crept into the edges of her heart. He'd probably laugh. Look, *worthless* is in love with me.

No, Piper, stop thinking like that. She wasn't worthless, in name or in reality. Ethan never, ever gave her the impression he felt that she was.

It was sure disconcerting how she kept swinging from feeling inadequate to self-confident. Her emotions were all over the place in a way they hadn't been in five years.

She'd really thought she was mostly over the trauma...except now she knew that her biggest defense was avoiding anything that revived old hurts and memories. She snorted. Being around the Dark Haven people was totally messing up that avoidance strategy.

Falling for a Dom would only make it worse.

What if Ethan said he loved *her*? What would she do?

Her heart went into overdrive.

Okay, okay, don't panic. She had time. He wouldn't just blurt out protestations of love—not Ethan. Like her, he was careful because he'd been burned in the past. She'd have time to think of what to do.

I'm in love with a Dom. Just shoot me now.

CHAPTER EIGHTEEN

On Thursday night, at Xavier and Abby's home in Tiburon, Ethan petted Blackie's soft fur and listened to the couple argue about the amount of cayenne in bouillabaisse. Piper had joined Lindsey and deVries in the living room.

"I thought Dixon and Stan were coming tonight," Ethan said.

"Stan has some urgent Homeland Security case and is putting in overtime. Dixon didn't want to come by himself." Abby whacked Xavier's fingers with a wooden spoon.

With a low laugh, Xavier plucked the spoon away, spun Abby around, and swatted her on the arse several times, hard enough to make her squeal.

"You...you sadist. You *impolite* sadist," she sputtered, face red. "We have company."

Xavier added the cayenne pepper with a gleam in his eyes. "Be grateful there are people here, or I'd have stripped off your jeans before spanking you."

As her blush deepened, Ethan smothered a smile. The little professor hadn't lost her charming modesty.

She glared at her husband before giving in and laughing. "My Liege, the brute."

"That's me." Xavier kissed her. "Do you want help fixing the salad?"

"We'll help, Abby. I'm great at cutting up stuff." Lindsey entered the kitchen, followed by Piper. "You men can take all that testosterone outside."

"I like that idea," deVries said. "I was stuck inside on the computer all day."

"Then that's what we'll do." Xavier picked up the bottle of burgundy and refilled everyone's glasses except for his and deVries'. "Another beer, Zander?"

"No, it's my turn as designated driver," deVries said. "I'll take a soda if you have one."

Xavier handed over a cola, took another for himself, and headed outside.

Ethan stopped to give Piper a kiss, enjoying how she softened against him and how she clung for a moment. Her fears of touching a Dom—of touching him—had almost disappeared, and he loved her affectionate nature.

Outside, the wide stone patio held a pool and hot tub off to the right and overlooked the bay. The crisp brine-scented air was so clear that he could see past Angel Island to San Francisco. A good telescope could probably find his Russian Hill house.

At the railing, Xavier glanced at Ethan. "We missed you at Dark Haven last weekend."

It was good to be missed; however, Xavier would have to get used to his absence. "I've been meaning to talk with you. I need a couple of months off from monitoring."

Xavier frowned and waited.

"I believe that Piper will eventually be comfortable visiting the club with friends while I work, but that time is not now."

"You don't want her having a panic attack without you nearby." Xavier nodded. "Agreed."

Good. One problem was taken care of.

"Gotta say, it's a pain in the ass to lose you when those

fucking reciprocal visitors keep flooding in." DeVries dropped into a chair at the table. "I hate tourist season."

"It's a problem." Xavier swirled his cola in the glass. "Last night, one of the visitors started to jerk off while watching a scene."

Ethan snorted.

"Our members shouldn't have to put up with such behavior," Xavier growled.

Devries's brows drew together. "I still think you should've let me cane his little frank and beans."

Grinning at the thwarted sadist, Ethan considered. They needed a way to orient visitors quickly. "Perhaps this should be a discussion at the next DH board meeting."

Xavier gave him a quick smile. "Already on the agenda."

As a stream of laughter came from inside the house, Ethan tilted his head to listen. Just the sound lifted a man's spirits.

Xavier looked at him over his glass. "She's good for you, Worth. I like her."

Before he could answer, Piper came out the back door, carrying a tray. "Sirs. I've been commandeered for delivery service."

She laid out plates and napkins, set the platter of appetizers within Ethan's reach, and waited to see if there was anything else he wanted. *His* submissive.

"That looks splendid. Thank you, poppet."

Although she didn't smile, her eyes brightened. Because she'd pleased him.

Unable to resist, he pulled her down and into his lap.

"*Sir*." She stiffened, then melted against him.

"The appetizers look tasty, but I'm hungry for a soft, squirmy submissive," he murmured. "Let's see if I can please you as much as you please me."

He kissed her, taking his time, then before she'd recovered, fastened a ruby and diamond tennis bracelet around her wrist.

"What?" She stared down. "Sir, no."

The moment he'd seen it, he'd known it would suit her. She was sparkles and bright colors, a pocket-sized gypsy. He studied it on her wrist. *Yes.* The gold enhanced the radiance of her skin. Red was her favorite color.

Her brows drew together. "But-but I haven't done anything."

Done anything? Did she think presents were given for performance? The snippets she'd shared of her childhood made him think that was true. After she'd acquired a stepfather, she'd been virtually starved for affection.

"Piper." He rubbed his cheek against hers. "This is a present, not a payment."

"It's too expensive." She frowned at it. "I don't need expensive stuff."

He felt his lips quirk because she was as adorable as she was unique. She hadn't wanted her business to expand if increasing the profit would sacrifice quality. She said "rich people" as if it were an insult—and apparently, didn't crave expensive gifts.

Her wide brown eyes were open and readable in a way that Nicola's never had been. As something inside of him loosened, he realized she wasn't the only person with a neurosis-inducing past.

"Piper, I gave you this because I wanted to see you smile. Because the rubies reminded me of your favorite color and your big heart. The diamonds sparkle in the same way that you do. In the way that you light up my life."

He'd had women react to expensive presents with tears, with kisses, with hugs. It was the first time he'd gotten a frown for the gift—and tears for simple compliments.

As she wrapped herself around him, tear-streaked face against his hair, he hugged her tighter.

Yes, he really did love her.

The knowledge settled into his heart with the feeling of rightness. Of completeness. Now all he had to do was get her to acknowledge what they had.

That might be a bit trickier.

CHAPTER NINETEEN

On Thursday, in her apartment, Piper joined Dixon on the couch and showed him the bracelet Ethan had given her. "See? It's too much."

"Pipster, it's perfect." Dix heaved a huge sigh. "Maybe I set my sights too low. I should have gone for a millionaire boyfriend."

"Dixon." Even as she said it, she knew he was joking. Her friend was totally in love with Stan.

And she was in love with Ethan, God help her. "Why does he have to be a damn millionaire and a damn baronet?"

Dixon burst out laughing. "You sound so pissed off. But seriously, Pips, the money and title aren't what get you, not really."

"No, you're right. It's because he's also a damn Dom."

"Nailed it. That domliness is what floats your boat, you know."

"It is, God help me, it really is. What am I going to do?"

Dix's smile was smug. "Admit you're screwed, lie back, and enjoy it."

"You're not helping."

The buzzer for the building's front door sounded.

Piper trotted to the wall and pushed the intercom button. "Yes?"

"It's Lindsey."

"It's about time you got here," Dixon yelled from the couch.

Rolling her eyes at him, Piper pushed the door release button. "Door's unlocked. Come on up." Leaving the apartment door halfway open, she took her place back on the couch.

Dixon pointed to the door. "Stan would say that's really unsafe."

"Sure, it is." Piper squirmed into a comfortable slouch. "But this lazy woman has no intention of jumping up and down to let people in or to—"

Heavy footsteps came down the hallway. Too heavy for Lindsey. Piper tensed. Maybe Dix was right about safety.

"Is your boy home?" The man's voice drifting in from the hall was vaguely familiar.

"I don't know." That was Stan. "I don't keep him on a leash, you know."

"Probably should. Or, better yet, cut the leash."

Piper scowled. It was the pushy guy named Darrell.

Dixon pushed himself upright on the couch.

As Darrell continued to talk, Piper realized the two were standing outside Stan and Dixon's apartment across the hall.

"Christ almighty, JS, you can do so much better. Even if it isn't me, at least get someone with a few brains. Someone educated who can keep up with you. Who pulls his own weight in the relationship. You're probably paying for everything, aren't you? It's not like his third-rate job could pay much."

"It's not—" The sound of a door closing cut off Stan's reply.

Dix's face was white, his shoulders hunched.

Piper slid closer. "Darrell is a jerk. I'm sure Stan is telling him that right about now."

"Dumbass Darrell didn't say anything that wasn't true."

The sad slump of Dix's shoulder sent fury into Piper's heart.

"Hey, guys." Laden with two brown paper sacks, Lindsey

kicked the door shut behind her. "We need to celebrate. I just finished jumping through all the reciprocity hoops and I'm now an officially licensed clinical social worker. Xavier's promoting me."

"That's great, Lindsey." Piper pushed enthusiasm into her voice. Lindsey had worked long and hard to get her life back in order.

Lindsey also had a psychologist's keen eye when it came to people. She eyed Piper, then Dixon. "Hey, Dix, what's wrong?" Dumping her sacks on the coffee table, she dropped down on his other side and took his hand.

When he didn't answer, Piper checked that the door was closed. "He heard that creepazoid Darrell bad-mouthing him to Stan. The two of them are over at Stan and Dix's place now."

"Stan's place," Dixon said. "It's his name on the lease."

"You pay half the rent, and that means it's both of y'all's place," Lindsey said indignantly.

"Not for long." Dixon tipped his head back, eyes closed. "I don't think it'll be for long."

He was so miserable that Piper's heart ached. "But why? Stan adores you."

"I don't want to talk about it." Pulling free, Dixon scrubbed his face with his hands.

"Oh, Dix." The bouncy, fun-loving Dixon was only the surface of his personality. Stan and others might call him *boy* in the same way Doms called female submissives *girl*, but Dix was a man. A dedicated, caring, deeply emotional man. One who'd better share before he burst.

Of course, it was up to him if he wanted to talk about his relationship with Stan. She shouldn't push.

Yet Dix was totally a social animal. If he was hurting, he'd feel better with friends around.

Piper glanced at the bags lying on the coffee table. "What kind of world-famous drinks are you making us, Lindsey?"

Lindsey blinked. "I don't know about world-famous. Texas

famous, maybe?" Her gaze was on Dixon, then she nodded at Piper. Time for slightly inebriated comforting.

A few hours later, Lindsey muttered to Piper, "I hope you realize that alcohol isn't an approved counseling substance."

"Ah, well, it's good to be flexible about these matters." Piper glanced at the half empty pitcher.

How many times had Lindsey refilled it? Enough that Piper's tiny blender had burned-out while chomping up ice cubes. Since Dixon had a high-powered blender, they'd checked to be sure Stan and the jerk had left, and moved the party across the hall.

The seriously blitzed Dixon was closer to his bed this way.

It was nice that his place was as comfortable as hers, even while being a guys' haven. Stan's Texas roots showed in the décor, from the brass tack and brown leather furniture, the reclaimed barn wood coffee and end tables, to the red-and-black western rug on the hardwood floor. A California boy, Dixon had added quirkiness and color—dark red bookcases, stark black-and-white abstract tree prints, and black metal-and-glass pendant lights.

"I like alcohol," Dixon stated emphatically and lifted his glass. "Although I shouldn't drink. Makes me run off at the mouth. Like oral diarrhea, right?"

Piper rolled her eyes. Then again, if he was offering up medical jokes, maybe he'd also feel like sharing.

"Darrell sure seems like a jerk," she said, leaving the observation hanging in the air. It was something Ethan did. Make a statement and let silence prod her into answering. Even when she recognized his technique, it still worked.

"Dickless Darrell *is* a jerk," Dixon muttered. "No, not really."

Lindsey tilted her head. "Both? What makes him a jerk and not a jerk?"

"He's a jerk because he says I'm not good enough for Stan."

Dixon swirled his drink, and wasn't it impressive that he'd only slurred his words a little? "But not a jerk cuz he's right."

"He is *not* right." Piper had known that was what Dix believed. If Darrell had been within reach, she'd have punched him. "How could anyone say you're not good enough? Stan loves you."

Dix stared into the depths of his drink. "Love only takes you so far. Gotta have more than that."

"You and Stan share a lot of traits." Lindsey held up her fingers as she listed them off. "You have the same work ethic, same morals, same sense of duty."

"Not the same background—his family has lots and lots of land and money. I'm a street-rat." Dixon slumped. "He's got his masters. Me? Crickets. Even getting my associate's degree was tough."

That didn't make sense; Dixon was incredibly smart. "What made school tough?"

"God, it was boring. Sitting still, hour after hour. Numbers and books and tedious homework."

Piper got it. She hadn't found college easy, either, especially in subjects she didn't enjoy. She and Dixon were a lot alike.

"Oh, li'l dogie, you do have way too much energy to sit still for long, especially with books," Lindsey agreed. "You're a total extrovert."

Dixon tossed back the rest of his drink.

Uh-oh. He'd had more than she'd ever seen him drink. Piper moved the pitcher out of reach. "Stan doesn't listen to the jerk, does he?"

"He probably hears deadshit Darrell bleating about me all day long. They're working a case together." Dixon's face held such misery that Piper pulled him into her arms.

"It'll work out; I know it will," she whispered.

"You may not have the book learning, but you have other skills that Stan doesn't." Lindsey stopped as the door opened.

Stan—*alone, thank you God*—stood in the doorway. Exhaustion pulled at his shoulders, and harsh lines were carved into his face. His brows drew together as he took them in. "A party?" His Texas drawl was even thicker than Lindsey's. "Here? Now?"

His tone was so unwelcoming that Piper was on her feet before she knew it. "Sorry, Stan. It's later than we realized." And it was. Well past midnight on a weeknight. Guiltily, she grabbed up the glasses and pitcher and saw Lindsey sweep the debris into the empty grocery bag. "We're out of here."

Dixon didn't speak. Just stared at Stan, heart in his eyes.

"Christ, it's like coming home and stepping on a litter of puppies," Stan said under his breath. He rubbed his neck. "Sorry, ladies."

As Piper stepped past him, his gaze landed on Dixon. His mouth tightened. "You're blasted, boy. You wouldn't have a drink with me and Darrell, but you're all too happy to get shit-faced with your friends?"

Lindsey shot Piper an alarmed look.

Oh, God. "He didn't have much choice," Piper said hastily. "We—"

"Opened his mouth and poured the drinks in. Sure." Stan shook his head. "Get on home with you now. I'll put him to bed."

Because that's what he really wanted to do after working for —what, eighteen or so hours?

Piper saw from the set of his expression, there was nothing she could do.

She'd really messed this up.

CHAPTER TWENTY

Hand low on Piper's back, Ethan walked with Piper down the sidewalk toward Dark Haven. He'd missed her last night and was looking forward to the evening.

As they neared the club, he felt her hesitate. It took him a second to realize why she'd gone tense. This section of the sidewalk was where he'd bloodied her stepbrother and then threatened her with the police. "Piper."

When she looked up, he kissed her gently. "I'm sorry I overreacted when I met Jerry and gave you such ugly memories."

Her smile was rueful. "When it comes down to it, I'm the reason Jerry was here. And then you ended up swamped with your own bad memories."

Yes, he really did love this soft-hearted, forgiving woman.

He kissed her again, this time, long and deep. If there were going to be memories from this spot, he'd ensure the good ones wiped out the bad.

As he stepped back, he saw her dreamy expression from the kiss change to one of sadness. "You're frowning again, pet."

"Just remembering. When we talked that night, you said you'd left everything behind once. But"—she shook her head

—"you didn't do anything wrong. You even saved a woman's life. Why did you leave?"

"Ah, well. What happened with Nicola—her background, the violence—was quite scandalous, especially for my conservative father and our conservative companies. Then my involvement in the lifestyle made the papers."

"Oh, God."

"Exactly. Eventually, I simply left. Xavier and I had stayed in touch after boarding school. He convinced me to choose San Francisco and start a business here."

Her dark eyes held sadness. For him. "You lost...everything?"

He nodded. His home, the city he'd loved. People he'd known all his life. Bloody hell but it had hurt. "My father and I eventually reconciled. I'll admit leaving behind my friends was painful."

She hugged him. "I'm so sorry."

"I'm not. I found a new city and new friends. A lover, as well." Holding her firmly, he kissed his way down her neck and nipped the curve of her shoulder several times, so when he guided her into Dark Haven, she was giggling.

"Piper, Sir Ethan." Behind the desk, Lindsey beamed at them.

Piper grinned back. "Hey, how do you feel?"

"Like I got drunk as a skunk. Thanks for letting me crash on your couch."

Piper made a fuffing sound. "As if I'd let you drive with that many margaritas in your system."

She'd be just as protective with children, too, wouldn't she? The thought warmed his heart, and Ethan tucked her closer.

"Have you talked with Dixon?" The worry in Lindsey's voice was concerning.

"No, he's on the ambulance today. I left him a voicemail." Piper frowned. "Isn't he here?"

"Uh-uh. That's why I'm stuck on the desk." Lindsey took their ID cards, scanned them, and handed them back. "Stan's working another late night, and Dixon said he wasn't up to coming in. Xavier was displeased."

"Oh damn." Piper made an unhappy sound. "And here I thought the myths about unlucky Friday, the 13th were over-rated."

Ethan tugged a strand of Piper's hair. "What's going on with Dixon?"

"He's..." She shook her head. "Nothing I can share. Sorry, Sir."

Loyalty and discretion. Both frustrating and admirable. "I understand."

After they hung their coats in the reception room, Piper tucked her tiny purse and phone into the outer pocket of his toy bag.

Dressed in his usual black turtleneck and pants, Ethan smiled at the little submissive beside him. She'd been comfortable enough to wear less clothing this time. A dark red corset, short black miniskirt, fishnet stockings, and strappy sandals. He'd planned a Shibari scene, but she looked so enticing he was tempted to find a theme room and enjoy a fast bout of sex.

No. He wanted the intense connection that rope bondage could impart, the unspoken dialogue between top and bottom... and once she was bound, depending on her headspace, he'd indulge in some erotic edging.

Then, maybe he'd find a theme room...

With her small hand in his, Ethan escorted her across the main floor, answering various greetings.

Piper spotted Abby across the room. "May I, Sir?"

Her growing ease with being away from his side pleased him. Brave girl. "Yes. Return to me within ten minutes, please."

He took a seat at a table, visited with friends, and enjoyed the oddity of a dance floor filled with giggling littles bouncing around to the Hokey-Pokey. On the raised stage to the right, a Mistress was caning an errant schoolboy.

Piper returned from visiting with Abby, her eyes dancing

with laughter. She motioned to the black and silver watch he wore. "I have ten seconds to spare, Sir."

He did love seeing her spirit unfettered by fears. "So you do. Are you ready to go downstairs?"

"Ah..." Her eyes widened. "Are we doing something tonight?"

"We are." He ran his finger over her jawline. "I enjoyed tying you up at the camp; you enjoyed it as well. I want to do something more elaborate and thought you'd prefer to play here where someone will rescue you, if needed."

She took a slow breath, her muscles relaxed, and then her dimples appeared. "You're pushing me and dealing with my worries at the same time. That's pretty sneaky, Sir Ethan."

He tried not to smile. "Such an accusation."

Even as he spoke, his hands were anticipating being on her, wrapping her in his ropes, enjoying the fragrance of her lotion-scented skin, her heady arousal. Watching her thoughts and emotions slow as the embrace of the ropes took her under. "Is that a yes? I need more from you than a nod, poppet."

"Yes." She swallowed. "I-I'd like to try the Shibari again."

"I'll turn you into a rope bottom yet." Taking her hand, he picked up his toy bag and led her down into the dungeon.

This time, Piper felt far less anxiety in the dungeon. In all of Dark Haven, actually. Wasn't it awesome how familiarity was lessening her fears?

Sir Ethan's hand was warm around hers as he pulled her to a stop near the steel spider web. The bottom tied to the "webbing" was blindfolded, had a huge erection, and panted as his Top whipped a dragon's tail across his chest.

Moans in different octaves came from nearby bondage tables. Wax play was happening on one. A violet wand on another.

As they continued across the room, a woman screamed, high and shrill, and kept screaming. A man yelled, "Help! I need help!"

Piper spun. Suspended beneath the blimp, a panicking rope bunny struggled frantically.

Sir Ethan took a step in that direction, stopped, and looked down at her.

Her heart turned over. He'd considered her needs, even though he wanted to go help that woman. *My Dom.*

She let go of his hand and nodded toward the scene. "Go. I'm good."

He touched her cheek and was gone, moving so quickly everyone else seemed stuck in concrete.

Piper crossed the room at a slower pace, watching as the Top and others tried to get past the bunny's flailing extremities to cut the ropes. The woman's terrified shrieks set up a quiver in Piper's belly. She'd screamed like that...once.

She went past a flogging scene. A spanking bench. A sitting area where Doms lounged in the chairs, slaves at their feet.

One naked blonde slave was kneeling by an empty chair. Her pale skin was marred with red welts and purple bruises. She looked familiar. Had they met at the kink camp?

No. Piper's eyes widened. That was the Defiler's second slave —slavegem.

"Hello, worthless."

Her lungs stopped expanding; her heart stopped beating.

A man's hand closed painfully around her wrist. "I knew I wouldn't misplace my property forever."

Stabbing terror stole her breath, her voice, even her screams.

"Jerry told me where you were. I'm angry I had to fly here from Kansas to retrieve you." His annoyance chilled his voice. The grip on her wrist didn't loosen. "Slavegem, get this collar off of her. It has the wrong name on it."

His voice dropped. "*Doesn't* it, worthless?"

She couldn't speak. Couldn't breathe. Couldn't feel anything. Darkness flickered in her vision, growing rapidly. She tried to stiffen her legs. If she fell, he'd have her.

He was talking to someone. "... mine. I have a signed

contract that makes her my property. She signed it free and clear. She's my slave."

The pain of his brutal grip broke through the paralysis. She wrenched back and forth, trying to pull away.

At her neck, slavegem's cold hands were unbuckling Sir Ethan's collar. It dropped onto the floor.

Nooo. The loss of it stabbed into her heart.

"She's mine. Any Master here will uphold my claim to a slave who signed herself completely over to me." Serna's words sounded reasonable. Persuasive. That same forceful voice had convinced her to become his.

As she swallowed past a desert-dry throat, he continued. "Sure she ran. What slave hasn't had second thoughts? But returned to where they belong, they'll kiss your feet in gratitude. Hell, I've had them whine at the door to be taken back. Haven't you?"

Men were talking. Agreeing with him.

Forcing her head up, Piper saw the disgusted stare of a Master. One who considered her scum for having run.

"It's good to have you back, slave." The Defiler's tone was warm. With an arm around her waist, he drew her closer. His whisper in her ear held no warmth at all. "Beg me to take you back, worthless. Kneel—and *beg*."

Beg. Nausea swept through her at the word. At the memories. He'd loved to make her beg. If allowed to speak, she had to beg for food, to use the bathroom, to be unchained, to stop a whipping.

Never. Again. Her jaws clamped shut.

Around her, the world went fuzzy. Her knees were bending, crumbling like fractured twigs in front of a steamroller. Each gasping breath tore through her as she fought her body. Fought against the memory of pain, the training that forced her to respond to the slightest order.

Something smacked hard against the Defiler's forearm, and his grip loosened. Someone pulled her away and caught her as her legs buckled. She was held against a man's hard body.

A breath brought her the scent of leather and pine. *Sir Ethan. Her Ethan.*

"Slow breaths, Piper. Pursed lips. Breathe out. Feel my arm around your waist. Listen to my voice."

She tried, tried so hard. The band around her chest was tighter than his hold on her.

"Worthless, you get back—"

"Leave my submissive alone, Serna." Sir Ethan's voice was cold—and even.

"She's mine, you bastard." The Defiler's voice lifted. "Listen to this, people. The last time I saw my slave was at a party where Worthington insisted that slave contracts weren't valid. She disappeared not five minutes later. Now, here she is with him."

Against the whispering around them, Serna's voice turned ugly. "You're a fucking thief, Worthington, and I'm going to get you tossed out of this place, you bastard."

"That's quite doubtful. In case you didn't hear—slavery is illegal. You can have someone sign anything you want—that doesn't make it enforceable." Sir Ethan was rubbing her back. "Easy, poppet. I'm here."

Trying to force her legs to work, she leaned against him.

"The contract is enforceable for people in the lifestyle, and you are going to pay for what you've done." Serna's words were cold. So cold. "I'll get you blacklisted from every club in the world

Oh no. The Defiler would go after Sir Ethan. Piper tried again to find air as a new terror filled her veins. Sir Ethan would be hurt, would be—

"Take it upstairs, Masters." The dungeon monitor walked over. "You're disrupting the dungeon."

"Of course, of course." Serna exerted his charm. "Forgive us."

Chills crawled over Piper's skin, and her stomach turned over.

"Come, sweetheart, let's get you out of here." Sir Ethan drew her closer to his side.

She nodded. Her hand touched her bare neck. What if Serna grabbed her, put his collar on her, took her away. He'd beat her, chain her in the darkness, and...

Bile rose in her throat. Her stomach lurched.

"Can't. Sick." She tore out of Sir Ethan's hold and ran across the room to the woman's restroom.

In a stall, she dropped to her knees and vomited until only dry heaves remained. Dizzy, shaking, she choked on sobs.

Yet, with every passing second, she tensed more. Her back was to the door. He might come in.

Head spinning, she staggered to her feet and out of the stall. After rinsing her mouth, she braced herself on the sink. The porcelain was cold against her clammy skin.

In the dungeon, the angry voices were gone. The dungeon monitor must have forced both Masters to go upstairs.

But Serna never lost. He wouldn't here, either. Not in a BDSM club filled with Masters and slaves. So many owners felt justified in recapturing a runaway. Not everyone agreed, but even then, people in the lifestyle almost never interfered with how someone else practiced.

The Defiler would win and take her away.

Someone would soon come to check on her, possibly to hold her until a decision was made. *I need to get out of here.*

Footsteps sounded in the short hallway and grew louder. Piper stiffened. Was someone here for her already? Her hands fisted.

The person who entered was slavegem. Naked, bruised, lashed. One eye puffy. Several inches taller than Piper, she was whipcord thin. Her stomach was concave, her breasts were sunken.

"Time to go, worthless." Slavegem held a pair of handcuffs.

Just the sight of them made Piper's stomach almost revolt again. Serna had left her handcuffed to a pipe in the basement for an entire month once; she still had the scars on her wrists. "The people here won't let him take me." *Please, please, please.* Sir Ethan, at least, would do everything he could to prevent it.

"*People* won't know." Slavegem's face held no expression. "Cuz you and I are gonna leave through the emergency exit down here. Now, turn around, hands behind your back."

As slavegem confidently moved forward, Piper stiffened. Memories flooded her of the slave's jealous cruelty—tripping Piper, slapping her.

Piper had buckled under to everything—because she was worthless. "*No*."

Slavegem's expression turned to shock. *No* was a word never said by a slave.

When slavegem grabbed for her, Piper put all her anger and despair into a single punch. Right into slavegem's gut.

Wheezing, unable to even scream, the slave landed on the floor in a curled-up ball.

Picking up the dropped handcuffs, Piper snapped one end around slavegem's wrist and the other around the bottom leg of the stall.

Almost horrified at what she'd done, Piper looked down. Pity stirred her heart as she saw the cuts along slavegem's side. Bruises from beatings. The woman was younger than Piper, not as educated, but just as emotionally needy. She'd been easy meat for Serna's manipulations, and he'd loved setting them against each other.

She was as much a victim as Piper. So Piper offered the words that Sir Ethan had given her so many years ago. "The slave contract isn't legal. Can't be enforced. If you get yourself to a women's shelter, they'll help you."

Sprawled out on the restroom floor, slavegem just stared at her.

Piper pulled in a breath. "Girl, look at me and look at yourself. Which of us would you rather be?"

Anguish filled slavegem's face before she closed her eyes, blotting Piper out of her world.

All right then. On wobbly legs, Piper walked out of the restroom.

Near the sitting area where the Defiler had grabbed her, she saw Sir Ethan's toy bag on a chair. Hurrying over, she pulled her purse and phone from the outer pocket.

Her heart was pounding faster...the fear was much, much worse because of the glimmer of hope. She straightened her spine and walked across the dungeon. Didn't think. Didn't feel. Walked past the scenes. Past the subbie dog cages.

The door. There. She shoved open the emergency fire door.

As the alarm blasted, she fled down the alley toward the busy street.

The alarm from the dungeon's emergency exit blared out as Ethan was partway down the stairs.

Piper. He knew it.

He'd prevented Serna from following Piper into the restroom, but the bastard had refused to leave the dungeon until Ethan did. Once upstairs, Ethan had dumped Serna on Xavier—the only person here with enough authority to keep Serna in check.

Not bothering to check the restroom, Ethan hurried past the submissive cages, shoved the emergency door open, and stepped outside.

The alley was deserted.

Ice shivered through him. She'd been so terrified, so lost. Had she come this way? She didn't have the keys to his car. This wasn't a safe neighborhood, not in the least.

But there was a taxi stand out on the street. Piper had used it before when she and Dixon arrived together.

Where are you, Piper?

As he stepped back inside, Xavier was tapping the door's keypad to shut off the alarm. "You think Piper left this way?"

"I'll check the restroom to be sure, but yes." Ethan spotted Serna on the staircase landing.

The bastard wasn't hurrying to the restroom where he would think Piper was. After glancing around, Serna walked back up the stairs. Why wasn't he looking for Piper or his slave? Maybe because he knew they weren't down here?

A stab of fear had Ethan checking the room for the emaciated blonde. She wasn't in sight. He turned to Xavier. "Serna came in with a slave. She's not here."

Xavier's frown deepened as he caught on. He focused on the submissive caged in the dog kennel to the right of the door. "How many people left through this door?"

"My Liege." The tiny redhead bowed her head. "One. A black-haired woman. She was walking really fast."

"Thank you," Xavier said.

Piper had left on her own, hadn't been kidnapped. The fist Ethan had made unclenched. "Let's check the loo."

The knot in his gut eased as he heard a woman yelling from inside the ladies'. That wasn't Piper's voice. He pushed open the door.

Serna's slave lay on the floor, her wrist cuffed to one stall leg.

Undoubtedly Piper's doing. Ethan's thumb over his lips rubbed the smile away. "Well, slave, how did you get into this fix?"

"That bitch, worthless, she—" Her brain caught up, and her mouth snapped shut. "I mean, I was playing with Master's handcuffs, and I made a mistake."

A mistake, indeed. Ethan glanced at Xavier.

"What a mess," Xavier muttered.

Ethan studied the slave, visualizing what had happened. She'd probably tried to grab Piper and haul her out. Under Serna's orders—because the handcuffs would have had to come from him. Assault at best, kidnapping at worst. But this brainwashed woman would never incriminate her owner. She'd say everything was a misunderstanding, and the real criminal wouldn't be the one facing charges.

Even worse, publicity of this sort could damage Piper's business. She'd already had to rebuild her life once. A second time...? No.

He glanced at Xavier. "We handle this discreetly, yes?"

Mouth set in a flat, pissed-off line, Xavier nodded.

Ethan took out his spare handcuff key and unlocked the woman. "Serna is upstairs. Or if he left, you can use the phone in reception to call him." He moderated his tone because anyone belonging to Serna deserved compassion, not anger. "I'd rather have someone take you to a women's shelter."

Rubbing her wrist, she sat up. "I belong with my Master."

"As you wish." Without a crystal ball, he couldn't know if she truly wanted to be with Serna or was too frightened or shortsighted to leave him. "If you change your mind, we can help."

She shook her head.

Turning, he walked out. Now, where would Piper have gone?

The taxi driver had probably assumed she was a prostitute, considering her skimpy clothing and lack of a coat. After powering off her phone so it couldn't be tracked, Piper had sat rigid and silent all the way to her friend's empty apartment.

Once inside, she'd rushed to the bathroom and thrown up. *Again*. Huddled on the cold linoleum floor, she shook and threw up some more.

An eternity later, she rinsed her mouth and staggered out into Alberta's living room. The city lights streamed through the tenth-floor window and provided enough illumination to navigate across the room. She didn't turn on any lamps. Someone might see.

He might see.

No, she wasn't being rational. Not even close. But like any prey animal, she knew darkness was safety.

Dizzy, exhausted, she sat on the couch.

Too exposed.

Her legs wouldn't let her stand again, so she crawled across the floor to the blackest corner. With her back pressed against the wall, she sat and trembled and stared at the door.

Waiting for the handle to turn.

"Beg me to take you back, worthless." The Defiler's voice whispered in her ears. *"Beg me...beg me...beg me."*

He'd find her. He would. He'd hurt her. As memories dragged her into the abyss, her heart pounded against the rigid band around her ribs. She couldn't *breathe*.

"Piper." The voice was different. *"It's just a panic attack, poppet, it'll pass soon enough. Now breathe with me—only with me."* Sir Ethan's firm resonant voice, the clipped English accent, his hands on her upper arms. His calm watchful eyes.

Clutching the memory of Sir Ethan's voice like a lifeline, she fought to crawl out of the icy void. *Touch:* fingers to thumb. *Smell:* Alberta's cinnamon potpourri. *See:* the tops of the taller high-rises through the window. Square after square of golden light.

Eventually, she heard the ticking of the antique grandfather clock instead of the roaring in her head. As her breathing slowed, the tightness around her chest eased.

With a trembling hand, she wiped the tears from her face. Under the corset, her skin was damp with cold sweat. *I want Ethan.*

A raspy meow sounded from beside her knee.

She blinked down at the aged orange tabby. "Hey, Archimedes. Sorry if I scared you."

After a moment, the cat stepped with arthritic slowness onto Piper's lap, curled up, and settled in.

His weight and warmth were an anchor to reality. His fur was soft under her fingers. His purr the sweetest sound in the world.

"Thank you, ol' buddy. Are you all right with me staying here? I'll call Alberta in the morning to make sure."

In the taxi, all Piper could think about was finding an untraceable refuge. As she stroked the cat, her fingers still trembled. Boy, she'd really lost it this time.

Because she had a good reason. She shivered. The Defiler was here. In San Francisco. Here to *retrieve* her. Her heart slammed against her rib cage painfully.

Jerry and his vindictiveness. He would have told Serna everything about her.

Serna had come all this way to get her. That was just sick. She didn't belong to him anymore. She didn't.

But he didn't see it that way. She might be worthless, but he'd never tolerate a slave running away. Look at how he'd sent slavegem to handcuff and drag her out of the club. He'd do anything, legal or not, to get his "property" back.

Was she going to have to move again? Leave her life behind? Leave *Ethan*? The stab of grief was so painful she hunched over.

A furry cheek rubbed against her chin in an attempt to soothe. But there was no comfort to be had.

What could she do?

She shook with the longing for Ethan. For his warmth, the sense of safety with him, even his authority. Because he was compassionate and caring where Serna was evil.

Could she go to Ethan's home? Call him?

Her head was shaking no even before she finished the thought. He was a Master. He didn't approve of non-consensual slavery, and he'd defended her. However, slaves who broke an Owner/property contract fell into a gray area—at least as far as the BDSM community was concerned. Serna would point that fact out to Xavier and the rest of the Dark Haven leaders.

She knew Xavier and Simon, even deVries, wouldn't let Serna kidnap her. But there were so, so many other Masters there. They might decide against her.

Breathe. Slower. Slower.

Sir Ethan would defend her. He wouldn't hand her over to Serna. He cared for her, and he was proud of her for leaving Serna. For making a life.

But if Sir Ethan spoke up for her, Serna would ruin him the same way he'd done with Master Fenton in Kansas. He'd destroy Ethan's life. Get him thrown out of the BDSM community.

God, Ethan. When he'd talked about leaving everything behind in England, she'd seen the pain in his eyes. He'd lost his family, home, city.

Here, Ethan was one of the founding members of Dark Haven. His best friends belonged to the club. He had business interests with Xavier.

Serna would rip his world apart.

She couldn't live with herself if that happened.

Ethan was rich, gorgeous, a baronet. Brilliant and competent and wonderful. She was a slave who had broken her word and fled her Master. Not worthless—she wasn't—but it would be better for him to find a submissive who wasn't...damaged. One who wouldn't destroy his life.

She needed to stay away. Once her brain wasn't so fuzzy, when she wouldn't burst into tears, when her voice wouldn't shake.

Then she'd tell him it was over.

CHAPTER TWENTY-ONE

Where the devil was Piper? After leaving another voicemail for her, Ethan shoved his cell into his pocket. On Saturday morning, Simon's security business offices were almost empty. But the location had been the most convenient place to meet—and provided access to the search software.

Simon walked into his office and leaned a hip against his massive mahogany desk. His expression was bleak.

"No answer, I take it." Xavier had taken a chair in the sitting area.

Unable to sit, Ethan paced across the room. "Do you have any leads at all, Simon?"

"I'm afraid not. She must have turned her phone off. DeVries says she hasn't used her credit card or accessed any of her accounts."

Xavier leaned forward. "Could she be hiding in her apartment and not answering the door?"

Ethan rubbed his face, feeling the stubble alongside his beard. "Dixon and Stan have a spare key fob to her place, and Dixon checked for me. She hasn't been home. She isn't at Chatelaines. He's calling the friends of hers that he knows."

"He doesn't know them all?" Simon asked.

"No." Ethan closed his eyes, thinking of her brightness of spirit, how she drew people to her with just a smile. "She likes people—and in the vanilla world, she has more friends than I can count."

"It's reassuring to know she probably has a safe place, but it'll make it more difficult to locate her." Simon shook his head.

Ethan's gut tightened at the thought of her being frightened. Lost. "I should have stayed with her."

"If you'd gone after her into the bathroom, Serna would have followed. She was terrified enough." Xavier shook his head. "You got caught in a no-win situation, Worth."

He knew it. Logic didn't assuage his guilt. No one, especially his submissive, his woman, his love, should be afraid when he was around.

Simon's black eyes hardened. "What should we do about Serna?"

"I was a second away from starting a fight, but she would have panicked even more." As she had when he'd bloodied her stepbrother. "Now I'm sorry I didn't put him in hospital."

Xavier snorted.

"So much for our usual voice of reason." Simon shook his head.

"If you'd seen the way she reacted to him, you'd have held my coat." Ethan paced back across the room. "He actually thought we'd allow him to take her against her will."

"Some Masters believe they have the right to hold someone in slavery forever, no matter how illegal." Xavier shook his head.

"Assholes," Simon muttered. "Will Serna return to the club?"

Ethan flexed his fists. He'd like to meet up with the wanker without Piper to witness.

"Probably. Either to try to get Piper again or to cause as much trouble for her as he can." Xavier glanced at Ethan. "Once this is over, we're going to lay out Dark Haven's position on Master/slave contracts. I understand the appeal of a consensual non-consent contract—no matter how invalid—but one lacking a retraction/termination clause for both parties is quite simply unethical. Let's educate our membership."

Ethan nodded.

"You didn't answer what we do if Serna shows up tonight," Simon said.

"He essentially attacked a submissive in my club." Xavier's words were mild, but filled with a simmering anger. "He's *persona non grata* and will be turned away at the door."

Xavier's voice hardened. "With luck, he'll refuse and give me an excuse to throw him into the brick wall a few times."

"Not yet," Ethan said.

Both men stared.

"Don't hurt him and don't ban him," Ethan added. The words were difficult to say.

Xavier's growl said he was barely throttling back his fury. "Why?"

Ethan held up a finger. "First, Piper refuses to talk about what Serna did to her. I know it was abusive, but specifics would be useful to counteract the poison that lingers. If given a receptive ear, Serna is the type who will boast."

"I'm not sure I can tolerate having that bastard in Dark Haven." Xavier opened and closed his hands. "But I can suck it up if you need information from him. I'll ask deVries to have a conversation with him."

"Not deVries." Simon half-smiled. "He'd end up punching Serna before getting more than a tidbit or two."

"Good point." Xavier considered. "Either Alan or Michael, then. They're both Masters, would come across as sympathetic to Serna's cause, and can keep their reactions under control."

Simon glanced at Ethan. "Any other reasons?"

"One, although it might be reaching." Ethan watched a seagull fly past the window, then turned back to the room. "Serna had her convinced that her entire existence was all about serving him. That a slave who leaves her Owner is filth. She had enough spirit to run, but such indoctrination is difficult to shake off. If she saw others in the lifestyle call him out for the abuser he is, some healing might occur."

"Seeing him again is probably far past the courage of an abused slave, Ethan," Xavier said.

"I know." Ethan rubbed his jaw. "It's a long shot, no matter how brave she is."

In the silence, he turned toward the door. "Meantime, I have a little subbie to locate."

That morning, Piper left Alberta's apartment, having raided her friend's closet for gray drawstring sweatpants and a stretchy red tank top. She added a black hoodie to conceal her braless state.

Maia, another friend from Stella's, met her at a coffee shop, bringing a couple of cheap prepaid phones, tons of sympathy, and an offer of help.

Piper had gotten teary-eyed. She was lucky in her friends, wasn't she?

After Maia left, Piper ordered coffee and a donut—because sugar makes everything better, right? But the donut reminded her of how Sir Ethan had fed her in the camp, looking out for her with his compelling mix of authority and protectiveness.

There she went, getting all weepy again.

Time to take a risk and check her messages. Turning on her phone, she opened her voicemail. So *many*.

She listened to a few, skipped over several, then found one from Rona.

Rona offered her house, her help, Simon's help, and finished by saying that if Piper needed just Rona's help and didn't want Simon involved, she had it.

Sniffling, Piper skipped two more messages.

Then Abby's voicemail repeated the message, even to saying she'd help without Xavier's knowledge.

Piper cried a little after listening.

She skipped another message and opened Lindsey's.

Lindsey said the same as Rona and Abby but admitted she was shit at keeping secrets from deVries. Then she said her sadist Dom would love an excuse to beat Serna up. Just say the word.

All three offers were so very, very tempting.

Piper bit her lip. *No*. She certainly wouldn't have deVries run the risk of being jailed for assault. She wouldn't be the cause of a submissive keeping secrets from her Dom...and if the Doms knew where she was, they'd tell Ethan.

After skipping another message, she opened Dixon's. "*Pips, I heard about that rat-bastard who gave you shit last night. Is he why you get all antsy sometimes? Anyway, I know you're staying away from everybody—but I'm not everybody*."

She had to smile at that one. Such a Dixon statement.

"*You know, I can sack out wherever you're staying if you want someone close so you can sleep at night. Or I can watch your back while you're running around. Call me, sweetkins. I want to help. I won't tell Stan-the-Man if you don't want him to know.*"

Had she ever had a better friend?

She swallowed and, bracing herself, opened the first skipped message.

The one from Ethan.

He loved her.

Oh my God.

He said it right out loud, "*I love you, Piper*." She pulled the phone from her ear and stared at it, and played the voicemail again. "*I love you, Piper*."

Hot and cold chills streamed over her skin. He loved her. The feeling inside her was huge, as if her heart was straining to encompass all the world. *He loves me.*

And that was so impossible right now.

Hand over her chest, she played the next message.

He apologized for leaving her alone. He said he'd wanted to punch Serna but had been afraid she'd panic even further.

She scowled. Seeing him hit Serna would have been glorious. Or maybe not. She'd had an anxiety attack when he made Jerry all bloody, and with Serna, she'd already been panicking. Ethan had been right to worry about her reaction.

He said he'd gone upstairs with Serna because it was the only way to get Serna away from her.

The thought of Serna coming into the tiny enclosed space of the bathroom stall sent her heart rate skyrocketing. *Oh, Ethan, thank God you didn't let that happen.*

She felt a knot in her chest release, one she hadn't realized was there. She hadn't realized how betrayed she'd felt that Ethan had gone upstairs. But he was right. Serna would never have left unless Ethan did, too.

She played the next messages.

He said he loved her—again.

He said he'd come for her wherever she was. Would protect her. Would hide her if that was what she needed now. Would go with her to press charges against Serna if that was what she wanted. Or not. Her choice. Trust him to help. To be her shield.

And he loved her—yet again.

God. Every few messages he said that. Just that. *I love you, Piper.* He wanted to see her. To protect her.

I love you, too, Ethan.

He was strong, so very strong, and he'd never back down from Serna. How much would loving her cost him? How could she risk destroying his life? Her heart felt as if it was ripping into pieces.

"Ahem."

Piper looked up.

An elderly woman stood beside the table. "Honey, are you all right?"

Piper realized her face was wet from tears. "Yes. Yes, thank you." She forced the quaver out of her voice. "I'm listening to messages from friends, and I realized how much I miss them. But I'm okay."

The woman gave her a sympathetic smile and a *pat, pat, pat* on her shoulder. "It's hard to be away from the ones we love. It'll get better, honey. It will."

No, no it won't.

As the woman carried her coffee out of the shop, Piper blinked hard. Wasn't it amazing how nice people could be? Some people. Most people.

Finally, she reached the most recent message. Its timestamp showed it was sent just before she'd turned on her phone. It was from Dixon.

Her smile disappeared.

"*I'm leaving Stan. Packing up this morning. I'll still help you, no matter what you need, but I want you to know that I won't be across the hall, okay? So use the phone if you need me, sweetcheeks.*"

Dixon was leaving Stan?

Oh, God, what had happened?

As she powered-off her phone, Piper glanced at the time. Dixon would still be at his place.

She went into her apartment building by the back way—the one used to take garbage to the bins. After running up the stairs, she checked the hallway on her floor. Empty.

Her heart was pounding, more from fear than exertion. Because Serna must know where she lived. Surely, he couldn't have gotten in, though.

It didn't matter if she was scared. Dixon needed her. She wouldn't let him go through a breakup with Stan by himself. Dix probably hadn't told anyone else what was going on.

What if that night they'd all been drinking had made things worse between Dix and Stan? Remorse squashed her insides.

She tapped on the door. After a minute, it opened.

Pale face, dark circles under his reddened eyes.

"Oh, Dix." Even as she grabbed him in a hug, he did the same with her. Two messed-up fragile people.

He was crying as hard as she was. Because they'd both lost their strong, protective, loving men. And they'd lost the fulfillment that came with serving the Doms they loved.

Her soul had empty, aching craters.

Eventually, Piper pulled away and wiped her eyes. "Sorry. I came to help, not cry all over you."

Scrubbing his own face, he drew her inside and flipped the lock on the door. "If you hadn't, I wouldn't've been able to bawl my head off, too. Thanks."

"What can I do to help?" Piper saw a suitcase sitting beside the door. Another one was open on the coffee table next to a pile of DVDs and Dix's laptop. She sank into a chair. "Are you sure you want to do this? Does Stan know you're leaving?"

Dixon's eyes brimmed with tears again. "I tried to tell him last night. He came home after 3 am, and I tried, but he blew me off."

That didn't sound like Stan. Piper lifted an eyebrow.

"Yeah, okay, not blew me off. Not exactly. He said, '*Boy, I know something's wrong, and we need to have a long talk, but I'm past brain dead. I can't right now.*' "

"That seems reasonable," she said cautiously. Dix in this mood was like nitroglycerine—ready to explode at the wrong move. "You aren't going to wait?"

"I asked if we could talk four days ago and got the same shit." He flung out his arms as if to encompass the whole apartment. "These days, he's only around long enough to fall into bed for a couple hours, get up, shower, and leave. He doesn't even eat here."

"Is his work that busy?"

"It hadn't been up to now. He puts in overtime now and then, but never like this." Dixon dropped onto the couch next to her. "Of course, he never partnered on a case with Devoted Darrell, either."

Oh, damn. "I'd hoped Darrell would be gone by now. Isn't he from out of town?"

"He is. Was." Dixon's shoulders slumped. "I heard them talking on the phone." He grimaced at her reproving look. "Yeah, my bad. I even opened the bedroom door so I could listen. The Divine Darrell has a really loud voice."

She shouldn't encourage him to eavesdrop on his Master. But... "What did he say?"

Dixon gave her a half-smirk. *See? You, too.* His smile faded. "He might put in to relocate to San Francisco. Wanted to know what Stan thought."

"And?"

"Stan said he should do what was best for him."

"Well...but Dix, that's not exactly like he encouraged the guy. He could hardly tell him to keep his butt in Texas, after all."

"Yeah, he could've." Dixon pouted for a second. "After that, dildoneck Darrell went on and on about stuff he wanted to do with Stan. Hiking and skiing. Sampling restaurants and all the BDSM clubs, too."

"And Stan said...?"

"He said that'd be fun. He and me"—he pointed to his chest—"would enjoy showing Darrell the city."

"I'm glad Stan pointed out that he's taken, but I bet Darrell didn't appreciate the reminder."

"Yeah, no, not hardly. He went on and on about Stan tying himself to an uneducated, whiny, clingy wimp. That Stan deserved someone who'd have his back, could make his career, could be his equal. Not some gutter-rat." Bitterness and hurt was clear in Dix's voice.

He'd told her about growing up poor in a scummy part of Sacramento. His janitor dad walked away. His mom worked crappy jobs and still couldn't make ends meet. Dixon had worked hard to stand on his own feet, support himself, educate himself. He held three jobs, worked hard for his money, and saved it. How could anyone call him a gutter-rat?

Piper knew exactly how he felt. Gutter-rat versus over-educated Special Agent. He felt Stan was out of his reach... exactly how she felt about Ethan. Worthless slave versus aristocrat.

But this wasn't about her. She pushed her grief into a corner. "Darrell is a pig, a complete swine, but Stan isn't. He's not. Don't you think he deserves a chance to work things out?"

"Maybe." Dixon slumped against her. "But, God, Pips, what if he says it would be good to take a step back, or that maybe we moved too fast. It'd kill me."

Her heart chilled. She could almost hear Ethan saying those things. Only he hadn't. *"I love you, Piper."*

That right there was the core. "Does Stan love you, Dix?"

The expression on his face was heartbreaking. "He says he does. Or he used to say that." He sighed. "I haven't heard it in a long time."

God, god, god, she didn't know what to tell him.

Then the lock whirred, and the door opened, and it all became irrelevant.

Dixon sat up straight as Stan opened the door. The surge of hope filling his heart almost did him in.

But Stan stopped in the doorway and turned to speak to someone in the hallway. To the Divine Darrell. If Stan kissed the fartknocker, Dixon would...would do something ugly.

Darrell was gloating about something. "It was a fantastic arrest. Looks great on the old resume, you know?" His loud tenor just seemed to be begging for a good bitch-slap. Dixon's hand tingled to oblige.

"I suppose." Stan sounded as if all the energy had been sucked out of him.

Dixon wanted to draw him a hot bath, make him a drink, and—

"Fuck, lighten up, old man." Darrell made an irritated sound. "We got the bastards."

"Not soon enough."

"Well, Christ Jesus, if you want to sit here and wallow in your misery, then fine. If you'd rather celebrate, then dump your ball-and-chain and come on down the hall."

"Darrell," Stan growled.

Ball-and-chain? Dixon scowled. He didn't drag Stan down, didn't make demands. Then again, what dipshit Darrell called him no longer mattered. Pain hollowed an aching space in Dixon's chest. He'd be breaking those so-called chains himself.

"Sorry, just kidding." Darrell continued, "Come and celebrate with me. We could have some fun, you know?"

"Thanks, but no. See you tomorrow morning, Darrell."

Right. Once again, Stan and Darrell would spend the day together. A Sunday, no less. Dixon couldn't breathe against the rising tide of misery.

Closing the door, Stan turned, saw Dixon. "Hey, there you are."

Before Dix could answer, Stan saw Piper. His eyes narrowed. "Where the hell have you been?" The hell came out a very Texan *hay-yell*. Not good. When Stan's drawl thickened, Dix hid the canes and floggers.

Dixon leaned forward, ready to step in front of Pips. Even if it was Stan.

"I was staying at a friend's place." She rose. "I need to get back there, actually."

"You're going nowhere, girl. Plant your ass right back down." Stan pointed to her chair before scowling at Dixon. "Did you know where she was?"

Ball and chain, gutter-rat. The constant cuts hurt; Stan's anger made everything worse. Dixon's words dried up, and he could only shake his head no.

"All right." Stan noticed the suitcase by the door and the other on the coffee table. "You can certainly stay here, Piper, if you're worried about being alone. But it would be better if..." He stiffened as he realized Dixon's belongings filled the open suitcase.

Turning slowly, Stan stared at the entertainment center where gaps showed in the neatly lined-up DVD's. He picked up the snake-print boxer briefs from the suitcase—so not Piper's. The underwear dropped on the floor.

The smoldering gray gaze hit Dixon with the power of a punch. Dixon tensed.

"Were you going to talk with me before you disappeared?" Stan's voice was quiet, the hurt obvious.

An unwilling witness to a breakup, Piper edged toward the door.

But nothing escaped Master Homeland Security investigator. He pointed to her, then the kitchen. "Stay. There."

Pips didn't have what it would take to defy an angry Dominant, especially after what she went through last night at Dark Haven.

Shoulders slumping, Dixon gave her an *I'm-sorry* look. He shouldn't have told her he was packing up. He'd only wanted to help, but instead, he'd screwed up her life. He was scum, just like Darrell said.

Her return look held a friend's *it's-okay* and without a word, she walked into the kitchen. At least she'd be spared a part of their fight.

"Dixon? Was I supposed to come home and find all your shit just gone?" Stan's hurt was turning to anger.

Anger? What the fuck did *Stan* have to be angry about? Smoldering resentment flared to life. "When, exactly, was I supposed to talk with you? *Sir.*"

When Stan blinked, Dixon shot to his feet. "Oh, maybe last night? Like when you came home and told me you were too tired to talk?"

"I was—"

"Or all the days and nights before that? Same shit; rinse and repeat." Dixon's voice rose. He didn't have a temper, not really, but there were fucking limits. And the pain in his chest shoved him right past them.

He kicked the briefs Stan had dropped. "Wait, maybe we could've had a nice discussion over a meal—only there haven't *been* any meals or quiet evenings. Have there? *Have* there?"

"Hell." Stan sagged down onto the couch. "You did ask to talk with me, didn't you? I'm sorry, Dix. I fucked up."

The instant acknowledgment of error and apology broke Dix's spiraling anger, and he hesitated. He'd pushed a two-ton boulder of resentment up a hill, only to have it turn into a Styrofoam ball, leaving him scrambling for his balance.

Stan didn't move.

What the hell? His Master looked exhausted...as usual, these days. He'd been running on fumes for a week. But the devastation in his eyes—that was new. *Did I do that?* As guilt tunneled into Dixon's heart, he realized he wasn't the cause. Not yet, anyway.

Maybe Stan's investigation? When Darrell gloated about the arrest, Stan had said, "*Not soon enough.*"

Dixon took a step forward. "Stan? Now your case is done, can you tell me what it was about?"

Stan's hands closed. Opened. Then he rubbed his face, every movement exhausted. Grieving. "Darrell tracked a gang of child predators here from a kid who went missing in Texas. Using the internet, the bastards would lure children to where they could be grabbed, then use them for porn movies."

Oh, this was worse than all the fucks in hell. Dixon sat next to Stan, thigh-to-thigh, shoulder-to-shoulder, and pressed closer at the feel of the cold body next to his. His Master was almost shocky. "You're home. Did you catch the gang?"

"Oh yeah," The tone was emotionless. Stan was never emotionless. "Got them cold. Prosecution should be easy."

Dixon knew—knew—the answer before he asked. "The victims?"

"We found one alive. Another, just a boy, killed himself sometime yesterday."

The grief in his voice was so deep, so immense, that Dixon could only hold him, wishing to shield him from the world. "You tried, I know you did everything possible to save him, but you're not God. The assholes won't hurt any more children. You did good, Stan." His voice broke. "You did good."

When Stan pulled in a slow breath, Dixon knew his words were getting through. No one was stronger than his man. He'd gone into law enforcement because he wanted to help, to protect. It was more than a want—it was a calling. But the same compassion that made him a great Master was what was gutting him right now.

As a paramedic, Dixon knew the feeling— the frustration and helplessness and anger. He pulled his Master closer. "It'll get better, it will."

Far too soon, Stan straightened with a sigh. "Thanks, Dix. Sorry about that."

Sorry? Dixon blinked. "*Excuse* me?"

Mr. Macho Texas had trouble showing weakness. He wanted to be strong for Dixon—all the fucking time—and forgot a submissive could and should be plenty sturdy. After all, Masters were only human, no matter what their Domination for Dummies handbook said.

Stan winced at Dix's glare. "Yeah, sorry again. Thank you. You helped." There it was, the straightforwardness that Stan demanded—and practiced himself.

Unfortunately, the Dominant's acute insight hadn't taken a nappie today. Stan studied the suitcases again. "Yeah, I get that I've neglected you recently."

He set a blunt-fingered hand on Dixon's shoulder. "But it's happened before, and you never got distant because of it. Or wanted to leave. Why this time?"

Because Dixon had never felt like a hindrance before. A ball and chain. He glanced at the door and looked away quickly. *Shit, shit, shit.*

The criminal investigator had major skills in interrogation—although he called it a pussy name like interviewing—and could read body language like he was reading a kid's book.

Stan's gaze traveled between Dixon and the door. His brows drew together. "Darrell."

Although Dix didn't allow his expression to change, the stupid flinch he gave surely revealed his hurt feelings.

"You've heard Darrell spouting off, haven't you?" Stan sighed when Dixon nodded. "I didn't—and don't—agree with anything he says about you, Dix, but since I have to work with the idiot, I pick my battles."

The contemptuous tone made Dixon blink. "Wait, what? Isn't he your friend?"

"Not even close. He's a colleague and a fairly good agent. A bloodhound when following a trail." Stan's hand tightened on Dix's shoulder. "He's also a submissive who, unfortunately, I played with years ago. For a week. Then I realized his self-centeredness never stops, and the persistence that makes him a good agent is a pain in the ass when he won't take no for an answer."

"You don't want to make him your submissive?" Dixon asked slowly.

"Fuck no." The pissed-off swearing widened Dixon's eyes. That last one was not only anatomically impossible but also really gross. "Why the hell would I want anyone else when I have you?"

When Dixon's heart lifted like a helium balloon, he tried to yank it back down. This discussion wasn't done. Not really. He tried to keep the quiver from his voice. "You know, Darrell was right, though. I'm not good enough for you."

"You're not? Well, boy, you'd best explain. I must have missed something." The iron edge made the words an order.

Just fuck me with a floppy phallus. Dixon pressed his face against Stan's rock-hard chest, trying to figure out a way to escape.

"Talk to me, boy. Why aren't you good enough for me?"

"I'm not from a rich family like yours. Even a very nice family. I grew up on the streets; I'm a gutter-rat." Like the discerning Darrell had mentioned more than once.

"I see." Stan paused. "Guess I should avoid anyone who had a crap family or was broke growing up."

Dixon frowned. When he said it like that...

"I'll leave it to you to tell deVries why we can't be friends anymore. Because his family was far worse than yours."

"No!" Dixon's pride 'n' joys shriveled to tiny marbles. "Don't say anything." Stan sometimes let deVries play with him, and the sadist luuuurved cock-and-ball torture.

"Then keep talking, puppy."

Dixon pulled in a breath. CBT might be easier. "I don't have a bachelors or masters."

"True enough. Do you need one?"

"What?"

"Do you need a degree?" Stan asked patiently. "Is there a particular profession you want that you need a degree for? You hold down three jobs, and I thought you liked it that way. Did you want to switch to one full-time profession?" The reasonableness of the questions was irritating.

"Um." Dixon considered. He worked an ambulance part-time and loved the excitement. Worked in a clinic as a physical therapist assistant and loved the stability. Worked for Chatelaines doing whatever was needed and loved the variety. "No."

"Dix, you're one of the smartest people I know."

"Yeah, sure I am." Dixon made a scoffing sound low in his throat.

Stan grabbed Dixon's hair and yanked his head back. Painfully. "Have I ever lied to you?"

Dixon tried to shake his head. *Ow, ow, ow.*

"Do I lie at all?"

The growling annoyance melted every bone in Dixon's body —and woke up another bone. *Dammit.* "No, Sir."

"Just because you're lousy at sitting still when you're bored doesn't mean you're stupid. It simply means you have more energy than a greyhound on meth."

That didn't sound like a compliment.

When Stan's forbidding expression relaxed into a smile, Dixon's heart turned over. "As it happens, I like all that energy. I don't need someone with a degree. I need a boy with more loyalty and courage and compassion than any dozen people."

Stan used his grip on Dix's hair to pull him closer, and his mouth covered Dixon's. Brutally hard. But the angry kiss turned softer. Possessive. Amazing and wonderful. "I love you, Dix."

The last ounce of resistance faded away.

Stan lifted his head an inch, and his voice went to steel. "Girl, if you take one step closer to that door, I'll hogtie you and leave you on the floor till I get around to recalling your existence."

Dixon winced. He'd forgotten all about Piper. *Shiit-fucking-takkes.*

Stan turned his head, eyes fixing Pips in place. "You can leave if you give me your word that the only place you'll go today is your apartment."

Shoes in her hand, two paces from the door, Piper scowled. "I don't want to be in my apartment right now."

Stan jerked his chin toward the hall. "Then you can use our guest bedroom. Give me your word."

When her gaze met the Homeland Security agent's, she caved. "Fine. You have my word. My apartment or your guest bedroom."

She stalked into the spare bedroom.

Dixon grimaced. *Sorry, Pipster.*

When the door slammed hard enough to jiggle the chandelier, Stan chuckled. "The girl has a temper, doesn't she?"

Rising, he yanked Dixon to his feet. "Let's go burn off some of that energy of yours. I'm looking forward to hearing you make some noise. Lots and lots of noise."

As his Master towed him toward their bedroom, Dixon's head was spinning. A concussion, that's what he had. One minute in despair over leaving the only man he'd ever loved. The next minute, he zoomed up so high he'd smacked his head right into the fucking clouds. Because Stan was so soul-bearingly honest and... *He loves me.*

But—wait... Dixon planted his feet, stopping everything.

Still holding Dix's hand, Stan turned. Keen gray eyes focused on Dixon. "Boy?"

"I love you, too. You know that, right?"

Stan's expression turned Dixon's heart into a soft melty jelly. Yeah, he knew.

CHAPTER TWENTY-TWO

Piper flopped onto the bed and scowled up at the ceiling. Honestly, where did the damn Special Agent get off telling her what to do? This was...was kidnapping.

Kind of. She could have left—and Stan couldn't have stopped her, not really, only she didn't want to piss the Master off more than he was. Dix was already in trouble.

Would Stan call Ethan?

She snorted a half-hearted laugh. Probably not for a while. In fact, that'd been why she'd tried to leave. In the kitchen, she'd heard far too much of their conversation and could tell how they'd be resolving their fight. She'd heard some people liked that voyeur stuff, but not her. Sheesh.

Bunching up the pillow under her head, she sighed. At least the two had straightened things out.

Darrell's insults had sure messed with Dixon's head. Which was strange since Dix was one of the most confident people she knew. He could win over the crankiest clients while their grumpy sarcasm bounced off his cheerful shield.

But Darrell's derogatory comments had damaged Dix's self-image until her friend saw himself as a stupid, uneducated gutter-rat. A ball-and-chain dragging at Stan. Because of Darrell, Dixon's *mirror* lied to him.

Yet everyone else—especially Stan—saw him as the amazing person he really was.

Piper rubbed her fingers, which were tingling with the need to slap Darrell right across his condescending mouth. Had the creep spoken louder on the off chance that Dix was home and would hear him? The manipulative jerk.

Her eyes narrowed. Darrell's comments sounded a lot like the way the Defiler had talked about her. Everything Serna said had torn at her confidence...because she'd believed him. Thought he was telling the truth.

Had his words been chosen deliberately to tarnish her mirror? To warp her view of herself until she truly believed she was worthless. He'd told her slaves didn't think, that slaves existed only to serve. Had he wanted her to see herself as a slave named worthless because, that way, she'd never give him trouble?

Ethan didn't see her as worthless. He didn't use those tricks.

When her counselor had tried to discuss how an abuser would break down a victim, physically, socially, and mentally, Piper hadn't been able to talk about Serna. She still felt uncomfortable even thinking his name.

God, she was a wimp.

Dixon had faced up to his fears. Of course, his Master had made sure he did. Sir Ethan was like Stan only even more skilled and sneaky.

She shook her head as the men's voices, laughter, and a squeaking bed reminded her she wasn't alone in the apartment. When Dixon made a squealing sound, Piper pulled the pillow over her head.

Heavens, she was tired. Although Archimedes had been a sweet furry companion last night, Piper hadn't been able to sleep, knowing Serna was in the city. That he planned to take his property back.

I'm not property.

She was submissive, yes. She loved serving her Dom—a Dom she had the right to choose.

But she wasn't property.

Tucking her arms behind her head, she turned to look out the window. As the morning fog dissipated, the sky was changing from gray to blue.

Where was Ethan right now? Was he wondering where she was? If she was all right? He'd be worried...because he loved her. He really did, and she loved him, too.

Nevertheless, Serna would keep coming after her until he got her back. He was convinced the contract, no matter how illegal, gave him rights to her, and he thought every Master and slave in the lifestyle agreed with that.

Did they? Or had he convinced himself he was right?

He'd sure convinced her that he was a wonderful Master and would take care of her and...

Wait. She sat up in bed. If a burger place promised a person a hamburger and gave them a soy burger, well, that was illegal, wasn't it? It might be a verbal agreement—hamburger, not soy burger—but if a person got a soy burger instead, the burger place would give their money back.

With Serna, he'd presented himself as a loving Master. That was why she'd signed that contract. What she'd gotten was a selfish sadist.

That was just wrong. He was wrong.

Inside her brain, a light went on. He'd lied to her, manipulated her feelings and self-worth—just like that asshole Darrell—and tried to make her feel like nothing, just to get what he wanted from her.

Everybody had worth.

But some people—like Serna—were also real assholes.

Another smacking sound broke into her thoughts. Wet sounds. A shriek. A squeal. She crushed the pillow over her head to block the sound.

It didn't help.

As Ethan walked out of Piper's kitchen, he checked his watch. Almost noon.

Concern warred with rising anger. *Little subbie, you're going to be in some serious trouble if you don't get your pretty arse home.*

Taking a sip of the dark roast coffee he'd just made, he looked around. Since Churchill suffered if left alone too long, Ethan and Piper hadn't spent much time at her apartment.

But he felt at home in her place. The blue-and-white décor was a mix of old-fashioned, modern, and quirky that blended in a charming way. The sun streaming in the tall windows glinted off a dragon statue amidst the foliage plants. Low bookshelves held a mixture of business books, romance novels, and mysteries. One wall displayed photos of Victorian houses in ornate antique frames. On another wall, smaller antique frames showcased photographs of Piper with friends.

She'd also chosen very comfortable furniture, he noted with appreciation, as he settled into the overstuffed armchair. His sock-clad feet went up on the coffee table—an antique steamer trunk.

Absently, he picked up a rock from a wooden bowl filled with tumbled stones. It was cool in his palm, smooth against his fingers. Stress relief, indeed.

He rose as the apartment door opened, and Piper walked in.

Seeing him, she staggered back, fumbling for the door handle. Stark terror was on her face.

Bloody hell. "Piper." Not moving, he sharpened his tone. "*Piper.*"

"Ethan." Her voice cracked as she stared at him. "I thought you were..."

There, she was back in the rational world. Nonetheless, he slowed his approach.

Her hand was on her throat. "You scared me to death."

He closed his arms around her and pulled her close. "That makes us even, then, poppet. I've been worried sick about you."

"I'm so sorry." Her cheek was against his chest, and her arms tightened around him. "I panicked. Then I needed to think about...stuff."

About running? About leaving him? "I see." All night, he'd been imagining what she was going through—and wondering if he'd ever see her again. "I'm sorry, Piper. I should never have left you alone."

Never lifting her head, she snorted. "I read your texts. God, Ethan, if he had followed me into that tiny bathroom, I'd have lost it even more than I did. Thank you for realizing that."

The remorse that lay so heavy on his heart lightened a bit. "Then can you—"

"How did you get in here?" She looked around as if just realizing they were in her place, not his. "Wait, don't tell me—Stan let you in."

"When he and Darrell arrived, yes." Ethan rubbed his cheek over the top of her head. Her hair smelled different, no trace of lavender or lemon.

Her gaze lifted "That was a couple of hours ago."

"I thought you'd eventually return here. Or call me."

"I was going to." She pulled in a breath. "After I changed, I was going to call. So we could talk."

Relief filled him. "I left a note on the table at my place in case you showed up there." All right, time to deal with the elephant in the room. When he scooped her into his arms, she squeaked and clung to his neck.

He sat on the couch, settling her on his lap. "Now, tell me what kept you from calling me right away. From letting me help."

"Master Serna has a—"

"Stop." Was this a mistake? Maybe. But it needed to be said. "That abusive git doesn't deserve the title of Master, Piper. Don't give him that respect."

A wrinkle creased her forehead. "Right. You're right. Okay.

Serna is incredibly vindictive. If someone questions his methods, he goes after them. In Kansas, you were hoping to see Bob Fenton. Serna and other Masters drove Master Fenton out of the community because he intervened in a nonconsensual whipping and then later reported a Dom for rape."

"Ah, yes. We like to believe that we self-police, but too often, it's a cover-up, especially if a crime involves the so-called pillars of our community." Unfortunately, power inequities existed in even the most enlightened groups. "You're worried that Serna will drive you out of the lifestyle?"

She shook her head. "He'll go after *you*, Ethan."

Which was why she'd stayed away, trying to think of what to do. Warmth swelled Ethan's heart. She wanted to protect him.

"Have I mentioned that I love you?" he said.

Her eyes sparked with anger, and she gripped his shirt in tight little fists. "Did you not hear me? He'll get you kicked out of the community. You'll lose your friends—all your friends. *Again*."

"Yes, I do completely love you." His words reduced her to sputtering, which he silenced with a long, thorough kiss.

Ethan's arms were around her, his mouth on hers. Every breath brought her his scent, so clean and masculine. As the jittering worries inside her smoothed out, it felt as if she'd come home. She wrapped her arms around his neck and let herself go.

Here was where she belonged, right here.

When he eased her back, pulling her arms down and kissing her fingertips, her heart was so full she almost started to cry.

His deep blue eyes softened. "You had a nasty night, sweetheart. Can I assume you were at a friend's house and safe?"

He was still worried. God, she loved him. "The woman I've been cat-sitting for let me use her apartment, and I was at Dixon's this morning."

Ethan lifted an eyebrow. "Stan's been home for a couple of hours. He knew I was over here."

"Uh...he was a bit busy." She averted her gaze. "Dixon was leaving him, and they had a fight. I tried to leave, but Stan wouldn't let me. He made me give my word I'd only come here or use his guest bedroom. I was scared that Serna might get into the building, so I chose the guest bedroom."

"What changed your mind?"

She could feel her face heat. "Dix is...noisy, and the walls are awfully thin. I'm surprised Stan didn't gag him."

Ethan ran a finger down her hot cheek, and his lips quirked. "I daresay Stan knew exactly how loud Dixon was getting."

Because...he knew Ethan was in her apartment and figured he'd drive her over here.

That *sneak*.

Since Stan wasn't present, Piper punched Ethan in the arm.

His masculine laugh sent desire curling in her stomach. Until his expression went stern.

"All right, poppet. You warned me about Serna. Is there anything you want to discuss?"

Because Ethan undoubtedly had a whole long list of things he planned to scold her for. "I was planning to leave San Francisco. Fast. To stay safe."

"I'll keep you safe." His face was hard. Determined.

"I knew you'd say that, and I thought about running to you, but then Serna would ruin your life. You deserve better than that." Under her breath, she added, "Than me."

His jaw turned to stone. He opened his mouth. Closed it. "You were going to call me, so you must have changed your mind. I'm listening. Tell me why."

Because this was who he was. A Dom—but one who would listen first. Listen with his mind open. Even if they didn't work out, and she ended up a continent away, she would never forget this moment. His hands stroking up and down her arms, his gaze level, his patient silence.

"I—" She had to bite back her first words. *I love you.* No, this wasn't the time. Things were undecided. "Dixon was going to leave Stan without talking to him first. I heard them arguing. Dixon didn't think he was worthy of Stan. I understand how he felt."

"Because an arsehole trained you to think you're worthless?" Ethan asked softly.

She nodded. "Dixon doesn't see all the things that make him incredible, and I thought, maybe, my self-image might be a bit skewed, too. It hurt Stan when he realized Dixon was just going to leave. Dix wasn't right to do that."

"So you decided to talk with me." Brows drawn, Ethan gazed at the wall for a moment before his sharp eyes focused on her again. "Unlike Serna, I don't think anyone is worthless. Perhaps they haven't found what they have to offer the world, haven't realized their potential, but worthless? No."

She blinked. Although she told herself she wasn't worthless and believed it—mostly—his words cheered her soul.

"I agree that Serna messed with your self-image. So...let me tell you about Piper Delaney." The corner of his mouth kicked up slightly. "She's empathetic, fun, affectionate, loyal, and bubbly. It's no wonder that she's so well loved by her friends."

What? She stared at him.

"She's an excellent multitasker and persuasive, intelligent, quick-witted, forward-looking, and hard-working. That's why she's such a success in business."

He really saw those things in her? This was like being wrapped in a warm blanket.

"She likes to laugh—even at herself—and she makes me laugh more than I have in years. She apologizes when she's wrong, fights fair in an argument, and doesn't lie about how she feels, although sometimes I have to pry it out of her. She's giving, responsive, loving, and almost a mind-reader when it comes to knowing what someone else needs. I love how Churchill has her wrapped around his paws and how she stops to pet dogs in stores. She has a wealth of interests, and her mind bounces around when she lets it loose, so she's never boring."

She couldn't move.

"Even after fifty years, we'll probably find things to discuss—and argue about. And I'll still love her as much or more than I do now." He cupped her cheek, his thumb stroking over her lips. He kissed her, a promise in his warm lips, in the way he lingered.

Gathering her close, he wiped the tears from her cheeks.

She didn't know when she'd started to cry.

"We'll keep working on how you see yourself," he murmured. "Can we agree you're not going anywhere?"

She stiffened. "I don't want him to ruin your life. Your friendships."

"He can try." Ethan's voice was nonchalant. "Piper, the circumstances here aren't the same as in Kansas. The communities aren't the same. Xavier and Simon—all of us who run Dark Haven are on the same page when it comes to abusive relationships and ethics in the lifestyle."

Oh. She swallowed hard. "Are Xavier and Simon mad at me?"

"No, poppet. Simon is furious with Serna. Xavier even more so. He planned to ban him from the club."

Relief made her sag against Ethan. "But...'*planned to*'?"

His thumb rubbed his chin as he studied her face. "I asked him to wait. I wanted you to have the opportunity to face him in the club. Not for him to waylay you, but for you to be able to say what you need to say."

"Are you crazy?" She pushed against his chest, terror sliding cold fingers between her ribs.

"Think, Piper. Don't react blindly."

She sucked in air. *Think. Sure*. Just the idea of seeing the Defiler again terrified her. Facing him with people around and...

Deliberately facing him. Not having him sneak up on her from behind. The breath she took this time had an audible quaver. "You want me to exorcize him from my life."

"Mmmhmm. You have things you need to say to him."

Like that he was a liar. "Would you...would you be there?"

His expression held the gentlest of reprimands. "Do you really imagine I'd allow you to be in his presence without me there?"

Warmth filling her, she leaned into him. "I guess not."

"I'll be there. So will Simon, Xavier, deVries, Stan, and all your submissive friends. No one could keep them away."

She wouldn't be alone. "I...yes, then. I don't know if I can, but I want to try."

"Good enough. Do you want him tied-up and gagged first?" He grinned. "I'm asking for a friend."

And she burst out laughing.

CHAPTER TWENTY-THREE

After a while, Piper had wanted to go—Ethan smiled because she'd almost said "home"—and cuddle with Churchill. So he'd driven her back to his house.

As Churchill meowed his vehement annoyance of her absence last night, Ethan set them both on his lap. Bloody hell, but he loved having Piper in his arms.

Thinking he might never see her again had created an ache in his chest. Holding her eased it. Eased him.

As they talked about the night, Piper slowly went limp against him. It was time to move out of the past and look toward the future.

When he ran his hand over her curvy hips, he had to say that the immediate future held a definite appeal.

Piper must have felt his dick harden. She wiggled—which he couldn't complain about.

He trailed a finger down her cheek, along her jawline, down her neck. Under her thin shirt, her nipples were tiny peaks. "I missed you last night."

Her lips tilted up. "Are you planning makeup sex? I've heard it's fun."

She hadn't experienced makeup sex? Maybe not. She'd

mentioned that her lovers before and after Serna had been casual. Short-term. Serna had been her only serious relationship. "It is fun. I believe it's part of a Dom's duties to add to a submissive's experience."

And he had a craving to take her. To be inside her. No, more than that—to exert his will over her, to see her sweet submission, and to satisfy them both.

Gripping a handful of her hair hard enough that she knew he had control, he watched her pupils dilate. Rather than fear, her expression held dawning excitement.

"Piper. Go into the bedroom and strip. Kneel on the bed, facing the headboard. I need to notify Xavier and Simon that they can stop looking for you."

She winced. "I'm sorry."

"Don't apologize for being human. Xavier's sorry, too. And quite angry you weren't safe in his club."

"It's hardly his fault. The dungeon monitor got there right away. Can you tell them thank you for worrying?"

She could break a Dom's heart. "I will." He set her on her feet. "Go."

Giving her time to obey, Ethan let his friends know Piper was safe, as well as her decision to face Serna tonight. Xavier said he'd go in early and text if and when Serna showed up.

When Ethan entered the bedroom, he saw Piper kneeling in the center of the bed. He cocked his head, listening. She'd gone above and beyond his instructions. The playlist with Apocalyptica's most haunting music, starting with "Farewell", was playing.

The curtains had been closed to shut out the daylight. The flameless votive candles on the nightstands provided a flickering light that danced over her golden skin. It also showed the tense muscles of her back and arms. Why was she ill at ease?

After a second, Ethan caught on. She'd taken the initiative, something Serna would have found irritating. Serna was an idiot. "Very nice, poppet. Thank you."

Her tension drained away in an almost visible stream.

Ethan smiled and used the keypad to unlock the black leather trunk against the wall.

She turned to see what he was doing, and her eyes widened.

He cleared his throat. Initiative was one thing. Ignoring his orders about position was another.

Flushing, she returned her gaze to the headboard.

For a moment, he considered his canopy bed—custom-built to his tastes as a Dom. The top of the black heavy steel frame held three extra cross bars. The headboard was ornate as well as sturdy—a black steel geometric design that changed to black leather padding closer to the mattress. Because it'd only taken one time of fucking someone into the headboard to realize padding was useful.

Last night at Dark Haven, he'd planned to create an elaborate Shibari design on Piper. Share the intimacy of rope with her. Render her utterly helpless in suspension.

But... That scene wouldn't work this time. For the safety of a completely suspended submissive, he always stayed focused on her, which meant no sex for him.

Today, they both needed the closeness of making love.

So... Bondage? Definitely.

Total suspension, no. Partial suspension? Yes, that would be perfect. Just enough helplessness. "I'm going to tie you, poppet, and we're going to have some fun."

She stayed motionless except for a betraying quiver of her lovely breasts.

Reaching into the trunk, he picked up the silk ropes, ran them through his fingers, set them down. Stroked a finger over the jute. Too harsh for now. Hemp...yes. He'd use the set of ropes that were broken in and thus softer.

"Black and teal will look beautiful against your skin." He draped the hemp ropes over her shoulders, so she would smell the sweet grassy fragrance, and set the basket holding scissors and toys onto the foot of the bed.

Picking up the suspension rigging, he stepped up on the bed.

The rigging plate with several vertical lines was already set up and merely needed attachment to the bed's crossbars. Then, he could start.

Folding the blue-green rope in half, he located the bight and began to tie his favorite chest harness. "I like the way this compresses your lovely breasts and holds in your waist." With every glide of the rope, he followed it with a stroke of his hand over her velvety skin. As he wrapped her breasts, above and below, he took the time to play, filling his hands with soft flesh and using his mouth on her nipples until they were swollen and red.

The semi-corset around her waist would give her the feeling of being hugged and add comfort to the sense of helplessness that he intended to give her. The constriction of the rope around her breasts would add an erotic element.

Keeping his body against hers, enjoying the heat of her skin, how she'd begun to breathe in time with him, he continued, extending the knots down each arm in a beautiful pattern with loops for the swivels. The tension left her muscles as the ropes created a silent dialogue between them, reinforcing his authority, her helplessness. His love.

After pressing a kiss to her palms, he nipped her fingers to assess the warmth and sucked on her fingertips. A flush of anticipation rose in her face.

As he moved her where he needed her, and she gave herself fully over to his hands, he could feel her increasing surrender.

He did a set of basic frog-ties, fastening her ankles to the backs of her thighs. He loved the vulnerability the tie imparted. A submissive would know she couldn't escape, not with each foot pressed against an arse cheek.

Checking in, he kissed her slowly, gently. "Give me a color, poppet."

Her eyelids were already at half-mast. Her voice was husky as she whispered, "Green, Sir." Sliding into rope space.

"I'm going to position you now...solely for my enjoyment, sweetheart."

She didn't reject the idea—more the opposite. Her eyes held a glow of delight at being used to serve his needs. His beautiful submissive.

He ran a rope from her left knee to the side of the bed frame, then her right, adjusting them until her legs were widely spread. Her lower half was restrained to the bed, but her arms were free. She braced herself on her hands in doggy style.

Such a pretty arse and pussy. He ran a finger through the slickness. She was very, very wet.

Her breathing sped up as he penetrated her with a finger. Then another. His cock throbbed with its own urgency. *Patience.*

Reaching up to the suspension rigging, he attached one vertical line to the loop at the back of the chest harness and added another so her torso was supported. More support—rather than less—increased a bottom's comfort, so he hooked more lines to the loops he'd left on the backs of her arms. Her arms, held straight, were restrained alongside the long length of her upper body, like a bird taking flight.

The rigging's anchor point was closer to the head of the bed so the harness lines pulled her forward slightly. She was bent over with her torso not quite parallel to the bed, but angled slightly upward. Although some of her weight was on her knees, her upper body was fully supported by the ropes. Helplessly held in place.

And her pussy and arse were nicely available for whatever he wanted to do.

He sat down in front of her. Her expression was...interesting. She was relaxing into the ropes, the partial suspension, as she realized she was supported comfortably. Yet her breathing hadn't slowed completely because she'd also realized she was restrained in a very erotic, very vulnerable position

Gripping her chin, he kissed her roughly even as he reached

underneath her torso to play with a compressed, dangling breast. He could feel the shiver that ran through her.

Oh God, oh God. Sir Ethan was kissing her, his lips firm, his tongue demanding, even as he teased her poor throbbing breasts that the ropes had compressed into tight globes. As he rolled her nipples between his fingers, the sensation was so painfully glorious that she moaned.

He chuckled—and tugged at the aching peaks.

Her attempt to wiggle made her rock slightly, only slightly. She wouldn't be moving much—and the knowledge that she was tied with her pussy and ass so exposed just made her hotter.

"Now, we're going to play." His smile flashed, making her heart turn over. "I'm going to try to make you come—and you're going to try not to come. If you do, my reward is I get to spank you on the ass five times."

Her body froze as fear slid through her and disappeared almost as fast. Because he was watching her face, his gaze... understanding. Yet firm. He'd spanked her a couple of times before. Once for punishment, once for fun. Both times, she wasn't sure if she'd liked it or not; the memories of old pain hadn't released her enough to relax. "Um. So what's my reward, Sir?"

He chuckled. "That forbidden orgasm would be your reward, don't you think?"

Probably. An orgasm was really high on her list of things to do right this moment. Only...he'd spank her.

When he took out a wand vibrator and plugged it in, her eyes widened. "Sir, that's cheating."

His smile grew. "It is, isn't it?"

Holding the wand, he added an attachment—a short dildo that stuck up from a U-shaped curve. He moved behind her and set the bumpy dildo at her entrance. As it slid inside, she felt the ends of the U-shape putting pressure on both her clit and anus.

As the vibrator came on, it vibrated...everything. Her G-spot, her clit, even her anus, all at the same time. *Oh God.* Her butt went up, her back arching. And...*no, no, fight it*.

Useless. The pressure grew and grew, forcing her right to the peak with nothing she could do. It felt so good, so amazing. Unable to hold back, she came, pleasure singing in her veins... even as she gasped, "You-you-you *bastard*."

"Oh, little subbie..." He made a tsking sound and pulled the wand away and turned it off. "I can't believe you came that quickly. I'm not sure you even tried to hold out."

As he knelt beside her hip, his rough palm massaged her buttocks. "You know, poppet, by the time I finish, I don't think you're going to be able to sit down...or walk." He swatted her butt.

The sharp sting made her jerk her head up. As she rocked in the ropes, she couldn't move away, couldn't do anything.

Smack, smack. He rubbed the sting away.

Even as he did, her skin was absorbing the pain, sliding it into her recesses, creating a hot pool inside her.

Smack, smack. He leaned in and caressed her breasts, teasing them back into hard, aching points. Teasing her back into arousal.

"Such pretty breasts just cry out for adornment, don't you think?"

He didn't wait for her to answer. Holding her nipple with one hand, he fastened on a clamp, tightening it. Her nipple burned with the sharp compression, the pain making her try to rise up to get away. But the way she was balanced, her weight was too far forward. All she could do was squirm in the restraints.

"Breathe, Piper. Breathe through the ache."

Ache, my ass.

"Take this. For me."

For him. For her Dom. Letting her head hang down, she sucked in a breath. Another. The pain slid down to a nagging ache.

The second nipple was easier, but...harder. Both nipples were burning with just enough pain to make her aware of every breath she took. To feel how the ropes made her breasts swell and throb.

Her pussy had started to tingle, to ache at the emptiness inside.

How could she possibly be aroused again?

"You're such a good girl." Tangling his fingers in her hair, he held her head immobile as he kissed her. Deep and wet, taking his time as though she weren't in ropes, didn't have devices on her. Making her aware she was helpless. That her body and her arousal and time itself were in his hands.

"Let's see if you can hold out better this time since you got the first orgasm out of the way."

God help her, he pushed the wand attachment inside her again, held it so the ends of the nubby curve pressed against her clit and anus. He turned the vibrator on. Her entire pussy area, inside and out, came alive. Her clit swelled. Her muscles drew taut as the pressure built.

No, she wouldn't come this time. Teeth gritted, she fought the climax back, sweat breaking out on her body. Everything he did felt too good.

He tipped the vibrator slightly, hitting new spots. Two outside, one inside—and a violent release hit, sending pleasure searing through her.

"Aaaaaah, oh God, aaaaah." Her body bucked uncontrollably in the ropes. She gasped for air, her heart pounding.

The vibrator turned off.

"Tsk. You Yanks lack stamina." Amusement threaded his dark smoky voice. Before she could even catch her breath, he slapped her bottom. The burn was fiercer this time, only each time his hand hit, the sting slid straight into a heavy liquid pleasure.

"That's five." He flicked on the vibrator without any more warning, and the sensation drove the air from her lungs. He'd upped the power. The hammering inside and out meant no one could possibly fight it.

She came, screaming a protest.

The next spanking was painfully pleasurable, prolonging her orgasm. The spasms continued, on and on, until she went limp.

When he slid the wand attachment from her, her pussy was so swollen and sensitive, she could only quiver. She had a momentary thought of swearing at him, but her mouth didn't seem to be connected to her brain.

"Still green, poppet?"

"Mmmhmm."

"Wiggle your fingers and toes. Anything numb or tingly?"

"Nnnunuh."

His low masculine chuckle made her heart happy. Until he said, "Let's get you wiggling again." Fingers danced over her pinched nipples, around her breasts. He tugged on the clamps, sending zings of aching pleasure through her, then played with her breasts some more. As they swelled, her nipples throbbed even more.

And she wiggled.

Lifting her chin, he kissed her. "These have been on long enough."

These what? She felt his fingers on her left breast, on the nipple. The clamp loosened and came off. A second later, all the blood in her whole body rushed back into the tender nipple, and it burned like fire. She jerked, squirmed, tried to pull her arms down, but the ropes held her torso straight out over the bed with her arms flying behind her like wings. "You...you bastard."

"Sorry, love, but my parents were married." Laughing under his breath, he kissed her—and removed the second clamp.

"Ow, ow, ow. You sadist, you evil, mean, nasty sadist." Both nipples throbbed and stung...and somehow set up a matching burn in her clit.

"That's me," he agreed politely. "Only I think you should say, *Nasty sadist, Sir*."

She froze, hearing what she'd said. She'd been totally rude to a Dom. To a Master.

He...was grinning.

He nuzzled her temple. "When we're playing in bed and I push you, swear words and accusations are permitted. Expected, even."

His hand gripped her hair, lifted her head. His eyes were a deep intense blue as he said gently, "Swear at me at a table in Dark Haven, and I'll take you over my knee." The sun lines beside his eyes crinkled. "And I'll enjoy that, too."

She shuddered with helpless need. Because he wasn't angry. Because she'd probably enjoy it too.

"Prepare yourself, sweetheart. I'm going to take you now, and you're going to come again, whether you want to or not."

A whimper escaped her. She might die if she came again.

She heard his clothes coming off, then he was on the bed behind her. Her knees were wide apart, her thighs tied to the sides of the bed. Open and restrained for his use.

The head of his cock found her entrance, and he pressed in—so much bigger and thicker than the attachment. Velvety smooth and hotter than fire. He stretched her, even as her walls spasmed around him in aftershocks.

"I love being inside you, Piper," he murmured. "Although teasing you into orgasming might be almost as pleasurable."

His hips worked, moving his cock in a circular motion inside her. She was so sensitive that she wiggled, tried to move away, and only rocked back and forth on him.

His body covered hers, his hand on her belly, and his other hand... He tugged on her right nipple—the very tender abused nipple.

"*Owwww.*" Her hands tried to stop him, but her arms were tied too firmly.

"You can't stop me, poppet." He thrust inside her more forcefully, ignored her squirming, and teased her left nipple.

The instinctive need to fight left her panting, overpowered, at his mercy. The joy of being helpless, totally controlled slid through her. Sir Ethan had claimed her.

The mattress seemed to disappear, leaving her floating.

"That's right, sweetheart. I have you." His thick shaft moved in and out as he teased her nipples, as desire set up a throbbing in her core. "And this time, you'll come with me inside you."

She'd die. Simply die. "Please, I can't." Her sweat-soaked hair swung around her face.

"Now, pet, 'can't' isn't a good word to use around a Dom." He yanked her back on his cock. "You can. And you will."

She could do nothing. He knew her, had learned her body too well. He could—and would—ruthlessly force her into another orgasm and wring every last drop of pleasure from her. Knowing that was more erotic than anything she'd felt before.

The vibrator came on again. This time with no attachment. He pressed it steadily against her clit. Her entire body started to shake as he thrust, hard and fast, even as the wand hammered against her ever-so-sensitive clit.

She didn't have a chance, taken from inside and out. She was filled with so many sensations that she couldn't process anything. His cock was thick inside her, and her whole body spasmed with the maelstrom of pleasure.

"Oooooh." The storm of sensation poured through every nerve in her body.

"There's my Piper." He pressed deep and, with a low groan, came inside her. His arm tightened around her, holding her to him.

Everything went fuzzy for a while, and sometime later, she was out of the ropes and lying on her back. Her entire pussy felt like it was somewhere between numb and tingling.

Sir Ethan lay on his side next to her, idly playing with her breasts. Waiting for her.

"You're a mean, cruel Dom," she whispered.

"Indeed, but you love me anyway. It's time you gave me the

words." His stern gaze pierced through her, pulling her heart right to the surface.

"I love you. So very much." She'd done it. Said the words. And the way his eyes went soft with pleasure filled her world.

His lips curved with a satisfied smile. "I love you, too, Piper Delaney."

Eventually, when it was time to get moving, she found out he'd told her the truth—she couldn't walk.

As he helped her into the bathroom, he was laughing.

Damn Dom.

CHAPTER TWENTY-FOUR

Standing in front of the wall mirror in Ethan's master bedroom, Piper grinned. "Wow, I look good."

"Of course you do." On the bed, Lindsay slouched against the padded headboard. "I am a genius at the art of big hair."

"You really are." Piper's black collarbone-length hair was doubled in volume—and curly. Before leaving for Dark Haven, Ethan had come over to kiss her and hadn't been able to resist playing with the fat curls. From the look in his eyes, if they'd been alone, she'd have ended up back in bed.

Flirting with herself in the mirror, she turned her head. Her smoky eyes were huge with long curling lashes. Her cheekbones looked sharp enough to cut. Her lips were an *I-dare-you* red that matched her shoes. "You totally rock makeup, Abby."

Abby and Rona were sitting in the two armchairs by the windows. Abby smiled. "My little sister insists on keeping me up to date—and recruits me to help her dress for her big dates."

"You look perfect." Rona nodded her approval.

"The dress is perfect," Piper corrected.

Even as Piper had begun to worry about what she'd wear to the club, the three women had arrived at Ethan's to help her get ready.

Rona had wanted her to wear something that felt less... vulnerable. Piper couldn't wear as many clothes as a Domme would—it would indicate fear. But her normal fetwear was too inviting. Too revealing.

So Rona had given her a skintight black latex dress with a built-in bra. It was short, of course, but long enough to cover her butt. The lacing from belly button to sternum showed off her skin and cleavage, but also made those breasts difficult to touch. Thin straps kept the top up—again, making it difficult to mess with.

Pulling up the hem, she gazed at the matching black latex briefs. They were tight and sexy...and an excellent barrier to unwanted touch.

"Thanks, guys." Her red pumps with ankle buckles were perfect, and the steel-spike stiletto made an awesome defense.

For extra courage, she donned the ruby and diamond bracelet Ethan had given her.

"You do realize that this is simply for your comfort, right? None of the Masters will let that *bastardis* touch you." Abby's phone rang and she answered it. "Yes, My Liege?"

Although Piper strained her ears, she couldn't hear what Xavier was saying.

"We're leaving now." Abby tucked her phone away. "Xavier says Serna has arrived with his slave and is chatting up the members, trying to gain sympathy for the time he invested in his runaway slave. He's telling people that you really want to return to him. That you have a slave heart."

Piper felt her mouth go dry.

"It'll be all right." Abby glanced at Rona. "Although it might get messy."

"Messy?" Rona frowned.

"As I hung up, I heard Simon start arguing with Xavier on who gets to hit Serna first. Then Ethan...well, have you heard him when he gets all English and annoyed? He said if anyone got to punch Serna, it would be him."

Piper's mouth dropped open. Her Dom. Then the sweeping joy of being protected gave way to reality. "Don't let them hit him, okay? Serna is the type to sue."

"They'd have to find the body first." Lindsey sniffed. "Zander has ways...and he's really unhappy with that guy."

Rona studied her fingernails. "Simon's been teaching me self-defense. I wouldn't mind getting in a punch. Just for practice, you know."

"Yes!" Abby's eyes lit. "We all should. Mr. Macho would be too humiliated to sue women."

"I'm in!" Lindsey's voice dropped into a John Wayne drawl, " '*You tangle with me, I'll have your hide.*' " She adjusted an imaginary hat and bounced on the bed. "Maybe we should have a fem squad to terrorize bad Doms."

"No, not a good idea. No, no, no." Piper shook her head frantically. "Xavier would have a fit—and Ethan would blame me. God, my butt is already sore." Which was why she was standing now.

Her friends busted up laughing. They'd already teased her about the beard burn on her cheeks and the rope marks on her arms and legs.

"Time to get moving, people." Rona started to shoo them out of the bedroom, then stopped. "Piper, you need a coat. It's cold outside."

"Right." Ethan had mentioned he'd left her long coat in the bedroom closet. She walked over to the closet, reached for the doorknob.

No doorknob. She stared.

"Problem, Pips?" Lindsey asked, joining her.

"The door. It's a folding door."

"Uh-huh." Lindsey eyed Piper with concern. "I see that. Folding. Magnetic latch."

"This was a regular hinged door last week. With a doorknob."

Rona ran her hand over the doorframe, then leaned forward

and sniffed. "It smells like new varnish. Maybe Ethan prefers this kind of door?"

Piper couldn't look away from the closet. No knob. No lock.

An accordion-type door couldn't be secured. Couldn't keep anyone locked inside. Tears prickled her eyes.

He'd changed the closet door for her.

"Hey, Pipster." Standing in the Dark Haven entry, Dixon greeted her with a hug and grinned at the three women behind her. "I see you brought the female part of your crew."

"Hey, Dixonian." She looked him over. His lips were swollen, his cheeks and neck beard-burned, and the faint mark of ball-gag straps ran across his cheeks. He not only looked well-loved, but sweet contentment showed in his eyes.

She had a feeling that he and Stan were not only together, but stronger than before.

After Dix handed out hugs to her "crew", Piper held her membership card up to the scanner, then followed everyone into the main club room. From the speakers came the eerie-voiced Trivium, "The Wretchedness Inside" and a few people were dancing. Most of the tables in the center of the room were taken. People liked to socialize before and after scenes.

She could feel her breath turning shallow, and she kept reminding herself to stay alert. Regulate the pace. It was a stupid world when a person had to monitor her breathing. She looked around and didn't see Serna.

Relief was the uppermost emotion. Maybe he'd left.

Then she saw Sir Ethan heading across the room toward her, and she knew he'd been watching for her. Worrying about her. Her heart went into a complete breakdance. *Mine, mine, mine.*

It wasn't fair that he was so gorgeous. Or the way he looked like the English aristocrat that he was. Although the lethal look of his exquisitely tailored suit over a black turtleneck would probably get him kicked out of Parliament.

"Here you are. You do look lovely tonight, pet." He spotted her bracelet, and his look of approval warmed her. "I fear you're missing an essential item of clothing, though."

"I am?"

With a tender smile, he reached into his suit coat and pulled out his collar. ETHAN'S glinted at her. He lifted an eyebrow.

"Oh, yes. Please, Sir." She bowed her head and pulled her hair out of the way so he could put it on. The feeling of his fingers, the fleece lining, the fit around her throat was like having his body against hers, his strength part of her.

"There you go. Mine." The satisfaction in his voice matched the feelings running through her.

When he hugged her, she wrapped her arms around him, breathing him in, feeling the rock-solid muscular frame against her. The world grew firmer under her feet. Tipping her head back, she looked up into his unwavering, watchful eyes. "I love you, so, so much."

An eyebrow rose, and a smile lightened his stern expression. Cupping the back of her head, he leaned down to kiss her. Slowly, gently, letting her know that she was his.

And loved.

By the time he lifted his head, he'd had to tighten the arm around her waist to keep her from sinking into a puddle on the floor.

Laughter came from behind her, and he looked over her head. "Ladies. It's good to see you."

Her crew hadn't left to find their Doms. They were sticking with her.

Because Serna was here. She felt her stomach turn over. Could she do this? Face the man who'd reduced her to nothing?

"This is your decision, your choice, Piper. No one will force you into anything you don't want to do," Sir Ethan murmured.

"Where is he?" Her lips were having trouble forming words.

"He's in a group of men by the bar." Sir Ethan's voice was loud enough the others heard, and everyone turned to look.

Serna was barely visible inside a circle of four men—none whom Piper had met. Whatever he was saying received appreciative nods. He was probably talking about ownership and property. *The scumbag.* Slavegem was kneeling at his feet, posture perfect, but—as Piper used to do, she was sneaking looks around.

Her gaze met Piper's, and she looked down.

Piper felt bitter amusement along with pity. Serna would probably like to know Piper was here, but slavegem wouldn't tell him...because he'd be likely to punish the girl for looking around. Stupid so-called Master. Abuse ensured a slave would worry more about self-preservation than her Master's desires.

Eventually, Piper's crew caught the Defiler's notice. When he spotted her, a smug expression crossed his face. He strode confidently across the room, followed by the other Doms.

Piper took a step back. *Oh, God.*

"Courage, poppet," Sir Ethan murmured. His hand on her back reminded her he was right beside her.

Dixon took her hand. When Piper turned to give him a grateful look, she saw Stan had closed in, as had Xavier, Simon, and deVries.

"Worthless, I expected you to be here tonight." Serna exchanged a meaningful look with his followers. "A true slave wants nothing more than to be owned. Even if she can't say the words, she'll keep showing up, hoping to be taken back."

He looked down at slavegem who'd taken up her spot at his feet. "Wanting to be in her destined place at her Master's feet."

Through the buzzing in her ears, Piper heard Rona snort in disgust.

"Dear sweet Jesus," Lindsey muttered. "That dude is all hat and no cattle."

"Does anyone have a cane? I want to hit him," Abby whispered and got a rumbling negative from Xavier.

In the silence that fell, Piper couldn't speak. It was taking everything she had not to run.

"So, Worthington, you fucking thief," Serna said. "She's here, proving my point. Wanting to return to me."

"I doubt that." Sir Ethan's voice was easy. He didn't say more because...he was waiting for her.

Serna's gaze turned to her. His smile turned cruel in a way she recognized, a way that made her body start to tremble. Her mind might tell her she was safe, but her body recognized the signs. He'd hurt her. Horribly. "Get over here, worthless."

When she didn't move—*couldn't* move—he took a step toward her and tripped on slavegem.

Paralysis broken, Piper jerked out of reach.

Furious, Serna kicked slavegem in the chest. "Stupid cunt."

Whimpering, the girl curled into a ball as he drew his foot back for another kick.

"No!" Lunging forward, Piper shoved him away from slavegem. "Leave her alone, asshole."

"You *dare*." Face dark, Serna swung his fist.

Sidestep and block. Years of self-defense. Gut tight, form perfect, Piper punched him in the cheek. Even as pain flared in her right hand, she shot her left fist out to nail him in the jaw.

His head jerked sideways. Blocking his wild swing, she stepped forward, drew power from her toes all the way to her right fist—and punched him right in the mouth.

He staggered back. Lost his balance and landed on his ass in the center of his followers.

Arms grabbed her from behind. Piper tried to fight, but Ethan drew her back against his chest. "Easy, poppet. You got your blows in. Now it's time to talk."

"Huh. Good job, Pips." Dixon's voice rose. "But the dimwit dildo-dick is still conscious."

"I appreciate her restraint." Xavier gave her a slight smile. "I need him able to talk so we can finish this tonight."

Xavier wasn't angry. She'd punched a Master, and he wasn't angry?

Was Sir Ethan? She looked up at him. "Are you upset I hit him?"

"I'd rather have done it myself," he said gently. "But I think it was good for you."

She let out a breath.

"Good form, too, although you might stand more sideways to decrease the target area."

"Excuse me?" She was ready to panic, and he was critiquing her fighting style?

The men around Serna helped him to his feet.

A couple of women were trying to help slavegem, but the girl waved them away. Too frightened to even allow someone to care for her. *God.*

"You're bleeding, Piper." Rona lifted Piper's hand.

Looking down, Piper realized her knuckles were scraped and bloody...and really hurt. *Ow.*

Rona wrapped a ripped-up, cold, wet towel around her fingers. "Simon tells me I should hit the soft parts, never the mouth."

"Excellent advice. However, this time?" Sir Ethan winked at Piper. "You did well, poppet. Serna won't be able to hide his punishment under his clothing."

Piper's mouth dropped open.

Shaking free of his followers, Serna confronted Xavier. "I demand the right to punish that cunt."

Ice ran through Piper as he continued. "She's my property as is this one." He pointed to slavegem. "I hold irrevocable slave contracts giving me the right to punish them in any way I see fit. That's what nonconsensual consent means."

The sound of slavegem's sobbing brought back too many memories. How fear would overwhelm her. How her whimpering would escape no matter how hard she'd tried to clamp her jaws shut.

No. No, he didn't have the right to punish slavegem. Or her. *No.*

Anger burned a bit of her fear away. "Your contract isn't worth the paper it's written on." She froze, not believing she'd said that. But she had.

"Yes!" came a voice from behind her. Lindsey.

Serna's color rose. "Did anyone give you permission to spea—"

"Oh, honestly, try to follow the conversation," Piper said, heard Sir Ethan's low chuckle, and took strength from it. "Or do I need to use smaller words?"

"Piper, we've heard Serna's argument." Xavier's hands were clasped behind his back; his face was grave. "Dark Haven's members would appreciate hearing yours."

To her surprise, the people in the room, most of whom she didn't know, echoed Xavier's invitation.

When the Defiler went livid with rage, Piper shuddered. The words she'd planned to say disappeared. Under his cruel gaze, her gaze faltered, dropped...and landed on slavegem.

Bruised, emaciated, the slave was rocking back and forth. She was so very lost. How could Piper leave her to the monster? She had to have a chance.

"Go, girl. Go, go, go." Dix was chanting behind her.

"You can do this," Abby whispered. "Stand up for yourself."

A wave of love for her friends washed through her. Leaning into Sir Ethan, Piper blinked away tears as she looked up and mouthed, *I love you.*

His steady eyes held hers for a moment, and courage flowed into her.

Pulling in a breath, she laid out her hard-won truths for all to hear. "There are several things I'd like to point out. The first is the most basic. The 13th Amendment makes slavery in any form illegal. A contract to commit an illegal act isn't enforceable. Your so-called contract is illegal and unenforceable. Which means if you move someone anywhere without their consent, that's kidnapping. Hitting someone who has retracted her consent is assault and battery. That's the law. Period."

Serna sniffed and looked around at his friends. "Owners and property operate outside the law."

"Whoa, seriously?" Dixon said in a mock-whisper. "Someone's thinking with his little head."

Snickering ran through the assembled crowd.

Don't laugh. If she started, she'd end up in hysterics.

Raising her head, slavegem stared at Piper.

I can do this. I must. For her. For other slaves. "Second. Even if a Master wants to write an illegal contract—for clarity, say—*ethical* Dominants will write it so there is a way out—for both parties. Because no matter how willingly a person gives a vow, things change."

Serna scoffed, folding his arms over his chest. "Not for good people."

The few men around him nodded.

"*From this day forward until death should us part.* That's a common vow. I take it no one in this room is divorced?" The silence that fell was gratifying. A corner of her mouth tipped up. "I know Serna has been. Twice. His wives probably fled for the same reason I did. Now my third point is this..."

Wait for it, wait for it.

"Whoa, girlfriend, don't leave us hanging." Lindsey was the perfect straight man. "Give us the meat."

The rough rasp of deVries's chuckle sounded—because he loved his Texan's irrepressible spirit.

Piper peeked up at Sir Ethan and caught his tender smile. The one that said he was proud of her and loved her...just as she was.

She could do this.

"Third, right. If I ordered and paid for a fancy Rolls Royce, but the dealer delivered a Toyota, well, the sale contract wouldn't be valid, would it? Because I didn't get what I ordered."

She gave Serna a scathing glance, then spoke directly to

slavegem. "When I met Serna, he acted like a caring, wonderful Master. Firm, but gentle. Never going past my limits. Telling me he loved me, treasured me. That he wanted to help me grow and become the best person I could be. I slept in his bed and ate healthy meals. He built me up and made me feel special."

She paused, her voice dropping. "He promised he'd care for me tenderly."

The room had gone dead silent. Scary silent.

"I signed the contract in a haze of adoration. I wanted to give this wonderful Master...everything. My heart, my body, my soul." A shiver ran through her. She had to tell them of the hell her life had become. The false promises, but this...this was the part she couldn't face. Had never been able to talk about.

Thickness closed her throat, imprisoning her words.

When Piper didn't speak, slavegem's head bowed. Her hands were clasped so tightly the tendons stood out. Piper could see how her skin was stretched over the bony prominences. She had no spare flesh. Just a wealth of bruises and cuts.

Piper swallowed. *I'm free. No matter what happens now, I'm free. She's not. This is my task to do.*

Forcing past the strangling memories, Piper continued. "My wonderful Master had lied about who he was—and everything changed. I slept on a blanket on the wood floor. I cooked him healthy food, but I had to eat canned stew. Once a day." She looked down at herself. "I was under a hundred pounds when I escaped. And I admit, sometimes I was so hungry I stole the dog's food."

Shame filled her, the feeling of being less than a human, less than an animal.

She saw slavegem's tiny nod.

"That fucking asshole," someone said.

A murmur of distress ran around the room and let her keep speaking. "If he had trouble at work or was bored or irritated or depressed—whatever—he beat me. Or humiliated me. He'd lock me in a tiny coat closet or chain me in the backyard, naked, without water and without shelter. I spent a month chained to a pipe in the basement." She glanced down at the lumpy scars on her wrists.

"It wasn't like that," Serna tried to say, but Xavier motioned for him to be silent.

She pulled in a breath. "This was the Master who said he'd treasure me, would help me grow. Nevertheless, he took even my name away. The only thing he'd call me was *worthless*."

When no one spoke, a shiver started in her center.

But she could feel Sir Ethan's warmth against her side. His arm around her waist anchored her, holding the memories far enough away that she could think.

Finish. Time to finish. Every meeting should conclude with a summary.

"The contracts Serna has been screeching about are illegal. Even if I *was* property—and I'm not—we have laws about the abuse of animals, and if an owner isn't capable of caring responsibly for an animal, he's taken to court. Shouldn't the slaves in our community have the same protection?"

She saw people nodding. Heartened, she added, "Ethically speaking, the slave contract should have a termination clause where the entire relationship can be dissolved."

"Finally, that person there"—she pointed to him—"that so-called Master put on a show and lied through his teeth to get me and slavegem to sign his bogus contract. Is he really the kind of person you want in Dark Haven?"

As she pointed, she realized deVries was behind Serna with his hand over the monster's mouth and had forced Serna's arm up behind his back. No wonder she'd been able to finish without interruption.

Giving her a quick smile, deVries let go and stepped back.

"She's lying." Serna was so angry that spittle flew from his mouth. "Lying to you all. Don't be fooled by her. She was always lying to me and—"

"She's telling the truth." Slavegem—no, *Gemma*—pushed to

her feet, cowering away from Serna. "You lied to *me*. You said you'd take care of me, that you loved me. You told me she was bad, and that was why you treated her so mean, but when she left, I didn't change, but you beat me like you did her. You lied and lied."

Serna's face went blank with shock.

Gemma's voice rose. "I don't want to be a slave. I want to go home to my mom and dad. You won't even let me call them. I want to go *home*."

Stepping forward, Piper pulled the sobbing girl into her arms.

Rona joined them, taking Gemma from her and squeezing Piper's shoulder. "I've got her. Go see this through."

Piper slipped back to Sir Ethan—*my place*—and realized deVries stood beside Serna with Simon on the other side, bracketing the man with intimidation.

Serna's mouth was bleeding. His jaw and cheek were swollen, beginning to show the bruising.

Totally worth her scraped knuckles.

Xavier strolled into the empty center of the circle of members. "Since Serna's arrival, we've all been discussing the Master/slave, Owner/property issues. These types of relationships *are* important to us. However, the basis of our lifestyle is also consent. I feel that Dark Haven's position should be that contracts must contain a revocation clause, a way for either member to terminate the relationship. Does the membership agree?"

A chorus of agreement sounded.

Only two young men looked pissed off. From the way Stan and Sir Ethan studied the two before exchanging glances, Piper almost felt sorry for the idiots. They'd be getting additional scrutiny from the person supervising the club's Doms as well as from a Homeland Security special agent.

"Very good." Xavier smiled slightly. "It's my decision that a Master's pursuit of a slave after the slave terminates the relationship will result in a canceled membership along with dispersing information of that unacceptable behavior to every club and group we can reach. I intend to begin with the so-called Master here." Frowning at Serna, he crossed his arms over his chest.

Talk about intimidating.

Abby put an arm around Piper. "My Liege is in a mood to rip someone a new *cūlus*."

Piper choked. Wasn't that Latin for *asshole*? "You're such a professor."

"Serna, good luck to you if Piper and Gemma decide to prosecute. Our membership would be pleased to testify about your attempted kidnapping." Xavier's mouth went flat. "Get out of here. I suggest you get some counseling; you need it."

"Don't let me ever see you again, fuckface," deVries growled.

Serna's face had gone white, making the blood and bruises stand out garishly. He stared around him, his shock and disbelief obvious.

Near him, Gemma was surrounded by women offering their support.

When Serna took a step in that direction, a line of Masters and Mistresses formed to block him.

Serna turned toward Piper, and another line formed in front of her. Her crew's Masters...and others, as well.

Not moving, Serna stared at her.

She sucked in a breath and held her ground, chin up.

Serna took a step back.

Sir Ethan set Piper to one side. "I'll escort you out, Serna." Although Serna was already heading toward the exit, Ethan followed.

Piper took a step after them, but was stopped by Lindsey. "You rock, girl. Way to go." Fists up, she re-enacted the fight, right, left, right, adding her own sounds.

Behind her, deVries nodded. "Not bad at all, little Piper."

Piper looked at the door again. "Sir Ethan went out there. Shouldn't someone..."

DeVries shook his head. "Nope."

Before she could go after her Dom, Ethan came back in, strolling across the room, perceptive gaze on Piper. Despite the menace rolling off him in a heart-stopping wave, Piper flung herself at him.

His arms closed around her, and she could feel his cheek rub on the top of her head. “My Piper,” he murmured.

“Worth, do we need to call the asshole an ambulance?” Simon asked, his arm around Rona.

“No.” Sir Ethan chuckled. “He got into a taxi. Quite hastily, I might say.”

Rona made an exasperated sound. “You barbarians. I’ll get more towels.”

Pulling back, Piper turned to look at Sir Ethan’s hands. His knuckles were scraped and bleeding. “What did you do?”

“Sweetheart, I was content with the beating you gave him, until you told us how you were treated. I needed...” He sighed. “Well, I do hope you don’t mind.”

Hearing the barely diffused fury in his oh-so-calm voice, she burrowed back into his arms. “I hope he doesn’t bleed all over the cab seat.”

Sir Ethan laughed, and some of the tension left his body.

“I knew you’d had a rough time, but that was worse than I thought.” He rubbed his chin in her hair, then stepped back to look at her. “I doubt I’d have the courage to trust another Dom. You are magnificent, Ms. Delaney.”

Tears blurred her vision and spilled down her cheek.

Hand under her chin, he wiped them away gently. Her Dom. He could have pushed her to one side and taken Serna down without raising a sweat. Instead, he’d stood beside her in silent support as she’d had her say. Cheered her on without words.

He was everything Serna was not. The Dom she’d dreamed about, made up fantasies about.

She tipped her head up to him. “I love you.”

The kiss she received was far, far better than any fantasy.

EPILOGUE

Look at her. Smiling slightly, Ethan gave Piper's shoulder a gentle push and watched her rotate in the suspension. The lights of the dungeon danced over her bare skin as well as the black rope forming an intricate design over her naked body.

Perfect.

Ethan had used a chain dangling from the blimp in the Dark Haven's dungeon as part of his rigging. Piper was suspended on her left side, her left leg bent with her calf to the back of her thigh in a frog tie, and her left wrist tied to the ankle. Her right leg was straight and angled upward from her body, opening her pussy for his convenience. Another rope kept her right arm extended toward that leg.

At his usual pace, he had created his art on the canvas of her skin, meticulously lining up his knots, slowly drawing the rope over and around her body. The rough black rope against her smooth pale skin was beautiful. As he'd worked, her nipples had turned to hard peaks, and her skin had flushed a lovely pink. While building the chest harness, he'd caressed her breasts, even as the ropes slowly squeezed them into tightly drawn globes.

Muscle by muscle, she'd relaxed and grown increasingly aroused. By the time he'd reached her crotch to add a knot over her clitoris—the proverbial happy knot—her pussy was wet and glistening.

When he'd lifted her into the air, her body had stiffened for only a second before she'd relaxed into the rope's embrace. Because she trusted him. The knowledge warmed his heart.

Stopping her rotation, he adjusted her arm minutely and checked her fingers for warmth. "Do you have any tingling or numb areas, Piper?"

"No, Sir." Her voice was a bare whisper, relaxed yet husky with arousal.

Because he'd deliberately chosen to make this a very erotic session.

"Are you uncomfortable—too uncomfortable?" Rope suspension wasn't completely pain free...but that could add to the pleasure. The bite of the rope, the pressure...

"No, Sir. I'm good."

He'd stayed close to her while tying the knots, leaning his body against hers. Now, he stood with his chest against her back and put his arm under her head so he could whisper in her ear. "Yes, you are. You're a very good subbie."

The back of the dungeon was fairly quiet. The sounds of a whip cracking, moaning, slapping, groaning were distant. And he hadn't heard them at all when he'd been working.

Piper was sliding further into rope space, the place where only his voice, only his touch reached her. Even when a woman's voice rose in a wail, she didn't react.

He simply watched, treasuring the moment.

And then the time had come to torture his little submissive a bit.

Piper's mind seemed to be floating in clouds even as her body lay horizontally, swaying in the suspension. Around her chest, waist, legs, and arms, rope bound her so snugly that it felt as if Sir Ethan had wrapped her in warmth and safety. When he'd pulled on the rigging, the floor dropped away beneath her, and she'd left the earth behind. Yet the sense of being protected hadn't disappeared—it had deepened.

Now, he stood in front of her, and his hands stroked her bare skin, teasing her, enticing her into arousal. The ropes compressed her breasts, making them swell, and his fingers on her nipples pinched and rolled in erotically painful caresses. His gaze was on her face, holding her eyes as he played with her helpless body.

She sucked in a breath as excitement thrilled through her. She couldn't do anything except squirm.

His eyes crinkled. Then he tugged on the rope that ran between her legs—the one that had a big knot right over her clit—and a sharp lash of pleasure burst outward. Her clit was swollen, throbbing and urgent, and she moaned.

His smile flashed in his tanned face.

In the back of her mind, she knew she should be wary of a smile like that—a Dom's smile of ownership. Of seeing his submissive open and helpless.

But the ropes held her in safety and trust.

The knot over her pussy loosened slightly, and he positioned something soft and squishy directly over her clit before tightening everything again. A vibrator turned on, tingling over and around the sensitive nub of nerves.

Oh God. Her lips formed the word *evil*, but no sound escaped her.

His smile only deepened before he set her to rotating in the suspension.

As the wicked vibrator worked on her.

Her head hung down, and she could see the room slowly turning before her eyes closed. A shudder ran through her as her body roused, as her breasts swelled in the constricting ropes. Pressure grew inside her as her clit engorged and hardened.

"You're so beautiful when you're aroused." Sir Ethan's accented voice murmured in her ear. His arm was under her head, and his chest was against her back, warming her and holding her still.

His other arm reached over her waist, his fingers slipping past the vibrator and up inside her, wakening her nerves, inside as well as outside.

As the sensations swamped her, she tried to move. Nothing gave. Her right arm was over her right side, suspended by a rope. Her right leg was up in the air, her left bent in half.

He could do whatever he wanted to her—and the knowledge sent a shuddering heat through her. Need pulsed in her core as the pressure gathered.

His hand pulled back, and he added another wicked, clever finger, stretching her around his thick knuckles. "I'm not going to fuck you, poppet."

He rubbed his chin over her neck, his beard stubble sending a fresh stream of sensations down her spine. His fingers thrust in and out. "But you *are* going to come for me. In fact, you're going to beg to come."

Beg? *Never.* Even as she tried to shake her head, he pressed in deeper. God, she was so close, so very close. She wouldn't need to beg at all.

The vibrator slowed, eased to a faint tingle. His fingers stopped moving, but remained, thick and hard inside her...a physical symbol of his authority, marking his control over her body.

Like a tide going out, the need to come receded, leaving an ache behind.

Holding her still, he nibbled on her ear lobe. Kissed her neck and shoulder. Leisurely enjoying her...without withdrawing his fingers. The so-intimate hold made her shake inside.

Then he revved up the vibrator so it went harder, up and up in a hard jagged cycle, then slowing, pausing, and revving again. Right. Over. Her. Clit.

His fingers were circling and thrusting, drowning out any other sensations. She moaned as everything inside her coiled like a spring. Her muscles clenched around him as she hovered on the precipice.

He stopped.

The plea that came to her lips was halted by a shudder. No, she'd never beg. She couldn't.

"I have your body in my rope," he murmured. "Now trust me enough to give me this, too. I want to hear you whimper and ask me to let you come."

He kissed her cheek, and she turned her head so he could take her lips, wanting to give him that. Wanting to give him more. The realization held no fear. She could yield to him and be safe. Always be safe.

As if he'd heard her, his kiss went deeper, his tongue taking possession, sweeping her thoughts away.

And when the vibrator started and stopped again, she surrendered...everything. "Please, Sir. Please may I come?"

"Sweetheart." His eyes were so very blue, his smile a reward that filled her full to overflowing. "Yes, poppet. Come for me now. Give me your orgasm."

His fingers plunged in, deeper, harder, and the vibrator surged, driving her up and up as the incredible sensations rolled over her. Her core clenched around the hard fingers inside her, and the waves began, sending exquisite pleasure rushing through her. Even as her body bucked, as her entire world dissolved around her, her Dom held her in safety.

A while later, she realized she was sitting on the floor. A rope loosened and slid across her stomach followed by the slow stroke of a callused hand. Sir Ethan's lips brushed her bare shoulder as another rope eased and dropped onto the floor.

"Sir?"

"Back with me?" Hands cupped her face, lifting her head. His intense eyes met hers, like a fiery jolt before he kissed her.

The air went hazy again, like a warm fog closing in.

"Now, now, pet, stay with me here." His hands rubbed her upper arms.

"Sorry, sorry. I don't know..." Her thoughts crawled.

"You're rope drunk, sweetheart, and quite adorable with it."

Oh, that was okay then. As her eyes closed, she could hear him packing up his bag, fixing things. Her need to help disappeared in the clouds.

A blanket came around her shoulders, and he lifted her. Floating...

When she opened her eyes again, she realized she was curled up in Sir Ethan's lap, and there were people talking around her.

She lifted her head. They were in one of the sitting areas with three other couples: Stan and Dix, Lindsey and deVries, Angel and her Master, Malik, who Piper had finally met a couple of weeks ago. The Doms sat in the chairs with their partners at their feet.

"There you are." Sir Ethan sat her up and handed her a bottle of water, steadying her hand as she lifted it to her lips. After the first swallow, she drank eagerly.

His arm braced her from behind as she turned and scowled at him.

Innocence radiated from him...and his lips quirked. "That's a terrifying frown, poppet."

"I cannot believe you made me beg. *Beg*."

"And a very pretty job you made of it, sweetheart."

She'd actually begged him. To come. Yet she didn't feel diminished. Not when it was Sir Ethan. Still... She raised her chin. "Never again. Not for that, not for anything."

"Not for essentials like food or water, no," he said mildly before his unyielding blue eyes met hers. "However, you may count on begging to come—or not to come—quite often in the future."

His expression held a Dom's utter confidence, and the melting sensation in her core was messing with her resolve. She'd begged him for an orgasm, had surrendered—and her trust hadn't been misplaced. The bond between them had grown stronger.

"You two look pretty tight," Dix observed with satisfaction before his eyes widened with horror. "You're not moving out are you, Pips? I just got you trained to offer desserts at regular intervals."

Piper huffed a laugh because Sir Ethan had asked that question last night. "Maybe. Probably. Sorry, Dix."

Pouting, Dix curled his fingers in his iridescent blue chest harness. "Was it something I said?"

How could she possibly resist such an opening? She heaved a sad sigh. "Not...exactly."

"Wait, what?" Dix sat up, resting his arm on Stan's thigh. "I said something wrong? What?"

"Not exactly said. You're just too...loud. At certain times."

Lindsey snickered. "During sexy times?"

Sputtering, Dixon looked indignant. "You're being pissy because we sent you running back to your own place where Sir Ethan lurked in wait. Right? *Right*?"

"Lurked?" Her Dom had the sexiest laugh in all the history of mankind.

"It was just a little noise." Dix held his thumb and finger an inch apart.

"A little noise?" Piper shook her head. "Dixon, I've never heard howling like that in my life."

"Yeah, well..." Dixon scowled at Stan who was laughing his head off. "If I didn't make enough noise to send you home, he said he'd tighten all the clamps. In *all* the places."

DeVries gave Stan a respectful nod. "Great threat."

Oh, sheesh. Piper winced. Stan had a meaner streak than she'd realized.

"I love you, Pips, but"—Dixon cupped his loin cloth and contents—"I gotta protect my big boys here."

"Oh, well, we mustn't let the boys suffer." Piper couldn't subdue her giggles. "You sounded like a cat in heat. A humongous cat."

"Pretty good, huh?"

"She was the prettiest pink when she showed up." Sir Ethan nodded to Stan. "Thank you."

Stan grinned. "My pleasure."

"Since we're talking about our apartments...we have an empty one." Dixon's face brightened. "Stan put his foot down, and Dickless Darrell done went home to Tex-ass."

Stan choked.

Piper could feel Sir Ethan's chest bounce as he smothered a laugh. The British were so polite.

She wasn't. "Good riddance to him."

"Definitely." Lindsey grinned at Dix before turning to Piper. "Speaking of good riddance, did you know the guys have been keeping track of that pecker-headed Serna?"

The name hit Piper like a rock into her lake of happiness, a shock, but then the ripples spread out and disappeared into calm. Her counseling sessions over the last month were making headway. It didn't hurt that when she came out of her therapist's office, she'd find Ethan waiting for her.

God, she loved him. She tilted her face up, and yes, he was watching her. Making sure she was all right. She kissed him with every speck of love in her heart before turning back to Lindsey. "I didn't know. What's going on with him?"

"After Sir Ethan and Xavier called all the Kansas clubs, he got blacklisted." Lindsey grinned.

DeVries grinned and pointed to Stan. "And then our buddy here sicced the Feds on Serna and his friends."

"How did you do that?" Piper's eyes widened.

Stan smiled slowly. "I might have mentioned to some Kansas colleagues that a Master practicing nonconsensual slavery probably had friends with the same bad habits."

"Very good," Sir Ethan murmured. "Did your colleagues discover anything?"

"Two Masters had unwilling slaves—young women like Piper who'd been misled. Another was trafficking in Russian slaves. One had a slave who was perfectly content." Stan smiled at Piper and tilted his head toward Angel. "Not all slaves are there against their will."

"Some of us are far luckier in our Masters." Angel laid her head on her Master's thigh.

Malik ran his fingers through her hair, his gaze soft. "Some Masters know what a gift we're given."

Even as Piper sighed, she felt Sir Ethan's arms tighten around her and his murmured, "Yes. We do."

"Since you have Feds in the area"—Lindsay looked at Stan—"do you know if his slave, Gemma, is all right?"

Stan shook his head. "We had no reason to stay in touch with her. Sorry, girl."

"I know how she is." At the quizzical looks, Piper added, "I gave her my phone number in case she needed someone to talk to."

"Of course you did." Sir Ethan rubbed his cheek against hers. "Have I mentioned how much I love you?"

As her heart sang, she tilted her head back for his kiss. How could her love keep growing, more and more and more?

When he released her, Piper grinned at the "awww" expression on Lindsey's face. "Anyway," Piper said, "Gemma returned to her parents who were horrified at what she's been through. She's in counseling, and her mom goes with her."

"Her mother?" Dix shook his head. "A small-town mama? That would suck the big one."

"It started off pretty uncomfortable, I guess. Gemma took my advice to pick a kink-friendly therapist. So when Mama was critical of Gemma's bad choices, the counselor gave Mama some BDSM novels as *her* homework. Mom went from judgy to..." Piper giggled. "Well...Gemma spotted a paddle and nipple clamps in her parents' bedroom last week, and she was still grossed out when she talked to me. It seems parents aren't supposed to have sex—let alone kinky sex."

Dix's infectious laugh started everyone else off, and then they were all laughing.

"Gemma's enrolled for the fall semester at their community college and is working part-time in her dad's pharmacy."

"Excellent," Sir Ethan said. "That sounds like the perfect way to ease her back into her community and also help meet her need to serve."

Piper rolled her eyes. "You are such a Dom."

"Yes, I am." His arms around her were iron hard, a solid strength she could depend on. "And, as it happens, I'm *your* Dom. I recommend you don't forget it."

"No, Sir. Absolutely not, Sir. Wouldn't dream of it, Sir."

The Dom who held her heart merely chuckled and whispered, "Now, poppet, you're in trouble."

She grinned at him.

She should have remembered that he never forgot a transgression. In the wee hours of the night, he woke her, then deliberately and thoroughly reduced her to begging. Over and over and over.

Damn Dom.

Want to be notified of the next release?

Sign up to get a New Release Email at http://www.CheriseSinclair.com/NewsletterForm

Have you tried the Masters of the Shadowlands series?

Club Shadowlands

> *"Prepare to be lured to the world of the Shadowlands! Always fresh, intelligent, and emotional Ms. Sinclair knows exactly how to captivate her readers and she delivers it with stunning results..."*
>
> - The Romance Studio

Her car disabled during a tropical storm, Jessica Randall discovers the isolated house where she's sheltering is a private bondage club. At first shocked, she soon becomes aroused watching the interactions between the Doms and their subs. But she's a professional woman--an accountant--and surely isn't a submissive . . . is she?

Master Z hasn't been so attracted to a woman in years. But the little sub who has wandered into his club intrigues him. She's intelligent. Reserved. Conservative. After he discovers her interest in BDSM, he can't resist tying her up and unleashing the passion she hides within.

EXCERPT FROM CLUB SHADOWLANDS

An eternity later, Jessica spotted a glimmer of light. Relief rushed through her when she reached a driveway studded with hanging lights. Surely whoever lived here would let her wait out the storm. She walked through the ornate iron gates, up the palm-lined drive past landscaped lawns, until finally she reached a three-story stone mansion. Black wrought iron lanterns illumined the entry.

"Nice place," she muttered. And a little intimidating. She glanced down at herself to check the damage. Mud and rain streaked her tailored slacks and white button-down shirt, hardly a suitable image for a conservative accountant. She looked more like something even a cat would refuse to drag in.

Shivering hard, she brushed at the dirt and grimaced as it only streaked worse. She stared up at the huge oak doors guarding the entrance. A small doorbell in the shape of a dragon glowed on the side panel, and she pushed it.

Seconds later, the doors opened. A man, oversized and ugly as a battle-scarred Rottweiler, looked down at her. "I'm sorry, miss, you're too late. The doors are locked."

What the heck did that mean?

"P-please," she said, stuttering with the cold. "My car's in a ditch, and I'm soaked, and I need a place to dry out and call for help." But did she really want to go inside with this scary-looking guy? Then she shivered so hard her teeth clattered together, and her mind was made up. "Can I come in? Please?"

He scowled at her, his big-boned face brutish in the yellow entry light. "I'll have to ask Master Z. Wait here." And the bastard shut the door, leaving her in the cold and dark.

Jessica wrapped her arms around herself, standing miserably, and finally the door opened again. Again the brute. "Okay, come on in."

Relief brought tears to her eyes. "Thank you, oh, thank you." Stepping around him before he could change his mind, she barreled into a small entry room and slammed into a solid body. "Oomph," she huffed.

Firm hands gripped her shoulders. She shook her wet hair out of her eyes and looked up. And up. The guy was big, a good six feet, his shoulders wide enough to block the room beyond.

He chuckled, his hands gentling their grasp on her arms. "She's freezing, Ben. Molly left some clothing in the blue room; send one of the subs."

"Okay, boss." The brute—Ben—disappeared.

"What is your name?" Her new host's voice was deep, dark as the night outside.

"Jessica." She stepped back from his grip to get a better look at her savior. Smooth black hair, silvering at the temples, just touching his collar. Dark gray eyes with laugh lines at the corners. A lean, hard face with the shadow of a beard adding a hint of roughness. He wore tailored black slacks and a black silk shirt that outlined hard muscles underneath. If Ben was a Rottweiler, this guy was a jaguar, sleek and deadly.

"I'm sorry to have bothered—" she started.

Ben reappeared with a handful of golden clothing that he thrust at her. "Here you go."

She took the garments, holding them out to keep from getting the fabric wet. "Thank you."

A faint smile creased the manager's cheek. "Your gratitude is premature, I fear. This is a private club."

"Oh. I'm sorry." Now what was she going to do?

"You have two choices. You may sit out here in the entryway with Ben until the storm passes. The forecast stated the winds and rain would die down around six or so in the morning, and you won't get a tow truck out on these country roads until then. Or you may sign papers and join the party for the night."

She looked around. The entry was a tiny room with a desk and one chair. Not heated. Ben gave her a dour look.

Sign something? She frowned. Then again, in this lawsuit-happy world, every place made a person sign releases, even to visit a fitness center. So she could sit here all night. Or...be with happy people and be warm. *No-brainer*. "I'd love to join the party."

"So impetuous," the manager murmured. "Ben, give her the paperwork. Once she signs—or not—she may use the dressing room to dry off and change."

"Yes, sir." Ben rummaged in a file box on the desk, pulled out some papers.

The manager tilted his head at Jessica. "I will see you later then."

Ben shoved three pages of papers at her and a pen. "Read the rules. Sign at the bottom." He scowled at her. "I'll get you a towel and clothes."

She started reading. *Rules of the Shadowlands.*

"Shadowlands. That's an unusual na—" she said, looking up. Both men had disappeared. Huh. She returned to reading, trying to focus her eyes. Such tiny print. Still, she never signed anything without reading it.

Doors will open at...

Water pooled around her feet, and her teeth chattered so hard she had to clench her jaw. There was a dress code. Something about cleaning the equipment after use. Halfway down the second page, her eyes blurred. Her brain felt like icy slush. *Too cold—I can't do this.* This was just a club, after all; it wasn't like she was signing mortgage papers.

Turning to the last page, she scrawled her name and wrapped her arms around herself. *Can't get warm.*

Ben returned with some clothing and towels, then showed her into an opulent restroom off the entry. Glass-doored stalls along one side faced a mirrored wall with sinks and counters.

After dropping the borrowed clothing on the marble counter, she kicked her shoes off and tried to unbutton her shirt. Something moved on the wall. Startled, Jessica looked up and saw a short, pudgy woman with straggly blonde hair and a pale complexion blue with cold. After a second, she recognized herself. *Ew.* Surprising they'd even let her in the door.

In a horrible contrast with Jessica's appearance, a tall, slender, absolutely gorgeous woman walked into the restroom and gave her a scowl. "I'm supposed to help you with a shower."

Get naked in front of Miss Perfection? Not going to happen. "Thanks, b-b-b-but I'm all right." She forced the words past her chattering teeth. "I don't need help."

"Well!" With an annoyed huff, the woman left.

I was rude. Shouldn't have been rude. If only her brain would kick back into gear, she'd do better. She'd have to apologize. Later. If she ever got dried off and warm. She needed dry clothes. But, her hands were numb, shaking uncontrollably, and time after time, the buttons slipped from her stiff fingers. She couldn't even get her slacks off, and she was shuddering so hard her bones hurt.

"Dammit," she muttered and tried again.

The door opened. "Jessica, are you all right? Vanessa said—" The manager. "No, you are obviously not all right." He stepped inside, a dark figure wavering in her blurry vision.

"Go away."

"And find you dead on the floor in an hour? I think not." Without waiting for her answer, he stripped her out of her clothes as one would a two-year-old, even peeling off her sodden bra and panties. His hands were hot, almost burning, against her chilled skin.

She was naked. As the thought percolated through her numb brain, she jerked away and grabbed at the dry clothing. His hand intercepted hers.

"No, pet." He plucked something from her hair, opening his hand to show muddy leaves. "You need to warm up and clean up. Shower."

He wrapped a hard arm around her waist and moved her into one of the glass-fronted stalls behind where she'd been standing. With his free hand, he turned on the water, and heavenly warm steam billowed up. He adjusted the temperature.

"In you go," he ordered. A hand on her bottom, he nudged her into the shower.

The water felt scalding hot against her frigid skin, and she gasped, then shivered, over and over, until her bones hurt. Finally, the heat began to penetrate, and the relief was so intense, she almost cried.

Some time after the last shuddering spasm, she realized the door of the stall was open. Arms crossed, the man leaned against the door frame, watching her with a slight smile on his lean face.

"I'm fine," she muttered, turning so her back was to him. "I can manage by myself."

"No, you obviously cannot," he said evenly. "Wash the mud out of your hair. The left dispenser has shampoo."

Mud in her hair. She'd totally forgotten; maybe she *did* need a keeper. After using the vanilla-scented shampoo, she let the water sluice through her hair. Brown water and twigs swirled down the drain. The water finally ran clear.

"Very good." The water shut off. Blocking the door, he rolled up his sleeves, displaying corded, muscular arms. She had the unhappy feeling he was going to keep helping her, and any protest would be ignored. He'd taken charge as easily as if she'd been one of the puppies at the shelter where she volunteered.

"Out with you now." When her legs wobbled, he tucked a

hand around her upper arm, holding her up with disconcerting ease. The cooler air hit her body, and her shivering started again.

After blotting her hair, he grasped her chin and tipped her face up to the light. She gazed up at his darkly tanned face, trying to summon up enough energy to pull her face away.

"No bruises. I think you were lucky." Taking the towel, he dried off her arms and hands, rubbing briskly until he appeared satisfied with the pink color. Then he did her back and shoulders. When he reached her breasts, she pushed at his hand. "I can do that." She stepped back so quickly that the room spun for a second.

"Jessica, be still." Then he ignored her sputters like she would a buzzing fly, his attentions gentle but thorough, even to lifting each breast and drying underneath.

When he toweled off her butt, she wanted to hide. If there was any part of her that should be covered, it was her hips. Overweight. *Jiggly*. He didn't seem to notice.

Then he knelt and ordered, "Spread your legs."

Get Club Shadowlands now!

ALSO BY CHERISE SINCLAIR

Masters of the Shadowlands Series

Club Shadowlands
Dark Citadel
Breaking Free
Lean on Me
Make Me, Sir
To Command and Collar
This Is Who I Am
If Only
Show Me, Baby
Servicing the Target
Protecting His Own
Mischief and the Masters
Beneath the Scars
Defiance

Mountain Masters & Dark Haven Series

Master of the Mountain
Simon Says: Mine
Master of the Abyss
Master of the Dark Side

My Liege of Dark Haven
Edge of the Enforcer
Master of Freedom
Master of Solitude
I Will Not Beg

The Wild Hunt Legacy

Hour of the Lion
Winter of the Wolf
Eventide of the Bear
Leap of the Lion

Sons of the Survivalist Series

Not a Hero

Standalone Books

The Dom's Dungeon
The Starlight Rite

ABOUT THE AUTHOR

Cherise Sinclair is a *New York Times* and *USA Today* bestselling author of emotional, suspenseful romance. She loves to match up devastatingly powerful males with heroines who can hold their own against the subtle—and not-so-subtle—alpha male pressure.

Fledglings having flown the nest, Cherise, her beloved husband, an eighty-pound lap-puppy, and one fussy feline live in the Pacific Northwest where nothing is cozier than a rainy day spent writing.

Website
Facebook
Facebook Reader Discussion (Shadowkittens)
Bookbub

CPSIA information can be obtained
at www.ICGtesting.com
Printed in the USA
BVHW031155140819
555878BV00001B/54/P